THE SEDUCTION OF DUALITY

MIDWAY MYSTICS COLLECTION
BOOK ONE

GENAVIE CASTLE

CASTLE PUBLICATIONS

COPYRIGHT

The characters and events portrayed in this book are fictitious. Any similarity to real persons, living or dead is coincidental and not intended by the author.

ISBN: 978-1-962047-16-6 eBook

ISBN: 978-1-962047-17-3 Paperback

Cover design by: CRey-ative Designs

Edited by: EPONA Author Solutions

Printed in the United States of America

ABOUT THIS BOOK

This is a dark retelling inspired by Dr. Jekyll and Mr. Hyde. As a romance reader and writer, I wanted to give the classic a why choose twist with a touch of paranormal and a HEA. However, like the original there are dark themes within these pages. Please consider this list of potential content and trigger warnings before moving forward. Your mental health is important.

Graphic sexual content including MFMM scenes
Violence
Explicit Language
Kidnapping
Dismemberment
Torture
Emotional abuse
Parental neglect
Non-Consent/Dubious Consent
Death
Sexual assault
Mental illness

Suicide attempt

Dementia

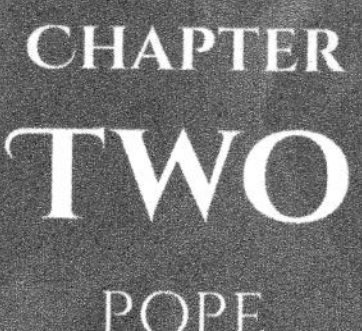

CHAPTER TWO

POPE

One drink turned into dozens. We skipped the OJ and went straight to the champagne. It was the guarantee to give you a morning headache type of champagne to boot. The four of us were completely sauced by the time we left On the Bend and had decided to enjoy the rest of the day by taking a short trolley ride to the Strand.

According to history, Port Midway began as a hub for the mystics. Supernaturals of every flavor started here and moved on to other parts of North America. It was no longer a port. Sure, we had fishing boats and boating excursions for tourists during the summer, but mostly it was a little seaside town. It was small and the residents liked it that way.

The Strand was a stretch of shops, restaurants, and bars located along the water. The weather was moderate during the summer months which brought out the masses. Tourism spiked, making Sunday at the Strand one big party.

I was walking on a cloud as we meandered down the Strand and not because we'd been bar hopping since we left brunch. It was the auburn-haired beauty holding my hand. Aisling was my dream girl.

I'd been lusting after her since the day she'd moved in. Unlike other women, she didn't succumb to my charms. In the beginning, I was determined to wear her down and get into her pants. No matter what I did, she kept me at arm's length and turned me down gracefully. Naturally, that made me want her all the more. Soon lust morphed into intense emotions. I couldn't stop thinking about her. I became obsessed. So much so, that I'd been watching her from afar. She was intriguing.

I wanted more than just her body. I wanted everything she had to offer. It was odd to feel so much for someone else. I was a selfish prick. Accustomed to doing whatever and whoever I wanted. Not this time. She was different. Strange. Unexpected. No matter how long it took, I was willing to wait, watch, and enjoy unraveling the mystery that was Aisling Lovelle.

"Does she know?" Ty asked from beside me.

"Does who know what?" I asked, my gaze fixed on Ash, who sauntered away from me to Nelson, who was trying on ridiculous-looking hats.

"Don't be bashful, Pope. We've seen you with a parade of women. But never have we seen one that's captivated you as much as she does."

I shrugged, unable to hide the stupid grin plastered on my face.

"You should make it official. Girls like that won't stay single for long."

He was right. My thoughts drifted to the first time I laid eyes on the girl next door.

Several months earlier —

A loud ruckus woke me and pissed me right the fuck off. The clock read six in the morning. Fuucck.

I pulled on a pair of boxers and stomped downstairs. As soon as I stepped out of my front door, the brisk fall air made my skin prickle and further soured my mood. There were moving trucks across the street and a couple of men making a racket as they shuttled boxes into the house. Did they have to be so loud?

I glared at one of the men. "Hey, you guys, mind keeping the noise down?"

The asshole laughed. "Sure man. Don't want to disturb your beauty sleep."

Fuck face. "Where's the owner or renter?" I growled.

"Inside. We'll let her know of your complaint." He stomped up the metal ramp leading into the back of his truck, making sure to emphasize each step.

Oh, fuck this. I don't care if the new neighbor is a little old lady, she's getting a piece of my mind.

Another guy stomped up the ramp, smirking at me as he went.

Fuck the old lady, I was going to deal with these fuckers directly.

"What the fuck is your . . ."

"Hey!" A feminine voice cut me off. "Keep the noise down."

"Sorry, miss," one of the guys said.

I stepped around the truck to find the owner of that voice. She didn't sound old and nope, she most certainly was not.

My heart leaped into my throat as my neighbor came into view. Her red locks were swept up into a high ponytail which swished against her nape as she moved. She bent over, giving me the perfect view of her plump, round ass. I was instantly hard.

She turned to face me and everything around me faded into the background. I closed the distance between us, drawn to those captivating golden-brown eyes.

"Oh! Hi!" she stammered. "Sorry about the noise."

She balanced the box on her hip and extended her hand. "I'm Aisling."

Her smile made my stomach do somersaults. Somehow, I managed to find my words and accepted her hand.

"Gaius Pope. You can just call me Pope." Her hand was uber-feminine. Smooth. Delicate. I held on to it as though it was mine to hold on to.

She tried to pull it away, but my grip tightened.

Someone bumped my shoulder and knocked me to my senses.

"Here let me take this." I stepped closer and took the box.

"You don't need to help. We um . . . obviously woke you. You should go back to bed." Her cheeks reddened and she averted her gaze.

"Might want to hide the boner," one of the movers muttered behind me.

Oh shit. I moved the box to hide my crotch.

Aisling stepped closer and placed her hands on the box, her fingers skimming mine.

"You don't have to help." Her gaze met mine and her tongue slid over her bottom lip. "Go back to bed, Pope." She winked and sashayed her way into the house.

"I'll see you later," I called out. And every day after that.

Aisling's laughter brought me back to the present. A gust of wind blew up her dress, revealing the string bikini underneath. My dick twinged in my shorts. She shot me a gorgeous smile.

I snagged her by the waist and pressed a soft kiss to her lips. She leaned in as I was about to pull away and gently slipped her tongue into my mouth. I opened for her, my hold on her body tightening.

Water sprayed my face. Nelson chortled, squirting us with water. "Simmer down you two! There are children present."

I scowled at the asshole for ruining my fun, but Ash beamed up at me and cuddled into my side.

That smile.

"Come on, I hear live music." Ty grasped his husband's hand. "And I need another drink."

Ash giggled and followed Nelson and Ty, pulling me along with her.

That laugh.

Hours and many drinks later, the sun had gone down, and we were dancing to a country music cover band. Well, they danced, and I happily watched from the sidelines. Ty was twirling my girl on the dance floor. She wore a radiant smile that made my heart swell.

A fresh beer was placed in front of me, and Nelson muttered something to someone. I didn't care what was happening around me. My sole focus was on my Aisling.

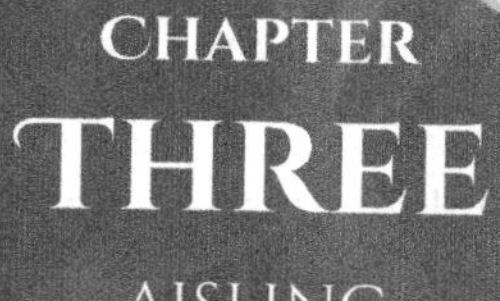

CHAPTER THREE

AISLING

The life of a chemist was equally rewarding and frustrating. I sat in a cold room and analyzed data for hours. I loved it. It wasn't a glamorous job, but it was good work. With my innate magical abilities as a low-level witch and the years I'd spent studying science and alchemy, I've created numerous products that benefited mundane and mystics all over the globe. As one of the lead scientists at Buchanan Pharmaceuticals, I was proud to be making a difference in people's lives. I'd created a variety of things from simple common cold remedies to non-habit-forming pain relievers. If only I could come up with a cure for two ailments that were personal.

I tapped my pen on the desk as though that would change the outcome of the data I'd been staring at for the last few hours. *What am I missing?*

"Hey, boss lady," Zoey approached me warily. "I'm heading out. Do you need anything?"

"No, thanks, Zoey. Have a great night." My voice was tinged with exhaustion. I glanced at the time. It was quitting time and there were still too many things that needed to be done.

"It's been a long day and you've been working non-stop. Maybe take a week or two off?" she offered meekly.

"No, it's all good. I'll have my usual three-day weekend to decompress."

"Um, right. That-uh doesn't seem to be helping. For the last couple of weeks, you've returned on Monday morning looking more worn out than when you left."

"I was hungover," I replied defensively.

"Right. That happened once. And I'm glad you're getting laid regularly, but maybe an extended break from this cold lab would do you some good. When was the last time you had a vacation?" Zoey asked while cleaning her glasses with the hem of her sweater.

I gazed into space searching for an answer to her question and came up with . . . never.

"It's been a while, huh?" She exhaled, then placed her red cat-eye glasses on her nose. "Think about it. Or at the very least, come over this weekend. Emily and the kids miss you."

"I miss them, too," I admitted.

Zoey was my best friend and office manager. We were roommates in undergrad. I went the science route while she traveled the world. When Zoey returned to Midway, she was getting out of a relationship and had just had a baby girl.

Her family had offered to support her and her daughter Millie, with the hopes that Zoey would take over the family business. Like her mother, Zoey was a seer. Zoey never took to her magic and she was adamant about supporting herself, which was fortunate for me. I needed help in the lab, and she needed a job with good pay and flexible hours. She organized my office and my social life. It worked out great for both of us.

Zoey was an incredible multi-tasker. She had to be. Zoey and her partners had a total of seven children. Before opening the lab, she met Emily and the women married soon after. The couple knew they wanted more kids and didn't waste anytime. Through artificial insemination, both women got pregnant. Emily had twins, a boy and a girl, and Zoey had a boy. They were happy with four kids but since they had leftover eggs from their first round of IVF, they decided to try again a year or so later. The sperm donor for the second round was Jacob. He was a waiter and a struggling student. He needed the money and so they agreed. Zoey had twin boys and Emily had a girl. Shortly after the kids were born, Jacob decided he wanted to be a permanent fixture in the kids' lives. Their love grew and soon they got married.

The throuple had loving parents and siblings who pitched in to help with their seven children. It was a lot and overwhelming. I couldn't imagine having that many let alone seven. Having children wasn't a grand idea for me and my mental health issues. I needed to get in front of all that first. The thought of never having children created a sharp pang of longing deep in my chest.

I blinked away those self-defeating thoughts and gave Zoey a small smile.

"The outreach program is having their annual fundraising event soon. It's the same as last year: games, rides, carnival food. You should come," she said.

"That sounds amazing. Remind me, please."

"You got it, boss bitch." She winked. "In the meantime, how about I refill your coffee before I leave?"

She grabbed my coffee cup, the one she'd given me as a gift, and turned on her heel.

I propped my elbows on my desk and palmed my face. Maybe she was right. A break might give my brain a chance to reset and then I could come back with fresh ideas. Unfortunately, time was a luxury I couldn't squander. I needed to solve the problem before something terrible happened. If I was being honest with myself, something terrible had already happened. Something I did. I wasn't one hundred percent certain, but my gut instincts were never wrong. And amazing sex with Pope was not going to erase those things.

Soft arms wrapped around me. "Take care of yourself, Ash."

Zoey's playful tone couldn't hide her concern. "I'd be lost without you."

My heart did a little flip-flop thing in my chest. I had very few friends, but the few I did have were the best. "Thanks, Zozo. I'd be lost without you, too."

Instead of leaving after Zoey, as I should have, I worked until my vision went fuzzy. The tonic I'd created required an intricate process that took time and precision. As far as efficacy, that was trial and error. I pressed the heel of my palms into my eyeballs. This had to work. Anguish replaced my frustration. If I didn't get the tonic right, the episodes would continue, and I'd be behind bars. Or in an asylum.

My limbs felt numb and heavy, which could have been a sign of stress and fatigue or . . . I glanced at the clock. Shit. It was past midnight. I'd been consumed with work and had forgotten my dosage. I hurried across the lab to the latest batch of tonics I'd created, removed the cap, and guzzled the elixir. The herbal mixture had a bitter medicinal aftertaste which lingered on my tastebuds. The formulation was a special blend of herbs, human medicine, and magic. To change things, I'd added more medicine which made it taste awful. I paused for a beat and nothing happened. In a panic, I downed another bottle. A prickly sensation rolled through my body and warmth flooded my veins. Taking in slow deep breaths, I sat there allowing the formula to work its way through my system. After a full minute, the prickly sensation abated, and I allowed myself to relax.

Two bottles in one go. Maybe that was the answer. I crossed my fingers. It used to be one bottle every twelve hours for four consecutive days. Then once a day for three days. I increased my dosage on the weekends and that didn't help. I'd blacked out twice since brunch. And that voice chirped up at odd times. I massaged my temples but the answers to my problems didn't come.

By the time I made it back to my place, I was beyond tired. It had been a long day, but it was productive and necessary. Along with my personal projects, I had other work orders I needed to complete. Zoey was the best assistant but there were things only I could do. Perhaps I needed to hire another chemist to help with the lab work. I certainly had the budget to do so, Dr. Buchanan had given me complete autonomy at the lab and a generous budget. The problem with hiring someone new was I'd have to reveal my personal projects which was a hard no.

Exhaustion seeped into my bones as I undressed and slid under the covers. It was Thursday and I had three days to recover. *Please, no more blackouts.*

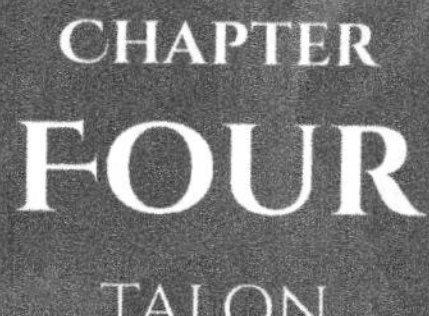

CHAPTER FOUR

TALON

Breaking News—

I'm Desmond Chang from MidwayChannel 5, coming to you live from the Blitzed Troll Bar on 5th and Brentwood, where a tragic scene has shocked the community. The bar known to locals as a late-night bar frequented by the after-hours crowd is the home of a gruesome murder. This is the second murder reported in the neighborhood. Police responded after a 911 call was made early this evening and as you can see behind me, first responders are still on the scene. So far, the local authorities have yet to release a statement regarding the victims and any leads.

"Boss?" Igor knocked on my door.

"Come in," I replied, my focus on the screen. Another fucking murder. And the latest had happened in one of my establishments. I had to deal with the shitshow before the police decided to make my life hell. Bloody. Fucking. Hell. This wasn't good for business.

I had many businesses, and all were legit. Well, mostly legit. Hard to walk the line when owning strip bars and sex clubs. I'd been in the process of installing the best surveillance and security systems money could buy after the first murder, just as a precaution. That hadn't helped. The cameras at the Blitzed Troll were on the fritz. All we'd been able to get were pixelated videos the entire night. And if that wasn't frustrating enough, all the cameras in the surrounding area had the same issue.

The sound of heavy footsteps alerted me to my VP's presence. "One of the waitresses at Blitzed Troll said she saw something. Do you want her brought in?" he asked, coming to stand beside me in my office.

"Has she talked to the authorities?" I asked.

"Yep. As well as the rest of the staff. None offered anything useful. The waitress, Freddie, said she didn't give the cops any details. She's been taken to the Carriage Motel, away from prying eyes," he answered.

I nodded. "Good call. Let's head there."

He didn't move.

"Now." I grabbed my coat.

He glanced at his watch and quirked his eyebrow.

"We can't ignore a murder on our doorstep," I explained. "Besides, I'm not worried about missing anything spectacular."

Nirvana, one of my clubs, had a sex party happening this evening. Sex parties were profitable. I wasn't one to partake, being the owner and all that, but this was going to be a masquerade which meant anything goes. And more than ever, I needed the release. My beast was a prickly ass as of late. Thus it'd been a dry spell that was making me feel uncharacteristically old even though thirty-four for a mystic wasn't old at all. Mystics lived double the lifespan of humans.

I shrugged off my inner pity party as Igor pulled into the parking lot of the Carriage Motel. It was a recently acquired property I was dying to blow up and rebuild. I'd worked in construction while putting myself through college and law school and still craved building things with my own two hands. Whenever I got a chance, I'd get my hands dirty and work alongside my construction crew. It was therapeutic.

The car door opened, startling me for a hot second. *Jesus, I needed to get laid*. All work and no play was making me . . . jumpy.

Igor led the way toward one of the bartenders from the Blitzed Troll, who stood in front of a room, vaping. Larry, if I remember correctly, bowed his head as I approached, then opened the door, where two of my employees waited.

"Hey boss," Kevin, the bar manager, greeted me. He sat upright on the double bed and pointed with his thumb to the woman on the other bed. "This is Freddie. She's in shock. We all are. But uh . . . Freddie said she remembers the victim speaking to someone."

Freddie, one of the waitresses I barely knew, leaned against the headboard with her arms wrapped tightly around her knees.

I stood at the foot of the bed, with my arms crossed, waiting for Freddie to acknowledge me.

"Freddie!" Kevin snapped.

The waitress startled at his voice, her eyes round.

"S-sorry, sir," she stammered.

"You're not in any trouble, Freddie. I need you to tell me what you remember," I stated.

"Uh . . . he, the dead guy," she gasped and wiped her eyes.

"Was he a friend of yours?" I asked in a soft tone. The way she was sobbing made me think they had a relationship.

Freddie shook her head vigorously. "No! Not at all. He's been in the bar a couple of times. He kept to himself. Was quiet and kind of creepy. It's just. The dead body. So much blood." Her body began to shiver.

I pulled a deep breath into my lungs. The musty scent of dust and old cigarettes tickled my nostrils as I waited for Freddie to collect herself.

"A woman was speaking to him when I delivered a beer to his table. I remembered this because he was always alone, and no one spoke to him. No one likes waiting on him. He never tips. He is always . . ."

"The woman," I prompted. I didn't have time for unnecessary specifics.

"Oh, um, yeah. She didn't stay long. I dropped off the beer, and she left the bar shortly after. He stayed. Had a couple more beers and shots."

"What did she look like?"

"She's never been in the bar before. I'd remember her anywhere. She was different, very graceful. Starlet-beautiful. Tall, but it might be the heels. Alabaster skin. Glossy red." Freddie pointed at her head.

I rubbed my chin. "And you think this redhead had something to do with this nameless guy's death?"

She shrugged one shoulder. "No. Yeah. Maybe. I mean the guy was an asshole. Paid cash, always. Never offered a name or anything. And then this beauty walked in and spoke with him directly. I mean . . . a guy like him would never get a girl like her."

"Did you see her leave?"

"No, I was busy with other customers."

I glanced at the bar manager. "Any recollection of the redheaded guest?"

He shook his head.

"I remember her boss. I was at the door when she came in," the bartender who had been outside vaping said. "Gorgeous girl. I saw her talking to him. She couldn't have been there long, because the next time I glanced at his table she wasn't there. This was before the shots. I didn't see her after that."

"Was she mystic?" I asked.

Freddie and the bartender shook their heads.

A human woman wouldn't have been able to commit the crime. The victim had been slaughtered with a dull blade. It would have taken someone powerful to hack through him. The woman could have been working with someone else, a mystic. It wasn't much but at least we had something.

"If anyone can think of anything else, contact me and only me. Got it?" I pushed a little of my dominant magic out, making my employees cower.

I wasn't an alpha. Not really. But I ran my businesses like one, and the people who worked for me, shifter or not respected me as such.

Igor dropped me off at Nirvana forty-five minutes later. I strolled through the club, taking in the heady atmosphere. The musky scent of sweat, sex, and cum wafted through the air like a thick fog. The music was drowned out by constant moans, groans, and bodies slapping together. It was a feast for the senses. I loved it. Or at least I had, once upon a time. The fact that my blood wasn't pumping with excitement was strange and frustrating. What the hell was wrong with me? Maybe it was the murders.

Feeling a sense of disappointment, I grabbed a bottle of scotch from one of the bars and stomped to my office. Maybe I just needed to relax and enjoy the view for a moment. Drink a little scotch, smoke a cigar.

As soon as my ass hit the leather recliner, she walked into the club. The ambiance seemed to transition into something more, as though she wove a spell, entrancing the crowd with every step. Men and women gawked as she passed them. A couple of brave souls tried to engage her in conversation. I couldn't hear what was being said but their disappointed expressions said it all.

Not sure when I'd gotten out of my chair, but I was leaning on the one-way window, studying her as she sauntered through the club. Her hair was piled high atop her head with loose tendrils framing her masked face. The top half of her mask was ornately designed with tiny rhinestones swirling around the eye area and a gauzy, transparent material covered her lower half like a veil. She wore a sheer black body stocking studded with a thousand rhinestones that looked like glittery stars.

I pulled my cell from my pocket and dialed one of the bouncers on the floor.

"Who is she?" I asked.

"Registered as . . . The Mistress," the bouncer replied.

I smirked at her chosen alias. It wasn't unusual in a place like this, and it added to the mystery.

"Bring her to me," I ordered.

Moments ticked by as I watched with anticipation.

My bouncer stood there slack-jawed as the beauty walked away.

Playing hard to get, are we?

My phone rang.

"Don't worry about it," I barked into the phone and headed downstairs.

I prowled through the club, watching her from a distance until she ended up at a bar located toward the rear of the club. She ordered, then scanned the crowd. She was hunting but didn't realize she was the prey. My prey.

Watching her made every nerve in my body come alive. My skin was buzzing, my pulse raced, and my cock inflated with every step toward her.

The bartender saw me coming and slid the glass of wine. "On the house."

I stood behind her and placed my hands on the counter, one on each side blocking her in.

She raised the veil just enough for me to see her plump lower lip and then she took a deep pull of wine.

"How's the wine?" I asked while inhaling her scent. Strawberries and creme.

She lowered the veil, turned slowly, and tilted her head to gaze into my eyes.

The mask I'd slipped on before leaving my office had partially covered my face. It wasn't much of a disguise, and I didn't care much about that but since it was the theme of the night, I was willing to play along.

Through the sheer veil, I watched her tongue roll along her red lower lip. My breath caught in my throat. The small movement stirred my blood.

"I've had better," she drawled. A loose tendril brushed her cheek. Red hair. *Could she be the murderer?*

"I bet you have." My nostrils flared and I leaned in closer, running my nose along her jaw. The veil was soft, her skin softer. I trailed my nose down her neck and flicked my tongue over the little pulse point that was thumping away.

Witch . . . and something I couldn't place. The wolf in me purred in approval. Murderer or not she was mine.

I hovered my face close to hers and whispered, "Yes or no."

"If I say no?" She raised her chin and slowly uncrossed her legs, revealing her crotchless bodysuit, and giving me the perfect shot of her pink slit.

My stiff cock ached in my pants.

"I'll walk away." I brought my lips to her ear. "But if you say yes, baby, I'll take you to heaven with my tongue, and then you'll be begging to ride my cock to hell and back."

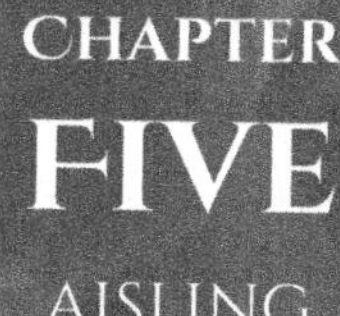

CHAPTER FIVE

AISLING

He was all over me, invading my senses. He had a unique scent, a mixture of ocean and earth. He ravaged my mouth, stealing my breath with hungry kisses. My skin was hot and tingly with intense need. Big, calloused hands roamed over my curves.

My fingers tangled through soft, short locks.

I spread my knees apart, accommodating his broad frame. Hot lips latched onto my taut nipples. His hand dipped between my legs, gliding over my wet pussy. Petting, stroking. My pelvis chased his hand, desperate for more. A thick finger entered my body. I moaned out loud and spread my legs wider. Another finger slipped into my core. Everything went tight. My orgasm cresting.

My nails dug into the stranger's muscular biceps. He rubbed the pad of his thumb over my clit and my climax tore out of me.

I panted for air while strong arms lifted me, making the room sway.

My back met satiny fabric. His manly scent was everywhere. Hard muscles pressed against me, and my pulse picked up. Pillowy lips roamed over my skin and landed on my pussy. Every flick of his silky tongue sent tantalizing jolts over my sensitive flesh. I writhed under him, losing myself in the sensations inflicted upon my body. I clawed his chest. His biceps.

It was too much and not enough.

Something smooth and blunt prodded my entrance. It felt thick. Hard. And too big. Panic flitted in my belly. Arousal overrode apprehension, my pussy weeping with need.

He entered my cunt with one strong stroke. His thick cock stretched me to the point of pain. The sharp sting mixed with a rapture so intense shot through me. My eyes rolled back in my head as I succumbed to the assault of pleasure swirling through my body. A dam broke, and my pussy spasmed around his cock.

He groaned. The sound was primal. Animalistic. He thrust into me hard, deep, and fast. With one final thrust, his release burst out of him, flooding me with his seed.

Overwhelmed with bliss, I drifted in and out of consciousness.

A moment later, his cock was inside me again and again.

His eyes, his face. I couldn't see him. He was faceless.

DAWN CRESTED over the horizon and my arms encircled my middle, warding off the morning chill.

I rummaged through the trunk, looking for. . . something.

"Whore!" The reedy voice spat the offensive word at my back.

Anger surged within me.

Red swam behind my eyes, like waves crashing against a rocky shore, spraying my face with its mist. Unnatural strength flowed through my veins, propelling my muscles forward with an exhilarating and strange force.

Screams of agony cut through the peaceful morning. My hands were bloody. My pulse raced. I felt . . . alive.

Dead eyes stared back at me.

I woke with a panicked breath, sweat covering my trembling body. The fuck?

I'd been having the weirdest dreams for the last few nights. It was either sex with a faceless stranger or those dead eyes. My skin prickled. It seemed more like a memory, not a dream.

Unable to go back to sleep, I dragged myself into the shower, my head and body confused. I was terrified and horny. Two opposite emotions that shouldn't be uttered in the same sentence.

The cold shower chased away the terror swirling through me, but it did nothing to douse my overactive hormones.

Maybe I should stop at Pope's for an early morning visit? He'd told me he was busy working last night. No, that wasn't right. I told *him* I had work to do, and he went to his place with a disappointed look on his beautiful face. Why did I send him away? *I was tired and being a moody bitch.* We agreed to keep things casual between us, and I hoped that hadn't changed. If he decided to end our friendship because of my moodiness, I'd be devastated.

I shrugged off my inner turmoil and went to the office before the sun rose. Knowing it was going to be a long day, I went to the Java A-Go-Go drive-through for a twelve-dollar cup of coffee and a bag full of overpriced pastries, then parked in my usual spot.

Shelby Centre was one of six high-rises in Port Midway conveniently located near a bunch of trendy restaurants and bars, all within walking distance.

It was one of those fancy places with a massive chandelier in the entryway, large statement art pieces on the walls, marble flooring, and e-card entry. I dug into my purse for my card while trying to balance my hoodie in the crook of my arm, my hot cup of coffee, and my bag of pastries.

My purse was an abyss. Put something in it and I'd never see it again. I fumbled with my belongings, sloshing hot coffee all over my hand. I dropped the bag of pastries and cursed.

"Mother fucking fuck!" I switched my coffee into my other hand and sucked off the hot liquid.

"Do you need some help?" A raspy voice startled me, causing me to spill my drink . . . again.

"Fucking, Jesus!" I yelped.

The stranger took the offensive hot cup out of my hand as I shook off the burn.

"Are you okay?" His brow bunched, and he regarded me with kind eyes that were a captivating shade of green.

I raised my gaze and stared. My brain went completely blank. I forgot my words. He was devastatingly handsome. Tall, brawny with corded muscle that filled out his light-blue button-down shirt and his gray trousers. He had a serious vibe to him that screamed boss. And . . . money. He seemed familiar, yet we'd never met before. But there was something else. Something that made me want to step into his personal space and run my tongue along the stubble on his jaw.

My lashes fluttered, and I felt my cheeks heat embarrassed by my scandalous thoughts.

He smiled at me. A smile so big it brightened his face and made his eyes twinkle.

There you are, my inner voice purred.

No, no, no. She cannot be here right now. I dropped my gaze, willing my inner voice to shut the hell up.

"You have quite the colorful vocabulary." He grinned.

I was beet red. And still, my damn mouth wouldn't utter a single word.

"I'm Talon." He extended his hand to shake mine.

"I'm wet and sticky," I replied and lifted my coffee-covered hand. What the fuck did I just say? Of all the things I could have said, I led with that?

Talon had the good nature to laugh.

"It's okay, I don't mind wet or sticky." He bit the inside of his cheek. "Um . . . how can I help? You were obviously searching for something."

"Yeah, my key card," I mumbled.

"*That* I can help with," he said. He bent, picked up the bag of pastries I dropped, and motioned me to the door.

"Thanks," I said as he held up his phone to the card reader.

"You seem familiar, have we met before?" he asked.

"No." *I would have remembered you.* "I'm Aisling, by the way. Sorry for my um . . . colorful language."

He chuckled. "Nice to meet you, Aisling. Apologies aren't necessary. What floor are you on?"

"Four, please. You don't have to walk me. My office keys are right here." I jingled the keychain hooked to my purse.

"It's no trouble. Can't have this hot cup of coffee burning you again." He sipped my coffee. My lipstick imprint left the tiniest hint of color on his lips.

His tongue slid over his bottom lip. "Mmmm . . . delicious. Tastes like cinnamon."

Why was that so hot? I couldn't remove my gaze from his mouth. My face felt warm again.

"After you." He stepped closer to me and placed his hands on the small of my back.

I entered the elevator and leaned against the back wall. Talon stood beside me. He was a big man, six and a half feet at least and his body radiated a warmth that made my insides tingle. He slid closer his arm brushing mine.

"Who do you work for?" he asked.

"Buchanan Pharmaceuticals," I replied.

"Really? I always wondered who was working for them here in Port Midway. Do they treat you well?"

"I have zero complaints. This is just a satellite office, so there are only two of us. Me and my best friend, Zoey." I replied.

The elevator doors opened, and Talon followed me to my office.

I unlocked it, and he strolled in like he owned the place.

"I wasn't expecting this." Talon's gaze swept the lobby as he placed the pastries on Zoey's desk.

Zoey and I went for a tranquil spa vibe for our waiting area. We didn't receive visitors much, but I wanted to give Zoey a peaceful space to work in versus the chaos she had to deal with at home.

"I was expecting a sterile lab," he added.

"Back there." I pointed to the door leading to the back office. "Would you like a tour?"

"I'd love one."

I smiled and led him to the lab. My domain. I loved my work and my lab. It wasn't grand, but Buchanan Pharma had given me a sizeable budget for lab equipment, which was more important to me than fancy furnishings.

The lab took up most of the back office space. We had a small bathroom in the far left corner and a kitchenette next to it. On the opposite wall was my tiny office.

"This looks complicated and expensive." Talon peered at the lab equipment while drinking my coffee.

"It's necessary," I replied, watching him glide through my lab. I liked the way he moved. Quiet, graceful, with a strong masculine edge that shouted *predator*. If I had to guess, I'd say he was a shifter. Alpha wolf, I presumed. He turned to the corner office and walked in.

"Alpha." The words left my lips without me thinking about it.

Talon slowly turned his gaze toward me. His eyes flashed golden, and I stepped forward, inexplicably drawn to him.

Mate. He mouthed the word, but no sound came out. I stopped inches away from him. My body shivered with need.

He drank me in with his gaze and said, "Dr. Aisling Lovelle?" He glanced over my shoulder at the certificates hanging on the wall. "I'm impressed. With all of it. And you."

His words brought me out of the trance I'd fallen into.

I laughed shyly and stepped away. "It's just a lab. Nothing glamorous about my work. And the space, well, if you can ignore the cold, it's not a bad place to work."

"Cold?" He raised an eyebrow.

"It's freezing in here. With as much money as they invested in this building, you would think they could have spent a little more regulating the temperature."

"Have you talked to building maintenance about this?" Talon clenched his jaw.

"I have, a number of times. And so has Mr. Roberts across the hall. Maintenance came over a few times when we first moved in, and they never got it right. I stopped fighting the issue and decided to dress appropriately instead." I waved a hand down my sweater and the oversized hoodie in my hand.

"That shall be fixed." He took another sip of my coffee.

"You have an in with building maintenance?"

"I better. My name is on the building."

I tilted my head at him as I set my purse down and propped my butt on the edge of my desk.

Talon removed a business card from his wallet and handed it to me.

Talon Shelby, Esquire.

Great. I just insulted my landlord.

"Sorry, I didn't mean to insult your building." I dropped my chin. He'd probably raise the rent now.

Talon stepped in front of me and hooked my chin to meet his gaze. My heart rate clamored in my chest. The sheer size of the man made me feel like he could protect me from anything life threw at me.

"You never need to apologize to me, Dr. Love," he started.

"Lovelle. Or Ash. Just Ash will do," I interrupted.

He grinned. "Okay, Ash. Same time tomorrow?"

I frowned.

"I owe you a cup of coffee."

"You did not drink the entire thing."

He chuckled then placed the cup on the desk behind me, lightly pressing his body against mine.

His nose grazed my cheek, and he dipped his face to my neck.

The warmth of his breath bathed my skin, making me shiver. I wanted him to kiss me. I wanted to feel those sinful lips all over my body.

"Say you'll meet me tomorrow morning, Red." His voice was low and raspy.

I nodded.

"Yes?"

"Yes," I replied

He stood abruptly and winked. "Till tomorrow then, Red." He backed away.

"Technically, it's auburn." I pointed to my hair, then picked up the coffee cup and sipped while lightly running my tongue over the area his lips had been.

Talon stopped, turned, and crossed the room with two long strides. He was in my space again so close but not touching. I leaned in, brushing my hard nipples on his chest.

He ran his thumb along my cheek and gently tugged on my lower lip. "Tell that to these rosy cheeks."

I flushed despite myself.

CHAPTER SIX

AISLING

I drummed my pen on the desk, waiting for my computer to spit out data. My symptoms had been getting worse for the last few weeks. The blackout episodes were more prevalent and the bits of visions I was getting were nightmarish. What had I been doing? I shook my head. It wasn't me. Couldn't be.

The computer beeped and I rushed to my desk, keeping my fingers crossed. Please work.

Like any medication, efficacy could be determined via monitoring symptoms and bloodwork analysis. Since my symptoms hadn't reduced, I was hoping my bloodwork would tell me something different. I analyzed my blood results and slammed my fist on the desk. No change. Damn it.

There was one thing I could do. The absolute last thing I wanted to do but I was out of options. I placed my palms over my face, praying for an epiphany.

An argument in the front office had me raising my head. I stood and moved to the door when it burst open.

"Sorry, boss!" Zoey said. "I told him to wait in the lobby, but he insisted."

"It's okay, Zoey," I said peering at her around the visitor's large frame. "I'll take it from here."

"I'm Dr. Lovelle, how may I help you?" I asked the dark-haired stranger.

His sable eyes took me in from head to toe, a mixture of surprise and desire flashing through them. He wore a light gray suit tailored to fit him like a glove, highlighting his athletic physique; muscular shoulders, a narrow waist, and thick thighs. His black button-down was open enough to reveal a bronze tan and a tattoo skimmed his collarbone.

He'd been standing in front of me a full twenty seconds and didn't say a word.

I waved a hand in front of his face. "Excuse me? What are you doing in my office?"

He blinked rapidly and then said, "Uh . . . you're Dr. Lovelle?"

"Yes."

"Dr. Ash Lovelle?" he asked again.

"Still yes."

"Sorry I was expecting something, I mean someone different."

"Male. Yeah, I get that a lot. Dr. Aisling Lovelle, Ph.D. in biochemistry. Not a medical doctor. The hospital is a dozen or so miles east." I waved him out the door.

"No." He grinned. "You're the person I wanted to speak with. I'm Dr. Jethro Buchanan. You can call me Jet." He held out his hand.

"Harlo's son." I shook his hand and he nodded. "Is he okay? I haven't heard from him in a while."

I studied Jet's face and didn't see the resemblance to his father. My boss.

"He's fine. I'm not sure if he's told you about his retirement, but I'm taking over operations and wanted to get to know everyone in the business. You included."

"Oh. Okay. Thanks for the personal attention. But um . . . didn't my personnel files tell you I'm a woman?"

"No, actually there wasn't much about you at all, which is one of the reasons I'm here."

"Odd. Anyway, yeah, happy to answer any questions. Can I get you something? Coffee?" I offered.

"Well, no. I have a better idea. Since it's nearly closing time, why don't we have an early dinner? Get to know each other better. Do you have a change of clothes?" He gave me a once over with his gaze. "Why are you wearing a turtleneck? It's ninety-two degrees with sixty percent humidity."

"No, I don't," I replied, ignoring his comment about my clothes not fitting the current weather. "Why don't we stay here? I can show you around the lab."

"We'll have time to review the lab over the next few days. I'd like to get to know you in a less formal surrounding. I've found meetings out of the office make it easier to develop a rapport. There's a trendy restaurant I keep hearing about. It's a short walk from here. As long as you don't mind getting hot." He flashed me perfectly white teeth.

I rolled my eyes and was about to insist upon staying in when Zoey interrupted.

"I picked up your dry cleaning a few days ago and forgot to let you know." She hooked her arm around mine and then faced Jet. "Give us a minute, she'll be ready to go in a jiff."

Zoey tugged me into my office and closed the door.

"Damn, he is hot!" Zoey sang while lifting one leg and pumping her hips.

"Is that how you have sex? I've never seen that move before. Do it again." I smirked.

She laughed. "Don't try to joke your way out of this dinner, Ash. You need to get some, girl."

"I am not getting anything," I retorted.

"Not with that attitude you're not. Or that outfit. Strip." She unwrapped a garment bag hanging on the back of the door.

"No, I'm not. And when exactly did you pick up my dry cleaning? I don't have dry cleaning."

"Yes, you are. And yes, you do. This has been hanging here for months. It's the skirt you wore the one time we went to happy hour, ages ago." She unhooked the skirt and held it out to me.

"I'm not going. I have work to do." I argued, taking the skirt from her and throwing it on the desk behind me.

"Ash?! This is the new boss. The man with the power to give you everything and take all this," she waved her hands in the air, "away."

She was right, but so was I. If I didn't get my tonic right, all of this, my entire life would be toast.

"Aisling you will always be the number one boss bitch. But that hot piece of man meat out there owns the entire freaking company. You must play nice," she insisted.

I shook my head, thinking about all the things I needed to get done. It was not the right time for an impromptu dinner. And the audacity of that man thinking he could just show up and demand my time.

Zoey wouldn't take no for an answer. She pushed and prodded until I was stepping out of my scrubs and into the skirt.

Before I knew it, I was wearing the pencil skirt and of course, Zoey had found heels that had been hidden in a box beside my desk.

She gave me a once over and shook her head. "Lose the sweater, Ash."

"Not going to happen." I crossed my arms over my chest.

She threw her hands up in resignation and pushed me and Dr. Buchanan out of the office.

"Enjoy your dinner," Zoey waved.

I scowled at her over my shoulder.

"You clean up nice," Jet drawled. "Just had to keep the turtle neck huh?"

Why was he so interested in my wardrobe? I wore a white bodysuit under my long-sleeved turtleneck with no bra. There was no way I'd be having dinner with my new boss while flashing my nipples.

Buchanan Pharmaceuticals was owned and operated by a family

of warlocks. I interned for Dr. Harlo Buchanan for two years. He had been one of my greatest mentors. I considered him a second father. After I graduated I had planned on opening a small lab of my own. I didn't have the funds, but I had big dreams. There were a few personal projects I wanted to work on and wanted autonomy to do so. Dr. Buchanan offered to bring me under the Buchanan umbrella and work in a small satellite office. The opportunity was everything I could have ever asked for and more.

It had been five years now and Dr. Harlo never complained. His son was a mystery. I could only hope he'd be as easy to work with as his father.

My lab was located in the professional district of Port Midway. It was surrounded by other businesses including retail and restaurants. Jade Gardens, the restaurant, Dr. Buchanan was dying to try, was a short walk. The happy hour crowd gathered at the popular establishment for its Asian Fusion cuisine and to mingle with other professionals. As soon as we entered, I remembered why Zoey and I hadn't gone out again. It wasn't my scene. I was the nerdy scientist who preferred staying in versus going out for after-work drinks. I sighed inwardly.

Despite the crowd, Jet had gotten us a table, and we were seated right away. I slid into the chair opposite him, stealing glances his way while pretending to read the drink menu. He had sharp features, almost severe. His full lips softened the sharp lines, and his deep brown eyes were framed by dark, thick eyebrows and long lashes.

I ordered a water which earned me a frown from the handsome doctor. "Are you always so uptight? I don't mean to insult you, it's just, first the reluctance to go out, then the turtleneck, and now . . . Don't tell me you never drink alcohol."

"Bourbon, chilled. Make it a double," I said to the waitress who returned to the table with my glass of water and his Cabernet.

"What would you like to know, Dr. Buchanan?"

"Call me Jet." He shrugged his shoulder. "Anything you want to share."

"What if I don't want to share anything?"

His eyes narrowed at me as he sipped his wine. "How about I start first?"

I nodded.

"For reasons I care not to discuss, the board members at Buchanan Pharma had asked my father to retire, and they put me in charge. I don't mind the added responsibilities. I just didn't think it would come so soon."

He paused while the waitress dropped off my drink. He ordered a bunch of appetizers and then turned his gaze to me. "Did my father mention it to you at all? This sudden change?"

"No. Not at all. We don't speak often. Maybe once every couple of months. May I ask what prompted the board to insist on him retiring?"

Jet swirled his glass of wine and then he eyed me the way one would scrutinize a puzzle. He was contemplating if I was worthy of his trust. I didn't care about family squabbles or corporate politics. So, I shrugged.

"You don't owe me an explanation."

Jet nodded. "I'm not sure what my father's plans are. He's been in and out of the office for the past couple of weeks, tying up loose ends. I've been analyzing a few things at the main lab. Everything's good. But then there's you."

Here it comes.

"You're the only satellite office. Hell, you're the only person on our payroll who does not report on the daily. You are completely autonomous. It's like you are your own entity here in the heart of Port Midway's business district. Your numbers are good all the way around. Production and profit are steadily climbing. It's a good thing. But what I can't figure out is why. Why you?"

"Simple. I asked. Your father agreed. And like you said, production and profit are steadily climbing." I stated.

"Alright, I'll ask plainly." Jethro propped his forearms on the table and glared at me. "Are you fucking my father?"

I choked on my bourbon. "Seriously? I am not going to dignify that with an answer."

"That means yes." He leaned back in his chair and narrowed his gaze. "It tracks. An attractive woman like you has probably been getting everything and anything she wants her entire life."

"You don't know fuck-all about my life." If I could have killed him with a look, I would have.

The asshole smirked. "No reason to feel ashamed. If I were in your position, I would have also asked the rich old man for the world. However, a man in his position would've expected something in return. I want to know what the terms of your agreement were."

"Fuck you. You looked at the reports. My work should speak for itself." My nostrils flared, and I gripped the table.

"Data can be altered."

Heat crawled from the base of my spine to the back of my neck. This motherfucker.

I downed the bourbon. "I'm out. If you need anything, send me an email. Or fire me."

We stood at the same time, glaring at each other.

CHAPTER SEVEN

JETHRO

I pulled into the parking garage and slowed as I passed the Prius in a reserved parking space for Dr. Ash Lovelle. I ground my teeth.

The asshole was somehow taking advantage of Buchanan Pharmaceuticals, and I was going to find out why.

The lab was tiny, with a waiting area that looked like a spa. Soothing colors and calming music sang through the speakers. A large fish tank took up the length of one wall opposite the reception desk.

The receptionist and the only employee other than Ash greeted me with a pleasant smile. Yep, they wouldn't know me from Adam. The son and only heir to the Buchanan fortune. Her boss. And the one person she should be ass-kissing. She didn't, though. Nope, the four-foot-ten, black-haired woman guarded the lab like a fucking Doberman pinscher. She was so much shorter than me, I pushed past her with ease, only to be flummoxed at the sight of Dr. Ash Lovelle.

Ash was a she, not a he. I suppose it was sexist of me to have made the assumption but . . . mistakes happen. And Aisling was lovely. Auburn hair piled into a messy bun atop her head. Her high cheekbones and sharp nose were splattered with freckles I longed to kiss. My tongue felt thick in my mouth, and I couldn't speak.

She said something to me and waved a hand in front of my face.

Use your words, Jet. "Dr. Ash Lovelle?" I asked for the millionth time. *Why was I acting like an insecure pre-teen?*

She smiled and rattled off something about a hospital nearby then waved me off like she was dismissing me.

My vocal cords managed to work, and I introduced myself. She placed her small hand in mine. Her skin was soft and freezing cold. I maintained contact with her skin a little longer than appropriate.

A flash of concern washed over her face when she asked about my father. I assured her the old man was good and asked her to dinner. Sort of. I unintentionally insulted her wardrobe. *What the fuck is wrong with me?* I was such an asshole.

She rolled her eyes at me which struck a nerve. I deserved it for being a dick, so I let it slide . . . just this once.

I turned up the charm which didn't faze her. Damn, I must be off my game. Thankfully, the assistant saved my ass, and in a few minutes, we were walking toward Jade Gardens.

The summer heat was on full blast and the path to the restaurant crossed solid cement. Ash changed out of her scrubs and sneakers into a tan pencil skirt that showed off defined calves and firm peach. On her feet were glittery, strappy heels which gave her a couple of inches of height, bringing her head to my chest level. She kept the turtleneck though, which had to be uncomfortable. I wondered why she kept it and of course, I had to open my big mouth and ask.

She rolled her eyes again, which only increased the iciness between us. Eye rolls to men were a direct insult. Like taking an ice pick to a man's ego. It did not sit well.

And of course, it got worse. I goaded her about ordering water, and then she ordered a double bourbon. The same drink my father and I drank when we were together. Was there something between them? Harlo Buchanan had a reputation for cheating on my mother.

The thought of my father sleeping with her? My Ash? Set my nerves on fire. *Wait, my Ash? Something was seriously wrong with me. Did I have a stroke?*

I pushed the issue. But she bit back, and I liked her fire.

"Fuck you. You looked at the reports. My work should speak for itself." She cursed me. And I was captivated even though the contempt in her honey-colored eyes could've killed me. She guzzled the bourbon and stood.

Oh hell no, she was not walking out. This was just getting good. I matched her stance.

And then my day went to absolute shit.

"Jethro Buchanan. What brings you into my establishment?" Talon Shelby, my old roommate from school, stood beside our table with a shit-eating grin.

Before I could say anything to him, he turned his attention to my Aisling. Yes, mine. I'd already claimed her in my head like a horny teenage boy.

Ash held out her hand and he kissed the inside of her wrist. I grit my teeth.

"Get your claws off my employee, Talon."

Ash hit me with a glare, her expression full of annoyance.

"My colleague," I corrected.

She rolled her eyes dramatically this time, telling me she was knowingly irritating me with those eye rolls.

"The lady can speak for herself," Talon quipped, still holding onto her hand.

"This is Dr. Aisling Lovelle. She runs our satellite office in Shelby Centre," I told him.

"Oh, I know. We've met." Talon ran his sausage finger over her hand. "I'm almost offended, Dr. Lovelle. You said you were too busy for dinner."

Ash dropped his hand. "I was. I am. New boss over here insisted." She pointed to me.

Talon nodded. "I see. Next time, no excuses."

The waitress came to the table with the appetizers I ordered.

"Ah, your food is here. I thought you two were leaving," Talon said after the waitress walked away. "Please sit, and order anything you want. On me, of course. We need to catch up, Jet." He clapped me on the shoulder. "It's been too long. I'll have another place setting brought over. Please, Aisling. Sit. It'd make me look bad if you refused the owner."

The asshole smiled at Ash, showing off his dimples, and she replied with a sweet smile of her own.

Fuck this guy.

"Actually, Talon, we're in the middle of a business discussion right now. Do you mind giving us some space? We'll catch up some other time."

"Nothing's changed with you, has it, magician?" He straightened his spine, glaring at me.

"I have no idea what you mean, pup," I retorted.

"You know exactly what I mean. Always competing with me. When are you going to learn, there's no competition. You're not even close to being in the same league as me." He straightened his back, staring me dead in the eye.

"You're right about that. I wouldn't want to be in the same league as you, dog. Flea shampoo is not my thing."

"Aww, did I ruffle the little wizard's feathers?" he quipped. "Or did you lose your magic wand again? It's probably where you left it last. Up your ass. Not sure what you learned at magic school, but according to the movies, that's not how it works."

"Wizard movies? How old are you nine? Your insult game is weak. I almost feel bad for you." I laughed.

"Can you believe this guy?" I asked Ash, who wasn't there.

"Where'd she go?" I asked Talon who was already heading out the door. I followed on his heels.

CHAPTER EIGHT

TALON

I sat at the far end of the restaurant watching the happy-hour crowd enjoy the food, drinks, and company. People liked to mingle after a long day at work. As an investor and part owner, I appreciated their need to slake their thirst at one of my establishments. I had nothing to do with the success of Jade. That was the chef's doing. He was the heart and soul of the place.

A familiar face strolled into the restaurant full of swagger. Jethro Buchanan. My former best friend. We were roommates during our undergrad years. But we were both competitive, and it was only a matter of time before we had gotten on each other's nerves.

It had been years since we'd last talked. Senior year if I remember correctly. We'd lost touch over the years. I wasn't even sure why. It wasn't like we had a falling out. Or did we? I rubbed my chin as college memories ran through my mind. We were both competitive. But not with each other. It wasn't a girl. It wasn't sports. Was it money? Perhaps? His family was loaded. Mine had it until my father lost the family fortune. I'd been working since I was twelve. I had to work hard from middle school and through law school. He never gloated. Was I insecure? Probably. He never made me feel like I was less than him. In fact, during our undergrad years, he had helped me with my studies because I was busy working and playing sports. Maybe I was the asshole and needed to apologize.

I was about to approach him when I noticed his date. Aisling. My Aisling. I'd just asked her this morning to join me for dinner. Did she reject me to go out with Jet? Were they an item?

Then again, she did work for Buchanan Pharmaceuticals. The asshole's family. *Maybe it was a business meeting,* I told myself, which calmed my testosterone-filled ego. I sipped my Scotch, intending to watch how the scene played out.

That plan went out the window fast. There was something about Aisling. A magnetic pull I couldn't deny. I'd thought she and I met before in my sex club. There was a familiarity I felt in my gut. *Is she my mistress?* Couldn't be. The stature was similar. The hair was a tad less fiery than I had remembered. And she had shown zero recollection of me. Curiosity, yes. Attraction, yes. Other than that, she didn't know me, but she was intrigued, and that I could work with.

Plus, Ash was so different from the woman I'd met a few weeks ago. She was shy and sweet with a spicy edge I was dying to explore.

My focus remained solely on Red. My Red. She was constantly on my mind. Our morning meetups the past couple of days were time well spent, but not enough. I needed more of her. I needed to make her mine. To hell with the woman I'd met at Nirvana. This woman, this Dr. Lovelle, was the one.

Abruptly, she stood and glared at him. He mimicked her posture. *Well isn't this interesting*? If it weren't for all the people in the restaurant, I would have been able to hear their conversation.

As if my body had switched to autopilot, I was gliding across the floor to their table.

I said hello to Jet and greeted her by grasping her hand and kissing the inside of her wrist. My nose grazed her skin, taking in her scent. *Mistress, my beast cooed.*

Jet muttered something about staying away from his employee.

I ignored him and focused on Ash.

We exchanged a few words all of which went in one ear and out the other. My focus was on my Aisling.

Ash removed her hand from mine, which would have been insulting if not for the rosy hue on her cheeks. "I was. I am. New boss over here insisted." She pointed at Jet.

Of course, the silver-spooned brat would insist on occupying her time. It was nothing short of a miracle they hadn't met before. I needed to learn more about their situation. "I see. Next time, no excuses."

She blushed again and shot me a sweet smile.

The waitress arrived with a platter of appetizers, and I invited myself to their table.

Despite my beasts' confirmation, my man brain wanted irrefutable proof. This was hardly the place or time, but fuck it took everything in me to refrain from dropping to my knees and gliding my nose along her pussy to take in her scent. It was a primal instinct. Pure wolf.

Dr. Lovelle released my hand, and I nearly snatched it back like it was mine to hold. I tempered my possessive beast and gazed upon her face.

Her shy smile and the way she blushed at every comment or lust-laced innuendo had me convinced, this was not the same woman I'd fucked for hours. *Was it?*

"Talon, we're in the middle of a business discussion right now. Do you mind giving us some space? We'll catch up some other time," Jet said, dismissing me.

Asshole. The memories came flooding back. It wasn't a rivalry. Not really. We both liked to annoy each other as much as possible. We were competitive and one day we'd taken that competitive edge a little too far.

We weren't kids anymore. The posturing was silly, and he was making me look bad in front of the beautiful doctor. I straightened my spine and began exchanging digs with my old friend. It was like old times, and it almost made me giddy.

"Can you believe this guy?" Jet pointed at me and looked at Ash who wasn't there.

I hurried out of the restaurant, trying to catch her scent, but there were too many people around for me to get an accurate read with my smeller. I scanned the parking lot in front of the restaurant looking left and then right.

A few stores down, she bumped into a guy holding a bag of donuts in one hand and a half-eaten one in the other. He leaned in to kiss her cheek. Shit. She knew him and followed him to a Tesla. Wanker.

They got into the vehicle and drove off.

"Who the fuck is that?" Jet asked standing beside me.

"Don't know. Did you drive or walk from the lab?"

"Walked."

I turned on my heel and headed to my office. There was a walking path that connected the office buildings with the retail section. It was convenient for worker bees, and the parking lot out front made it accessible during off business hours.

Jet kept up with my strides to my office where I turned on the television and accessed my security cameras. I never paid attention to the security cams placed around and in the building unless there was a need, making this the first time in years. I entered my access codes and flipped through the different cameras.

"Surveillance? Really, perv?" Jet frowned.

"I own the building asshole. Of course, I have surveillance cameras," I deadpanned. "You can leave if this bothers your good boy sensibilities."

"Why do you care about her?" he asked.

"I know her. Sort of," I muttered.

"Parking lot, third floor," he replied.

Not bothering to ask how he knew that information, I panned through the garage surveillance to the third floor and saw the Tesla pull up behind a parked Prius.

The Tesla moved to an empty parking spot. I scrambled, tapping on the keyboard until I found a camera angle that gave me the perfect shot of the inside of the car.

Jet and I focused on the screen.

The donut guy tilted her chin and leaned in for a kiss. Ash's lips met his and then it got a hell of a lot more interesting.

Her turtleneck sweater came off and his hands disappeared between her legs. Next thing I knew, her skirt was bunched around her waist and she was straddling the lucky fucker.

Blood rushed to my cock. Jet groaned beside me.

"Dude, you need to go," I rasped.

"Fuck off. Keep your dick in your pants until I leave," he told me, not taking his eyes off the big screen. "Can't you enlarge the video?"

I tapped on my keyboard and the camera angle in question took up the entire screen. I groaned.

Jet moved the client chair to the other side of my office, giving us space to enjoy the show.

CHAPTER NINE

AISLING

Dr. Buchanan, the elder, was a kind man. His son, not so much. I wasn't sure why he was goading me into a fight, but I'd had enough. The fucker had the nerve to come right out and ask if I was having sex with his father. Gross. And fuck-all insulting. I couldn't believe the asshole.

As I was about to leave, a gorgeous man wearing a navy blue suit arrived at our table. Talon. I'd been purposely coming to the office before dawn for the past few days in hopes of running into him. He didn't disappoint.

There was something about his raspy voice and pale green eyes that drew me in and put me at ease. He seemed familiar, yet I couldn't place him.

Tingly shivers ran through me as soon as we made skin-to-skin contact. *Easy, Ash it's just a handshake.* He turned my palm over and ran his nose along the inside of my wrist. The gesture was gentle and brief, yet those shivers shot straight to my core.

I withdrew my hand and looked longingly at my now-empty glass of bourbon. Between the infuriating yet sexy Dr. Buchanan and the smoldering gentleman, Talon Shelby, my libido was in overdrive.

The food arrived and Talon invited himself to join us. Not that I'd planned on staying but the banter between him and Jet was intriguing. At first.

I took in their appearances, appreciating their similarities and differences. Jet was a tad shorter and not as broad. He had a darker, edgier sex appeal. Talon was smooth as whiskey, with rough hands and a devastating smile. Add Pope to the mix and my imagination was doing a happy dance through Slutville.

I bit the inside of my cheek, giving my dirty thoughts the boot. Not the time, Ash.

The men were familiar. From the way they teased each other, they'd known one another for a while. It was freaking hilarious. Magic wand? Flea shampoo? I wanted to know more about them but considering Jet had insulted me moments ago, it was not a situation I wanted to be a part of. While they exchanged barbs, I took the opportunity to escape.

As soon as I exited the restaurant, I recognized a swathe of blonde hair and tanned skin. What was he doing here? I crossed the parking lot and he met my gaze.

"Hi!" Pope smiled, a bag of donuts in one hand, a half-eaten one in the other. "What brings you here? I didn't take you for a happy hour kind of gal."

He bent down to kiss my cheek.

"I'm not but I could use a ride." I opened the passenger door to his Tessie and sat down.

Pope tucked the bag of donuts under one arm, opened the door, and slid behind the wheel.

"Uh . . . is everything okay?" He placed the bag in the back seat and started the car.

"Meh." I shrugged. "Just had a brief meeting with my new boss."

"New boss? Well, it sounds like the meeting sucked. I'd offer you a donut, but you don't like . . ."

I leaned in and took a big bite of the chocolate's deliciousness. Creme dripped down the corner of my mouth.

"Sugar," he finished stating.

"It's good." I chewed then flicked my tongue to the corner of my mouth to lick the creme that had oozed out of my mouth.

Pope leaned over and kissed me while licking the creme coating my lips.

"You missed some." His voice had a sexy tone that added fuel to the fire brewing in my lady bits.

I noticed Talon and Jet across the parking lot, looking right at us.

"Drive, please," I said and tried to take the donut from Pope's hands.

He moved the donut out of reach and drove out of the parking lot. "You're welcome to have more, but only if I can feed you."

"You're driving," I told him.

"So?"

I didn't have a witty response, so I dove in for another bite running my tongue along his finger.

"Aww fuck. You're killing me, angel. Please tell me I'm driving you home, so I can sink my cock into your pussy."

"Nope, office, please. I need my car. After the light, take a right into the next driveway." I ate the last bite of his donut. "The parking garage is on the other side of the building." I swallowed the dessert and began sucking the chocolate off his fingers.

Between fighting with Jet and Talon's presence my body was brimming with need. Running into Pope was the cherry on top of a delicious hot man dessert.

Pope drove as I'd directed, all while sliding his fingers down my throat. Perhaps we should have gone straight to my place.

"Third floor, to the left, you'll see my car." I released his finger.

Pope brought his car to a stop behind my car. "Come here." He tilted my chin and pressed his lips against mine.

His tongue dove into my mouth, tasting of chocolate and creme. My thighs clenched; my pussy throbbed with want, making me squirm in my seat.

"Maybe we should continue this at home," I said between kisses.

Pope drove the car a few feet and parked in an empty spot, then brought my face to meet his.

Or maybe not. It was risky, anyone could have walked by. But I didn't care. The thought of being watched heightened my arousal. And there was something to be said about seizing the moment. My body was on fire, and Pope was there stoking the flames.

He palmed my breasts through my sweater, prompting me to shrug out of my turtleneck. Pope pushed the straps of my bodysuit down my shoulders, granting him access to my nipples. I gasped as his teeth scraped the taut buds.

He slid his hands under my skirt, seeking my pussy.

"Spread those legs," he told me.

I bunched up my skirt and drew my knees apart.

Pope undid the snaps of my bodysuit and his deft fingers worked over my drenched cunt, slipping up and down my sex. He sunk two fingers into my core while rubbing the pad of his thumb over my clit.

I moaned into his mouth and reached between his legs. My climax was soaring, but I was just getting started. Slipping my hand under his gym shorts I sought his length, pleased to find him rigid and ready for me.

"Pope, I want you. Need you," I moaned, rocking my hips to clash with his fingers.

"No. Not yet. I want you to come for me. Then you can sit on my cock and ride me until you come again."

His filthy mouth drove me wild. I came, gasping for breath. If someone peered into the windshield, they would have a clear view of my pussy coming all over Pope's fingers. That made me want more.

"Cock." I pushed on Pope's chest.

He chuckled. "Clean my fingers first." He raised his sticky digits in front of my face. I sat up a little to meet his hand and closed my legs.

He drew his hand away and shook his head. "Keep your legs spread."

I did as he asked, and he brought his fingers to my mouth. I sucked them clean, keeping my eyes on him the entire time.

"Good girl. Sit on my cock." He sat back and brought his shorts down.

I straddled his lap, my skirt and the top of my bodysuit bunched at my waist. I wanted to be completely naked but didn't waste time with the details. I wanted his cock more.

Pope reclined his seat as I positioned myself over his tip. I sank over his crown and breathed, allowing my body to adjust to the intrusion. He had the perfect girth that made my pussy gush every single time.

Pope wasn't in the mood to take things slow. He thrust into me from below, making me cry out in pleasure.

I captured his lips with mine, moaning and groaning while rocking over his cock. I worked a steady rhythm, my walls squeezing his length. Visions of Jethro, Talon, and Pope flashed in my mind. The three of them together. With me. I rode Pope harder and faster. Talon, Jet, and Pope. They were equally thirst-quenching. I wanted them all. Together.

Hot skin. Hard muscles. Thick cocks. Oh my fucking god. My imagination was going wild, and I was riding Pope like a bull-rider.

"I fucking love your pussy." His big hands gripped my ass. "And I love it when you use my cock for your pleasure. Tell me, Ash. Who was the asshole that left you wanting, baby? The attorney? The new boss? Someone else?"

"Both."

"Oh fuck. Two of them?" He groaned.

I pressed my forehead to his, my hips slowing to a gentler, slower pace. "Would that bother you, Gaius? If I fucked two other men?"

"No. As long as you tell me every sexy detail," he rasped.

Pope was the perfect man. He was always open to my needs, wants, and dirty talk. Since I met Talon, I'd been coming home from work needing to scratch an itch. Pope knew I'd been riled up by another man. It didn't bother him at all. He asked for details and I gave them, loving the way it turned him on.

"I'd rather have you right there with me," I replied, bouncing up and down on his length.

He groaned, his eyes rolling back in his head.

"Watching you get fucked by a big cock while mine is in your mouth would be so hot. Fuck, Ash. You're going to make me come." He guided my hips, setting a harsh pace that had us both grunting. Sweat dripped down my spine. His face was between my breasts, muffling his moans. My fingers were tangled into his hair, and I tugged, feeling another orgasm rise.

"That's it. Squeeze my cock when you come." Pope let out a guttural moan.

I erupted, my walls clamping down on him. Warmth filled my channel as his release mixed with mine.

I folded on top of him, heart hammering, lungs gasping for air. We were silent for a moment, blissed out. His lips ghosted over my shoulder and he lazily trailed his fingers up and down my back. I closed my eyes.

CHAPTER TEN
POPE

My typical day consisted of working in front of my computer station at home. I was a wanted fugitive due to my hacking skills, but they'd never find me. I had an innate affinity for electronics. Computer coding came naturally to me, and I had perfected my skills over time, allowing me to erase my presence online and making me the perfect and most sought-after hacker.

It also made it easy to track my sexy next-door neighbor, who should be on her way home. I took a brief shower and glanced at the clock. The tracker on her car showed it was still parked at her office. Odd.

I checked her phone, which showed her walking out of the office and heading in the opposite direction of the parking garage. That was even stranger.

Ash was a creature of habit. The only time she went out after work was for Zoey's birthday, which, according to her calendar, was nine months away.

My internal alerts went up, and I hopped in my car heading

toward the restaurant area near her office building. I reversed into a parking spot and sat for a time, staring at the tracker. She was in an Asian Fusion restaurant. The after-work crowd was swarming the place for what looked like happy hour. I thought about my options for a second. I could walk into the bar area or wait in the car until she finished whatever she was doing.

A horn blared breaking my train of thought. I shook my head telling the anxious driver I wasn't leaving. *Guess I can't just sit here.* With the decision made for me, I stepped out of the car into the muggy heat.

Jade Gardens had large windows, facing the street. I took a chance and casually strolled by but didn't see her. I passed the restaurant, continued to the end of the shops, and turned around. It was stupid and quite obvious, but I had to know what she was doing there. Okay, that was a lie. It wasn't what she was doing that made me curious. It was who she was doing it with.

On my second pass, I got a glimpse of my Aisling who stood at a table facing a man dressed in gray slacks and a black button-down. He was reasonably handsome if you liked dark broody types. Ash and the unknown man were glaring at each other, and I stood outside gawking.

Another man strode up to their table. He was dressed in a suit that fit snugly over his thick body. Too snug if one were to ask me. He turned to the side, and my stomach bottomed out. It was him. The fucker that hooked up with Ash's alter ego - the Mistress in Nirvana. Shit. Shit. Shit. I moved along and headed into a donut shop to order a half dozen donuts. Why? Fuck if I knew. I had a sweet tooth, but half a dozen donuts were overkill. If that wasn't enough the girl behind the counter gave me a chocolate-covered creme donut freebie. I waved thanks and bit into the sugary confection.

The sugar rush appeased the anxiousness rolling through my gut. Somewhat.

I hit the unlock button on my key fob and decided to wait in the car. I was certifiably insane. I wasn't jealous, not really. I liked watching her at Nirvana. It was sexy as fuck. But that guy was different. Mistress had spent the entire night with him, telling me she liked the guy. And that made me jealous. I wanted to be the main man in Ash's life. That was stupid considering she told me straight up she didn't do relationships. What are you doing Pope?

I turned my gaze back to Jade Gardens and was surprised to see Aisling walking toward me. Her creased brow told me something hadn't gone well. I should have been outraged on her behalf for whatever had happened and a part of me was. A larger part of me was doing a little jig inside because they'd pissed her off and now, she was coming to me.

"Hi! What brings you here? I didn't take you for a happy hour kind of gal." I bent down to kiss her cheek.

"I'm not but I could use a ride." She got in my car.

Smug satisfaction rolled through me as I got behind the wheel.

She said something about a new boss, then took a big bite of my donut. Except for bacon candy, Ash didn't eat sugary sweets. Something set her off, and I was glad I was there when she needed someone. Again. Stalking her was paying off.

My cock swelled as she began licking chocolate off my fingers. Well shit. This was going better than I planned.

She directed me to her car which was unnecessary, but I played along. The high from her licking my fingers lingered and shot straight to my dick.

"Maybe we should continue this at home," she said in that husky tone that made me melt.

Nope, not home. We were finishing this right here. I parked in the corner of the empty parking lot, right in front of a surveillance camera.

A few days ago, Ash had mentioned meeting Talon Shelby. She talked about him as though they hadn't met before. I knew differently because I was there when they'd met at Nirvana. It was obvious then that she wasn't aware of what she'd been doing when her alter-ego took over.

It made me wonder if Talon had recognized her. He had to. But she'd been wearing a mask at the club, and although I hadn't had direct interaction with the Mistress, I knew there were stark differences between the two.

I began researching Talon Shelby and knew he owned the building as well as other establishments around the city. There was a lot I hadn't uncovered about the rich prick, but I had mostly wanted to know what his true motivations were in regard to Aisling.

From what she said, she ran into Talon one morning on her way to the lab. And they'd been running into each other ever since. Accidentally on purpose, of course. If my hunch was correct, the asshole was in his office, spying on Ash at that moment. I would have if I were him. And since I had to sit there while he banged the Mistress for hours, I decided to return the favor and allow him to watch me and Ash fuck in his garage. What could I say, I was a giver.

In no time, I had Aisling writhing on my fingers, soaking my seat with her cum. She was fucking magnificent. She licked her juices off my digits and I turned toward the camera and winked. *You're welcome, asshole.*

By that point, I was hard as a rock, precum spilling over my tip. Ash sheathed with my length with her cunt and before I knew it, she was enticing me with dirty talk. Thoughts of me and him taking her at the same time had me exploding into her pussy. Completely bare-back. Again. Fuck yes. It wasn't something I did, ever. But with Ash, it was the only way I wanted it.

We sat in silence, catching our breath. Ash's heart rate steadied to a normal pace, her breathing evened out, and her body went heavy. Ash was sated and asleep with my cock still tucked into her pussy. Pride soared through me.

I held in my laughter and raised the seat to its upright position. Ash didn't seem to notice, so I buckled us in, reversed, and drove us home. It was a bit unsafe. Not really. Self-driving cars had their perks. And we lived less than five miles away.

Parked in my garage, I kissed her shoulder, her neck, and the side of her face. She released a soft sigh, making me chuckle.

I parted the seam of her lips with my tongue. She kissed me back and shifted her hips causing her core to contract around my dick, making me hard again. She moaned and then opened her eyes.

"Hi," she said in a sleepy voice. "Where are we?"

"My garage."

"Oh shit. Did I fall asleep? How did you drive with me in your lap? You should have woken me."

"Relax, angel." I rubbed her back. "You're with me. You're safe. You can sex me up until you pass out anytime you want."

That earned me a real kiss and round two in my garage.

"Do you want to talk about your meeting?" I asked Aisling over dinner. Ash and I had mediocre kitchen skills, but we managed to put together a salad and a pasta dish.

"Umm . . . not much to say except he's an ass," she said, then swallowed a mouthful of pasta.

"Who is he?"

"Boss's son. Jethro Buchanan."

"Interesting," I murmured making a mental note to cyberstalk the dude. "Does this mean the old man kicked it and Junior is taking over?"

"No, Harlo is still alive, just retiring. But yes, Jet is taking over. I knew that was an eventuality, but I didn't realize it would come so soon."

"I take it you've met this Jet dude before," I said with a little too much sarcasm in my voice. Jesus, I needed to reign in my jealous streak. Wait, I thought I didn't have one. Okay, I was lying to myself. I was totally jealous when it came to Ash.

"Nope. First time. Harlo mentioned him of course. Jet's older than me by a few years. By the time I met Harlo, his son was doing an internship abroad."

Ash set her fork down and regarded me with a pensive look.

I smirked. "Ask your questions, Aisling."

"What makes you think I have questions?" Her brows furrowed.

"The big question mark blinking above your head." I swirled my finger in the air.

She threw a paper napkin at me.

I chuckled. "Seriously, babe. Ask me whatever you want."

"I just realized I don't know anything about you."

"I don't know anything about you either," I retorted, which was a bald-faced lie. I knew everything. Aisling Marie Lovelle, age thirty-two. Mother: Gillian, lead witch of the Moon Serpent Coven. Father: Donovan, human. Parents lived in a commune located in Clarenceville, a small town in the mountains, north of Port Midway. Aisling visited them but not as often lately. My research revealed her father had dementia. Something had happened during her last visit a few months ago because soon after, she began her late-night excursions.

"I asked first," she replied. She tapped her pointer finger on her chin. "Tell me everything, Gaius Pope."

I chuckled. "Not much to tell aside from what you already know. I'm twenty-eight, a work-from-home coder. I was adopted by human parents at the age of six. I have one brother, who is also adopted. My parents and brother live on the West Coast. I moved to Midway almost ten years ago for work and stayed."

"You're not a coder are you?"

"I am. Sort of. Most of my income comes from my hacking skills," I admitted.

Her lips curved into a devious smile. "And here I thought you were the innocent boy living next door?'

I barked a laugh. "I am innocent."

"Please. That's like me saying I'm a nun."

She pushed her dinner plate to the side and rested her forearms on the table. "What type of magic do you have?"

I frowned. "What makes you think I have magic?"

"You said you were adopted by humans, telling me that you are not."

My frown turned into a smile. She was smart. I needed to remember that. "I do. Not sure what kind, though. I have speedy healing and an affinity for the elements. Metal in particular."

"Hmmm . . . Interesting. My dad does, too. He's not mystic, though," she said thoughtfully, trying to figure out what those traits meant. There were many different flavors of magic; some, like shifters and vampires, were more obvious than others. I was unsure, and my adopted parents didn't know either. Aside from family, I never talked about my magic with anyone. But Ash meant more to me than any woman or man that I'd ever met.

"I," I cleared my throat. "I don't know much about my magic. Where it came from or how to use it entirely. It's a mystery. I gravitated to computer science because I'd hoped to find my biological parents to piece together the puzzle. So far, nothing."

"That's interesting. I always thought I was adopted." She casually rose and began clearing the table.

My eyebrows shot to my forehead. "Why is that?"

"Red," she pointed to her head. "Both of my parents have dark hair. Everyone on my mother's side has dark hair. My father isn't close to his family, so I don't know them. But my mother insists there's a redhead somewhere in the family tree."

I stood behind her at the sink where she was rinsing dishes and pressed my lips to the top of her head. "I like your red hair."

"Thank you. And thank you for bringing me home and dinner." She angled her head giving me access to her neck.

I feathered kisses down her neck to her shoulders. She pushed her ass against my crotch, waking up my dick . . . again. My hand snaked around her belly, working my way under the rolled-up waistband of my sweatpants she put on after our shower earlier.

She wiggled free and said, "I have another question."

I reached for her, and she slipped away. "Ask," I stalked after her. She went upstairs to my loft which was my working space.

She stopped in front of my desk which was wall-to-wall monitors. But Ash wasn't interested in my gear. She sat in my chair and swiveled it to face the window on the adjacent wall of my monitors, showcasing the perfect view of her front door. "See anything interesting happening across the street?"

A lump formed in my throat. Shit.

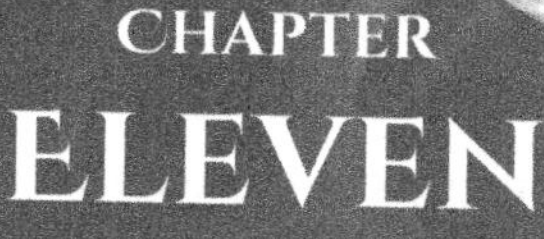

CHAPTER ELEVEN

AISLING

"Thanks, Pope." I leaned over the center console and planted a gentle kiss on his cheek.

"Anytime, angel." He kissed me back and then covered his yawn.

My hacker was not a morning person. I giggled to myself and got out of the car. I told him I was fine taking a rideshare to work since I'd left my car at the office overnight, but he insisted.

Waking up with Pope wasn't as terrifying as I'd thought it would be. I had my issues with commitment, and yet falling asleep with him and waking in his arms felt . . . good. The more time we spent together, the better it got. Considering my issues, I suspected it wasn't going to last. Because of the impending separation I had envisioned in my mind, I gave him a temporary pass for his lame response to my question about him having the perfect view of my front door. According to the computer-coding savant, he never noticed my comings and goings. I called bullshit.

"Good morning, Red."

I jumped back, nearly tripping over my own feet.

Large hands braced my elbow, and my gaze followed the

appendage, craning my head to peer into my landlord's beautiful face.

"Apologies, I didn't mean to startle you." Talon regarded me with unrestrained amusement.

"Dammit, Talon." I swatted his arm. "Didn't your mother tell you not to sneak up on women like that?"

We'd been running into each other since the first morning we met. It was kind of an unspoken agreement between us. Although I expected him, the big man managed to sneak up on me every time.

He tilted his head to the side, stared into space, and then shook his head. "No. I must have missed that lesson."

"Ha. Ha. Not funny." I rolled my eyes.

He chuckled. "You left Jade in a rush. I hope it wasn't something I said."

"No. Not at all. I just wanted my meeting with Jet to be over."

"Guess my intrusion wasn't so bad then?"

"It was perfect timing. You saved me."

Talon had charm and sex appeal in spades. The way he looked at me made me feel like he was born to worship every inch of me. It was deliciously arousing and unnerving.

"Well, I don't want to impose or cause any complications with you and your boyfriend, but maybe you can save me from having coffee alone. Would you like to join me?"

"No boyfriend." Those two words came out in a rush.

He frowned and canted his head to the side. "The Tesla?"

"Oh, no, that's Pope. It's uh . . . complicated." My stomach began to sour. It wasn't a lie, yet it made me uncomfortable dismissing my relationship with Pope. "He's a really good friend, and we have an . . . understanding. And I yeah. I need to get to work. Enjoy your coffee."

Stop rambling Ash and get to the lab.

"I wasn't trying to pry." Talon's voice was sincere, and he regarded me with a genuine look of something I couldn't place. Understanding. Acceptance. Intrigue.

The fantasies I'd had about him and Pope flashed into my mind, making me feel hot. He wasn't a mind reader but the way he was smiling at me made me feel like I was wearing my lust-filled fantasies on my face.

Talon stroked my cheeks which were flushed with warmth.

"It's fine." I began fishing in my purse for my key card. "And thanks, but I need to get to work."

"Lose your key card again?"

"Yes. It's like that damn thing vanishes somehow." I dug out a hair brush, my wallet, a tampon, lip gloss, lipstick, and two scrunchies and handed them to Talon. I found my car keys, keys to my office, another tampon, breath mints, hand sanitizer, and mascara.

"How much crap do you have in that thing?"

I looked over at the man holding two fistfuls of my belongings.

Jesus, Ash.

"Shit. I'm sorry. It's in here somewhere."

"Here, why don't we put your treasure trove back into the abyss, and I'll walk you to your office."

I began placing my things back into my purse and something started to buzz.

"Shit!" Talon jumped back. "What the fuck is that?"

My belongings fell to the ground while one item, in particular, began vibrating in his palm.

"Wait. Is this a . . ." Talon scrutinized the item.

"Forget about it. It's nothing." I reached for it and he held it away from me with a big grin on his face.

"This is a vibrator. You bring a vibrator to work?" He chortled.

"Stop. Give it back." My cheeks were hot. "Seriously, Talon." I tiptoed and snatched it from his hand while he bowed over laughing.

To make matters worse, I couldn't get the darn thing to shut off. Laughter bubbled out of me. It was just too ridiculous. Talon and I stood there laughing for a good minute.

"Okay, okay, you've had your fun," I pouted.

"Sorry. It's just. . . you are unexpected." He dabbed his eyes and began helping me gather the rest of my things. "Let's get you to your office."

"Are you, um . . . rubbing one out at your desk? On your lunch break? How many times a day?" he asked while swiping his key card for the elevator, a playful grin tugging at the corner of his lips.

"Seriously? Can we pretend you didn't see that?"

"Not possible." His heated gaze traveled the length of me. "I'll be thinking about you and your special lipstick all day."

My thighs clenched. For some perverse reason, I wanted to give him a live show. Something was seriously wrong with me. I blamed him. As much as I craved his presence, I was uncharacteristically bashful around him.

We entered the elevator, and I chose the farthest corner from him.

Talon closed the distance between us and pulled the hairpin which was holding my bun in place, causing my locks to fall around my shoulders. His body heat slid along my skin, making me tingle . . . everywhere.

"Do I make you nervous, doctor?" His voice had a sexy rasp that made me do a weird wiggle, thrusting move with my hips.

"Nope," I squeaked like one of those puppy toys. *God kill me now.* I hurried out of the elevator.

He chuckled lightly.

I managed to unlock the office door without doing anything else embarrassing. "Thanks, Talon."

"No, thank you." He smiled. "I love our mornings together, Red."

He leaned in and whispered in my ear. "Think of me when you play with your toy today."

"I don't do that." I trembled as his minty breath caressed my neck.

Talon stroked my cheek, and I leaned into his touch, yearning for more.

"Sure you don't. I'll be thinking about you when I stroke my cock," he said in a low husky tone and then sauntered away from me, leaving me bereft.

"I can feel you checking out my ass," he said, not bothering to turn around.

"It's a nice ass," I muttered under my breath.

"I heard that."

Mortified, I hurried into the office and heard him laughing before I closed the door.

CHAPTER TWELVE

TALON

"Here you go, sir." The cashier at Middle Urth Cafe handed me a paper bag. "We can deliver this. Free of charge."

"I got this. But thanks." I signed the credit card terminal and dropped some cash in the tip jar.

"The redhead, huh? Nice," he commented with an approving nod.

I gave him a hostile glare.

"I didn't mean to offend, sir. She's hot. I mean, you make a great couple," he stammered. "I'm going to go now."

The cashier scurried into the kitchen like his ass was on fire.

It didn't surprise me that he knew Aisling. She left an impression. The manager of the cafe immediately knew who she was and what she always ordered, which worked out in my favor. There was something about Dr. Lovelle that made me want to take care of her. Sure, asking around about her was a bit stalker-ish, but I had good intentions. Mostly.

Ash's assistant was on the phone, so I strolled past her desk and entered the lab.

"Motherfucker!" Aisling cursed.

Her potty mouth made me chuckle. I followed the sound of her voice to the breakroom, where she was removing her sweater.

"Dammit." She began rinsing the coffee-covered sweater in the kitchenette sink.

"What is it with you and coffee?" I asked.

She jumped back, eyes wide. "Bloody fucking hell, Talon! Can you stop with the sneaking up on me?!"

I laughed. "Sorry, Red. I wanted to stop by and see if you were making use of that special lipstick of yours."

"Ssshh! You said you'd never speak about that again!"

"I did no such thing." I gave her a teasing grin.

She narrowed her gaze and the corner of her top lip curled up into a snarl. *Is that supposed to be her mean face?* Fucking adorable.

"Teasing. I wanted to surprise you with lunch." I held up the paper bag.

Her gaze softened and a sweet smile graced her lips.

"According to the manager at Middle Urth, your favorite is the Mediterranean Salad with chicken and Zoey's is the Thai Crunch Salad, no protein." I placed the bag on the table and withdrew the take-out containers.

"You bought lunch for me and my best friend?" she asked, her shoulder brushing my arm.

I breathed her in and said, "Not a big deal, Red. To be honest, I wanted an excuse to see you."

"Thank you, Talon. That was very thoughtful." She tiptoed, lifting her face and aiming for my cheek. I leaned in meeting her halfway and then tilted my head, surprising her by lightly pressing our lips together.

The kiss was soft, exploratory. I had to remind myself to breathe. My tongue slipped into her mouth, savoring her sweet taste of cinnamon and vanilla. I wound my arms around her waist and pulled her body flush against my chest. Our kiss deepened and she released a soft moan that turned my cock into steel.

"Ash! Oh, sorry!" Zoey exclaimed.

Ash disengaged herself from me and stepped away.

"He just waltzed in here like he owned the place," Zoey continued.

I am the owner, cockblocker.

"It's fine, Zoey. This is Talon Shelby. Talon, Zoey," Ash said.

"Shelby? Shit, you do own the place," Zoey muttered.

"He also bought us salads," Ash added.

"Salads from Middle Urth?! Awww. Thanks, big guy. You can go back to snogging my best friend." Zoey smiled, then pointed at the salad. "I will tuck into that when I return from my errands. Do you need anything, Ash?"

"I'm good. See you soon." Ash placed the to-go containers into the refrigerator while Zoey disappeared into the lab.

The kiss was sweet. But not nearly enough. I hoisted Ash onto the counter and settled myself between her legs.

"We can do better than that." I crashed my lips to hers. Our mouths melded, and our tongues danced. She threaded her fingers into my hair, holding my face to hers.

"Mr. Shelby!" Zoey's screech startled me and Ash. "Someone is here to see you. He's from the maintenance department."

"Shit fucking timing," I groaned.

Ash giggled and slipped off the counter. "You should do something about that." She pointed at my crotch.

I adjusted my erection before meeting with the crew I'd asked to take a look at the cooling problem in the lab. The issue took longer than I thought, and it still wasn't fixed.

"Hey baby," I called out, realizing half a second too late that I may have overstepped with the term of endearment.

"Yeah?" she answered, still looking at a clipboard then turned to face me.

A big smile took over my face, and my six-foot-four, two-hundred-plus-pound frame felt lighter. Unconsciously, I rubbed my chest. *So this is what it feels like to find your mate.*

"Do you have a second? I wanted to introduce you to the guys who will be fixing the cooling issue."

"Sure." She ran her hands up and down her arms.

I shrugged off my suit coat and helped her put it on.

By the time the maintenance supervisor gave us the rundown of what needed to be fixed, I had to say goodbye to Ash.

"I hate to leave but I have an important meeting on the other side of town," I told her. "Dinner, tomorrow."

It wasn't a question, but Ash wasn't so easily swayed.

She cupped my face and brought my lips to hers. "Maybe. I have a lot of work to get done."

A low growl rumbled from my chest.

"Soon, Talon. I promise." She kissed me again, then nipped my lower lip.

Holding her to her word, I exited the lab and then turned back around.

"Baby," I called out.

She peeked her head into the lobby.

"I forgot something," I said and crossed the small space.

"Oh, of course." She began taking off my coat.

"Don't."

She froze. My voice was more curt than I'd intended. I placed a light kiss on the top of her head, then reached into my coat to retrieve my keycard from the inner breast pocket, scraping my knuckles across her nipple.

Her breath hitched, and I felt myself harden.

"Damn it. If I don't leave now, I never will," I muttered.

Ash giggled and ushered me out the door.

Before I stepped into the elevator, I heard her call my name.

"You forgot something." She met in the hallway, stuffed her hand in the coat pocket, and pulled out a foil packet.

"How did that get there?" I murmured.

"Honest, Red." I held up my hands. "I didn't come here expecting anything."

She laughed and slipped the condom into my pants pocket.

"Sure, you didn't. Go be a lawyer." She delivered a hard smack to my ass and stepped toward her office.

"Hey, Red?"

She glanced over her shoulder just as I tossed the condom, which she easily caught. "Hold on to that. I don't plan on getting naked with anyone but you." I winked and got into the elevator.

CHAPTER THIRTEEN

AISLING

Zoey and I had lunch at Middle Urth Cafe at least once a week. Their food was always delicious and yet the salad Talon dropped off was a thousand percent tastier. I wasn't sure if it was the gorgeous man who delivered it. His thoughtfulness. Or perhaps it was just him. Or perhaps it was that kiss. I brushed my fingertips over my lips, reliving the way his molded to mine.

I tightened his suit jacket around me wishing it was his arms enveloping me in a hug. Talon Shelby had me floating in a dreamlike state, making it difficult to concentrate on the graph in front of me.

Images of Talon's muscled chest and big hands swirled through my head. Clenching my thighs together, I added Pope to that mix and almost reached for my special lipstick when Dr. Buchanan arrived. And he was even more of an asshole than the day before.

He strolled into the lab, went straight to the breakroom to make himself a cup of coffee, and didn't say a word. That didn't bother me. What did bother me was the way he made himself at home like he was planning to stay awhile.

"Good afternoon, Dr. Buchanan," Zoey chimed. "I wasn't expecting you again so soon."

"Get used to it," he replied with an icy tone. "Things are about to change around here."

His frosty response had my hackles up. "Dr. Buchanan, a word please?" I motioned to my office and mouthed an apology to Zoey.

She flipped him off behind his back and skipped back to her desk.

"Did you have a fun evening?" Jet asked.

I stopped short at the doorway, blood boiling in my veins as he leaned back in my chair.

"Yes. I um . . . had plans I'd forgotten about. So, I had to leave early."

He gave me a dry look and then said, "Bull. Shit."

"Excuse me?"

"Never mind, not important. We have a ton of things to go over." He motioned for me to sit opposite him as though I was the guest. In my office.

"Okay, first never talk to Zoey like that again. Second, get off my chair," I seethed.

The fucker ignored what I'd just said and continued ranting.

"I'd like a report of everything you're working on. Your projections for the rest of the week. I also need a full accounting of expenditures . . ."

Jethro rattled on a long list of shit. I closed my eyes and inhaled a deep cleansing breath.

"Are you having a female moment? I'm sure you have something in here for cramps or bloating." He rummaged through my desk.

I wanted to punch him in his handsome sexist pig face, but being the mature adult that I was, I chose a calm, professional tactic.

"Dr. Buchanan, we got off on the wrong foot yesterday. Why don't we start with a tour of the lab?" I motioned to the lab.

He studied my face with a narrowed gaze.

I smoothed my hands down Talon's jacket, feeling uncomfortable under his scrutiny.

"Yes," he stood. "A tour would be a good start. Not sure I approve of your two-thousand-dollar lab coat, though. Or are you pining over your boyfriend?"

His comment made me feel like a teenager with a schoolgirl crush, because yes, he was right, I was pining over Talon. Reluctantly, I took off the suit jacket and swapped it for the lab coat hanging behind my door.

A week or so ago, I was eager to show off the lab to Talon. His nods of approval and compliments had me beaming with pride even though I was sure he had no idea what half of the stuff was. He was a businessman and attorney, not a scientist.

Showing Jet around elicited different emotions from me. He wasn't just my boss, he was a respected colleague. Anxious butterflies crowded my belly, and my hands felt clammy.

My lab was a scaled-down version of what Jet had at BP headquarters. It was microscopic in comparison, but it was perfect to me. I designed every aspect of it and was proud of what I'd created. At that moment, I wanted Jet's approval.

With an impassive expression on his face, he perused the shelves lined with herbs, powders, and roots. He analyzed the purification system, the centrifuge, the incubators, and even the microscopes with a trained eye. At one point he slid on a pair of gloves and picked up a beaker, held it up to the light, brought it to his nose, and then moved on to a pipette.

All the while, he hadn't uttered a single word.

I wrung my hands together as he continued his meticulous inspection of my lab, waiting for a response.

Beads of sweat began to accumulate at my nape when he finally turned his attention to me.

"Impressive, Dr. Lovelle. Tiny, but well organized and efficient. You have expensive taste in equipment, and I can see why. All of it is necessary for such a small operation."

A breath of relief came out of me in a whoosh.

"You should be proud of yourself." He smiled. At me.

My ego grew ten times its normal size. I wasn't sure why I was being so weird about needing his praise, but there it was, and it felt euphoric. I dug my nails into my palms to keep myself from falling to my knees and thanking him for his approval.

"Tell me about this." He pointed to a project I had been working on before Talon's arrival earlier.

For the next couple of hours, I walked him through my current projects, leaving out anything pertaining to my episodes, of course. It wasn't all bad. Jet was smart, and he got me. He understood my lab language, and I found myself enjoying his company.

"I couldn't have created a better lab myself. It makes me wonder if we should entertain duplicating this setup in other parts of the country." Jet tapped his chin.

"I'm glad you approve," I said. "And I uh . . . I mentioned duplicating this setup to your father."

Jet's jaw clenched and his posture stiffened. "Did he help with this design?"

"No. He gave me the okay to do as I wish," I stammered.

"Has been here to visit?" His question made me feel like I was being interrogated.

"No. Never."

The expression on Jet's face was pure disdain. "Thanks for the tour. Let's move on."

"I'll need you to work on that list I mentioned. More importantly, I'll need your access codes?" His hostile tone had me on guard.

Okay. Whiplash.

"My what?" *What the hell just happened? Was his father a sore subject?*

"Access codes to your computer. I want to analyze every detail of what you've been working on." His haughty attitude returned, and I wasn't having it.

"Why? I send reports every week. On time. As always." I glared at him.

"Because I'm the boss and you are to do what I ask."

Now he was getting on my nerves. What the fuck? Dr. Asshole was back.

Jethro shot me a challenging glare and it got worse from there.

A few hours later, I was pulling into my garage, exhausted. Jet and I had bickered endlessly after the tour. Mentioning his father set him off and since it had nothing to do with me, I wasn't willing to back down. It wasn't my fault he had daddy issues.

Pope was heading toward me when I got out of my car. It was like he had a sixth sense of my whereabouts. Or perhaps he was watching me. That was likely considering he had the perfect view of my front door from his workstation. That should have been alarming, but there was nothing about the man that seemed threatening, and after dealing with Jet all afternoon, seeing Pope's smiley face was welcoming.

"Hey, angel. Another long day?" he asked.

I nodded and leaned into him for a hug.

Pope tilted my head and pressed his lips against mine. Slowly. Softly. It was a chaste kiss that was comforting. A kiss from earlier in the day floated into my mind.

I pushed away from Pope, guilt churning in my stomach.

"I kissed Talon," I blurted.

He blinked and said, "Was it awful?"

"No." I shook my head. "It was amazing."

I cleared my throat. *Why did I just say that*? Pope liked dirty talk, but he probably didn't want to hear *that*.

"I'm confused. You had a sour look on your face when you got out of the car. What happened?"

"Jet." My shoulders slumped.

"The new boss?" Pope rubbed my arms.

I thumped my forehead on his chest. "Yes. I don't get that man."

Pope chuckled. "I'm sorry you had a rough day, angel. Did you eat anything?"

"I had lunch. Talon brought salads for me and Zoey." *Again, Ash, why are you spewing details Pope probably doesn't want to hear?*

"That was nice of him," Pope replied without a trace of jealousy in his tone.

I peered up at him, searching for a sign of annoyance or discomfort or something.

"I'm not a jealous man, angel. But I am concerned. Lunch was hours ago. You need to relax and eat something. Why don't I whip up some food while you take a bath?"

"How are you still single?" I asked.

"My beautiful neighbor hasn't taken me off the market." He flashed me a genuine smile.

I wrapped my arms around his middle and snuggled into his chest. Grateful for having him in my life.

"What are you hungry for?" he asked.

I released my hold on him and shrugged. "I'd be happy with an apple."

He laughed. "I can do better than that. Oh, I know!" He snapped his fingers. "I'll meet you inside."

"Hey," I tossed my keys at him so that he could let himself in. "What's for dinner?"

"You'll have to wait."

"I don't like surprises," I retorted.

He continued walking across the street to his place, ignoring me.

Fifteen minutes later, I emerged from my bedroom and followed the scent of bacon.

Pope was in the kitchen, pulling the crispy, salty goodness from the oven.

"Breakfast for dinner? My favorite!" I reached for a slice of bacon.

He smacked my hand. "Let them cool down for a minute."

I chuckled and peered around his biceps to see what else he had going on in my kitchen.

"Pancakes, too? I didn't realize you were a chef."

"I'm not. I followed the recipe on the box."

"That explains why those are burned." I pointed with my chin to the pancakes stacked on a plate.

"You're welcome to take over, angel," he challenged.

Pope scooted out of the way and handed me the spatula. My mother and sister were great cooks. I did not inherit those genes. My pancakes came out just as bad if not worse. Burned on the outside, undercooked on the inside.

"Those are worse than the overcooked ones," Pope chortled.

I laughed with him. "It's my first two tries."

After a couple of fails and tons of laughter, we discovered turning down the heat made for evenly cooked pancakes.

We were having so much fun teasing each other I hadn't thought about Jet or Talon at all until we settled on my couch after dinner. Jet was a thorn in my side, but Talon was a harder subject to tackle. I cared about Pope and wanted him in my life without hurting his feelings. But I wanted Talon, too.

I leaned into Pope's side and sighed.

"Do you want to talk about it?" he asked.

Not really. But I had to.

"I like him," I whispered.

"And it sounds like Talon feels the same way," he replied.

"How'd you know I was talking about Talon?"

"The way you reacted when you told me about the kiss."

"I don't want to hurt you, Pope. But there's something about him. In some ways, it's like we've met before which never happened. And yet there's a connection I can't deny."

"I'm not asking you to choose, Aisling." His voice was tender, almost vulnerable.

I sat upright to peer into his eyes. "I don't want to lose you, Pope. I don't expect you to be okay with my choices but I . . . I would break into a million pieces if you unfriended me."

He laughed and pulled me into his arms. "I would never unfriend you, Ash. I'm not sure what kind of relationship you and I have or what our future holds. I just know that I'm not going anywhere until you tell me to go."

Fuck, my heart.

Pope was my sunshine on the darkest days. He was my laughter when all I wanted to do was cry. He had a way about him that made the most difficult, uncomfortable things seem easily surmountable.

He was incredible. And that should have been enough. But there was also Talon. There was no denying that the wolf fit into my life somehow. Was it fair for me to ask Pope to stay? No, not at all. But I would hate myself if I didn't tell him how much he meant to me.

I buried my face into Pope's neck. "You're more than just a friend to me, Gaius. The connection I have with you already exists. I don't want you to go."

"I'm right here, Aisling. This is where I want to be." Pope's words filled my heart with a love I'd never experienced before and maybe, just maybe I'd be able to tell him about my blackouts.

CHAPTER FOURTEEN

AISLING

"Good morning, Red." Talon sauntered into the lab with a cup of coffee and a paper bag.

My tummy went a flutter, which seemed to be my normal reaction every time he was around. Ever since the day he'd brought me and Zoey lunch, we'd been running into each other until this morning. His absence had made me feel jilted, which was silly considering we didn't have a relationship at all.

It was mid-morning and I'd been buried with work. "Good morning, what brings you to my humble lab?" I said, trying to mask the effect he had on me.

"Yeah, Talon, what brings you to *my* lab?" Jet interjected.

I scowled at Jet for souring my mood and was about to tell him to fuck off, but Talon squared his shoulders and held out a hand to me.

"I'm here to see Aisling, of course." He smiled.

Jet clenched his jaw, and I took his reaction as a good sign. He had been a complete dick since the day I'd given him a tour of the lab. The man who had been pleasant to be around for those brief few hours never returned, which led me to believe "asshole" was his true nature.

I grasped Talon's hand and pressed my body to his in a way that suggested we were more than friends. After that kiss, I'd hoped we were something more, but we never had another opportunity to explore the simmering chemistry between us.

"Hi," I said.

He trailed a finger along my jaw and kissed my cheek. "I missed you this morning and wanted to make sure you had decent coffee and something to eat."

"You're the best." I guided him to my office and closed the door.

He set down the coffee and paper and then cornered me against the desk.

"One day, very soon, I want more than these brief minutes with you, Red." His face hovered inches from mine, as he studied me with a curious expression on his face. Sometimes he was sweet and playful. Other times he smoldered with heat so intense I could barely breathe.

"Okay," I managed to say.

"I'm sorry, boss." Zoey's voice chimed over the intercom. "There's an important call for you on line one."

"Alright, thanks, Zoey," I replied.

A low growl rumbled from Talon's chest. His eyes flashed gold. I cupped his cheek.

"Soon," I told him.

His lips brushed over mine. It wasn't quite a kiss, but the unspoken promises were loud and clear.

"Soon, my Aisling," he purred.

As per my usual weirdness, I watched Talon leave and felt a keening in my chest. I didn't want him to go and couldn't figure out why. And the worst part of it all, I'd been too busy with work and dealing with my personal issues; I hadn't had the time to take him up on a dinner date.

I shrugged off my errant thoughts and picked up the phone. The important caller hung up and refused to leave a name with Zoey.

From the way Jet was smirking behind a microscope, I had a feeling he had something to do with it. I glared at my new boss.

Dr. Asshole had been taking up space in my lab. Sure his family money paid for said lab. But it was still my fucking lab. It had been mine for five years. I did good work and produced incredible results for a tiny operation. It was profitable all on its own. Maybe it wasn't during the first couple of years, but it was now. None of that was good enough for Dr. Jethro Buchanan. The overbearing prick had been crawling up my ass the entire time.

He continued to pester me about my access codes to our computer files. He was never getting his hands on my computer. I had personal shit I was working on. He didn't know that and he wasn't going to find out. Ever.

I sat behind my desk and wrote down codes to give him access to pertinent files that weren't personal to me. I'd have to get the data off at some point just to make sure he didn't override the system. Pope could have helped me conceal my projects easily enough, but I wasn't ready to talk to him about my issues just yet.

I was just about to reach for the cinnamon scone Talon had brought me when Jet said, "How is it that you get here before nine a.m. and you don't seem to get any work done?"

He was leaning on the doorframe of my office, scowling at me over the rim of a coffee mug.

"I'm tired of you hovering over my shoulders."

"Do as I ask, and I won't have to hover," he retorted.

"Fine. Here. Your precious codes. Now leave me in peace. I have shit to do." I slammed the sticky note on the edge of my desk.

He glanced at the note and tilted his head. "Was that so hard?"

"Why are you still here?"

"I need you to work on these samples." The fucker picked up my scone and walked out of my office.

"Hey! Give that back." I stormed out of the office.

He placed the scone on the desk beside my desktop centrifuge and a row of pipettes.

"I don't know what it's like in your lab, but in mine, we don't eat near our experiments," I scoffed.

"I'm not doing the experimenting, you are." He picked up the scone and bit into it.

I gaped.

"Oh sorry, does this have sentimental value?" he asked with his mouth full.

"You are a repulsive person."

He swallowed, then chuckled. "Sorry for eating the scone that your boyfriend bought you. I'll buy lunch. Sit." He pointed to a chair and started barking out orders.

I pinched the bridge of my nose.

"The faster you get this done, the faster I'll be out of your hair."

His words perked me up, and I went to work.

Lunchtime rolled around and I refused Jet's offer to buy lunch. "I know I'm a hardass, but I won't make you starve. You need to eat," he said.

"Thanks, but Pope is on his way," I replied.

"Pope?" He raised his eyebrow.

"Friend of mine," I replied. "Speak of the devil."

Pope's voice floated from the lobby. I grabbed my purse and said to Jet, "I'll be back in an hour."

I stepped into Pope's embrace and held onto him for a moment. Jet was being a dick and I needed some fresh air.

"Hi, angel. Ready?" He kissed the top of my head.

"Do you need anything, Zoey?" I asked.

"I'm good, boss. See you in a few." She waved.

"Hi." Jet approached us, his hand extended toward Pope. "I'm Dr. Jethro Buchanan."

The way Jet formally introduced himself made me cringe. What an asshole.

The men shook hands and chatted while I held the door open.

"I'll have her back in an hour," Pope announced.

"Please do. I'd hate to keep Aisling here after hours."

As soon as we got into the elevators, Pope started laughing.

"He seems nice, in a possessive, she belongs to me kind of way. When do I get to meet the wolf?" he teased.

"Don't start." I groaned.

True to his word, Pope had stayed by my side despite knowing of my rendezvous with Talon in the mornings.

Would they both be okay with sharing? I sure hoped so. Was I being greedy? Probably. If both of them were okay with it, then why not? Zoey had a polyamorous relationship and seven kids. They were one big happy family.

"I thought shifters were the possessive ones. Guess I was wrong. Still, the wizard has a stick so far up his ass, he probably doesn't realize how dickish he's being." Pope's comment brought me out of my musings.

"I don't even know where to start with that one," I admitted. "Fucking Jethro Buchanan is hellbent on being a pain in my ass."

Pope draped his arms around me, chuckling about my problems. His take on how I should handle both men had me laughing even though I knew Jet was going to be fuming when I returned and was probably going to insist on overtime for the foreseeable future.

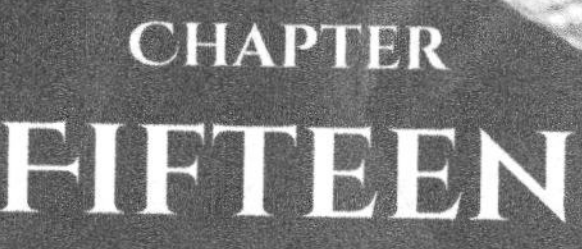

CHAPTER FIFTEEN

AISLING

Not only did I have to work late the night before, the next morning, there was no sign of Talon and Dr. Asshole arrived before me.

"This is not part of my contract," I snarled at Jet as he directed a team of techs to set up lab equipment. For him. The fucker was moving in.

"Well, it is now," he scoffed.

"What the actual fuck is your problem with me?" I rested my hands on my hips.

"You are. You have way too much privilege within this company and nearly zero accountability. You take three-day weekends every fucking week. Do you know how many hours I work? How many hours my other chemists work?"

"Not my fault you suck at your job!"

"Insult me all you want. I can make this worse. In fact, I will. I want your access codes by the end of the day tomorrow."

"I don't work on Fridays." I crossed my arms over my chest.

"You do now. No more three-day weekends, unless it's an official holiday. And I want access to everything you're doing in this lab."

"I've already given you access codes. You have everything you need. What the hell else is there?"

"I'm not an idiot, Ash. You made me an administrator which means I have access to pertinent files in this office, but not everything."

"You don't need my specific codes to see what I've been working on. And I sure as hell don't need you to micro-manage me, Jethro. Get the fuck off my back." I was shouting at that point and wouldn't be surprised if steam was coming out of my ears.

Jet stalked toward me. I backed up until my butt bumped into the edge of my desk.

He wore a severe expression, his brows knitted together, and his jaw clenched tight. He looked like the handsome villain in every girl's fantasy. His handsome face hovered so close to mine that his breath fanned my lips. "Let me be clear, you and everything in this lab belongs to me. I will be all over your back. And all over your front. Anytime I fucking want. You will submit to me, Dr. Lovelle, and enjoy it."

His words were thick with lust, his eyes roamed over my face and landed on my lips. The sexual tension between us had my chest heaving and my thighs clenching. My overactive hormones were short-circuiting. I wanted to strip him naked and ride the smug, sexy, prick and strangle his cock with my pussy and make him beg for more. I bit the inside of my cheek, causing enough pain to bring me to my senses.

"In your fucking dreams." I shoved at his chest. He didn't move. My hands remained on his chest, and my lips parted. He groaned.

"Move."

"No." He placed his hands on the desk trapping me between him.

"You're an asshole." *And you smell good. And I want to run my hands all over your firm, muscular chest. Whoa! Shut. The. Fuck. Up. Brain.*

"You're an insufferable little monster." He leaned closer and ran his tongue over his bottom lip.

A knock on the door made him straighten his posture.

"We're done, sir," a tech said.

"Tell them to take it back," I snarled.

He gave me a dramatic eye roll, then thanked the techs.

Fucker.

"Get out of my office."

He laughed, straightening his suit. "Careful, Ash, I may implement a mandatory uniform which I assure you will not include turtlenecks or long sleeves. I think tight skirts and bodysuits will be the only acceptable clothing for female doctors working in this lab."

This was sexual harassment 101, but the way his dark eyes smoldered when he looked at me made me ache with need. The fucker smirked as though he knew how he was affecting me. Smug asshole.

"You're a pig!" I grabbed my purse and headed out the door, fuming.

I stormed past Zoey, who looked at me warily.

"I'm going to lunch." I yanked the door open and stomped out.

As soon as I approached the elevators, the door opened. A woman stepped out, and I stepped in. The elevator soared and stopped at the tenth floor.

"After you," an older gentleman gestured for me to step in front of him.

"Oh, sorry, not my floor." I gazed at the elevator panel and noticed floor twenty-three, Shelby and Associates. I pressed the button.

The elevators opened to a grand lobby, where a middle-aged woman dressed in an expensive dress suit was sitting behind a credenza. I waltzed right in like I had every right to be there.

The woman stood to address me. "May I help you?"

"I'm here to see him," I pointed to a placard on the door of an office located behind her.

"Oh, he is in a meeting now and doesn't have any available appointments," she stammered

I maneuvered around her and headed straight to his office. "I'll wait." I waved her off.

"You can't go in there," she called after me.

I ignored her, still fuming about my new boss.

Fucking Jethro Buchanan. I paced up and down the marble floor. I should sue. Talon was an attorney. And he did say something about contacting him if I needed legal advice. That time was now. He probably meant to make an appointment but in my current state semantics wasn't part of the equation.

I continued pacing, clenching my fists at my sides. I should sue for sexual harassment, even though I wanted a taste of those unspoken words. The thought of his big hands caging me in at my desk made my heart rate climb and not in a bad way. I bet he'd enjoy bending me over that desk and . . .

"Dr. Love." A deep voice made me pause mid-step.

I took a deep breath, exhaled, and faced Talon.

"Do not call me that." I glared. "Just call me Ash."

"As you wish. What brings you to my office? Are you okay? Your face is flushed."

I turned away from him and began pacing again. The last thing I wanted was to admit to anyone how much Jethro affected me physically speaking. I focused on my lab and Jet's hostile takeover.

"I need an attorney. You said I could come to you for advice. And I need advice." I pointed a finger at him stabbing the air.

"Sure I'm happy to help, why don't . . ." he began.

"I need to sue that asshole," I cut him off. "There must be something in contract law that will put a stop to his meddling." I shrugged out of my lab coat and slammed it on the white leather sofa.

"The man is a menace." I resumed pacing.

"I'm assuming you're speaking about Jethro."

"Yep, Dr. Asshole." The rage inside me was making me sweat. I tore off my sweatshirt and threw it on the chair. That didn't help. "Why is it so freaking hot in here," I removed my T-shirt, leaving me in a cropped tank top and loose-fitting pants that slung low on my hips.

"Don't stop there," Talon murmured.

I glared at the man I'd come to for legal advice. Talon had the decency to drop his gaze even though the corner of his lips turned up.

"I meant, please continue," he said, sucking in his cheeks.

"Are you mocking me, Mr. Shelby? I assure you this is not fucking funny."

"I would never." He placed a hand to his chest as though offended. His eyes twinkled.

Talon was totally laughing at me, and truth be told, I'd already embarrassed myself in front of him. First the vibrator and now the crazed lunatic. I ignored the smirk on his face. What's one more thing? So long as he helped me with my problem. I had money. I could afford to hire him. Maybe. In my state of fury, I failed to notice the expensive furnishings in his office. Maybe not.

"Like I said, I need to sue the smug prick. I want him out of my lab, like two days ago! He can't show up and . . ."

A whirring sound cut off my tirade and the curtain behind him opened revealing the most incredible view of Midway.

Storm clouds rolled in from the east, promising a night of rain, lightning, and thunderstorms. In the distance, waves crashed against rocky cliffs, and the few boats docked at the harbor rocked restlessly with the whims of Mother Nature. We were miles away yet if I closed my eyes the briny scent filled my nostrils, and I could feel the ocean spray on my skin.

Tall crags surrounded the cove which, according to history, had been the main port for supernaturals to cross. To this day, it remained an open hub for all types of supernatural species no matter what their power level was. Urban legend said the seaside town was founded by mystics and had always been a safe harbor for humans and supernaturals alike until a demon horde invaded. Mystics, along with the help of angels, had defeated the horde and banned demons from entering its borders. It had been touted as one of the safest cities in the world since. I fell in love with Port Midway immediately and seeing it like this hurt my heart to have spent most of my time in the lab.

"Even on stormy days like today, I find this view calming," Talon said, standing directly behind me.

I hadn't noticed him until I felt his breath brush my shoulder. I took a half step back feeling his body heat caress me like a lover.

"It's beautiful," I said.

"You're beautiful."

I focused on his reflection, and our gazes met.

"Mistress," he said in a voice that was all animal.

His eyes flashed gold.

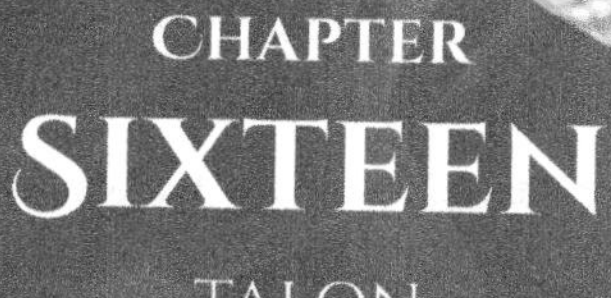

CHAPTER SIXTEEN

TALON

"We need to get ahead of this situation, Talon. There have been three reported murders in the last two months. Who knows how many more have happened that we have yet to discover," Thomas Hayes, Midway's Chief of Police said.

"And you're coming to me with your problems, because why?" I frowned at the shifter. He wasn't just the chief of police, he was Midway's pack Alpha. He had been my father's beta and closest friend. That was until my father lost his mind.

Once my father gave up control of the pack, my entire family was shunned, me, my mother, and my baby sister. The pack turned their backs on me and mine, and I'll never forget it. I worked hard, rebuilt my fortune, and established myself in the community. I didn't owe the pack a goddamn thing.

"Talon, two of the murders had happened at your businesses. You . . ." Thomas started.

"My employees have already given their statements as have I," I cut him off.

"You have a reputation in this city and have access to people we don't. The people will respond to you if you ask around."

Although I didn't have a title, I'd become a leader in the community since I began revitalizing downtrodden neighborhoods and helping small businesses grow. Some needed financial help. Some needed legal advice. All needed business coaching to help keep their doors open.

I wasn't magnanimous. Nor was I greedy. I just found a niche that helped those in need and increased my influence.

As a result of my good deeds and increasing wealth, I skirted the political game, lending a helping hand whenever I was needed.

The serial killer situation was a pain in my ass. Two of the three reported incidents occurred near my bars. The other happened at a business where I had ties with the owners. The police didn't have leads and my security team didn't have any either. Everyone was on edge. This serial killer nonsense was unusual and ultimately not good for business.

Although one of my waitresses had mentioned seeing someone who resembled my mistress, I knew she wasn't responsible. She couldn't have been. The woman I'd fucked for hours was not a killer. She had a voracious sexual appetite, but fucking wasn't the same as killing.

Aisling was another story. My wolf was certain they were the same. I wasn't so sure. In the few short moments I'd spent with Dr. Lovelle, she appeared shy and conservative. However, the little rendezvous she'd had in the parking lot with the donut guy and her little lipstick vibrator proved otherwise.

I couldn't figure her out and at first, I thought that was the allure. The mystery of who she was that captivated me. But that wasn't it because the more I thought about it, the more it didn't matter. I wanted to be near Aisling all the freaking time.

"We need your help. I have other important matters to deal with. There's been an increasing number of disturbances on the east side of town . . ." Thomas's voice interrupted my wandering thoughts.

"Not my problem," I interjected before he could finish. His nagging was beginning to wear on my patience.

"Talon, do not pretend like you don't care about Port Midway. All I'm asking from you is to talk to the people."

"What makes you think I haven't already?"

"If you have, I hope you'd share your findings with us. The authorities of this city."

A scuffle in the lobby had me gazing out of the conference room's glass wall. We usually kept the elevator for this floor on lockdown but since I'd had a meeting, we kept it open. Dr. Aisling Lovelle stormed past my secretary like a boss. *Well, this is unexpected. And very much welcomed.*

"Meeting adjourned." I stood to address Thomas and one of his cohorts. "Apologies, I have an important meeting I forgot about."

"We just started," Thomas complained.

"Good luck with this. We can reconvene when you have solutions that will help us find the killer."

I exited the conference room ignoring his protests and found Ash pacing in my office.

"Sorry, boss," Addie apologized. The older woman was loyal and damn good at her job. For Aisling to have steamrolled past her said a lot.

"Don't worry about it, Adeline. I was expecting her. Hold my calls for the rest of the day," I told her. "And show our guests out, please." I jerked my chin toward the conference room.

Jokingly, I called Ash, Dr. Love, which she did not find humorous. Her face was scrunched and pink. She paced back and forth, ranting with each step. She was fighting mad.

Jethro had done something to set her off. Just as I knew he would. After the sexy show she and her boyfriend, Gaius Pope, the donut guy, gave us the other day, I thought maybe he'd loosen up. We had shared a bottle of whiskey talking about the good old days.

The asshole had the balls to tell me to leave her alone because she belonged to him. Thinking about our conversation made me smile.

"Ah, that would be a negative, old friend," I told him, leaning back in my chair.

"Do you want to make a wager on who can have her first," he challenged me.

I laughed. "Dude, are we even talking about the same woman? She walked out on two alpha males and fucked some no-name surfer-looking dude less than thirty minutes later. Aisling Lovelle is not a sport. If that's what you think she is, you've already lost. And if you try to play that game with her, she'll chew you up and spit you out."

"I don't even know her. And for some reason, everything I said came out wrong. It was like I'd never talked to a girl before." He sipped his whiskey.

"Well, I for one am looking forward to seeing her again."

"If she'll see you again. She may have gone home with donut guy, but she will return to my lab in the morning."

I shrugged. "I don't give a rat's ass about you or donut guy. I care about her. And besides, I can share."

He scoffed. "She belongs to me, back off."

I snapped my finger. "That's it right there! That's your problem. You don't know how to share."

"I do too." His eyebrows quirked.

"No, you don't man. You've got only child syndrome." I leaned back in my chair and swiveled around in a circle.

He thought about it for a moment then said, "What makes you think she wants to be shared?"

"Don't know, but the donut guy has one up on us already. And I have a feeling he won't go quietly into the night. If you can't beat 'em, join 'em, I say." I spun my chair in the opposite direction.

"The man is a menace." Ash's shout brought me back to the present. I hadn't stopped watching her every move, but I'd tuned out her tirade. Rude. I know. But I'd already decided to help her with any problem that came her way.

"I'm assuming you're speaking about Jethro," I added.

"Yep. Dr. Asshole," she snapped and then began doing the oddest thing.

She'd already taken off her lab coat, which was understandable. But the strip tease had just begun.

I'd been on the receiving end of some very entertaining and satisfying strip shows before, but this one was the absolute best.

"Why is it so freaking hot in here?" She shrugged off her T-shirt.

It wasn't hot, she just wore too many layers. There was an issue with the air conditioning vents on her floor which would be fixed, whenever she gave the maintenance crew the green light to begin. She hadn't scheduled it yet, since she was working all the time and Jet had shown up. Not that I was complaining because Ash was down to a cropped tank top and pants that highlighted the curve of her ass and slender waist.

"Don't stop there," I whispered.

She hit me with a glare that could have shot me dead. Fuck she heard me. It took every muscle in my face to keep my lips from curving into a smile.

"I meant, please continue," I said aloud, sucking in my cheeks.

"Are you mocking me, Mr. Shelby? I assure you this is not fucking funny."

With every ounce of self-restraint I possessed, I managed to bottle up my laughter. It wasn't a laughing matter. She was adorable, with the bun slipping to the side of her head and her flushed cheeks. She was a mess, and it was so fucking cute. Don't get me wrong, I loved the sexy siren in her, but this side of her was real. We hadn't spent much time together and here she was, exposed and vulnerable.

My curtains opened. The window beside my desk faced east. Even with the special glass tint, and the AC during the summer months, the rising sun cooked my office interior, so I typically kept the drapes closed. For convenience's sake, I had a timer installed on the curtains which automatically opened daily around lunchtime.

The view of Port Midway drew Ash, and she moved across the

room to stand at the window. Awe washed over her face and her body relaxed as though she was standing on the shore. She looked peaceful aside from the flicker of sadness that flashed over her posture. She loved the ocean but didn't visit as often as she'd like to. Too busy working, I presumed. On what? I wondered.

I stepped behind her, aching to wrap my arms around her middle. She was so close; her strawberry scent filled my senses.

Our gazes met in the window's reflection.

"Mistress," my beast rasped, and my golden eyes reflected off the glass.

Her eyes flickered in a way that made my skin prickle. She mentioned being part-witch and part-human, but there was something else.

Ash rounded on me, her eyes wide. "Mistress? Why would you call me that?"

"What are you?" I asked, awe in my voice. She wasn't a shifter. I'd be able to pick up on that immediately. She was a mystic, but not one I was familiar with.

"I'm a potential client. Answer me. Why would you call me mistress? Are you married?"

Uh oh. She was back to being pissed again.

"Not married." I showed her my ring finger. "A mistress can be someone who is given authority, like a queen," I added.

She eyed me suspiciously.

"The way you blazed through my office earlier was like you owned the place. Only someone who held a special place in my life could pull that off. I liked it. A lot. I could have used the term *wife* or *mate*. It'd fit. But I have a feeling that would scare you off."

She placed her hand on my chest trying to push me away. "Sounds like bullshit. But you're an attorney, which means it comes with the territory. So, I'll forgive the slight. Just this once."

I chuckled. "I assure you, babe. I'll never lie to you."

Her eyes narrowed at me. "Do I have a case?"

I tilted my head. Case? "Ah, Jethro." I shrugged. "Perhaps. I need to look at your contract."

Her light-brown eyes searched my face. She was a unique creature. And so captivating.

"Have we met before?" She regarded me quizzically.

I smiled.

"I mean, before meeting downstairs?" she added.

I knew what she was talking about, and I wanted to say yes. It had to be her. I couldn't recall the freckles though. I did, however, remember those breasts and those taught buds poking through her tank.

"I was wondering the same thing." I smiled and dipped my head to run my nose along her jaw, inhaling her scent. "You seem very familiar to me."

What was she? I had to know. And I would find out.

CHAPTER SEVENTEEN

AISLING

Talon leaned closer, his muscular chest pressing into my palm. Aside from a few innocent kisses, we hadn't kissed like we had the day he brought lunch to my office, and I was dying for it.

"I like your freckles," he rasped. He leaned even closer, his nose grazing my shoulder, his lips brushing over the spattering of freckles on my skin.

The gentle contact made my entire body quiver. A wanton moan escaped me as his tongue flicked the pulse point on my neck.

He breathed in deeply, sniffing my skin.

I drew away from him. "Are you smelling me?"

He gave me a boyish grin. "Sorry. My beast is um . . . being a bit forward."

"Ah, the golden eyes."

He nodded.

The way Talon looked at me made me feel like I was the only woman in the world for him. For some reason, I swore we'd met before. And it wasn't at the entrance to Shelby Centre.

He leaned a little closer to me, then stopped. My palm lay flat on his hard, muscular chest. Why was I still touching this man? Instead of moving my hand as I should have, I traced a button on his shirt and studied his face.

His eyes were a pale green, with gold striations through the iris. Mesmerizing. My hand traveled upwards, gliding along his neck to his square jaw. I traced the outlines of his high cheekbones, up to his brow, and along his forehead. He closed his eyes and a deep, contented rumble emanated from his chest. Or was he purring? The thought made me smile, and I caressed his skin down toward his lips. He leaned his head into my palm and then his tongue flicked the inside of my wrist.

Goose flesh prickled all over my skin.

"Sorry. Again," he murmured.

"Wolf?" I asked.

The iris of his eyes turned from green to gold. It was intriguing. I'd never been this close to a shifter. My momma had warned me to stay away from shifters because they were temperamental creatures and couldn't be trusted. She had strong opinions about mystics, which was hypocritical considering she was a witch and my father was human. And thus, I ignored her warnings and continued exploring the gorgeous man in front of me.

Thunder boomed, and I turned toward the window. Clouds rolled in, no rain, but it was coming. I sighed. Rainy days were meant for lovemaking or at the very least snuggling with a romance novel.

Talon rested his chin on my shoulder. I pushed my hips back, seeking . . . something. A steel rod pressed against my butt. I gasped and was a second from pulling away when he snaked a hand around my belly and held me still.

"Don't," he breathed. His voice was soft, deep. Commanding.

That one word nearly brought me to my knees. My body quaked with need. He pushed his hard, long, cock against my ass, stroking himself and making me drip.

"You smell delicious, Ash." His big hands splayed over my belly.

"What do I smell like?" I braced my hands on the windows and rubbed myself against him.

"Lust." His hand roved over my abdomen, then between my breasts. He palmed my breast and squeezed hard. "Mine."

I mewled in agreement, my arm hooking around his neck. I hadn't come here for sex, but that's what I was getting. And I wasn't the least bit ashamed.

"Sir? I do apologize. This couldn't wait." A female voice shrilled through the office intercom. Breaking my lust haze.

"I told you to hold my calls." Talon's voice was gruff and lethal.

"I know, sir. It's Dr. Buchanan. He's called several times. I told him you were in a meeting, and he's threatened to come up here. I thought you may want to prevent that." His secretary trailed off.

"Fucking pain in the ass." Talon rubbed a hand over his face.

I maneuvered out of his hold. "Are you two friends?" I hadn't thought of that before seeking him out. This might be a conflict of interest. Fuck my life.

"No. Not really." His brows furrowed. "We used to be. We were roommates in college."

I stepped away.

"Don't leave." He fixed me with his golden gaze. "I'll only be a second."

Hello wolfy.

He held my gaze until I nodded and then moved to his desk to make the call.

I decided to use the bathroom and put some space between me and the big bad wolf. A part of me wanted the beast to chase me. I glanced over my shoulder to find him tracking my every move. Yep, that would be a lot of fun for another time.

Talon's office screamed wealth. He had to have an ensuite and so I chose the first door on the other side of the room and stepped in, the light flickered on and the door closed behind me. My eyes widened. Okay, not a bathroom. I found myself standing in a small room with dark walls and a spiral staircase leading up.

My gaze followed the stairs which seemed to go on forever, and then I glanced over my shoulder at the closed door. I probably should have turned around and gone back to the office but what the hell. He did see me come in here. Before I could change my mind, I hurried upstairs only to arrive at another door, which was locked.

My shoulders sagged with disappointment and then a buzzer sounded followed by a clicking sound. I tried the door again and smiled as it unlocked. Thank you, I said, even though he couldn't hear me. Or could he? He had to have seen me approach the door and buzzed me in.

I paused mid-step. Maybe I shouldn't be here. He could kill me. Or keep me in his secret rooftop dungeon forever. I was about to turn around when a trickle of water caught my attention. I continued down a short hallway and had to pick up my jaw from the floor.

Talon's hideaway was a rooftop apartment. The trickling water was a water feature in the foyer, that led to the main area of his home. Across the foyer was a living room, to the left was a kitchen, and to the right were three doors.

Since I was a nosy busybody, I explored the rooms. Beyond the first door which was a half-bathroom, the next was an office, and the double doors at the end of the hallway led to the bedroom.

The bedroom reminded me of walking into a hotel room at check-in. It had all the typical appointed furnishings, and the king-sized bed was neatly made. Like his office, the furniture looked like expensive, hand-crafted, custom-made art pieces. The decor was sleek, modern, and masculine with dark grays and pops of color here and there. It had everything one could ask for yet it seemed impersonal. Maybe he didn't live here. I peeked into the closet and found it full of men's business suits. Maybe he did.

The walls in his room were floor-to-ceiling glass offering an unobstructed view of Port Midway. Damn. And I thought the view from his office was amazing.

The bathroom was spotless and appeared unlived-in. There wasn't even a toothbrush on the counter. He probably had a maid. Or girlfriend. A man like him had girlfriends. Lots of them. I glanced at my reflection, shocked. *Seriously, Ash?* My bun had slid from the top of my head to my ear, and strands of hair were everywhere. I spent a few seconds fixing my hair then continued snooping.

I moved back into the living area and out the sliding door where I discovered a rooftop garden. Wood-paneled flooring led to a seating area surrounded by potted plants filled with shrubs, herbs, and flowers. There was a bar area that seemed to have access to the kitchen inside.

It was impressive. But it paled in comparison to the ocean view. *This was the life.*

A warm hand slid across my waist, making me jump.

"Jesus, Talon!" I breathed.

He chuckled. Strong arms wrapped around me, and his warm body pressed against mine. I closed my eyes for a second, allowing his presence to envelop me. It was comforting. Safe. Arousal slid through me and pooled in my core.

"This is incredible. Do you live here?"

"Sometimes. My home is by the shore. But I stay here when I'm working, which seems to be all the time."

As soon as he said *work* my thoughts flashed to Jet and I turned in his arms. "How did it go with Jet?"

"He's . . ."

"Actually. Don't. I. Umm . . . I shouldn't have asked you for help. I didn't realize you two were close," I stammered. "This was a bad idea."

I stepped back and Talon stepped with me.

"Jet and I have history. That doesn't mean you and I can't have a . . ." His gaze dropped to my lips, then down to my chest. "Relationship."

A tingly sensation prickled at the base of my spine. I'd entertained the idea countless times since our first meeting.

"Something, or someone, ruffled his feathers today. And he was looking for a drinking buddy. I told him I was busy with someone much more deserving of my attention."

"Does he know I'm here?" I asked.

"Yes."

"Why would you tell him that?"

"Why not? He asked. And like I said, I don't lie. Does it matter?"

His question sounded more like a challenge. And he was right. Why should I care if Jet knew I was spending time with Talon or Pope? Or anyone else.

Talon closed the distance between us. "Does Jet have a say in what you do?"

"No." I tilted my head back to meet his gaze. Damn, he was tall.

He leaned toward me, then stopped. He was so close, I could almost taste the mintiness of his breath. I leaned in, my nipples grazing his chest. His lips feathered over mine. Too soft. Too gentle. I needed more.

As though he read my mind, his hands were in my hair and he pulled, tilting my head back. He kissed my lips with a fiery possessive passion. I parted my lips, granting his tongue access. My hands roamed over his chest. I undid one button. Then another, and another. My fingertips glided over his smooth, hard chest.

Talon released his hold on my hair and tore off his shirt. Buttons flew. And he discarded the fabric to the ground. He picked me up in one smooth movement. My legs wrapped around his waist, and I cupped his face, sealing our lips together.

Talon laid me on a lounge chair and settled on his knees between my legs. His gaze drank me in. Something splatted on my face. And then again on my torso. We both glanced at the sky as more raindrops sprinkled over us.

He smiled at the storm overhead. I stared at him, appreciating his beautiful body as water droplets trickled down his chest. He was one delicious snack. No, not snack, he was the whole meal.

Talon began kissing and licking raindrops from my body. I

moaned, arching into him. The rain picked up, cooling my heated skin.

"Let's take this inside," he started.

I reached for his length and squeezed. "Or not."

CHAPTER EIGHTEEN

TALON

I watched Ash walk into the corridor that led to my hideaway and smiled. Just where I wanted her to go.

I dialed Jet's cell.

"About time," he answered.

"What's got your knickers twisted in knots? I'm busy," I snarled.

"You're not that busy. I need advice. Meet me at the bar."

"No can do. Like I said, I'm busy."

"Listen. I know you don't care, but I could use your help. Ash and I fought and she's been gone forever. She's not answering her cell, and her car is still here. I went to Jade Gardens and a couple of other places looking for her. I'm worried. I was hoping you could have your surveillance team look at today's videos."

I rolled my eyes at his dramatics. At most she'd been gone for an hour not . . . forever.

"Not necessary, Jet. She's fine." I pulled up the video leading to the entrance of my apartment and buzzed Ash in as she approached the door.

"How would . . . wait is she there?" His voice shrill.

"Yes," I replied.

"Son-of-a-bitch!"

I winced and pulled the phone away from my ear.

"Why the fuck is she there?"

"Why do you think? She needed legal advice because you're being an ass."

"Listen, I . . . fuck." He growled. There was a long pause.

"Jet, if you care about her, give her some space. She'll be back to work in the morning."

He growled and muttered a string of curses. "Fine. Hey, Tally. . .You can't keep her to yourself."

"You know how this works, Jethro. Aisling makes the rules." I hung up the phone and hurried after Ash.

She was in the garden, gazing at the scenery, a smile lighting up her face.

I watched for a moment, admiring her. I still wasn't sure if the Mistress and Ash were the same person. After that kiss, I didn't even care. Ash was the one I wanted. The one I'd keep.

I snuck up behind her, making her jump. I enveloped her in my arms while her nerves settled. And then she spun around asking about Jet.

"Does Jet have a say in what you do?" I asked, gauging her reaction.

"No," she replied, a hint of hesitation crossing her beautiful features.

She stepped closer and tilted her head to meet my gaze. Her posture said she wanted me, but there was something about Jet that intrigued her. My lips spread into a genuine smile. I wasn't lying when I told Jet I could share.

I grazed my lips over hers. Teasing. Tasting. My cock had been hard the minute she arrived in my office and now it ached to be inside her. Fuck she was driving me mad. I gripped a fistful of her hair and claimed her lips. Hard. Her fingers glided over my skin and made me feral. I tore off my shirt, lifted her in my arms, and laid her on the lounger.

I settled between her legs and then it started to drizzle. I chased each drop as it fell on her skin and was about to take her into the house when she grabbed my cock.

"Baby," I growled. My claws elongated and I sliced through her tank top, making her big breasts spill out.

I latched onto her nipple with my teeth, massaging her tits, while raindrops slid down her chest. She wasn't deterred by the weather and neither was I. I moved down her soft skin to her pelvis and shoved her pants past her ass.

Once her pants were off, she flipped me over. My beast growled in appreciation. Her lips fastened to mine. The drizzles turned into a steady rain.

"Sit on my face, baby," I gripped her hips and guided her body to straddle over my face.

She hovered. Rain soaked her hair, plastering it to her head. I pulled her body down, smacking my face with her pretty pussy.

She was delicious. My mouth salivated and I ate her cunt like my life depended on it. She rocked her hips, fucking my face. Her juices dripped down my throat. My cock throbbed. I was ready to come without even touching myself.

Ash moaned. Her head tipped back as rain streamed down her body. I flicked her clit with my thumb, while I tongue-fucked her pussy. Her breathing came out in rough pants, her nails dug into my forearms. She was close. I slipped my hand under her body and into her tight hole. She let go, drenching my face with her cum.

I flipped us over and crashed my mouth to hers. She was gasping for air, but I didn't care. I had a primal need to make her mine. I whipped out my cock and pressed into her entrance. Her tiny pussy resisted my size, and I should have taken greater care. I didn't. I slammed into her. Hard.

"Oh! Fuck!" she cried.

I stilled my hips. Had to. I was ready to blow.

"Don't you dare stop!" She cupped my face and fused our lips.

"Never. You. Are. Mine," I stated between kisses. A strong urge to mark her as my mate rolled through me.

Not yet.

I moved my hips. She moved with me. I picked up the pace. She kept up with me.

Her moans spurred my movements. I was on edge, ready to lose control.

"Give me everything, Talon."

"Ash. You can't say things like that. Not now."

She angled her neck, giving me full access to that special place where wolves marked their mates.

"Fuck, baby." I pressed my forehead to hers. I wanted this. Wanted her. My Aisling. My mistress. She'd have more than one mate, though. And I was okay with that. As long as I could mark her first.

"You like my cock, baby?" I pulled out a little and pushed back in.

"Yes," she groaned. "So big. I feel so full."

"You like to fuck don't you."

"Yes!"

"This is my pussy. I will fuck you anytime I please."

"Yes. Yours. All yours."

"And the only time another cock enters this pussy is if I say so."

"Yes! Whatever you want."

She was in a haze of lust. And again, I should have been more careful, but my beast was ready to pounce.

Mark her. She belongs to us, my wolf growled.

His persistence and Ash's request were making it hard for me to hold back. My wolf was a surly bastard at the best of times, but he had never steered me wrong.

Ash and I hadn't been on one date. Hadn't professed our love for one another. And yet this was more than that. It was more than a dinner and a movie. It was more than saying I love you. It was more than the exquisite feeling of her pussy milking my cock. It was a soul-deep knowing that I was hers and she was mine. It was branded in my being. Everything about Aisling became crystal clear. She was my mate, and I was going to mark her, right the fuck now.

"Ash, baby, I'm going to mark you as mine. And everyone will know who you belong to." I pumped into her pussy, hard and deep.

She met my gaze. Her golden-brown eyes regarded me with lust, want, and something more.

"Mine," she declared. "You are mine."

Oh fuck. She was perfect.

My fangs elongated, and my eyes golden. My wolf was front and center, ready to stake our claim. Aisling didn't flinch. She met each thrust of my hips with her own.

Thunder rolled. Rain pelted our bodies. We didn't care. We slammed into each other. Pushing and pulling. Her walls closed in around my cock. My balls drew up tight, making my toes curl.

Aisling brought my face to hers, sealing our lips together, then said "Do it."

She turned her face giving me her neck, and I bit into her flesh. Coppery liquid filled my mouth. My magic burst out of my chest, and dove into hers, connecting us forever. Aisling's pussy spasmed, choking my cock as she came. I followed her off the edge, with my fangs still embedded in her neck. My hips sputtered as jets of my cum shot out of me, filling her tunnel. My vision went spotty, and I floated in pure pleasure as my wolf magic settled around me and Ash. An overwhelming sense of peace filled my entire being.

I blinked the raindrops from my eyes to gaze upon my mate. A content smile splayed across her beautiful face. I pressed my lips to hers and said, "Mine."

Her eyes flicked open, her cheeks reddened, and she cupped my face. "Mine."

I deepened our kiss, doing my best to shield her from the rain. We were soaked in more ways than one. Lightning flashed overhead.

"Time to go inside, mate."

CHAPTER NINETEEN

JETHRO

Watching Aisling storm out of the office rankled. I'd been a colossal ass since. I lashed out at Zoey, the office manager, and sent her home when Ash hadn't returned an hour later.

I waited, pacing in the lab like a scorned lover. After wearing a path on the tiled floor, I decided to get out of the office. I checked the parking lot, and her car was still there. Next, I went to The Commons. The retail and restaurant area. She wasn't there, either.

The next thing I knew I was dialing Talon. We were friends, sort of, and I could use the company. His secretary was the ultimate gatekeeper. He finally called back after I threatened to go up there.

Talking to him didn't help. Ash was with him. Of course. For the past few weeks, they'd been meeting before work. It seemed innocent enough, but I knew Talon. It seemed like he was courting her, which meant she wasn't just a fling. And her going straight to him after our fight meant she thought of him as more than a friend also.

The thought of the two of them together made me envious. And jealous. And angry . . . with myself. I infuriated her so much and pushed her straight into his arms. Way to go, Jet.

I couldn't stand being in the lab knowing they were together, so I got in my car and drove around for a while. I was driving around aimlessly and found myself in my old stomping grounds near the university.

It was a small private college that had a good curriculum for undergrads and graduate programs as well. I decided to continue my studies overseas, while Talon stayed on and studied law and Aisling got her doctorate in chemistry and alchemy. *Stop thinking about them, Jet.*

Doing that was nearly impossible while sober, so I chose a random local bar. After a few beers and polishing off the largest, greasiest burger, I was feeling somewhat settled until my phone rang.

I almost declined the call but knew if I did, he'd just call back every five minutes.

"Father. What can I do for you?"

"What's going on? When I signed over the documents making you CEO that didn't mean you could take time off to fuck around in Port Midway!" he snarled through the phone.

Knowing this was going to be a shouting match, I pulled out some cash from my wallet and left it on the table.

"First off, it was the Board of Directors that unanimously made me CEO. And part of my responsibilities is to figure out why we have a satellite office in Port Midway, spending resources we don't have." I replied as I slid into the front seat of my truck.

"That's ridiculous!" he screeched. "Aisling Lovelle has an exemplary track record. She's worth four scientists combined. Why would you be out there harassing her?"

"I'm not harassing her father," I began.

"Jethro Bartholomew Buchanan, do not lie to me. Did you do something to piss her off? If she quits, I will never forgive you!"

"Why?!" I fumed. "Why is she allotted so many privileges in this company? What is it about her that's so special?! Why did you spend so much money on that tiny lab in the first place?" My temperature spiked, and I turned on my truck's AC full blast.

"Do not question me, Jethro. She's special to me. That's all you need to know."

"Not good enough, Father. Are you having an affair with her?"

"Don't be ridiculous. She is half my age!"

"That's never stopped you before!"

"If this is about Jessica . . ."

"Not everything in my life revolves around my ex!"

"Watch your tone, son."

"Answer me! You're a selfish asshole to everyone else, except her. What is so special about Aisling Lovelle?"

Silence.

My father was not a faithful man to my mother. Never had been. The sad thing was my mother knew about his many affairs and did nothing. It was one of the many reasons I was allergic to commitment, well love in general. I used to think my mother stayed in her loveless marriage for me, but I was a grown man. Her life was empty and sad and honestly a tad embarrassing for both of us. I wouldn't be surprised if my father had a thing with Aisling. I'd asked her about it which thoroughly pissed her off. Her reaction made me think my assumptions were wrong, but Harlo was being evasive about the entire situation. Like he always was when hiding something from my mother. Another disgusting thought crept into my mind.

"Oh fuck! She's your daughter isn't she?!"

"No! Absolutely, not. I met her mother for the first time at Midway U when Aisling graduated. Before then I never met the woman, so that theory of yours is preposterous."

"Are you sure? It wouldn't be the first affair you've ever had."

"Christ, Jethro. Trust me when I say this, Aisling is not related to you or me. I've checked her DNA myself."

That was a relief. I'd been lusting after Ash since the moment we met. If she was my half-sister, I'd puke all over myself and then pluck my eyes out.

"Wait, why would you check her DNA?"

"Because, CEO, we do drug tests on all of our potential employees, and I have an interest in mystic genetics. Call it academic curiosity."

Sounded like bullshit, and I was ready to call him on it but he droned on.

"Your responsibility is to get Buchanan Pharmaceuticals back on the top. And picking on Aisling is not the answer. Leave her be!" he added.

"No. You still haven't answered my question. Why is she so special to you? Is she working on a secret project?"

"What is your fascination with her? She has always done good work for the company. She's an excellent scientist. Why are you even there?"

"Because it's not right! Something is not right. She's hiding something in that lab, and I want to know what it is." I was like a dog with a bone. I wasn't going to give up on this and I would find out.

"Ask her yourself."

"I did!" I punched the steering wheel.

My father, the asshole, fucking laughed. "I see what's going on. She said no. She's not giving in to you like the others. Serves you right! You've always been a stubborn boy. Selfish. Always thinking about yourself. Remember this, Jethro, this company provides you with a lavish lifestyle, one that has given you many privileges your entire life. You might be CEO, but I can easily disinherit you which would make you ineligible to hold the title, and it would make you penniless. Leave Aisling alone, Jet. This is your only warning."

The phone line went dead, and I just stared at it, waiting for an epiphany. The fucker always knew how to control me. It was always the same with him . . . give a little and remind me how fortunate I was for being bestowed his generosity.

This situation with Aisling was unique. He'd never cared so much about another person. Not even his wife of nearly forty-odd years or his only son. Her importance sparked my curiosity, and I just couldn't let it go. What would my father want from her? Did he expect Ash to fall in love with him? It was a ridiculous notion, considering the age difference, but it hadn't stopped him before.

And more than that, Buchanan Pharma was bleeding money from somewhere and my first instinct was Aisling Lovelle. The small lab had been a costly start-up. From what I could gather after being in the office for the past few weeks and comparing the financial records, the company had spent way more than what was in that lab. I thought she had pocketed the money but when I compared the lab accounting records with the account at Midway Bank, it all added up. It was like the money had vanished into some unknown account. Presently, the small lab was turning a profit and had been for the past six months. Still, the lab Ash was working out of should been a million-dollar setup not twelve.

Unable to let the topic go, I called HR in the corporate office for her home address.

Hours had gone by since she left the office; she had to be home, if not I was prepared to wait. Except when I got there, I was greeted by Gaius Pope. The first time I'd met him I wondered, who the hell was this guy? Turns out, he was the boyfriend aka neighbor aka the donut guy she fucked in his car. He wasn't any help, but he was concerned. I told him she'd gone to see Talon after leaving the office hours earlier. Info I didn't need to share, since it was none of my business. I wanted to drive a wedge between him and Ash, and Talon and Ash, all because I was a petty prick. The worst part about my scheming was Gaius—or Pope as he liked to be called—seemed like a decent dude.

Tail tucked between my legs, I went home to stew in the unknown of when I'd see her again. The more I thought about it, the more frustrated I became.

The next day I expected her to return to the office. She didn't. Aggravation and concern mounted on my shoulders. It was annoying as fuck even though it was her scheduled day off. Her schedule was about to change. Three days off every week meant she was working part-time hours making full-time wages. Not that that was an issue. Ash was smart, and she did good work. I was just being a control freak.

The minute I laid eyes on her I wanted to occupy all her time. I wanted to make her mine. I wasn't sure why that was. Sure, she was gorgeous and brilliant. But it was more than that. I had this primal urge to claim her, embed my seed in her womb, and lock her away.

What was it about her that made me want her so badly? Maybe it was because she refused to give me the answers I sought. Maybe the fascination would fizzle as soon as I'd gotten the answers. Maybe the strong desire to be with her would die after the sex.

I didn't understand it. It wasn't like I envisioned a long-term relationship for myself with anyone. Yes, I'd wanted that at one point, but that was a long time ago.

Before coming to Midway, I'd been thinking about getting a vasectomy. That was how strongly I felt about commitments. I'd rather snip my balls than be tied down. Hook-ups were great. I highly recommend it, but a long-term commitment? No, thank you.

Oh god, did this mean I was just like him . . . my father?

Hell no. Not having it. I'd bite my arm off before becoming like him; the man who was too busy chasing skirts to spend time with his family. That man was gross. I'd seen what his actions did to my mother and the countless women he preyed upon. Jessie included.

I scrubbed my hand down my face. The way I saw it, I had two choices. I could walk away from Ash and let her continue whatever secretive projects she was working on. Buchanan Pharma would be fine and Ash would be happy with me out of her hair. Or I could let down my guard, and get to know Ash, which might mean sharing.

If I kept my dick in my pants, which I'd been trying to do, maybe I could get to know her a bit more before we took it farther. And maybe sharing would be an option.

The concept was a tall order. Being around Aisling, my beautiful little monster made every inch of me ache to touch her. *Fuck, Jet. You are like your father. Thinking with your damn dick all the damned time.*

No more. I was going to be professional and keep my pants on until I figured out what was so special about Aisling that made my father give her carte blanche.

This was my opportunity to change the man my upbringing had turned me into.

CHAPTER TWENTY

AISLING

It was past midnight and my phone had been buzzing nonstop. Talon and I had barely come up for air since he'd found me gazing at the view on his rooftop terrace. He was all-consuming, and we'd done something that couldn't be undone. I'd never dated a shifter before, but their mating rituals weren't a secret. I knew it wasn't something to take lightly. And I just had to dive into the deep end headfirst. I was mated to a wolf. Bound to him for life. For some reason, I wasn't freaked out about it. It felt right. We were connected on a soul-deep level that was undeniable.

My phone buzzed again. "Mate," Talon crawled up my body. "It's your boyfriend again. You should talk to him before he files a missing person's report."

Pope had called and texted a zillion times. Talon didn't seem bothered by it at all. I, on the other hand, felt weird. Pope was important to me, and I didn't want to cut him out of my life. I should have talked to Talon about this before allowing him to mark me. Shit. I wanted them both. Now what.

Talon kissed the side of my face and handed me the phone. "Go ahead, babe. I'll be right here."

Of course, he wouldn't give me privacy. I couldn't blame him. I called Pope.

"Ash? What the fuck? Are you okay?" Pope sounded frantic.

"I'm sorry, Pope. Don't freak out. I'm fine."

"Where are you? What the fuck happened? Your boss came knocking on your door."

"What? Why?"

"Not sure, he said something about you leaving early and wanted to make sure you got home okay. Are you sure you're okay?"

Talon kissed my back. A soft moan escaped me.

"Pope, umm . . . listen," I began.

"I don't need details right now, angel. Unless you want to share. I just want to make sure you're okay."

"I am."

"He's being good to you?"

"What makes you think I'm with someone?"

"You're making sexy noises. If those noises are just for me, then, damn, I'm here for it. But I suspect you're being entertained. So, I'll ask again, is he being good to you?"

"He is." I released another moan as Talon flipped me over and fastened his mouth on my pussy.

"Fuck, you sound so good, Ash. I can imagine how wet you are right now." He groaned. "What is he doing to you, baby? Does it feel good?"

His questions shocked me into silence. I looked down to see Talon staring up at me.

"Tell me, Ash. I want details," Pope commanded with a sultry tone that made me want to tell him everything.

Talon reached for the phone and hit the speaker button. "Tell him what he wants to know, mate." He resumed running his tongue up and down my slit.

I moaned, and Pope moaned with me.

"Are his fingers in your tight hole? Or is he licking your sweet cunt?"

Between Pope's words and Talon's tongue, I was soaring, ready to fall off the edge.

"Licking." I threaded my fingers through Talon's hair and pressed his face into my pussy.

"Mmmm . . . baby, you like that don't you. You sound so hot when you moan. I want to hear you come."

"Does that turn you on, Pope? Listening to me come while another guy is licking my pussy."

"Fuck, yes. Listening. Watching. You have me so hard, baby. I'm going to come in my boxers."

"Stroke yourself for me. I want to come with you."

Talon let out a groan.

"Anything for you, baby."

"Yes, Pope." My breathing became ragged.

"You like that angel? You like fucking his face."

I moaned in response.

"That's it, baby. Are you close? I'm stroking my cock so hard and fast right now. Fuck, I wish I could watch you come."

I clawed the sheets, my hips undulating. Talon's moans vibrated on my clit.

"Yes!" My climax erupted. My body trembling.

"You sound so fucking hot when you come."

Talon drank me down, then took the phone.

I peered at him under my lashes and watched him aim the phone at my pussy.

"Ffffuuckk." Pope groaned.

I propped myself up on my elbows and saw Pope's hooded gaze on the screen. Talon had switched the call to video and aimed the camera at my cum-drenched cunt, all while fingering me nice and slow. I groaned, pumping my hips, chasing Talon's fingers. I was ready for another round.

Pope gasped. A lazy, content smile spread over his handsome face. I know that face.

"So fucking beautiful." Pope's voice was filled with awe.

Talon turned the phone to face him. "That's all you get this weekend. Leave us alone. Understand?"

"Lucky motherfucker. You better take good care of our girl."

"Of course." Talon disconnected the phone and mounted me.

I DIDN'T GO to work the next day. I didn't go anywhere the entire weekend. Not even home.

The storm that started Thursday lingered for days, keeping me and Talon sequestered in our love nest. Or was it lust? It was definitely more lust than anything else. For nearly three and a half days all we did was fuck. Even sleeping and eating came with sex. It was . . . the absolute best.

Interestingly enough, I hadn't taken a tonic once and didn't have any blackouts. I'd thought I was cured until my internal companion made herself known. It'd happened one night while in bed. In his sleep, Talon pulled me on top of him. The movement woke me and the voice in my head purred. I startled awake which earned me a shriek.

-No! Go back to sleep.

The voice was so clear and insistent, that I laid back down, resting my head on Talon's chest. She purred again, and I lay awake for some time until his thumping heartbeat lulled me into a deep sleep. She seemed to be content as long he was near. I didn't know what to make of this and decided to leave it alone.

If being mated to a handsome wolf shifter with a big D meant no more blackouts, I was all in.

"Red?" Talon called from the bedroom.

"I'm in here," I replied, sinking into a warm tub of bubbles.

"I should've known." He sauntered into the bathroom and placed a kiss on my forehead.

He had been on a business call earlier and I'd snuck off to soak in the tub. I'd been soaking in his monstrous bathtub as often as I could. All the sex had me aching in places I didn't know existed.

"Your boyfriend's been calling," he sat on the edge of the tub.

I smiled at my wolf. "I'm surprised you haven't answered it."

"I'm not jealous, baby. You're mine."

"I know you're not. And yes, I am but . . ."

"But . . . I might be willing to share." He gave me a sexy grin.

I climbed out of the bathtub and onto his lap. He was already hard, and I was desperate to have him fill me. The thought of him and Pope sharing me unleashed a fire of arousal. I sank onto Talon's engorged length and rode him until we were both gasping for air and then we opted for the shower to clean up since the tub water had gone cold.

I took my time toweling off and drying my hair while Talon proceeded to use my phone. The phone on the other end rang and Pope answered.

"Good morning, angel."

"Not your angel," Talon replied with a smirk.

"Who might this be, exactly? You failed to introduce yourself."

"Aisling's mate."

Pope chuckled. "Does Aisling's mate have a name?"

Talon laughed. "Talon. Why are you calling. . . again? I told you not to bother us this weekend."

"It's Monday morning."

Talon grunted in response.

"Where is she?"

"Good morning, Pope."

"Hi, angel. You good?"

"Great. Thanks for checking on me."

"Need anything?"

You. I leaned into Talon's side. "No, thanks."

"Okay, if you think of something you need from home, call me. I'll see you for lunch."

My heartbeat quickened. I was excited to see him.

"Looking forward to it!" Talon answered.

"You're not invited. You've had her to yourself the entire weekend, you selfish prick."

"New rules, as of now; I'm always invited."

"The lady makes the rules," Pope replied.

Talon fixed me with an intimidating gaze. But I had to make a decision. Set some boundaries.

"I want you two to meet," I said.

"Anything for you, angel. See you two at noon." Pope hung up.

"Are you okay with me and Pope?" I sat on the bathroom counter and pulled the towel around me a little tighter.

He released a heavy sigh. "Aisling. I know this is sudden. I don't have a single ounce of regret, except I should have given you time to get to know me."

I silenced him by placing a finger over his lips. "I don't have a single regret either."

He smiled and cupped my face. "There will be questions and things we will need to learn about each other. But I want you to know, I'm not going anywhere, ever. No matter what happens. This thing with Pope, I am willing to keep an open mind. I wasn't lying when I said I was willing to share. But, if I discover something I don't like, I will send him away. In a body bag."

I swallowed hard. The way he'd said it so casually made me believe every word.

CHAPTER TWENTY-ONE

POPE

As soon as I'd heard Talon call her mate during that first phone call, I knew he was going to be a permanent fixture in her life.

Did he know about her alter ego? I was dying to find out.

I'd arrived at Ash's office fifteen minutes early to see if I could have some time with her before Talon joined us. No such luck. I bumped into the shifter in the hallway.

"You're early." Talon narrowed his gaze.

"So are you."

"Haven't we met before?" he asked.

"Nope. Not that I can recall."

He opened the door to Ash's office and motioned for me to enter before him.

"Hi Zoey," I greeted Ash's friend.

"Hey, Pope, um . . ." She glanced at Talon.

"We're here for Ash," he told her.

"Sure, I'll get her for you. Wait here please," she said nervously and slipped through the door that led to the lab.

As soon as the door opened raised voices filtered into the waiting room. Talon stormed through the lab.

"No, Jet. I already have a full workload." Ash shouted. "I'm not taking on any additional projects all of which are due this week. It's impossible."

Shit. I'd never heard her yell before.

"Yeah, you are. And no it isn't. The solution is simple. No more three-day weekends for you." Dr. Buchanan retorted.

Those two were glaring daggers at each other, but the sexual tension between them was thick.

Talon crossed his arms over his chest and cleared his throat.

Aisling's fiery gaze softened when she saw him. She stepped forward and practically melted in his arms. *Fuck, she was in love.*

She peered around his massive biceps, and her eyes lit up. "Pope!" She greeted me with a kiss on the lips.

My inner turmoil relaxed. She was still mine. Or at least in part. A part of her was better than none. I'd be wrecked if she didn't want anything to do with me. Or pushed me into the friend zone.

"Hi, angel." I held her close. "Sounds like you could use a break."

She drew away from me. "Yes. Perfect timing. Let me get my purse."

She trailed a hand along Talon's arms as she passed and disappeared into her office.

"Uh, what the hell is going on, Talon? Pope?" Dr. Buchanan regarded us with suspicion.

"We're going to lunch," I replied.

"Don't talk to my mate like that ever again," Talon seethed.

"Mate?" Jet's eyebrows shot to his hairline. "And lunch? With both of you?" Jet's gaze flicked to mine then back to Talon's.

"Yes, yes, and yes. I'll be back in an hour," Aisling answered. She tugged on Talon's arm. He didn't budge.

Wolf and Warlock were mad-dogging each other. Talon clenched his jaw, his eyes flashed gold. Sparks of magic danced along Jet's palms. Cue the popcorn, people, this was entertaining shit.

Aisling didn't find it as funny as I did. Instead, she approached the shifter with a soothing voice and gentle touch.

"Talon," she said. His eyes were glued to Jet. "Mate?"

He turned his face.

"I'm hungry."

He grabbed her hand, and we exited the lab with Jet following us out to the waiting area. Before the main door closed, Talon turned back and said, "This isn't over Jethro."

Lunch with Aisling and Talon wasn't as awkward as I'd anticipated. Ash was openly affectionate with me and Talon, which put me at ease about the situation. Talon seemed perfectly fine with his mate and me sharing a kiss or two, which was unexpected. I wasn't going to complain.

I'd done more research on the shifter, and he had an impressive story. He wasn't only rich, smart, and handsome, he was also well respected in the community. He'd been revitalizing some of the older neighborhoods. Had set up a non-profit for small businesses and had been taking care of his sister and mother for years. His sister was in college out of state. His mother lived in a mega-mansion near the water. And to top it off, I liked the fucker. He was kind of funny and had an easygoing personality.

I was beginning to think we'd become good friends until he dropped a bomb in the middle of the table.

"Mate," he draped an arm around her shoulders. "I have to work tonight."

She nodded. "It's okay, I'll be working late also, it seems, and I need to go home anyway."

"I'd like you to move in with me."

"Not tonight, Talon. Maybe soon, but not tonight."

He smiled big. Then gave us a serious look. "I'm okay with waiting, but I want one thing."

I knew what he wanted without hearing him say it.

"No sex with Pope." He glared at me.

I crossed my arms over my chest.

"I'm sorry, what?" Ash cleared her throat.

"You heard me, mate. No sex with Pope. Unless I'm there."

The fuck face was being a territorial prick, and I would have been pissed off if it wasn't for the sight of Ash's flaming red face. I took it as a sign that she had at least entertained the idea of fucking me later.

"You can't put those kinds of limitations on our love. I wouldn't do it to you, asshole." I said finally finding my voice.

Ash beamed at me. *There's that smile.*

"I'm not saying no, forever. I'm saying, wait, for me. I want to be there, mate. I need to be sure he's good enough for you." His tone was sincere and protective.

Ash melted for him. "Okay. Just this once," she agreed.

Talon faced me, arms crossed over his chest.

"Fine. But I'm still sleeping next to her."

"Keep your dick in your pants, Pope," he added.

As it turned out, Ash was not a rule breaker. She worked late and came home exhausted. I strolled over to her place and pampered her. I drew her bath and sat on the bathroom floor while she told me what had happened with Talon, which was a bit concerning.

"I don't know, Pope. It just happened. He asked. And I said yes. No, I asked him for it. I wanted him to mark me."

I angled her jaw, allowing me to see the marks on her neck.

"He loves you." *And you love him.* Mating was something people couldn't fake. I would know. I'd fallen for a shifter once. I loved her, but we weren't mates. I didn't realize this at first. I wanted to fight the myth. Three years later, her mate had walked into her life and something in her changed. She became a beacon of light and happiness. Something I'd never come close to giving her. It hurt but I got over it. I hadn't fallen in love again. Until Ash. Was she going to leave me, too? My stomach bottomed out.

"Hey." She caressed my face with wet hands.

"I need you. Both of you. I don't know how this is supposed to work. It's sudden. And out of character for me. But I want both of you in my life. Now. And always."

Her words made me smile so big I could feel it in my bones.

"Be patient with me while I figure all of this out, okay?"

"Aisling, nothing in the world could make me walk away from you."

She kissed me deeply and pulled away.

"I know it's asking a lot but give Talon time to adjust. Please. He's trying to figure this out, too and he's willing to give us a chance. He just needs to get to know you."

"Okay, angel."

Talon called before Ash fell asleep, stating he would be working late. She curled up next to me, and it took every ounce of will power I had to keep my hands to myself. Mating for shifters was intense, and it said a lot about his character for him to be okay with me sleeping in her bed. I had to do my part or at least give it a try. For Ash, it was worth it. It wasn't like I hadn't seen her having sex with him before. She'd probably hate me when she found out how much I'd been stalking her. Cross that bridge, later.

I buried my nose in her hair and closed my eyes, allowing her steady breathing to pull me into a deep sleep.

Sometime later, I rolled over to find her side of the bed empty.

"Ash?" I called out.

No response. I got out of bed and searched the apartment. She was gone. So was her phone and car. I pulled up the tracker, thinking she'd gone back to Talon. She didn't. She was heading east toward the edge of town.

There was a main highway that led north of Port Midway which took you across the nation. The interstate was well traveled and one Ash had taken frequently when visiting her parents.

The road she was traveling veered off the main highway and went east heading toward the border which was surrounded by dense woodlands. It wasn't the safest area for her to be in. My nerves spiked.

As far as I could recall, Talon didn't have a business out there. Maybe he was there for something else, and she went to him. Doubtful. I panicked. Was she having one of those episodes again?

In minutes, I was in my car and speeding down the street. Perhaps I should have called Talon, but Ash had a good fifty minutes on me. I punched the gas pedal, eating up asphalt as quickly as I could.

According to the tracker, she had stopped. That didn't make me feel any better. *What are you doing Ash?*

Less than a mile away from her location I parked and approached on foot. She was at a brothel. Was it a sex thing? Couldn't be. I knew Talon had been sexing her up good for three days straight.

I scratched my head, thinking through my next moves. *What now Pope? Go in and track her down or wait by her car?*

Her familiar laughter filled the air. I moved toward the sound and found her between two men. One at her back, the other on his knees. Ok, maybe it was a sex thing. A glint of metal flashed in the dark. A knife appeared in her hand. She flipped the blade and ran it through the heart of the man standing behind her. The man on his knees stumbled, backing away. Ash stalked him with a maniacal grin on her pretty face. She was still beautiful. Crazy. But beautiful.

The man begged for his life. Ash laughed and then ran the blade across his neck. He lay there on the ground bleeding out, while his friend lay dead a few feet away from him. Ash threw the dagger on the ground and walked away.

I stood there, frozen in place. *Jesus, Ash. What the hell is going on with you?* I scanned the area, then made a wide circle around the body to retrieve the discarded murder weapon and went back to my car. Just as I started the car, a hand clamped over my mouth.

CHAPTER TWENTY-TWO

TALON

"I'm still working baby," I said to Ash while Igor drove me to the police station. "I'll come over when I'm done, okay?"

"Okay, don't work too hard, mate," she replied and disconnected the phone. The way she called me mate made my dick hard. I was with her during lunch and was already missing her something fierce.

Thomas Hayes, Port Midway's chief of police stood when I entered his office. If I hadn't seen him shift, I would've sworn he was human. His forehead was deeply lined and his hair was more gray than black. For a mystic, he hadn't aged well.

"Why did you want to see me, Thomas?"

"The recent murders, of course." He motioned for me to take a seat. "There's been some new developments I know you can help me with."

He slid a file across the desktop to me. I scanned the autopsy reports, noting the DNA analysis as an unknown mystic.

I snapped the file shut and threw it on the desk. "I don't see how I can help with this."

"The victims had a residual magical signature on their skin that can't be placed."

"I can read Thomas. What does that have to do with me? I'm a shifter. Find yourself a wizard that can help you."

"I tried that, asshole." He scrubbed a weathered hand down his face. "Listen, I've taken this to the head of the alchemy department at the university and was advised to take it to an elite witch or warlock who may have some insights into this anomaly."

"Again, shifter." I pointed at my chest.

"Jesus, Talon, do I have to spell it out for you? I don't want to scare the public by making it known that there might be a mystic serial killer. Buchanan Pharma's headquarters is a seven-hour drive across the border. Lucky for us, they have an office here in Port Midway. Get it now? Or do I need to send a patrol car to your building?"

"You want me to question my tenant?" My mate. Unease pricked at my skin. It wasn't her. Couldn't be.

"He's not a suspect. I just need his expertise."

"He?"

"Dr. Jethro Buchanan, the heir who is now the new owner. I called the HQ, and they said he's there."

"Fine. I'll do your legwork. I'll call you when I have something." I took the file and strolled out of the police station, with a million what-ifs running through my head.

It had taken a few hours to finish making my business rounds. Being an attorney was one thing, managing different enterprises was another. I'd always enjoyed working long days and nights until Ash. Things would need to change now that I was mated.

I got into the car just past midnight with Igor behind the wheel. He should have been done for the day but since I'd given him three days off while I was with Ash, he insisted on working late.

"Where to boss?" Igor asked.

I gave him Ash's address. As we turned down her street, a familiar Tesla raced past us.

"Turn around, Igor." I tapped on his seat. "Follow that car."

Igor followed the Tesla to the east side of town. The Tesla parked and out walked Pope.

I opened the door. "Go home, Igor. I'll see you in the morning."

"I'm happy to wait, boss," Igor asked.

"Go." I exited the car and caught up to Pope, sticking to the shadows.

He crouched behind a parked car, and I followed his gaze.

Ash was with two men, then suddenly blood sprayed everywhere. The man behind her was on the ground. And then she sliced the other's throat.

Mistress? I recognized this the moment I tasted her on the rooftop. Knowing Dr. Lovelle and the Mistress were indeed the same person didn't matter then since I'd already known she was my mate. The more time we spent together the more insignificant that fact became.

Witnessing the sudden act of brutality sent a wave of shock and disbelief through me. I knew then that not only was my mate the woman I'd met at Nirvana—who did not recognize me—she was also responsible for the murders the chief had just asked me about.

My mouth went dry. Like Pope, I froze in place while Ash sauntered away like she hadn't just murdered two men and got into her vehicle.

By the time, I refocused, Pope had already disappeared. I jogged back to his parked car which was unlocked. No sign of him. *Where did he go?* Knowing he'd be back, I hid in the back seat.

As soon as he entered I covered his mouth. "Why the fuck did my mate just kill two men? Did you put her up to this?"

He mumbled something, and I released him.

"Fuck, Talon," he gasped. "Of course, I didn't put her up to this. Where the hell did you come from?"

"Explain, Pope," I snarled. "Who the hell were those guys?"

"Sit up front, please. I'm not playing Miss Daisy with you." He motioned for me to move into the front passenger seat with the weapon still on his lap. "I don't know those guys. What are we going to do about the bodies?"

"I'll take care of it. Someone owes me a favor." I tapped into my phone. There are many advantages to owning a bar. Getting to know the regulars was one of them and some of them just happened to be the types to get rid of dead bodies without leaving a trace.

Pope drove us back to Ash's place and told me everything. And boy did he have a lot to share. He'd followed Ash to where she'd killed the two men, and she'd done it before. Three times before this evening. Fuck my life.

"You've been stalking my mate? For how long?"

"Long enough and that is not nearly as important as what I've seen. And for the record, she's only been your mate for the past few days."

He was right. I drummed my fingers on the armrest, trying to understand. My Ash and the mistress I'd met a few weeks ago were the same person. And she was responsible for all of it. Three murders. Now five.

"You've witnessed these murders, and you haven't talked to her about it? Why didn't you do anything?"

"What was I supposed to say? Hi, babe, how was the killing last night? And no, I had, have no intention of turning her in to the police. I've been protecting her every single time."

"What?! How? And why?"

"Why do you think?" He side-glanced me.

"You're in love with her." Of course, he was. I gazed out the window into the darkness.

"I've been messing with surveillance in the neighborhood." Pope's voice was so soft, it took a second for his words to register.

"Oh shit. You're not just an ordinary computer geek. You're a hacker."

He cast me a furtive glance. "*A* hacker? Try *the* hacker."

"Unfuckingbelievable. Quit messing with my surveillance, asshole," I muttered.

"I've only done it if Ash was involved." He smirked.

"What else have you seen while stalking her?"

"Lots of things." He shook his head. "I'm not doing it to be creepy. Like I said, I'm protecting her."

"What is she going to say when you walk through the door . . ." I glanced at the time. "At two a.m.?"

"I'm not sure. I've never slept beside her when she's disappeared to go kill people. Thus the stalking. The first time I followed her, she left her place in the middle of the night and drove out to the Last Resort. Ash is not one to party on the weekends so I was intrigued. Until tonight, this has happened only on the weekend."

"What the fuck does this mean? Why is she doing this?"

"No clue. The day after each incident, she wakes with a hangover, and seems to have no recollection of what she did for the previous two-to-three days."

This was insane.

"Did you notice anything while you were with her?" Pope asked.

I thought about it. "She was with me the entire time."

"That's a good sign. While she was with you, I spent the weekend searching the dark web for clues as to what may cause this. Nothing's surfaced." His throat bobbed as he swallowed hard, and a putrid scent filled the car. His discomfort was leaking out of his pores.

"What aren't you telling me?" I growled. "This isn't the time to be keeping secrets."

He sighed. "I also looked into her past. She grew up in a commune north of here. And they're not big on using the internet up there so there wasn't much to find until she began studying here at the U. Even those records were hard to dig up. Someone with a lot of pull sealed her medical records, but I managed to find something strange. She'd seen doctors and experts for periodic blackouts. The diagnosis stated 'findings inconclusive'. Could be a mental health issue. Or it could be supernatural. Something maybe to do with her lineage."

Fuck. My heart galloped. Mistress was mystic and she was very different from Ash. Both were vastly different beings residing in the same body. *How do I fix this?* I resumed tapping the armrest. This was bad and I had a niggling feeling it was going to get worse.

My visit with the chief of police rushed to the forefront of my mind. "She's leaving evidence behind."

"Yeah, I was afraid of that. I don't know what we're dealing with. If I did, I might be able to help her find a way to stop it. I love her, Talon. I'll cover it up as best as I can with my skills, but it might not be enough."

"It's not, Pope. It's not enough. The police know a mystic is involved. There's mystic DNA on the bodies left at every scene. And they want me to ask the doctor slash warlock in my building if he can look at the data."

"He? Jethro?"

I nodded.

"Oh fuck. He hates her. He can't get involved."

"He doesn't hate her. He hates himself because he's attracted to her."

"That makes no sense."

"I agree. Still, you're right about one thing, he can't get involved."

"Well, what are you going to do about him? About her?" Panic laced his voice as he turned into their neighborhood.

"I'll deal with the Jet situation. As far as Ash, she's my mate. I will die to protect her."

He parked in his garage and pulled out the dagger Ash used.

"Uh, you may not want to stick around for this part," Pope said, staring at the blade.

"What are you planning to do with that?" I asked.

"Get rid of it," he said.

"How?"

"My magic, I guess. I've been magicking the murder weapons away," he told me.

"Let's see it then." I waited for the show to begin.

Pope shrugged. He focused on the blade, his face scrunched with concentration.

The smell of burned ozone filled the car and soon the blade disintegrated.

Pope faced me. "I'm adopted. I don't know about my magical lineage. This is a new development. Ever since Ash's first incident, my goal was to get rid of the evidence and this is what happened."

"Okay. This has been an interesting night." I opened the door. "And umm . . . Thanks, Pope. For watching out for her."

The sound of a washing machine greeted us as we entered Ash's place together. She was sound asleep and didn't stir when Pope slid in beside her. I took a quick shower, which I noticed had been recently used, and sighed.

Jet was a situation I could handle, but Ash. Fuck, I had just found my mate and now she was in trouble. Big trouble.

I slipped into bed and drew Ash into my arms. Her curves molded around my body, and she nuzzled the crook of my neck.

"Talon?" Her voice was soft and sleepy.

"I'm here, baby. Go back to sleep."

"I didn't hear you knock," she said.

"Pope let me in," I replied.

The hacker pressed his body to her back.

"Hi, angel." He kissed her shoulder.

"Hi. I'm glad you're both here. I was having a bad dream."

I released a heavy sigh into the dark room.

"It's okay, Red, we're here. We'll protect you from those nightmares and anything else that comes your way."

I meant every word, even though she needed more than protection. Ash needed help. There's no way she could continue killing random people in the middle of the night. She was out of control. But she was mine now. As her mate, I would fix this for her. Somehow.

CHAPTER TWENTY-THREE

AISLING

Talon and Pope were in my bed, snoring. It was too cute and almost enough to relieve the headache I had woken up with.

I wanted to stay in bed with them and enjoy all those muscles, but I had to get to the lab before Jet. The thought of that man annoyed the shit out of me.

I leaned over and placed light kisses on Pope's cheek and then on Talon. My wolf woke and pulled me on top of him.

"Morning, baby," he rasped. "It's still dark out. Why are you awake so early?"

"I need to get some work done at the lab," I whispered, trying not to wake Pope.

He groaned, rubbing his growing erection on my pelvis.

I kissed him deeply, then moved to get off him but Talon kept me in place, his hands massaging my butt.

"How did you sleep? Any more nightmares?" he asked, nuzzling my cheek.

"No nightmares after you came home, but I woke with a headache."

"Do you want to talk about those dreams?" He drew away to gaze into my eyes.

I shook my head and pressed a gentle kiss on his lips.

"Stay in bed, mate. It's our first morning in your place. With Pope." He nipped at my jaw.

"Talon. I can't. I don't have time." I tilted my head, allowing him to suckle his mark on my neck.

His hand dipped between my legs. He pushed my panties to the side and began stroking me gently.

"Your wet pussy tells me you want to stay right here," he rasped.

"But Pope. I don't want to wake him," I said.

"He's already awake," Talon rasped, strumming my clit with a light, steady touch.

I ground my pelvis on his palm and peeked a glance over at Pope.

"Don't stop on my account," Pope said in a deep sleepy voice.

He was laying on his side. His gaze roamed over me and landed on my ass.

"Good morning. Sorry to wake you," I said.

"He doesn't mind. Do you Pope?" Talon asked.

"Not at all." Pope leaned in for a kiss. His hand roamed over my back down to my butt. And his fingers matched what Talon was doing to my dripping pussy.

I expected Talon to give me more resistance before letting the three of us travel down this path together. I wondered what Pope had done to make Talon decide he was good enough to be with me. With us. It wasn't a question I had time to ponder. I had dreamed of this moment ever since I met Talon and told Pope about him. My skin felt heated, and my pussy was throbbing. I was not going to pass on this opportunity.

Talon rolled me onto my back and he and Pope pushed my panties down my legs. I tugged off my tank and bra and spread my thighs as far apart as I could, giving both men access.

They worked me in tandem, sucking my nipples while stroking

my slit. Their fingers entered my core, making me quiver. My body ached for release.

"Mmmm . . . yes make me come."

"Not yet." Talon pulled out of me, and Pope followed.

"Guys!"

They laughed.

"Let us make you feel good, baby. Eat her pussy, Pope." Talon's voice was rough. Demanding.

Pope didn't hesitate. He dove between my legs. His tongue slid from my clit to my entrance.

Talon hooked my chin to face him and locked our lips together while pinching my nipples and making me arch off the bed.

I groaned, pumping my hips. There were so many sensations rolling through me, I was a quivering, wet mess. Having one man lick my pussy while another sucked my nipples was sending me through the roof.

"Does that feel good, mate?"

"So good," I moaned.

"Do you want him to fuck you? You want his cock?" His voice was thick with lust.

"Yes!"

"Beg me," Talon ordered. "Beg me to allow him to fuck you."

"Please, mate. Please, let Pope fuck me and make me come."

"What will you do for me, if I allow him to fuck you?"

"Anything you want. Please."

"First, lick your juices off his tongue."

I reached for Pope and brought his face against mine. His mouth and chin were glistening, I sucked his face.

"That's my good girl. Suck his face clean, baby."

Talon snaked his tongue between mine and Pope's. "So fucking good."

"Fffuck. Let me fuck her, Talon." Pope's voice was hoarse. Restrained.

My wolf chuckled. "Beg me. Both of you."

"Please, Talon," we said at the same time.

Talon chuckled.

"You want his big cock, mate? Look at it weeping for you."

Pope was kneeling, one leg on either side of me. His cock, hard and swollen rested on my pubic bone.

Talon surprised me by reaching for him. He smeared the precum over Pope's head, making his cock jump in his hand.

"Oh, fuck!" Pope tossed his head back.

"You want my mate's pussy, Gaius?"

"Fuck yes," Pope groaned.

"This cock is ours. No other hands or mouths touch you. And this is the only pussy you'll ever have, understood?" Talon all but commanded.

"Yours. All yours," Pope said, rocking his hips, begging Talon to stroke him.

My wolf turned his gaze to me.

"Is this what you want in your pussy, mate?" Talon guided Pope's crown to my entrance and ran it up and down my slit.

"Yes. Please, mate. Please let him fuck me," I begged.

"Tell me you're mine, and you can have his cock."

"I'm yours, Talon."

"Fuck my mate, Pope."

"Thank fuck," Pope rasped. He gripped my hips and sheathed his length in my pussy with one long stroke.

"Nice and tight, isn't she?" Talon hooked one of my legs, spreading me wider, and began massaging my swollen clit.

"So tight. And so wet." Pope pumped his hips.

"You look so good getting fucked, mate. Feel how hard I am."

He guided my hand to his thick length and began stroking himself. His large palm covered mine and showed me exactly what he needed.

Pope's thrusts became wild and fervent, making my tits bounce with each thrust as he used my body to chase his release.

My orgasm bloomed. Everything went tight. It was too soon. I didn't want this to end. I wanted both of them to use me for their pleasure and pleasure me in return. I wanted to keep going. But Pope's cock began to swell and my body was teetering on the edge.

I squeezed Talon's cock and locked my ankles behind Pope's back, keeping him deeply seated in my pussy. He drove himself deeper and deeper into my body. Jolts of pleasure danced over my skin. My walls clenched.

"Oooh fffuck. I can feel you coming," Pope gasped.

"That's it, baby, let go," Talon encouraged.

I free fell over the edge. Pope cried out, his hips sputtering as he emptied himself inside me.

"Fuck. That was intense." Pope swiped the sheen of sweat from his brow.

"Beautiful. So fucking beautiful, Aisling," Talon praised.

Pope rolled off me and Talon took his place. He pressed his forehead to mine and whispered. "I love you." His crown pushed into my entrance.

"I love you, too," I moaned.

He pushed forward another inch.

"You are mine." He slid in deeper.

"I'm yours." I squeezed his length.

"Fuck, your cunt feels so good." He sank into my depths, filling me deep.

Talon's golden gaze bore into me. "You love this, don't you? Getting fucked by two cocks at the same time?"

"Yeeess." I mewled and reached for Pope. He pressed his body against ours.

Talon drew himself up, giving Pope access to my breasts. Pope's mouth latched onto my nipples. His teeth grazed the stiff peaks.

"We are going to fuck you like this every fucking day." Talon picked up the pace. His thrusts were rough and punishing as he claimed my pussy.

I clawed the sheets as Talon pushed himself deeper and deeper into me. Pope massaged my breasts while kissing my neck and sucking over the mark Talon left on my neck.

My wolf let out a deep primal growl. Pope glanced at him.

"Keep going. I can feel your mouth on her mark," Talon told him.

Pope flicked his tongue over the mark, driving me and Talon crazy.

I threaded my fingers through Pope's hair as a wave of pleasure threatened to drown me.

"I'm coming!" I gasped. Pope's mouth clashed with mine, smothering my screams as I breathed him in, and my pussy squeezed around Talon's dick. I couldn't control it. My orgasm came crashing out of me, making me feel light-headed.

"Oh fuck, baby. You're the tightest cunt I've ever been in." Talon gripped my hips and bounced my body up and down on his thick cock. He came with a roar, his hips driving into me pushing his seed deeper and deeper into my tunnel.

"You're fucking amazing, Ash." Pope left gentle kisses on my shoulder. "I'm so glad you're ours."

"Me too," Talon crumpled on top of me.

I murmured something which meant to be *I love you* but wasn't quite sure if the words left my lips before I passed out.

A knock on the door had me bolting up in bed.

"I'll get it, babe." Talon leaned over to kiss my cheek. He smelled like my body wash and his hair was wet. "It's Igor, coming to take us to work."

"Shit. What time is it?" I scrambled off the bed and ran to the bathroom where Pope was getting out of the shower.

"Why'd you let me sleep?! I'll be late." I moved past him and took a quick shower.

Pope chuckled. "You have an hour to make it there on time."

I didn't want to be on time. I wanted to be early. But staying in bed to have sex with two hot as fuck men was so worth it. For some reason, I couldn't wait to tell Zoey.

A few minutes later, I was showered, dressed, and ready to go. The guys were in the kitchen drinking coffee and eating bagels.

"You need to have breakfast, mate."

"Nope. No time. Where are my keys?" I scoured my living area.

Pope held up my key chain. "What's the rush?"

"I'm trying to get to the office before Dr. Asshole arrives." I pecked him on the cheek. "Lock up for me, please." I kissed his other cheek. "And have a good day. Gotta run."

Before I could say goodbye to Talon, he had already swept me off my feet.

"I'll get the car started. You can eat in the car, Mistress," Igor stated.

My gaze fixed on his back as Talon and I followed him out.

"Why are you driving me to work? I have a car." I asked as we cruised down the road.

"We work in the same building, babe. This is eco-friendly."

"My car is eco-friendly. This thing is a gas guzzler."

"And bulletproof," Talon added.

"Why would you need a bulletproof vehicle?"

"You wouldn't be asking that if you saw the neighborhoods I do business in."

I decided I didn't want the details.

The office was empty when I arrived, giving me space to work on my personal projects while Talon worked on his phone at my desk. I'd finished a batch of tonics and had another project in the works with a few minutes to spare.

"Hey, baby," Talon greeted me as I entered my office space, which felt smaller with his broad frame in it. It was more important for me to have a larger lab area since I spent most of my time there. The office was used mostly for admin work and analyzing data.

"How's it going out there?" he asked me, not bothering to take his eyes off his phone.

"Excellent. What are you working on?"

"Emails." His gaze landed on me, and he flashed me his dimples. "Come here." He extended his hand.

I straddled his lap. He immediately nuzzled my breasts. "Talon, everyone will be here soon."

"I don't give a fuck." He pulled my sweatshirt, T-shirt, and tank off my body in one swoop, and he flicked my hardening nipple.

"Talon," I hummed.

He smirked. In minutes, he had my bottoms off and my ass propped on the desk. I unbuttoned his jeans and guided his tip to my slick entrance. Talon speared me with his hard cock in one smooth thrust. With our lips locked to muffle our moans, he brought me to climax. Twice.

We stumbled out of my office thirty minutes past the hour. Zoey was red in the face and Dr. Buchanan wore a deep scowl.

I guess we weren't as quiet as I thought we were.

Talon, my mate, made a show of adjusting himself as we passed Jet. "Good morning, Jethro."

"Whatever." Jet shouldered past me and went to his lab station.

I walked Talon to the elevators and returned to my office to find Jet sitting behind my desk.

"What now?!"

CHAPTER TWENTY-FOUR

JETHRO

One would think having a three-day weekend away from the office was a gift. Not in my case. After speaking with my father and talking to Pope, I'd decided to give Aisling the benefit of the doubt and treat her with the utmost professionalism I'd shown everyone else who worked for Buchanan Pharmaceuticals.

By Friday evening, I was seething and decided to do something to take the edge off and so I had myself a little orgy. Worst orgy ever. I wasn't into it and ended up drowning myself in booze until I regurgitated it all on my bathroom floor. Talk about frat boy party foul. Fucking embarrassing. Needless to say, my host skills sucked, and I'd never see the new friends I made, which wasn't a bad thing.

Monday morning came and the hangover I'd had was gone. I was thinking more clearly and went into the office fully intending to be the consummate professional. That plan disintegrated as soon as I laid eyes on Ash. She was radiant, with glowing skin and a gorgeous smile. Aisling was always beautiful, but she looked even more so. I knew immediately it had something to do with Talon. The thought of the two of them spending the weekend together made me bristle. It was my doing after all and made it even more difficult to swallow.

Instead of sticking with my original plan, I went with my default behavior which was . . . supreme asshole. And of course, that blew up in my fucking face.

Seeing her with her new mate and Pope twisted me up inside. Her expression and tone softened as soon as she saw Talon. She greeted him with love so raw and pure I could taste it. To add salt to the gaping wound in my soul, she greeted the donut guy, Pope, the same fucking way.

You could be right there with them, Jet, if you would just check your ego at the door. I dismissed the rude thought and stewed for the rest of the day and all night long.

After hours of tossing and turning, I was able to admit to myself that I needed to rethink my game plan.

The whole uncovering of Aisling's secret project wasn't as important anymore. Gaining her favor was. Why? I wasn't entirely sure, to be honest. I'd become obsessed with her since we met. And I didn't like to lose.

Maybe my father was right. Maybe it was the fact that she hadn't succumbed to my charms, my looks, or my money. The only thing I knew for sure was that walking away from her was out of the question.

If I wanted to repair the damage I'd already caused, I needed more time. Time to get to know her and allow her to get to know me. That wasn't hard. I could be charming when I wanted to be.

The next morning I arrived at the office a few minutes before nine with the sole intention of apologizing to Ash for my asshole-ish behavior and starting fresh.

As soon as I opened the main door, their sexy noises reached my ears. And just like that, my plan evaporated, and I became green with envy . . . again. *Why was I allowing this woman to derail every rational plan I devised?* I didn't have the answer to that question. The only thing I could hear were her moans of pleasure.

Jesus, couldn't they at least close a door? They had plenty of options to give them privacy. There was a door that separated the lobby area from the lab, and Ash had a private office within the lab. With a fucking door.

I stood in the entryway, slack-jawed when Zoey entered, running into me.

"Oh! Sorry." Her eyes rounded as she looked toward the lab. "Is that?"

"Yep. Why don't you get some coffee? Or something. I'll break this up." I ushered her out of the office.

Thankfully, she didn't protest, and I locked the door behind her. The moans and groans continued as I entered the lab. Envy bubbled in my gut, but curiosity hijacked rational thought. I crept closer.

Ash wasn't in the lab. She was in her office with the door slightly ajar. *Is that an invitation?* Probably not but I wasn't about to look away.

If I were a gentleman or even a moderately decent person, I would have knocked on the door, cleared my throat, or done something that would have alerted them to my presence. Since I was neither, I nudged the door open just a little more to get a better view.

It was so worth it.

Aisling looked like a sex goddess. Her pale skin glistened with sweat. Her red hair cascaded down her back like a river of lava. She was draped over the desk, with her legs wrapped around Talon's waist. His big hands clenched those luscious thighs, as he pumped into her. I had to admit they were fucking sexy together. Ash with her soft feminine curves. And Talon, the big man with his pants down to his knees, muscles flexed as he pumped into her. His perfect muscular peach clenched as he fucked her senseless. All the blood in my body surged to my cock. I couldn't tear my eyes away from them.

Moments later, they both released strangled gasps, telling me they had come, and their ill-timed sexiness was over.

I was wrong.

The kissing and licking started again. Soon more grunts and wet suckling noises followed. Son of a bitch. Now they were just showing off.

By the time they were truly done, my pants were unbearably tight in the crotch area and Zoey had returned to her desk. She had the decency to close the lab door, sealing off the cries of rapture from any visitors. Not that this office received any visitors, but it was the decent thing to do.

I stuck around, watching and listening to the entire show. I was equally aroused and livid. Damn them for looking and sounding so good. And damn them for making it difficult for me to go with my original plan. All I could think about was fucking her while she was sucking him off. Or maybe the other way around. The combination of being with them and Pope ran rampant in my head, making my already engorged cock unbearable.

And the fucked-up-ness of it all was the way my body was reacting would make it impossible for me to walk away from her. And I wasn't sure if it was just the sex.

Talon made a snide remark about something stupid and irrelevant. I passed them both, not able to look either of them in the eye.

They walked out together, and I waited, jealousy, envy, and desire roiling through me like a thunderstorm. Five minutes later they were still in the lobby chatting with Zoey and it dawned on me. Her computer.

I beelined to her office, saved a small lacey fabric from the floor, and sat behind the desk. The scent of sex and cum filled the small space like a dense fog. I could almost taste it. There was a wet spot on her desk that made my dick ache to be inside her. *Would it be gross if I licked it? Yes, Jethro. It would be horrifyingly gross.*

I patted my pants where the wet lacey fabric sat securely in my pocket and grinned feeling somewhat better to have at least found myself a little souvenir. *Act right, perv.*

Before walking into the lab that morning, I'd already tossed the whole secret project thing into the irrelevant pile. At the moment, it was the only thing, other than sticking my dick in her, that made any sense to me. It was the only rational reason for me to stay in Midway. And give her grief. It was stupid and irrational, but it was either harp on making her life hell or letting my cock think for me. The thing was, I knew I'd lose myself to her if our relationship became physical.

For the time being, I decided to stick with business . . . aka make her life hell.

Ash still hadn't given me her access codes and that was something I wanted to pursue. Legally speaking, I didn't think I had the right to ask for those, as long as she wasn't doing anything illegal and her work was being done. Her codes would have given me access to all her files, including personal ones that were on the desktop. To be honest, that's what I was truly after. Ash was working on personal projects. I wanted to know what.

I wiggled the mouse. The screen came to life. I scanned her desktop looking for something. Anything. I clicked on an open file. Huh? She'd been working on one of the projects I assigned to her yesterday.

Over the weekend I'd come up with a dozen different projects to throw at her. My goal. Keep her busy. Keep her in the office. With me.

"What now?" Ash glared at me from the doorway.

"I'm working. In case you forgot, this is a lab. Not a brothel." I kept my expression passive and my eyes glued to the screen.

"Piss off." She stomped over to where I was sitting, snatched the mouse out of my hand, and tried to shove me aside. "This is my office! Use the computer in the lab!"

Ash was closing out files while making scathing remarks about how I needed to respect her personal space. I tuned out her voice and focused on her. She was so close. I could feel the warmth of her body and her heady scent of strawberries and sex filled my nostrils. She bent over the desk a little, making her top rise above her waist and popping her butt out.

My gaze roamed over her exposed flesh and the roundness of her ass. Perky. Round. *And just enough meat to grip when I'm pounding into her from behind.* I inhaled slowly, drawing the scent of her cum mixed with Talon's deep into my lungs. I bet her cunt was still wet. The urge to drag her leggings down her hips to get a glimpse of her pussy was so strong, I clenched my fist, digging my nails into my palms.

"Are you even listening to me?" Her sharp voice brought me back to focus. "What the fuck are you doing in here, Jethro?"

"Like I said, working. I was about to make notes on the Cyrus project. The new setup is not synced with yours. Since you were busy, I took it upon myself to get started."

She crossed her arms over her middle, which pushed up her tits. Of course, that's where my gaze landed. What was a man to do?

"That's ridiculous. Why would you install new tech and not ensure it was working with our internal system."

"Installing tech is different from installing software. Someone is coming from corporate in the next week or two. Until then, I'll be working from here."

She gaped at me.

It wasn't exactly true, but plausible. I'd need to ensure my techs from corporate delayed their plans to come here. It wasn't that important anyway. Ash and I could share for the foreseeable future. The office was tiny and a little messy. Aisling was meticulous in the lab, but her office could use some order. That would be an easy fix but not that important either. The goal was to be close to her.

"You cannot be serious. I will not work in here with you breathing down my neck." She glared. "Where do you expect to put another chair in here?"

I patted my leg.

She narrowed her eyes and her top lip curled into a snarl. It was so fucking cute.

"Try it. You might like sitting on my lap," I teased.

Her gaze dropped to my crotch and her breath hitched.

Yep, raging boner. I couldn't hide it if I tried.

Ash's throat bobbed and then she licked her lips.

She liked what she saw. I leaned back, stretching my long legs. My cock strained against the waistband of my pants, begging to be set free. *Please sit on my lap.*

She cleared her throat. "Does this office look big enough for two?"

"Sounded like there was plenty of room for two this morning."

Thwack. My face snapped to the side.

Owww.

Ash's eyes were full of fury, her fists balled at her sides. I smirked. "Go ahead, hit me again. Get it out of your system."

She wound back and swung. I caught her wrist, twisted her arm behind her back, and shoved her face down on the desk. All thoughts of business evaporated and all I could envision was Ash's naked writhing flesh under mine.

"You were in here fucking all morning and you're mad at me?"

She snarled curses at me, which I ignored.

"I should spank this ass for being such a brat." I ran my palm over her ass while my other hand kept her down. She was at my mercy and so fucking stunning this way.

Her snarling turned breathy.

I chuckled. "But I think you'd like that." I gazed between her legs and noticed a wet spot on her crotch.

I pressed my face against her covered pussy, and . . . bit. Not hard but just enough to get her attention.

She squealed.

"That's for being a royal pain in my ass."

I released her. "Now get the fuck out before I shove my cock so deep into your pussy you won't be able to walk right for weeks."

She stood on shaky legs and stepped toward the door. Her face flushed, her nipples protruding from her shirt. "I fucking hate you." Her voice was low and breathy.

"Sure you do. That's why your pussy is wet and your nipples look hard enough to cut glass." I pinched the taut buds.

She smacked my hands away and turned on her heels.

"Dr. Lovelle?" I stood. She glanced at me over her shoulder. "Lock the door on your way out."

I popped the button on my pants and palmed my length.

Ash backed out of the office, her gaze fixed on my cock as I freed it from my pants.

CHAPTER TWENTY-FIVE

TALON

"What's the latest from MPD?" Pope asked.

We'd been crashing at Ash's place mostly because she didn't want to leave the hacker by himself, and he was making a big deal about sleeping at my place, even though my place was bigger and much more convenient for Ash and me. I didn't care where I slept. She was my mate, and I wasn't going to sleep anywhere but beside her.

"The what?" I replied.

"The police department," he whispered. "You know? The inquiry about the murders."

"Oh. Yeah. I forgot about that. I haven't even brought it up to Jet. And the MPD hasn't questioned me."

It had been over a week since my last visit with Thomas. I'd been so busy managing my businesses and keeping Ash entertained it had slipped my mind.

"Do you think that's wise?" he asked.

"No. I've been busy. And the chief hasn't pestered me," I replied.

"Yeah, I get it."

Pope and I had been on the receiving end of Ash's overactive libido. She had two men pleasuring her body multiple times a day and that was barely enough to keep our girl sated. I was a wolf, a mystic, and was more than capable of having multiple orgasms a day, unlike human men. But I had to admit, over the past couple of days, I was glad to tap out and let Pope take my place.

I wasn't sure what Jet was doing to her in the office, but she often came to my office during her lunch hour horny as fuck, and after work, she was ready to go again. It was fun actually and it made me want to buy Jet a gift or something.

She was in the bath, relaxing after our latest fuck-a-thon, while Pope and I sat around drinking a beer.

"Well, at least no nocturnal escapades," Pope murmured.

"Dude, don't jinx it."

My phone rang. I glanced at the screen and then glared at Pope. "What can I do for the chief of police this evening?" I answered.

Pope grimaced.

"Nope. I've had a busy week. I'll be on it first thing in the morning," I said into the receiver. "Thomas, seriously, take a breath. I will speak with Dr. Buchanan tomorrow."

Ash plopped on the sofa between me and Pope. Her gaze made the side of my face feel hot.

"Yep, alright, gotta go." I hung up.

"Talk to Jet about what?" she asked.

"About what an asshole he's being to you in the office," Pope answered for me.

I hated lying to Ash. Should we just come out and tell her? What would we say?

"I'm sure whoever that was wasn't asking about my working relationship with Jethro." She stretched out, laying her head in his lap and her feet over mine.

"How do you know that? Do you have wolf hearing now that you're mated to one?" Pope asked. "Is that a thing?" He looked at me.

"No." *Don't be ridiculous,* I wanted to add, but knew he was bailing me out. I couldn't continue lying but I didn't know how to approach the truth. I decided half-truth to start. "That was the chief of police. He wanted Jet's opinion on a case he's working on."

"Interesting. Can I help? We have the same credentials. I think."

"You think?"

"I'm honestly not sure what his specialty is. Yes, we both have PhDs in alchemy but there are various branches. All I know for sure is he's an expert in being a pain in my ass."

I chuckled. "That's an easy fix, babe."

"Oh? Does that mean you've looked at my contract?"

"I did. Do you want to good news first or the bad."

"Bad," she said.

"Basically, you're fucked."

She smacked me on the arm.

"Teasing. Sort of. Buchanan Pharma is flat out the owner of everything in that office and everything that is produced in that office. The good news is both parties can renegotiate at any time. It doesn't expressly state that they cannot come in and do periodic checks, which I believe that's what Jet is doing. Still, he cannot make contractual changes without your approval, and as the new owner, it might be a good time to renegotiate." I began massaging her foot and continued.

"Walking out is not a bad option. I have plenty of money, babe, you don't have to work. And if you do, I can buy you a new lab. The thing is, anything you've done there stays there. All intellectual property derived from that office is left behind. The contract is clear. You have free reign to work on anything you want as long as you're producing according to company guidelines. However, all studies, inventions, data, equipment, tech, and even pens and paper belong to them. So the question is, are you willing to let Jet have everything you've been working on?"

"I fucking hate that asshole," she growled.

"I know an easier fix," Pope said.

Ash and I faced him and waited for his solution.

"Fuck his brains out," Pope quipped.

Ash rolled her eyes.

"He's not wrong. This sweet pussy will get you whatever you want."

Hours later, I rolled over, reaching for my mate, and came face to face with a muscular back. Pope grabbed my hand and pulled me closer.

"Ash," I rasped.

He released my hand and thumped the mattress on the other side of him then bolted upright.

"Ash?" he called out.

Shit. I rubbed my sleep-crusted eyes and searched for my mate though my wolf senses told me she was gone.

I went downstairs and found her phone sitting next to mine. "Her phone's here," I told Pope as he appeared in the living room.

He ran to the garage and returned. "Car's here. Can't you do a wolf thing to track down your mate?"

I shifted and followed her scent to the front door. Pope opened it, and I tracked her scent, which was faint. She'd gotten into a car. I shifted back into my human form and told Pope.

"Fuck!" Pope ran his hand through his already mussed hair. "I jinxed it, didn't I."

"Stop. This isn't your fault," I told him. "Let's think this through. She had to have taken a rideshare. Or maybe someone came to pick her up." I ran the scenario through my mind. We'd gone to bed around midnight. It was almost five in the morning. Too early for the office then, but it was a possibility. As well as a million other places.

"Are there any cameras set up outside?" I asked.

"I need to go to my place."

In minutes, we were both dressed, and he was opening the door to his place which had the same layout as Ash's. It was a cookie-cutter neighborhood. Newish and conveniently located near the Strand and the business district.

A few steps into the front door we were at the base of the stairs, which led to the bedroom slash loft area. Pope bounded upstairs, while I remained on the first floor checking out his place. It was sparsely furnished as though he just moved in or was moving out. On the ground level, the living room extended from the front of the house, into a small dining area and then to the kitchen. Under the stairs was a half bath and against the far wall a door led to a small courtyard.

"Talon! What the hell are you doing down there?"

I went upstairs taking two steps at a time and whistled. Unlike Ash's, there was no separation between the bedroom and the loft. It was one wide open space with a bathroom in the far corner. His mattress was on the floor and the rest of the place was wall-to-wall computer crap. *So this is where the hacker spent his money.*

Six monitors were mounted on the wall, three more on the desk in front of him. Pope was tapping on his keyboard. His fingers were moving so fast it made me dizzy to watch. He was in his element.

"I think I found something."

The monitors flashed with different street angles.

"Are you hacking into your neighbor's surveillance cameras?"

"Of course, how else are we going to find her?" He continued tapping away, then stopped. "Right there!"

He pointed to a screen which showed a sedan of some sort. He enlarged the screen and jotted down the license plate. It was pixelated but clear enough to see the digits and letters.

"Here, check this out." He pointed his chin to the screen in front of him.

Ash was leaving the house and got into the same vehicle. Her hair was in a high ponytail, and she was dressed casually, in jeans and a T-shirt.

"How did she get a rideshare without a phone?" I asked.

"I wondered the same thing. She must have a burner," he replied.

Well, shit. Either Ash knew exactly what she was doing, or the Mistress, her alter-ego, was smarter than we thought.

"Where are you going, baby?" I murmured.

The screens flashed again, zooming all over the place. I focused on Pope. His brow furrowed and his pupils darted between the screens. He looked like he was possessed. And glowing. I sniffed the air. He was emitting something different, magic.

"Are you smelling me?"

"You're releasing a magical pheromone. A cross between warlock and I don't know . . . I'm trying to figure out what you are."

"I'm a hacker."

"I meant what kind of mystic." I cuffed his head.

"Hey!" he griped. "I don't know. I'm just me. Does it matter? We've crossed swords. A few times. I think you know me well enough."

I shrugged. He meant well when it came to Ash, that was all that mattered to me. Watching him work gave me a newfound respect for him though. With his talent, he could have ruined me with a keystroke. He probably had millions if not billions of dollars at his disposal, and yet he lived a humble, low-key lifestyle. He'd been covering up her indiscretions, okay yeah, murders were more than a simple indiscretion, nonetheless he'd been protecting her. To be fair, I couldn't have picked a better man for my mate.

I stepped away, giving him space to work. To the left of the wall of monitors was a huge window that had the perfect view of her front door. Stalker.

A few minutes later, Pope popped up. "Got it. The car is here." The screen indicated a residential neighborhood. A posh one. Shit.

Aww, baby girl, what are you up to?

"Time to go. You're driving." I told him.

He stuffed his laptop into a satchel and we headed out the door.

CHAPTER TWENTY-SIX

AISLING

I woke to an empty bed and a wicked hangover. How much did I drink last night? Talon and Pope had left while I was still asleep, which was odd and disappointing. I loved our morning threesomes.

I trudged into the office dying for my morning dose of caffeine and found Jet leaning against the sink in the breakroom, sipping coffee.

"No wolf, today?" He glanced over my shoulder. "I guess that means no."

I ignored him and turned on my heels just as Talon walked into the lab.

"Hi, baby," Talon greeted with a big smile, showing off those dimples.

I hugged him tightly, burying my face into his chest. "Don't do that again," I murmured. "I didn't like it. I didn't like waking up and not finding you next to me."

Talon pulled me into the waiting area.

"Hey," he tilted my chin to look into his eyes. "I'm sorry. There was an emergency. Are you okay?"

I nodded.

He kissed me deeply, stealing my breath. I clung to his broad shoulders, my body writhing against him. He shoved his hand down my leggings, his deft fingers probing my entrance. I parted my thighs, moaning.

Oh my god, this man. Talon could do anything to me. Anytime. And I was one hundred percent willing. I ached for my men. Both of them. I needed them constantly. Wasn't sure when I became so insatiable. But I was. Talon. Pope. Jet . . . my mind screeched to a halt. *No, not Jet, Aisling, he's an asshole.*

I focused on my mate and stroked his engorged cock through his trousers. He moaned into my mouth and then his stupid phone rang.

"Fuck," he growled and drew away from me to glance at his phone. "Sorry, baby. It's important. I need to deal with this. Call you in a little while." He ran wet fingers along my lips, shoved them into my mouth, then kissed me again.

Talon exited, leaving me slumped against the wall, panting. I collected my breath then went to my office and froze.

He didn't. Last week Jet had insisted we share the same office. It was uncomfortable and confusing. On one hand, I was furious at his insistence on making my life hell. On the other, the handsome control freak was edging me daily. Being around him was arousing and maddening. Luckily, I had two men who satisfied my needs. Not today though. I wondered what had been so important for both Talon and Pope to leave so early.

"Do you like what I did with the place, Dr. Love?" His breath slid over my nape and sent shivers down my spine.

"Do not call me that," I snapped.

He chuckled and shouldered past me into the office. "This seat is yours." He patted the folding chair he parked at the far side of the desk against the wall, while he sat in the comfy leather chair. *My* chair.

"I so fucking hate you."

"Don't pout, Aisling. It doesn't suit you. Come, sit, we have a lot of work to do."

After speaking with Talon about my contract, I needed to approach this situation differently. I wasn't going to win the battle, but somehow, I'd win the war. There had to be something Dr. Asshole wanted which would get him out of my hair.

"That's the spirit," Jet crooned, as I climbed over his lap to get to my seat.

"Shut. It."

He got on the phone, while I worked on a project. The lab was used when we dealt with chemical compounds and formulations. Most of the time it was all numbers and data analysis. Unfortunately, we'd finished the formulations over the weekend. Yep, the fucker made me work. I'd only agreed to it because I wanted to work on my personal projects. I'd gotten a few things done but he showed up, crowding my space again.

The only good thing about working with Jethro was watching him use his magic. I had a proclivity for working with plants and other natural elements. It was helpful with creating potions, tonics, and other formulas. But that was the extent of my witchy powers. Jet was a powerful warlock. He could multi-task with his magic using telekinesis while he cast spells on other things simultaneously. Even though Jet was an asshole, generally speaking, I admired his magical talent.

"Good morning, boss," Zoey waved from the door.

"Good morning," Jet and I said simultaneously.

"She was talking to me. You're not the boss. You're a massive nuisance." I gritted my teeth.

"You and I both know how much you like being bossed around," Jet rasped.

"Okay, how about I close the door?" Zoey gripped the door handle.

"No," I said.

"Yes, thank you." Jet's booming voice drowned out mine.

"Oh boy. Ash, lunch today. I'll knock." Zoey quickly shut the door.

"I was right. If she thought of you as *the* boss, she wouldn't have called you Ash. Boom."

"Did you take an extra dose of annoying pills this morning?"

"Sure did. Strap in, little monster, the morning has just begun."

He was right. He was just getting started and my patience for dealing with him was wearing thin.

Out of habit, I grabbed the cup of coffee, sipped it, and then spit the disgusting sugary drink back into the mug. "That is so gross."

"Hmmm . . . I figured you for a girl who likes to swallow," he teased.

Here we go. The sexual innuendo was endless.

"Guess, you'll never find out," I chirped.

"I don't know about that, little monster. One day soon, you'll be begging me to swallow."

"Enough! You can't talk to me like that. That's sexual harassment!"

I should have asked Talon about pursuing a sexual harassment case, but who was I kidding? Jet's filthy mouth and domineering attitude stirred something in me.

"Sexual harassment? Really? Says the woman who fucks her mate in the office, with the door open," he retorted with a sly grin.

"That happened once . . ." My voice trailed off. He wasn't wrong. We did have sex in the office last week. And a part of me knew the door was open and wanted him to see. Talk about creating a sexually charged environment. *Sexual harassment works both ways, Ash.*

"Once? So, him fingering you moments ago in the lobby isn't considered sex?"

Did he see that? Why was that so hot?

"What no, sassy comeback?"

"Fuck you."

"You wish," he drawled.

"I wouldn't fuck you if you were the last man on earth," I snarled.

"And if you were, I'd demand a fucking recount and then become a lesbian."

Jet belted out a laugh. "It's hilarious how delusional you are. You're dying to sit on my dick right now, even though you have two other men tag teaming your cunt twice a day."

He leaned back in his chair, giving me full view of the massive erection straining to be set free from his pants.

"In your fucking dreams," I muttered, while crossing my legs and clenching my thighs. I hated that he was right and hated myself more for being such a greedy little ho.

Not even five minutes later, he leaned over my shoulder. "That's incorrect. If you're not going to do this right, why bother?"

His cheek grazed mine and an image of him standing in front of the mirror with a towel wrapped around his waist flashed into my mind. The scent of his aftershave lotion tickled my nose.

"Stop telling me what to do."

"Never. You're doing this all wrong. Look." He pointed at the graph. He was right. Again. Fuck. I'd swapped the values of A and B, fucking up the entire report.

I bit the inside of my cheek, refusing to admit I was wrong. I couldn't be. I'd checked the numbers twice over the weekend. "Did you mess with this?"

"Of course not. Don't blame me for your mistakes," he scoffed.

I glared at him. His biceps flexed as he picked up the phone and dialed. "Edmond, talk to me, what's the status of that shipment?"

Although not visible, I knew there was a tattoo running from his left arm over his chest and touching his clavicle. It was one of those intricate patterns that was very masculine and very sexy. *How did I know that?* He always wore a long-sleeved shirt. He leaned back, and his outstretched leg touched mine.

"One second," he said and then covered the phone. "Did you need something?"

He cocked his eyebrow, waiting for a reply.

"Nope." I turned and continued my task which was painful for many reasons. Jet's loud voice continued to disrupt my concentration. And he was just too close. I was practically hugging the wall trying to get away from him but for every centimeter I moved away, he moved an inch closer.

My office was a tiny sweatbox with Jet in it. At some point, the turtleneck had to come off. Thirty minutes later I climbed over Jet to open the door. Ten minutes later my T-shirt was off, leaving me in a strappy tank. Yes, I wore layers. It made sense when it was summer outside and winter in the office. Jet had me working non-stop; there had been no time to allow the maintenance crew in to get the AC fixed.

I reached over Jet's wide frame to use the phone, crowding his space.

"An excuse me would be nice," he muttered.

"You're excused. Now get out," I replied and continued with my call.

His hand slid against the small of my back when I returned the phone to the cradle. Goose flesh pebbled my skin at the contact.

"This isn't going to work," I rasped.

"Seems like it's working just fine to me," he drawled, his gaze landing on my chest and my pointy nipples. "Am I making you hot?"

His thick thigh pressed against mine. The contact was making me squirm in my seat.

"Please. I'm not that easy."

"Oh, I don't know about that, you fuck two guys daily, more than once a day, I bet."

"Are you jealous, Dr. Buchanan?

He tipped his head to the side. "A little. More than anything, the thought of you being spit roasted by two cocks makes me rock fucking hard."

His half-hooded gaze was full of lust as he adjusted his big dick.

Oh hell, I was going to come in my panties. I stood and tried to move around him. Jet gripped my thighs.

"What's wrong? Did I scare you, little monster? If you run, I'll only chase you. And when I catch you, I will destroy that sweet pussy."

My gaze dropped to his crotch. His thickness tented his trousers. I was suddenly . . . Very. Fucking.Thirsty.

Time to take control of the situation. I leaned over and whispered into his ear. "Good luck with catching me."

I moved past him making a hasty retreat. Before I reached the door, it slammed shut and Jet was on me.

"Caught you," he growled. "Now, what should I do with you?"

He ground his hard length on my ass. I pushed my hips back wanting more friction.

"You're killing me with this ass." He gripped my butt cheeks. "I bet you love getting your ass fucked, don't you?"

My body stiffened. I hadn't done that. Yet. I hadn't trusted anyone to try it until I met Talon and Pope. So far, we hadn't ventured down that path.

"No ass play? I'm surprised. You're going to love it, my little slut. Save that for me," he rasped.

"Enough. You've had your fun," I protested out loud while silently begging him to continue.

"Fun? Not even close." In one sharp tug, my pants and panties were down past my hips. Jet smacked my ass. "Now this is fun. Push your ass out let me look at you."

Apparently, I was a brainless idiot when it came to Jet because I gave him exactly what he wanted. He placed one hand on my lower back, the other caressed my butt, and then dipped between my legs to cup my pussy. I let out a breathy sigh. This was new. Last week, it was his filthy mouth that kept me on the edge of my seat. His hands all over my sex was a first, and he had my cunt weeping.

"Beautiful. And so fucking wet. You're dripping. Is this all for me?"

"No!"

"Such a bad liar. I've been watching you clench your thighs and squirm in your seat all morning. You want me to make you come, don't you?"

My pussy throbbed. I was a panting, writhing, wet fucking mess.

"Tell me you want me to make you come, my little slut." He smeared my juices all over my pussy lips and along my back entrance.

"Yes. Make me come, Jet."

His fingers gently ran down my slit. His touch was feather-light, the complete opposite of his bossy personality.

"I can feel you trembling, little slut. You're close, aren't you?"

"Yes."

"How bad do you want it?"

"Bad."

He jammed a finger into my pussy. The sudden intrusion made me gasp. I nearly came undone.

"Fuck, Ash, your tight, wet cunt is driving me insane." He slid a finger in and out of my opening while another rubbed my swollen clit.

"That feels so good. Make me come, please." I pushed back against his hand, needing him to fill me.

"Nope." He withdrew his fingers from my body. "Time for you to go."

"You're fucking kidding me!" I glared at him over my shoulder to find him staring at my ass and licking his fingers. I pulled up my pants.

"You're delicious." He grinned. "Now get out."

"What the hell is wrong with you?!"

"Boss? Lunchtime." Zoey knocked on the door.

"I'm coming," I replied.

"Almost. But not quite." Jet smirked.

I reached around him for my purse, then slapped his face before exiting the tiny office.

Zoey was in the lobby waiting for me, and I took a minute, leaning on the door to catch my breath.

The next thing I knew I was on the floor. Jet was behind the desk, staring down at me. Fucker used his telekinetic magic to open the door.

"You have two seconds to get out of this office or I'm going to fuck you right there on that floor." His hand covered his length.

I scrambled to my feet, face flushed and breathing hard. "You're such an asshole."

Fucking Jet. He was toxic, and I was such a fool for letting him have his way with me whenever it suited him. He was fucking with me. Fucking with my head. I needed to get away from him or I was going to murder him in his sleep.

CHAPTER TWENTY-SEVEN

TALON

Being a shifter had many advantages. I was stronger, faster, more agile, and could fuck like a maniac all night long. One of the biggest advantages was heightened senses, which came in handy. Usually.

My wolf was, for the most part, easy to manage. Sure, he got surly now and then and was fiercely protective of those we claimed, which only included my sister, my mother, and now Aisling. Ash's nocturnal disappearing act had happened twice since we mated. My wolf wasn't concerned about it at all, and although I trusted my wolf instincts, it still drove me mad. The first time I witnessed her running a blade through two men was jarring. My wolf had napped during the entire ordeal.

Pope had been there that night and the three other times she'd killed. The police were looking for her and thankfully Pope had covered her tracks. I did my part that evening by calling in a favor to have the bodies burned. My contact took care of it, and there would be no police investigation on those murders.

The second incident happened a week or so later. Ash had disappeared while both Pope and I were sleeping by her side. Although

Pope had been able to track the rideshare she'd taken, we'd lost her near the Strand, the four-mile stretch of restaurants, bars, and shops along the pier. The rideshare stopped near three hotels and so I'd changed into my wolf form to track her by scent. It was almost like she vanished even though our mate connection was strong. My wolf wasn't much help, which meant she was safe or the fucker was being lazy.

Pope and I spent hours looking for her and came up with nothing. By the time we'd returned to her place, she'd already gone to work.

I went to her office, and she was fine. She missed us and looked a little tired, but she was fine. A week had gone by, and I was still on pins and needles thinking that she had killed someone even though nothing had been reported . . . yet.

Jet was keeping Aisling busy with several projects. The two doctors didn't get along much, but I believed it was a love-hate situation. Soon one of them would give in. Aisling didn't mind the work. Instead, she took his demands as a challenge. She was a perfectionist when it came to her job and dear old Jethro had been using that part of her to make her work harder. It was a shitty thing for him to do, but my mate loved being a scientist, thus I hadn't interfered.

On top of his work demands, Jet had been edging her daily which was almost cruel. I say almost because all it did was prime her up for me and Pope. I'm sure he had a reason for being such an idiot, but I wasn't complaining about her coming to my office in the middle of the day and needing me to make her come as many times as she could handle in one hour. After work was the same. She was a sexy beast and fucked both me and Pope until the three of us passed out. There were times when Pope and I wished the asshole doctor was with us so we could take a break.

In many ways, Jethro was helping us out. Ash was a savage in bed, and she hadn't disappeared in the middle of the night.

Plus, I still hadn't talked to Jet about the mystic DNA analysis. I told the chief the warlock was busy, and he would get to it. I was hoping it would magically go away. That was highly unlikely, and thus I wanted Jet on our side.

Everything seemed to be going well and I thought maybe Ash's situation was a passing phase, that would never happen again. As soon as that thought entered my mind, fate had to prove me wrong.

As usual, Ash wore us out. She'd made me come so many times I was fuck-all dehydrated and woke to get a drink. To my surprise, Ash wasn't in bed. *How does she slip out of bed without me knowing?* My wolf senses should have alerted me to her disappearance, but my wolf was not in the least bit concerned.

By the time I made it downstairs, she was getting into a rideshare. I dressed quickly, got into her little Prius, and followed.

The rideshare had dropped her off at a hotel. But Ash didn't enter. Instead, she walked to the Strand and rented a bicycle. It wasn't what I'd consider murderer transportation, so I took it as a good sign. I sent Pope a text, stashed my stuff in a nearby shrubbery, shifted, and began following her on four legs.

Unlike last time, I had eyes on her and used my shifter stealth to stay on her heels. She wouldn't be getting away from me.

It became apparent that Ash had put plenty of thought into what she was doing. The route she took led to a residential neighborhood. The wealthy one we had lost her in the last time.

She parked the bike at a nearby school and began walking through a residential area. Streetlights gave me plenty of shadows to conceal my movement and the quiet neighborhood made it easy to follow Ash's hurried footsteps.

Ash approached a two-story Mediterranean-style home and came to a stop in front of the six-car garage. She glanced around her, then took off at a sprint. In front of the house was a cement block wall that rose twelve feet in the air. Aisling scaled the wall in four easy strides and walked along its ledge like a cat.

I was astounded. Ash had a firm body. Not sure how because I hadn't seen her exercise once, but even if she did, the level of athleticism she had just displayed was supernatural. What was she? I couldn't spend another moment thinking about the situation, as Ash jumped off the ledge to the other side of the cement wall.

In my wolf form, I could easily hop over, which might attract too much attention. The other option I had was to scale the wall in my human form but that would make me recognizable in the event there were security cameras. I stretched my haunches in a perfect downward dog with my muzzle close to the pavement when a recognizable scent filled my nostrils. I spent a few seconds sniffing around and panicked. Without another thought, I jumped the twelve-foot wall.

No, Ash. Not him.

CHAPTER

TWENTY-EIGHT

POPE

Bleary, I glanced at my texts not comprehending the words.

Followed A.

Strand. Bicycle.

Bring my stuff.

I opened the attachments which were a picture of a bike rental stand, the next was a picture of a hibiscus bush.

It's too early in the morning for riddles, Talon.

"Talon? Ash?" I called out then glanced at the bed. It was empty. *Oh shit!*

I hopped into my clothes, grabbed my shit, and sped toward the Strand.

Fuck. Fuck. Fuck.

Ash was on another nocturnal excursion again. What triggered these things? She'd been good the past couple of weeks. Okay, maybe the last ten days. Whatever. It hadn't happened in a while and I, no we, were grateful.

It was a relief to have Talon with me on this. For a while there I thought I was going crazy. Aisling meant everything to me. There was no doubt in my mind that I would do anything to keep her safe and protected. But as each murder progressed, they got bloodier and more brutal. I wasn't sure how much longer I could continue covering for her if she kept killing.

Talon was a big help. He got rid of the bodies somehow, and he was proactive in getting her help. What kind of help, we both didn't know. We were researching her condition and so far the closest thing I could find pointed to schizophrenia or dissociative identity disorder. Mystics didn't get human diseases, but she was part-human and part-witch which was close to the human genetic makeup. It was a possibility. She was taking some sort of tonic which she said was vitamins for ladies only. She told Talon and me not to try it unless we wanted to start having periods. No, thank you. Talon and I backed off.

I imagine it was something she had created at the lab and one of the reasons she was butting heads with Jethro. That ass face was something else. He was a control freak and from what I could tell, not a cool dude. The sexual tension between them was obvious though. They probably should hate fuck and get it over with. Maybe then they wouldn't be at each other's throats.

Talon at least was fun to be around. I enjoyed his company. He loved Ash. And he was down with sharing. Aside from these nocturnal escapades, we were all happy.

As much as Jethro aggravated Ash, I was certain he would become part of our happy, weird family. The wolf, the hacker, the asshole warlock, and the gorgeous murderer.

Murderer. That's what Ash was. *What she is, Pope.* That should freak me out, but it didn't. It worried me. I wanted her to be well. If she did indeed have some sort of mental illness, she needed to be on medication. I think. Fuck, I truly didn't know. She'd gone to psychiatrists, and they all said nothing was wrong with her. Or maybe their diagnosis was wrong. I was completely clueless when it came to that stuff. I just knew that she needed help.

I found the bike rental station easily enough. I hacked into the payment system, which then allowed me to track the bike. Once I locked in the location, I searched the area for Talon's stuff, which was hidden under a bush.

The location of the bike was only a couple of miles away, in a wealthy part of town. Because, you know, wealthy people liked living by the water. *Why would she choose to come here?* The bike tracking system on my phone led me to a park surrounded by multi-million-dollar homes. Unable to discern which direction she'd taken, I decided to drive around.

As I passed wrought iron gates, brick walls, and manicured lawns, I wondered how Aisling chose her victims. Talon and I talked about this, and I started digging up information on the men she'd already killed and found nothing linking them together. Nor did I find any similarities.

Her last kill had happened in the roughest part of Port Midway. This area was the complete opposite. The streets were clean, the cars were expensive, and I was sure they all had the best security systems available. Hacking into them was going to be fun.

I drove for some time, lost in thought, circling the park, going up one street and down the next, until suddenly a big as fuck wolf jumped in front of me snarling. I stomped on the break, and the beast prowled toward my car then hopped onto the hood. His fangs were elongated and dripping with saliva. A deep rumble rolled from his muzzle. In less than a minute, the wolf shimmered into a man. A naked one with his big dick swinging in the wind.

I shook my head as he jumped off the hood and got into my car.

"Did I scare you, hacker?" Talon purred.

"Blow me," I huffed. "Put your clothes on. I don't want your sweaty bare ass on my leather seat."

"What, this ass?" Talon rubbed his butt on the chair.

"So juvenile. Who the hell gave you a license to practice law?"

He chuckled and got dressed.

"Did you find her?" I asked.

"Yep. Park there." He pointed to a spot under a tree.

I parked and we got out of the car.

"Where is she?" I asked.

"Ssshh," he admonished me and led me to the side of a two-story Mediterranean home.

"How did you find me?" I asked.

He stopped short and glared over his shoulder. "This is supposed to be a stealth mission," he whisper-shouted then continued moving through someone's yard.

We crouched behind a large and very loud mechanical contraption which I assumed was some type of pool cleaning equipment. Before I could get a closer look at it, Talon elbowed me in the ribs and pointed.

I followed his finger which was aimed at Aisling. She was statue-still, peering into a window. Whoever she was watching had to have been asleep. Dawn was still a few hours away. We stood there for a while, watching her watch whomever. Was she stalking her next victim? I didn't realize she did that. Suddenly she walked away, scaled the brick wall, hopped off the ledge, and landed on the other side.

Talon nudged me to follow. I thought we were going to follow Ash, but he went toward the window she had been standing in front of.

I peered into the house and my jaw hit the ground. Oh shit. This can't be good.

Talon pulled my arm, urging me to follow him without saying a word until we made it to my car.

"What the fuck, Talon?" I started the car.

"I don't know." He shrugged.

"How the hell did you get down here?" I asked.

"Ash's car. I already had Igor pick it up and drop it off back at her place."

Damn. The guy thought of everything.

"Should we follow Ash?" I tapped on my phone which was still tracking the rental bicycle.

"She'll have to return the bike. But I think she's going home," he said.

"I don't know, it's still dark out. This could be a stakeout situation and now she's going to find her real victim."

"Well, shit. In that case, yeah, follow her." He scratched his jaw.

"Was she standing in front of that window the entire time?" I asked as I parked the car waiting for Ash to return the bike.

"Yep. I'm not sure why. It's either love or hate. He's been such an asshole to her, it might be hate."

"We can't let her kill him. Can we?"

"No. Yes. I don't fucking know, Pope. She seemed intrigued by him. But not in an I'm-going-to-kill-you way."

"Aren't all stalkers like that? Intrigued by their victims."

"True. But her other kills weren't personal, were they?"

"Not that I could tell. They all seemed to be random innocents on the surface. I need more time to research that."

Ash returned the bike and got into a rideshare.

"I hope she goes home. I'm beat and hungry," Talon sighed. "Did you bring snacks?"

"What do I look like, Mary Poppins? I'm not the nanny, Talon."

I ignored his laughter and followed the rideshare.

CHAPTER TWENTY-NINE

JETHRO

"You're late," I said without looking up from my phone. She didn't respond but I could feel her fuming.

"When you stare at me like that, I'm not sure if you want to fuck me or you're planning to kill me," I added.

"The latter. Definitely the latter," she deadpanned.

I chuckled. "Don't just stand there gaping at me, Aisling. Get me a cup of coffee."

"Get it yourself. I'm not your slave!" She slammed her purse on the desk.

"Fine." I met her gaze and stood. Her eyes dropped to my crotch where my dick had been docile until she showed up.

"See something you like?" I asked, my cock inflating under the scrutiny of her gaze.

"No." Her tongue slid over her lower lip. "Why aren't you dressed?"

"What? You dress casually every day and I can't?"

Ash wore leggings or scrubs to the office with layers of sweaters daily. The lab was cold, but our shared office would get hot and the layers of clothing she wore came off one by one until she was down to pants which hung low on her hips and a cropped tank. It was a cock tease and I liked it. I was sure she knew exactly what she was doing to me.

To even things up in the clothing department, I decided to show up in sweatpants and a T-shirt versus my usual suit and tie. Yeah, I was a lab rat like Ash, but my role in the company had me wearing three-piece suits for meetings and such.

"You look ridiculous," she muttered.

I laughed and then said, "Are you sure about that, my little slut? I think you like what you see."

The sultry glint in her eyes had me straightening my posture. She tilted her head to the side as she studied my tattooed arm then paused on my chest. Her brows furrowed like she was trying to see through my shirt.

"Eeeww. Get over yourself." She came over to the other side of the desk to her chair, brushing her tits on my arm.

"Someone's in a mood. What happened? Your boyfriends didn't take care of your needs . . . again?"

"That's none of your business," she said in a breathy voice.

"Don't worry, my little monster, I'll take care of you today." I stroked her cheek, making her shiver.

I'd decided a couple of days ago that I was leaving. What prompted the decision were two things. One, my father insisted I needed to return. He wanted to ensure I handled things as the new CEO and according to him, I needed to be there for the transition to happen smoothly. The second reason was Ash. I enjoyed being around her too much for my own good. Flashes of my not-too-recent broken engagement had me deathly afraid of what Ash would do to me once I laid my heart out at her feet.

Leaving wasn't going to be easy though. Edging Ash was my favorite thing to do. I wasn't sure why I was being such a sadist. But I couldn't stop. It was the best part of my day. I knew she was fucking Talon or Pope, or both of them during lunch and as soon as she got home. I didn't care. I loved making her squirm in her seat while she worked beside me.

I kept fucking with her reports, forcing her to redo things. After the third day, she figured it out and tried to come at me with her fist, which was a fun time. I had her face down on her desk in seconds with her pants around her hips and her juicy ass in the air. I played with her until she was ready to come then pushed her out the door. Keeping my dick in my pants wasn't an easy thing to do. It was hellish and painful and kept me awake at night. But I knew what would happen if I went down that path. I'd never want to leave. And I had to.

I stepped out of the office to grab a cup of coffee and returned to see she had papers strewn all over the desk.

"Do you mind? We share this desk."

"This," she pointed at a stack of papers, much thicker than the other pile next to it. "Is your stack."

I sat in the leather office chair beside her to see what she was working on. "What the hell is this?"

"The reports from the labs I finished yesterday. You're welcome."

"We didn't finish labs yesterday."

"*We* didn't. I did. I came back last night."

"Your men must've been pissed about you working all night. Trouble in paradise?"

"No. And stop asking. I'm not discussing my love life with you, Jethro." She tapped on the papers. "Focus. I did my part. You do yours."

I grinned. I'd been adding to her workload continuously, so much so I even made her come in on the weekends. Aisling balked of course, but she loved the work.

The gorgeous doctor was truly brilliant. Her work was meticulous, and she had an innate ability to work through numerous problems at once. I'd given her projects I'd been working on alone for years and yet, Ash pulled solutions out of thin air. There was not a single bad thing I could say about Ash's work ethic. I was impressed and if I was being honest, it added to her allure.

There were times like these when we worked seamlessly together. We weren't bickering and we were so involved with our tasks, we didn't speak for hours. The sexual tension was still there though, and we took care of that by maintaining physical contact somehow.

For the first few days after I moved into her office, I kept my leg against hers on purpose. My actions irritated her to the point where she scooted her chair as far as she could to get away from me. As of late, it seemed like she needed the contact just as much as I did.

To test my theory, I moved my leg. She didn't react for a whole three minutes. The absence of her body against mine was frustrating, and I was about to pull her onto my lap when Zoey's voice intruded.

"Ash, Mabel is on line one."

"Thanks, Zo." Ash reached over and grabbed the phone, invading my space in the process. I loved it.

Ash settled back on her chair, and I casually leaned my leg against hers. The conversation had droned on for over twenty minutes. Mabel was a scientist in the main office. The woman was a talker. One of those people who kept speaking even after saying goodbye.

Soon Ash began squirming in her seat. Then she shrugged out of her sweater and T-shirt in one swoop. She was hot and bothered and so distracting.

Feeling generous, I slid her chair back and reached into her panties. The little slut was wet again. Just for me.

She shoved my hand away and then covered the phone. "I'm having a business discussion!"

"So? Take your pants off."

"No." She glared at me and resumed her call.

Well fuck that. I wasn't going to be ignored.

I pushed her to her feet, leaned her over the desk, and dropped her pants.

She had the most beautiful cunt. I smooshed my face into her wet pussy, making her squeal.

"I'm sorry, Mabel. Umm . . . do you mind if I call you back?"

I stopped licking her pussy. She glared at me over her shoulder, and I shook my head.

"On second thought, let's finish this up."

She talked, and I ate. She was delicious. So fucking delicious. I'd licked her juices off my fingers before, but this was extraordinary.

I fucked her with my tongue, shoving into her pleasure hole as far as my tongue would go. I licked her inner walls, making her entire body tremble, then plunged in two fingers. Every time her pussy began to contract over my digits, I backed off. Mabel droned on forever. Every time she wanted to hang up, I backed off. I had so much control over her, it was empowering. But it was hard on me, too. Literally. Usually, I'd kick her out of the office to take care of myself. Not this time. I wasn't going to last.

I pulled my dick out, spit into my hand for lube, and began stroking myself. Eating her pussy while choking my length had me ready to shove my cock in her.

Don't do it, Jet.

I didn't want to relinquish control. Not to her. With Ash, I needed to hold onto the reins or she would own me. In all honesty, she already had. It was more than just the sexual attraction between us. It was everything. Ash was intelligent, and she challenged me continuously. The woman didn't tolerate my bullshit and dished out as much as I gave. The thing was I couldn't stay. And she probably didn't want me to anyway. She had Pope. And Talon. If I wasn't in her face daily, or pussy for that matter, she wouldn't have given me the time of day.

Edging her and not submitting to my base desire made me feel like I wasn't completely lost. I was still me, and Aisling hadn't obliterated me entirely. Self-preservation was a thing.

Sitting next to her every day was a fight. Especially knowing she desired me just as much.

For now, her sweet cunt was in my face, wet, pulsing, and ready to come. And that was enough for me. I didn't want to fall in love with Aisling. That wasn't the reason for me being in Midway. That last step would ruin me. I had to leave before she could do that.

"Yes! Right fucking there." Her body quivered.

I blinked. She'd hung up the phone. Oh fuck. I stopped my assault on her beautiful, delicious pussy and backed away.

"God damn it, Jet." Ash rounded on me. Her chest was heaving. "Fuck it. Fuck this. Fuck you! Never touch me again."

She pulled her pants up and pushed past me.

Nope. Hell no. I knew if I let her walk out the door, I'd lose her forever.

"I didn't say you could leave." Using my magic, I slammed the door shut, then strode to her and pressed her against it.

"I don't need your permission," she said through clenched teeth. "Get. Off. Me."

"No." I groped her ass. She slapped my hands away. I snaked my hand down the front of her pants and shoved my fingers into her wet heat.

Aisling ground herself on my palm. Her lips parted and a raspy moan escaped her. For a moment I had her writhing on my hand. And suddenly, she went still.

"Jet! Stop," she ordered.

She pressed her ear to the door. I mimicked her pose. Children's laughter and squeals came from the other side.

What the . . .

Ash pushed me away. "Put your dick away. And don't ever touch me again. I'm done with you."

Before I could stop her, Ash was out the door.

CHAPTER THIRTY

TALON

Ash didn't go straight home. She stopped at a bar, had a few drinks, and then made it home an hour later. Pope and I snuck into bed while she was in the shower. She didn't seem to notice that we'd been gone also.

I was emotionally wrung out. I hadn't even heard her leave for work.

By the time I got out of bed, it was mid-morning. Igor had been waiting for me, causing me to hustle to get ready. Pope was still snoring, the lucky shit. Some days I envied his carefree, no-responsibility lifestyle.

My secretary cleared my morning schedule, giving me time to stop at the lab before going to my office. I needed to talk to Jet, and I wanted to see Ash.

She was stalking him. And I wasn't sure if that was good or bad. I suppose if she wanted to kill him, she would have done it already. I was hoping she was captivated by him and had no ill intent.

Did it matter to me if she killed him? Not really. He was a friend. Sort of. Until recently, it had been years since Jet and I had last talked. Did I want her to kill him? No. Not at all. Jethro's family had money. He was in a powerful position in the community. Scratch that. The world. If she killed him, everyone would be on a witch hunt. Between me and Pope, we could cover her tracks, but it wouldn't be easy.

Worrying over what Ash might do created a pit in my gut. I hurried out of the SUV and made my way to the lab.

I swung open the door and stopped short. The waiting area was crawling with kids and women. Zoey was at her desk speaking to a woman I hadn't met. Ash was seated on the floor with two babies on her lap and a couple more kids were clamoring all over her.

Ash, the real Ash, not her alter ego that I'd met months ago was forever imprinted in my brain. I cataloged her different looks during our time together. She had the adorable bashful smile, the one that reddened her checks. Her sultry gaze when she was horny and ready to fuck. She had the sated post-orgasm look that made her glow from the inside out. And now this. She was shrouded in an aura that bespoke of maternal unconditional love. A vision of me petting Ash's swollen belly flashed in my mind.

I crossed the room and kissed her lips. "Hi, baby. Who do we have here?"

"These are Zoey and Emily's children." She pointed to the woman standing near Zoey.

She introduced me to Emily and their seven kids just as Jet came to stand in the doorway. He stared at Ash with a puppy-love look all over his face. *Maybe there was a way to diffuse the situation before anyone got killed.*

Ash noticed me staring at Jet and said, "And that over there is Jet. He owns this lab."

"Like the airplane?!" The eldest boy, Adam, I think, exclaimed. It was going to take me a while to remember all their names.

The boy turned his attention to Jet. The warlock took a sheet of paper from Zoey's desk and folded it into a paper airplane, then used his magic to make it zip around the room.

The kids watched in amazement and that gained him new fans.

Too soon after the magic show, Zoey rallied her children. "Come on kids, let Aunty Ash and her men get back to work."

The kids complained.

"Listen to your moms," Jet said in a gentle but firm tone. "There'll be another magic show."

"Promise?" One of the twins, asked.

Jet took another sheet of paper, tore off two strips, magicked each into a paper flower and handed one to each of the two girls.

"I promise," he said.

The girls beamed at him with adoration. *So the asshole could be charming. Why couldn't he be that way with Ash?*

I helped my mate stand while kissing her cheek again. Seeing those kids in her arms with a big smile on her face made me want to put a baby in her belly.

"We're going roller skating," said one of the boys.

"Can you come with us, Aunty Ash?" Millie, the eldest daughter asked.

"Mommy Em said we're going to get pizza!" A boy who looked to be about five-ish pumped his fist.

"Kids, don't pester your aunt!" Zoey scolded her children, while taking a sleeping child from Ash's arms and placing her in the stroller by her desk.

"It's okay, Zoey. I don't mind. It's been too long."

Emily took the other twin from Ash. "It has been too long. We've missed you at home and the shelter."

I learned Emily worked at a homeless shelter on the east side of town. Zoey volunteered monthly, and Ash did so on rare occasions.

"Yes, it has been. I'll be sure to come by and help out," Ash promised. "And we need to get together soon. I miss all these babies."

Ash kissed each kid on the cheek.

This maternal side to her was slaying me. My heart ballooned in my chest. I felt like I was floating on air.

"Can you come with us today?" Millie asked. "I learned how to roller skate. You can watch me. Mommy Z said she can't because she's working."

"I'd love to sweetheart, but I'm afraid I can't." Ash kissed her forehead and glanced at Jet. "My new boss is here, and he makes me work all the time. But your mommy can take the time off."

She smiled at her best friend. "Take the rest of the day off, Zoey. You deserve it."

"Umm . . . thanks Ash, but I have plenty of work to do. I don't mind staying."

The kids protested all at once.

Ash laughed. "Seriously, Zozo. It's okay, take the time off."

The two women hugged, and Zoey said, "Join us, Ash. At least for lunch. It'll be fun."

Jet and Ash's gaze met. He gave her a warm smile and a nod. Then she turned to me. "I have lunch plans with my mate. Next time. I promise."

The kids whined which made me chuckle.

I wrapped her in my arms, keeping her back to my front. "Go baby, I need to speak with Jet. Come to my office later, and we'll go home together." I nuzzled her neck.

"Okay, guess we're having pizza for lunch," Aisling said, earning her a cheer from the kids.

Jet and I said our goodbyes and went to the office.

The scent of lust and sex was heavy in the room. It made me hopeful. And hard.

I crossed my arms over my chest and gave Jet a questioning glance. Ash had asked me and Pope if it would be okay if she and Jet had sex. Pope and I were on board with the idea. Still, I didn't want to ask him anything, I wanted him to volunteer the info.

He looked sheepish and his cheeks were flushed. That was different.

I was about to tease him about it when soft curves pressed against my body. "I forgot my purse."

Ash snagged her purse from a shelf beside the desk, then pulled my face down to hers for a wet kiss. I was fully hard by that point and all I wanted was to sink my dick inside my mate.

Jethro cleared his throat. "Talon, may I speak with your mate for a minute?"

The tension between them was thick and heated. I glared at him, then kissed Ash's cheek. "I'll wait for you in the lobby."

I closed the door behind me and used my shifter hearing to eavesdrop.

"I don't want you to go," he said.

"Too bad. You just told me to take the afternoon off!"

"No!"

There was a brief pause.

"I mean, yes. Take the afternoon off. I meant I don't want you gone. I want you to come back."

I breathed a sigh of relief.

A longer pause.

Everything would be so much easier if you just kissed her, dude.

"I fucking hate you!" Ash said, venom coating her words.

"I know. I deserve it." His voice sounded closer.

"Don't Jet. I'm sick of this. Sick of you." Her voice lacked the anger she was trying to portray.

Now would be the time, Jethro.

"I know. I don't blame you. Still, I want you to come back."

She gasped and moaned a little. I could feel her arousal through our mate bond. My dick throbbed in my pants.

Something pushed the door. Sexy noises had me palming my erection. She sounded so hot when turned on.

"Tell me you'll be back tomorrow."

"I have to go. My mate is waiting. Zoey is waiting."

"Aisling."

She moaned a little louder. "Yes. Yes, I'll be back."

"Tell your mate to come in after you're done."

I scrambled to the waiting area, not bothering to hide my boner.

Aisling entered, her face flushed and lips swollen.

"Come here. I'm going to put my babies in you."

She sealed our lips together for a heated kiss.

In seconds, I had her bottoms off and my dick fully seated in her wet cunt. In minutes, she was choking my cock with her climax, and I was filling her womb with my cum.

Fully sated, I pressed another kiss to Ash's lips before she left and waltzed back into the office where Jet was staring blankly at his computer screen. He gave me a knowing look and then shook his head.

I shrugged as I plopped on the folding chair opposite him.

"So," he stated.

"So," I repeated, studying his face.

He raised one eyebrow at me. "Happy?"

I chuckled. "Hell yeah. Ash is going to have my babies. That's my new mission in life."

He smiled. A genuine one that told me he was probably thinking the same thing. I returned his grin. We could fix this.

"Were you just wanting to brag or was there a reason for this visit?"

"Did you have anything to say?" I retorted.

He scrubbed a hand down his face. "Fuck, Tally. You know I want her. Do you want me to ask for your permission?"

"Yes."

He gave me an exasperated look. "Fine. May I pursue your mate?"

I held his gaze for a moment until he lowered his and said nothing for a full minute.

"I suppose. If she says yes."

He let out an audible breath.

"Don't hurt her, Jet. If you hurt her, then I'll have to kill you."

"I know you will. And I won't." His tone was hesitant but sincere.

I studied his face. He looked scared. Something about the situation made him nervous.

"You'll have to share," I said.

"I'm okay with that," he replied without hesitation.

"Are you sure?" I decided to press.

"No. But if I don't, I lose her forever." He shook his head. "I'd rather share."

I nodded. I understood that. We all did. "She's amazing, Jet. Let your guard down and love her. She's worth it."

"I know she is. I know." He rubbed his chest.

My old friend looked like a tortured man. It was obvious he was conflicted over how he felt about Ash. He'd always been resistant to relationships, and I never really knew why. We'd been college kids and relationships weren't the thing back then. Not for us anyway. Jet was more resistant to getting close to people. He'd always find a way to become a total ass when things got too real for him. I wasn't much different but at least I knew a good thing when I found one.

"Was there something else? I don't like being in here when she's not," he asked after a long pause of silence.

I grinned. He loved her. I fucking knew it.

"Umm . . . yes. Thomas Hayes, Midway's chief of police wanted me to ask you about something."

CHAPTER THIRTY-ONE

AISLING

It had been hours since I left the office, and I still felt them on my body. Talon's cum leaked out of my pussy. Jet's kiss lingered on my lips. And Pope was a comforting presence I carried with me no matter how far apart we were.

"Earth to Aisling," Emily sang. We were watching the kids on the roller rink. Zoey was out there along with a couple of instructors teaching the four-year-olds basics. I held one of the eighteen-month-olds in my arms, while Emily held the other. Jacob, their husband, and had one of the eighteen-month-olds in a baby carrier strapped to his chest while he skated.

"Sorry, I'm lost in thought I guess," I replied sheepishly.

"Zoey told me about your men and the new boss. That's different. For you."

"Yeah, it is, isn't it? How do you and Zoey manage it all?"

"It's easier for us, Ash. Dealing with that much testosterone must be exhausting."

"Dealing with seven children must be exhausting," I retorted.

She giggled. "It is. Luckily, there are three of us. Not exactly even, but we figure it out."

We sat silently for a minute.

"Oh! I forgot to tell you. Remember the last time you came to the shelter?"

I shook my head. "Not really; it's been months."

"Right. Well, there was that woman who came in beaten and drugged. Her drug dealer and his partner raped her, shot her up with a lethal dose of drugs . . . some new thing on the market. Anyway, those guys have been reported missing."

"What? That can't be good."

"No, it's not. Other women had been brought to the hospital in the same state. The police have been scouring the neighborhood for some time. I hope they're dead."

I was about to ask for more info when Zoey skated up to us.

"Hey! You're up, Em. I need a break."

I laughed as Emily and Zoey switched places.

"So? Three men, huh? Good on you!" Zoey winked at me.

"Two, yes. Not sure about the third. Jet's a pain in my ass. He challenges me at every turn."

"From what I heard, challenging can be fun." She gave me a sly grin.

I laughed. "Sorry for making the work environment awkward."

She chortled, waking her son who was just about to fall asleep.

"It's not, Ash. It's entertaining. And hot as fuck," she said, rocking her son in her arms.

My face heated as I thought of all the things that had transpired between me and Jet. It was hot. And cold. I couldn't figure him out.

"I'm not sure what to make of Jethro Buchanan."

"You like him though. As much as the others?" she asked.

I shrugged. "He's intelligent. Smarter than any man I know. I like working beside him and . . ."

"And?" she crooned.

I couldn't say it out loud and didn't have to.

"You want his dick."

Leave it to my best friend to put things bluntly. I couldn't hide my ear-to-ear grin.

She laughed. "Give it a chance, Ash. What's the worst thing that could happen? He moves back to the Meridian City? You'll always have Talon and Pope."

The thought of Jet leaving me made the pizza in my stomach turn rancid. He wouldn't leave me. Would he? I hadn't thought about it, but it made logical sense. I couldn't keep him. I didn't even want to keep him. Or did I? Of course I did. But his life was in Meridian City. Not here with me.

"On another note, are you feeling okay?" Zoey asked, just before my mind went down the rabbit hole of what life would look like without Jet.

I shook off the thoughts of my new boss and focused on her question.

Zoey was the only person not related to me by blood who knew about my issues. I'd been in the doctorate program when the episodes reappeared, and Zoey had been traveling the world. Since it hadn't occurred till recently, I never mentioned it.

I'd told her about them weeks ago over lunch. Talking about it had been such a relief. She was understanding and didn't judge me at all.

"I'm working on it. Since the guys have entered my life, I haven't noticed any episodes for a couple weeks. I changed my tonics. Hopefully, that's enough," I replied.

"Have you talked to them about it?"

I shook my head.

"They would understand, Ash. Those men love you."

I chuckled. I wasn't so sure about that. Unconsciously, I rubbed my belly. "Talon wants children," I said in a small voice.

She squealed. "That's amazing! You are going to have beautiful babies. And you'll be an incredible mom, Ash!"

Then she gave me a dubious look. "Why aren't you excited?"

"Zoey, I have a mental disorder that might be hereditary. I need to find the solution before I start popping out kids."

"Oh, Ash. You'll figure this out. You're a badass bitch and the smartest person I know." She draped an arm around my shoulders, and I leaned into her side.

"Have you considered going home?" she asked.

"I have. But that will only happen if I have no other choice." The thought of seeing my parents again made my heart hurt.

"You have me, Ash. If you ever need anything, I'm here for you."

"Thanks, Zozo. I appreciate you. And Emily. I hope you two know that."

"Ash, you're family. There's nothing we wouldn't do for you. We love you."

For a man who did illegal things online all day, Pope slept like he hadn't a care in the world. He fell into a deep sleep nightly and often slept in unless Talon and I were awake and going at it.

Talon didn't seem to need much sleep, but like me, he passed out after our sex marathon.

I'd gotten up to pee and then went back to bed to stare at them. I'd been watching them for a while. Zoey was right about one thing. My men loved me. Jet didn't. He was all about the sex. Our parting words earlier in the day were different though. His words were tender, and that kiss was more. More than lust. More than just passion and unfettered arousal. It was desperate. The type of desperation one displays when pleading for a chance. I brushed the thought aside and gazed at my wolf and hacker.

Talon and Pope loved me. I felt it more strongly than anything I'd ever experienced. Would they still love me if they knew I had a mental disorder? Was their love that deep? Perhaps. I was too afraid to test the theory. I loved them too much to risk losing them. Love. Yep, that's where I was now. Pope was fun, gorgeous, and a loyal friend. What started as friendship had turned into something more. And then there was Talon. My sultry protector who always made me feel safe and cherished. Those innocent walks from the entrance of the building to my office started as playful banter and transformed into a lifelong mating. I was so lucky.

Then why was I so eager to have a relationship with a man who vexed me every second? Yes, there was the sexual chemistry and we were on the same intellectual wavelength, which was equally stimulating. Despite those two significant things, he was still an intolerable asshole.

Because he will help us. All three of them will, the voice in my head said loud and clear.

I froze. My hand covered my mouth to hide the gasp that escaped me.

You know I'm right.

Shut up! I said to . . . myself, I guess.

You can't silence me forever.

Oh shit. I scrambled off the bed. *Yes, I can*!

No. You. Can't. It's just a matter of time.

Shut up. Shut up. Shut up. I made it to the kitchen, snagged a tonic from the fridge, and guzzled.

That won't help you for very long, the voice trailed off with a giggle.

I was so fucked.

CHAPTER THIRTY-TWO

JETHRO

Sleep didn't come easy last night. Ash was on my mind. Had been since the day we met, so that wasn't new. The way we'd left things was great. Amazing. I kissed her and she kissed me back. Best kiss of my life, if I was being honest and that said something. I'd kissed men and women and after kissing Ash, I couldn't remember any of the others. Maybe it was the way she affected me in general. I was treading on dangerous ground with her. See the thing is once your heart was stomped on, no one wanted a repeat performance. The dreadful part had been my reactions to Aisling were infinitely more intense than anything I'd experienced before. She could so smoke me. The thought made me shudder.

The minute I pissed her off, my body had gone into panic mode. My mouth went dry, and my stomach lurched. I knew I'd gone too far. She said she was done with me, and I couldn't blame her. I was a complete prick and she'd put up with me for weeks. Thankfully, Talon gave us a minute alone, allowing me to smooth things over, hence the kiss. She said she'd be coming in today. She had to. I wasn't ready to say goodbye to her. Not yet. *You have to, Jet.*

The thought of never seeing her again kept me awake. It took forever to fall asleep and when I did, my dreams were plagued with nightmares of me chasing Ash. She wasn't running from me. She was there, but not with me. Not mine.

I woke before sunrise, restless. Sleep wasn't an option, and Aisling wasn't lying next to me so sex wasn't either. The only other option was to go for a run. I scrubbed a hand down my face and then changed into my running gear. Dawn was approaching, making it the perfect time to head toward the Strand, a short mile or two run. I set a steady pace, swallowing deep breaths of the cool morning air.

Port Midway was beautiful. Like any other city, there were a few unsavory neighborhoods but for the most part the little seaside town was clean. The people were friendly, and it was safe, aside from the murders that had happened in the last month or two.

Talon mentioned the police department had requested my help with DNA analysis. It was my area of expertise since my fascination had always been genetics, and I was happy to help, of course. Why he didn't ask Aisling was a mystery. Maybe she said no. I wasn't sure. But I was certain she could decipher the reports just as well as I could. She was intelligent and yeah, she was smarter than me, although I'd never admit that out loud. I was the boss after all.

Buchanan Pharma was lucky to have her. Especially now, since she was mated to money bags. Talon could easily fund a new lab for her. Maybe he offered already. That would suck. I couldn't let her go. In the end, I'd have to, though.

Port Midway wasn't my home. My home was in the big city across the border and several hours away. If I wanted my family's legacy to survive, that was where I needed to return. And soon.

As much as I loved working beside Ash, it wouldn't have worked out in the long run. It wasn't like I could take her with me. Not that she would want to. She was too independent for that. And she'd never leave Talon or Pope. Or Zoey and all those babies.

Watching her with those kids unlocked something deep in me I never knew existed. Ash was beaming. She practically glowed with maternal love. The minute I saw how utterly happy and radiant she was surrounded by the children, my world turned upside down. And it scared the shit out of me.

I should have kept my distance. I tried. Okay, not really. I couldn't help myself. I was addicted to being around her, to touching her.

Tasting her yesterday didn't help. Her special flavor lingered on my tastebuds and was branded forever into my psyche. She was sweet and juicy. And I loved the way her pussy contracted around my fingers. Thoughts of Aisling's sweet pussy made me misstep, and I barely shot my arm out in time to catch myself before I face-planted into the sidewalk. I rolled with the fall and slowly sat up, wincing at my scraped knee. *Jesus, Jet.*

I shook it off and resumed jogging down the Strand. The pier itself was a good four-mile stretch. I'd been running nearly every morning, appreciating the quiet. The briny air filled my lungs and the sound of the ocean lapping on the pier cleared my head. Somedays it didn't work.

Aisling. What was I going to do with her? My plans to get to know her without involving sex didn't work. At. All. I'd wanted to see if my feelings for her were more than just physical, and I believed they were. According to me, the man who couldn't keep his hands to himself and his tongue in his mouth.

I should have let her stay mad at me instead of asking her to come back. It'd make things easier if she swore me off and never wanted to speak to me again. Who was I kidding? That would never happen. If she did that, I'd just force my way into her life no matter what.

Leaving of my own volition was an option. I'd already established I wasn't man enough to do that either. Still, no matter who left who, I'd have to leave Port Midway, sooner rather than later.

The right thing to do was talk to her about it before taking the physical part any further. That was downright laughable. I couldn't keep my hands off her whenever she was near.

I was a confused, tortured mess. Leave her or stay and never touch her again. Leave her or stay and fuck her, thus putting myself at risk for her to eventually rip my heart out. I didn't like any of the options available to me. Wracked with indecision, I slowed to a walk, panting.

Maybe we could indulge in the physical and then I'd tell her I was leaving. Would she understand? Or would she hate me? Of course, she would hate me.

Thoughts of Jessie floated into my mind.

"What are you saying, Jet?" Jessie whimpered.

"I'm saying this is too fast too soon. I need a breather."

"We've been planning our wedding for months!" Tears streaked down her face, smearing her makeup all over the place.

"Would you rather me go through with the wedding and leave later or worse, cheat on you at every turn like my father does to my mother?" I shouted.

"Fine. Take as much time as you need." She sniffled.

The wedding had been postponed indefinitely, even though Jessie and I were still living together. After several weeks, I realized Jessie truly loved me. She put up with my need for a break without making a fuss, and if that wasn't love, I didn't know what was. I was ready to spring the news on her when it happened. My ideal expectation of the definition of love exploded in my face.

I'd left the lab early to get ready for a big dinner date I'd planned where I'd give Jess the good news.

I expected an empty apartment but it wasn't. She was home. Whimpering. I crept toward our bedroom and my blood went cold. She wasn't alone. Her voice was loud and clear. And so was his. He was consoling her.

"He doesn't love me, does he?" she cried.

"I believe he does, in a way. He just prefers men. It's disappointing. I was hoping with you he could at least produce an heir . . ." he said.

I rounded the corner to peer into the room. They were naked.

"I can give you that and more." She straddled his nakedness and sat down on his cock.

I pushed the door open so hard it slammed against the wall, startling my ex and my father.

"Get the fuck out before I kill you both."

I lay on the front lawn of my rental gasping for air. *How did I get here?* I must've run at top speed with how much I was sweating. Or were those tears? That had happened nearly five years ago. I never spoke with Jess again and my father well, he and I came to an understanding of sorts.

"I was doing you a favor, son. She didn't love you. And you didn't love her. You're just like me. Commitment is not meant for men like us. Next time you fall for a woman, you'll remember this and think twice."

Unwilling to give my father another opportunity to ruin me, I went into the rental, showered, and packed up my shit.

My phone rang just as I was reversing out of the driveway, and I hit the accept button on the steering wheel without bothering to look at the caller ID.

"Jet, I'm leaving the file for you on the desk."

"Talon? What are you talking about?"

"The file. The DNA reports from the police department. I thought maybe it wasn't needed but the chief called last night and this morning. So, it's urgent. I was waiting for you but you're late and I have a meeting."

Shit.

"Right. I'm on my way."

"Thanks, man. Call me when you're done, I'll be on my cell."

He disconnected the line, and I sat in my car knocking my head on the steering wheel. Guess I was stopping at the office first.

CHAPTER THIRTY-THREE

AISLING

He was an hour and twelve minutes late. He was never late. Most of the time he was early. At worst, he was on time. Was he okay? Did he leave without saying goodbye? Unease flitted in my belly making me anxious.

I was about to hit the intercom to ask Zoey if she heard from him, again, when I heard his voice.

I exhaled a breath I didn't realize I was holding and dialed a colleague.

He leaned on the doorframe and watched me. I ignored him. It was a childish move, but I didn't know what to say. The thought of him not showing up did not sit well with me. The thought of never seeing him again would have wrecked me.

Cool your tits, Ash. He's here.

I finished my call and resumed working, pointedly ignoring him.

"You're in my chair," he drawled.

"You're late. I thought you left us for good. Zoey and I were about to pop the champagne," I replied with all the nonchalance I could muster.

"You'd miss me if I left," he replied.

"You flatter yourself."

"Move." He tapped my knee.

"No. You're late. You, sit in the kiddie chair." I pointed to the stupid fold-out chair I'd been sitting on *like a good girl*. I was an idiot.

He chuckled. "I'm not going to ask again, Ash. Move."

"What's the big deal, it's just a chair."

"It's my chair."

"Not today it isn't," I replied.

That made him laugh. He didn't laugh much but it was like the sun warming my skin when he did. I turned slightly to hide my smile.

"Ash, don't make me . . ."

I rolled my eyes and made a phone call.

He picked me up, sat down, and placed me on his lap.

And that was all it took for my brain to shut off and my greedy pussy to take control. But I wasn't going to make it easy on him. He liked to call me a brat, and so I felt obligated to not disappoint. I continued my phone call with a colleague in the corporate office Jet happened to despise.

"Hi Mark, it's Ash in Midway calling about the last report you sent."

Jet reached over and tapped a button on the phone. The call went to speakerphone.

I rolled my eyes and continued my conversation, while Jet's hands snaked under my shirt. His heated skin against mine made me squirm, and he began to harden. God damn this man was killing me with his big dick. I rubbed my crotch over his lap, making him groan.

Before our call was over, Mark asked, "Ash how come you don't have an Insta account? I saw some of Zoey's posts from the rink and looked you up and you weren't there."

"Right. According to HR, doctors at Pharma aren't allowed to have social media accounts."

Jet pushed my sweatshirt over my head.

"What? No way? Dr. Jet has one."

"Does he now?" I began tapping into the computer to find Jet's profile.

My breath caught in my throat as pics of him and a pretty blonde flashed on the screen. I stood.

Jet hung up on Mark and moved around me to close out his profile account.

"I can explain," he said.

I picked up my shirt from the floor, threw it on, and left the office.

"Ash?!" Jet chased me.

I got into the elevator and made it out of the building only to remember I didn't have a car.

Jet caught me and carried me back to the office.

"Put me down." I punched his back.

He slapped my ass. "Stop fussing, we're almost there."

"Let me go, Jet!"

Zoey stared at us slack-jawed.

"You may want to take a few hours off, Zoey." He told her, carrying me into the lab and slapping my ass again as soon as the doors were shut.

He dropped me on the desk, his big body caging me.

"You can leave me, Ash. I wouldn't blame you if you did. But never because of that. Never because of her." He pointed at the computer. "That was years ago. And not my profile. I don't have one. My ex created that account, and I never bothered to take it down."

"I don't believe you." I raised my chin.

"I don't fucking care. It's the truth." His lips crashed against mine in a searing kiss. His tongue probed my mouth. Claiming. Possessing. He was stealing the air from my lungs, and I gladly gave him every last breath.

"Jet." I gasped for air and pushed his chest. He didn't budge.

"That was the past, Aisling. Ancient history. This is now. This is what I want. You are what I want. What I need . . ." He claimed my mouth, my heart, my everything.

We groped each other's bodies. Hands were everywhere. I was

desperate for his skin. Clothes came off. I guided his hand to my slick heat.

"I love how wet you are." He knelt between my legs and fastened his mouth to my pussy. Jet feasted on me like I was his last meal.

"So fucking good," I moaned, riding his face. "You're going to make me come."

As soon as the words left my mouth, I nearly panicked, afraid he would suddenly stop, like he always did.

And he did. He peered at me through his dark lashes. I was ready to punch him in his handsome face.

"Did you fuck your men this morning?" he rasped.

I nodded.

"Did they come in your cunt?"

I nodded.

"Such a good little slut. Your pussy is so delicious. Especially when I can taste your men's seed mixed with your sweet juices." He ran his tongue over his bottom lip.

I pulled him toward me needing to taste myself and Pope and Talon from his mouth.

"I want yours, too," I said between kisses.

He pulled away. "Not yet. Come in my mouth, little slut. I want to drink every drop."

He knelt before me. His tongue probed my entrance, lighting up every nerve. I writhed under him, fucking his face. He sucked and licked and sucked and licked.

I clenched my thighs, and threaded my fingers into his hair, keeping him in place. Suffocating him with my pussy.

Every part of me was vibrating. His teeth grazed my swollen clit and I let go, drowning him with my juices.

He moaned as he drank me down. The vibration spurred me into another round of bliss.

Jet stood. His half-hooded gaze was full of primal lust. He tugged off his shirt with one pull and then hovered his cum-drenched face over mine.

"Lick your delicious juices off my face, little monster."

I did as he asked. I wasn't shy. Tasting myself off my men made me want them more.

He pressed his smooth shaft against my opening and plunged in without warning.

Ungh! I gasped. I clung onto him, my nails digging into his shoulders. "What the . . ."

"You like that?" He moved his hips, stroking himself along my walls. Pushing and pulling.

"You feel so fucking good, Ash. I've been dying to be inside you since the day we met."

He bucked his hips harder and harder and harder. Jet sealed our lips together, our cries of pleasure in perfect sync while he drove his cock deeper inside me.

Talon had girth for days. Pope had length. Jet was somewhere in between and . . . pierced. I felt the nubs of him scraping my inner walls.

"You take my pierced cock so good baby. You're going to feel me for days."

"Fuck yeah," I moaned. My orgasm snuck up on me. "You're going to make me come."

"That's it, baby, drench my cock with your cum."

I did just that. I came so hard that my heart slammed in my chest. My body shuddered.

Jet didn't slow down; he fucked me, branding me with his cock. I was floating in the clouds and murmuring incoherent words of needy lust. He held me flush against his chest.

"Fuck, Ash," he groaned and let go, coming deep into my pussy.

We held each other for a while, catching our breath. Jet was still inside me and something clicked. I felt complete.

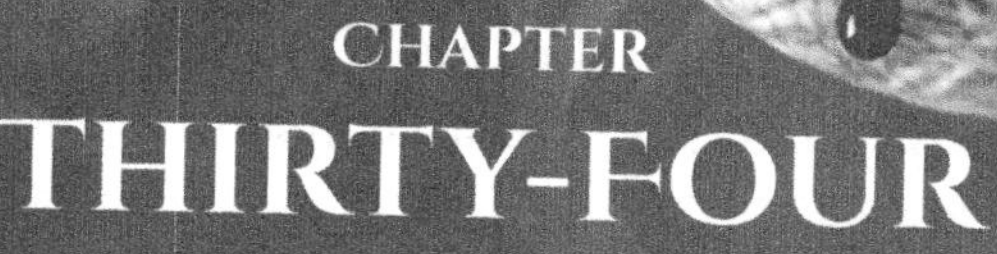

CHAPTER THIRTY-FOUR

TALON

Jet was being cagey as fuck. If it weren't for Aisling looking at me expectantly I would've chewed him out until he fessed up. For her sake, I plastered on a fake smile and said, "He's on his way, Red."

She shrugged her shoulder as though she didn't care, but my wolf senses immediately noticed the drop in pheromones. She was relieved and happy. And eager to see him.

The fucker better not hurt her.

For once my wolf and I agreed.

Ash wrapped her arms around my middle and tilted her chin up to peer into my eyes. "What are you up to today?"

"Besides missing you," I pecked her nose and her cheeks flushed. *There it is.* "Business as usual, babe. I'll see you after work."

She saw me to the door and before I exited I said, "Don't take any shit from Dr. Asshole, babe."

She giggled.

"I second that." Zoey held out her fist for me to bump.

I winked at my mate, bumped fists with her friend, and went to meet with Pope. We were working to find solutions for Ash's . . .

condition, if that's what you could call it. Whatever it was, it seemed like Ash didn't speak openly about it, and we tried to keep our meetings under wraps.

As I turned down the street Ash and Pope lived on, I sent the hacker a text telling him to meet me outside. I expected him to exit Ash's place but instead he strolled out of his.

"What, no driver today?" he asked, setting his satchel on the floor between his legs.

"Nope. I'm trying to limit Ash's exposure. I trust Igor, but until we know what we're dealing with, the fewer people who know the better."

"Smart move."

Pope didn't offer another word and neither did I. It was one of his best attributes. He wasn't guarded like Jet, and he didn't feel the need to fill the silence with mindless chatter, either. Overall, I liked the man. Or kid. He was younger than me and Jet by a few years. I glanced at the twenty-eight-year-old.

"What?" he asked without looking up from his phone.

"You're pretty mature for a man your age," I replied.

He faced me with a puzzled expression.

"I meant it as a compliment. When I was your age, I wasn't in the right headspace to even contemplate a serious relationship. And look at you."

"Oh. Well, I'm not mature. Just smarter." He smirked. "I've been with plenty of women to know a good woman when I find one."

"Watch it," I snarled.

He laughed.

"At least I'm smarter than fucking Jethro," I added.

The situation with Jet had me questioning his intentions. I'd hoped he and Ash would kiss and make up. We needed him with us on our quest to protect her.

"Oh yeah. What'd he have to say about the file?" he asked.

"He wasn't there. I had to leave it on his desk."

"Late to the office. Hmm . . ." He tapped on the armrest contemplating this info. "Sounds cagey."

"My thoughts exactly."

We drove the rest of the way in silence, both of us probably trying to figure out Aisling's other mate. I know I was. Jet and I had history, and yet I didn't know how to help them or if there was anything I could do.

Forty minutes later we were in East Midway where I'd seen Ash murder the two men. Since the men were together, the hacker had been able to track possible associates. Or friends or whatever they were.

Following Pope's directions, we arrived at a caravan park and cruised through until we found the unit we were looking for. MPD squad cars were parked in front of it, and we continued driving.

Shit.

"I hope you have another option," I muttered.

Pope nodded and directed me to another neighborhood. We came upon a cluster of two-story buildings that had seen better days. Over the years I'd been revitalizing neighborhoods like these. Well not as big as the one in front of us, but similar circumstances. I was only one man, though, and I wasn't infinitely wealthy. There were only so many projects I could tackle at a time. I'd have to put this one on my list at some point.

"There." Pope pointed to my left. "Building C, Unit 114. Are we going in?"

I glanced at him and realized Pope seemed like he was a mystic. What flavor of mystic? He didn't know. And that meant I had to classify him as human. Squishy.

"Maybe you should stay in the car," I offered.

"I can take care of myself," he deadpanned. "I was only asking because of the cops."

We were in the type of low-income housing sector cops only frequented if there was a shooting.

"We should be good. Just don't shoot anyone. Do you know how to shoot a gun?"

"Yep. Video gamer." He pointed at his chest.

I gave him a flat stare.

"Teasing. Geez." He lifted his shirt and pulled a Glock out of his waistband. "Leave it?" he asked.

Surprise. Surprise.

"No. I'd rather you be prepared to defend yourself."

There was no one in Unit 114 so we continued our journey visiting four more addresses. Each neighborhood was worse than the last. As luck would have it, at our sixth place we struck gold. The conversation we'd had with Marvin at the corner Sac-N-Save lasted all of five minutes but gave us a shit ton of information. Pope didn't waste a second. As soon as he got in the car, he pulled out his laptop and did his thing while I drove back to Shelby Centre.

We hit some afternoon traffic and I decided to turn off the highway to pick up some food. I pulled into Roadkill, an infamous BBQ joint, and parked. Pope didn't look up from his screen until I opened the door.

"Where are we?" he asked.

"Food, Pope. We need to eat."

"Thank fuck, I'm starving." He snapped his laptop shut.

After having our fill of burnt ends and a mountain of ribs, Pope got back online, and I called Ash. She didn't answer. I called the office, but Zoey didn't answer. I called Jet, voicemail.

I texted Ash. No response.

"We need to go," I told Pope.

"Everything okay?"

I told him about not being able to reach Ash or Jet.

"She's probably not answering you," he replied and started tapping into his phone.

We were approaching Pope's place and Ash still hadn't called either of us back. I was worried, but Pope was losing his mind.

"Hey, maybe she and Jet are having some alone time. That is good news," I told him.

"What if she lost her shit and killed him!" His voice was shrill.

"Calm down! Christ. Listen, why don't you meet me at the Shelby Centre? We can hang out at my place. If we don't hear from her by the end of business, we can knock on the door."

"You're leaving me? Here? Alone? While Ash could be out murdering people?"

"Alright, alright. New plan. We'll tell Ash that we're staying at my place. You included. And nope, I don't want to hear it. It's bigger. It's upstairs from the office. And it has 24/7 security. We'll know if she leaves in the middle of the night."

He didn't hesitate. "I'm in. Give me a second, I'll pack. Maybe you can pack some of Ash's things, too."

He bounced out of the car and went to take care of things.

A COUPLE of hours later and still no word from Ash or Jet. I left Pope to wander around by himself while I went to my home office and pulled up the building's security surveillance. I was watching the elevators on Ash's floor when Pope found me.

"This place is siiickk." He flopped on the chaise lounge. "You even have a rooftop pool. Does Ash know that? Wait don't answer that. You kept her here for days. Of course she does."

I continued searching the security feed.

"You left all this to stay with her. You really do love her, don't you?"

I arched my brow. "I let you fuck my mate, and only now you're figuring that out?"

He shrugged. "No. I mean, yeah, I knew you did. I just . . . I don't know, Talon. When I first met Aisling, she rejected me. Not in a mean way. It was elegant. I became obsessed with her. She has that something, you know. That sweetness. That liveliness. That special something that draws you in. It is so addicting to be around. I began stalking her. Then stumbled upon her slicing someone to death. And I didn't hesitate to do what I could to cover it up. I've been covering her murders since. Three times before you showed up. I thought I was losing my mind. I thought I was being ridiculous. I was risking so much, but I knew it was the right thing to do. I wanted to and would do it again. Knowing you'd do the same makes me feel less . . . I don't know. Less crazy?"

"You love her, Pope. As do I. And she loves us just as much. I know she loves me because she asked for my mate mark. She knew what that meant, and yet she didn't hesitate. She bound herself to me for life."

I strolled to the mini-bar and poured two shots of whiskey.

"I also know she loves you, too. Do you know how I know that?"

He shook his head.

"She refused this because she wanted to be near you, too."

A huge smile splayed across his face. He looked like he won the lottery.

I handed him a glass of whiskey. "To the love of our lives."

We clinked glasses and took a sip. "Thanks, Talon. What are you working on?"

"Checking surveillance, doesn't look like they left."

He moved around my desk to peer at the screen while standing behind me.

"Can you see her car?"

"She didn't drive."

"I know that, I was just wondering if you had a camera in the parking lot."

I turned to face him. "You know I do."

His face turned red. It wasn't cute or sexy like when Ash did it.

"You're such an asshole." I punched him lightly in his gut.

"What?" He feigned innocence.

"You knew damn well you were on camera that day."

The fucker laughed. Watching Ash ride his dick in his car was hot. But I wouldn't tell him that.

"Umm . . . since we're kind of confessing." He swigged the rest of his whiskey. "I saw you with her at Nirvana."

I nearly choked on my own saliva.

"Say that again?"

"I was stalking her. Like I said. I followed her to Nirvana. She strolled into the place and turned everyone down until you walked up. You went down on her in front of the entire place. Then you took her to your lair where you two fucked for hours."

"Pervy much?"

"Stalker. Obsessed. Crazy in love. You know these things about me," he said matter-of-factly.

"It was hot," he added.

"Go fill up my glass, you perv."

He chuckled and went to refill our glasses, while I continued searching for clues.

CHAPTER THIRTY-FIVE

JETHRO

I was well and truly fucked. And I'd never been happier in my life. Aisling was everything. Plus more. We'd been in the office all day and hadn't done a stitch of work. We were enthralled with one another and hadn't bothered to take a break for hours.

It wasn't just the mind-blowing sex. That was beyond anything I'd ever imagined. It wasn't just her intelligence. Nor was it just her beauty.

It was just her.

Being with her. The silkiness of her skin. The sweet scent of her hair. The way she claimed me with her mouth. The way she looked directly into my eyes as though she was peering into my soul.

She didn't say the words and yet being with her made me feel . . . loved. Valued. Cherished. It was reflected in everything she did. Every touch. Every smile. Every look.

I'd never experienced this type of love or love, period. It was foreign, yet invigorating. It was a high like no other. I was utterly in love with her. Love . . . yeah. She owned me. And if I was being honest, despite my assholish behavior, my feelings for her had grown over the last few weeks.

A phone buzzed, and I went in search of it. We were still in the office and Ash had gone to the bathroom. I passed the clothes scattered on the floor following the buzz which led me to the lobby where my phone was sitting on an end table near the plush waiting room sofas. Ash and I learned the sofas in the lobby were great for fucking. I smirked.

"What are you smiling at?" Ash wrapped her arms around my waist.

"You, my beautiful little monster." I kissed her again and again. "Are you feeling okay?"

"Perfect," she replied, craning her neck to kiss me.

She had hickeys all over her neck and chest. I couldn't mark her like Talon did but hickeys were fun, and I'd put them *everywhere.*

My cock woke up again. *How was I not exhausted?*

The phone buzzed again. Talon.

"He's called several times. Surely looking for you."

"Or you. Didn't he want you to look at something?"

"Right, I forgot about that." He'd left an envelope on the desk this morning, and I'd been too busy. I plopped on the sofa and patted the cushion beside me. Ash straddled my thighs instead.

"Aisling." I buried my face in between her breasts, savoring the scent of her skin. Being with her was equally calming and frightening. My last break-up snuck into my mind. "I need to tell you something."

"That sounds ominous," she replied.

"It's not terrible. But it's something you should know."

She drew away from me, forcing me to look at her. "Continue, please."

"I had a umm . . . relationship with a guy. Once. My father found out, and he throws it in my face when it suits him. He told my ex about it, and it was one of the reasons she —the one on that profile and I broke up. I'm not gay. I suppose bisexual if you had to label it."

Ash hadn't said a word, and I averted my gaze.

"Oh, okay. Is that all?" Her tone was casual as she shrugged.

"It doesn't bother you that I uh . . ."

"Like to suck dick." She gave me a teasing grin.

I chuckled. "I'm not a fiend for dick. And I don't crave it like I crave pussy. And I don't and never had feelings for men. But I don't dislike being with men, either. It's more physical exploration than emotional."

Her light laugh untied a tense knot in my core allowing me to breathe easily.

"It doesn't bother me, Jet. It would if you hid it from me or if you were a cheater. That's different. This I understand. We're all just flesh and bone."

"Aisling," I breathed her in. "You are too good to be real."

My father had made me feel ashamed of my sexuality. It was my greatest insecurity and the reason I hadn't told him to fuck off for sleeping with my ex. He made me feel like I was less of a man for exploring a side of me that I couldn't ignore. He said no one in our family and business would respect me if they found out. And no woman would truly love a bisexual man. But Harlo said he would keep my secret if I did exactly as he wanted. And so I did because I wanted his approval.

Ash was different. She didn't have a judgmental bone in her body. She accepted me for me.

"There's something else. It's not a big deal, but I guess I am weird about it." I swallowed past the lump in my throat.

Ash waited patiently for me to continue.

"They had an affair. My ex from the profile. And my father."

Ash blinked rapidly and then shook her head. "That's revolting." She crushed her body to mine and held me for a moment. "Now I understand why you thought I was having sex with him."

"Yep, I don't trust him. Guess I am more affected by what had happened than I thought. He told her about my ex, James. And uh, yeah, things went to shit. Not complaining since it led me here to you."

Aisling peppered kisses all over my face and just like that I felt a thousand pounds lighter.

"Thank you for telling me, Jethro. I respect you for being open. And fuck her. And fuck him, too. Don't let your father's antiquated ideas on sexuality bother you. After all, it's just a penis. I love penis." She traced my tatted chest with her fingernail.

I barked out a laugh. "Just a penis, huh? Well, just so that we're clear, I don't go out chasing dick, and I won't make moves on your men."

"That's between the three of you." Her voice came out a little breathy, and she squirmed on my lap and tugged on the elastic waistband of my boxers.

"You like that idea?" I nipped at her jaw.

She was wearing my T-shirt and nothing else. I cupped her pussy, making her groan. The slightest touch made her wet. She ground herself against my palm.

"Yes," she moaned, tipping her head back giving me access to her neck.

My phone buzzed again.

"Jet." Her voice husky. "You should probably answer him."

"Do I have to?"

"If you don't he'll break down the door."

She was right. Not that it mattered since he owned the building, but it had been a great day and I didn't feel like fighting with the big brute.

I pressed the accept button while using my other hand to stroke her silky slit.

"Thank fuck, Jet! I've been trying to reach you for hours!" Talon screeched into the phone. "Where's Ash? She hasn't answered me either."

"Calm down. She's fine."

"Is she?" Talon growled.

"I'm fine, Talon. Sorry, I missed your calls," Ash said.

"Hi, baby. I'm glad you're okay."

"Angel? I missed you. Are you ready to come home?" Pope shouted in the background.

"Yes. Say yes, Ash. It's time to come home. Bring Jet. We're upstairs. No protests from you, Jethro. Like you said, you cannot keep her to yourself. We'll cook dinner. See both of you in a few." Talon hung up.

What an asshole. But Aisling was giggling in my lap, and I couldn't be mad at anything.

"Guess we're going upstairs," I said.

"Are you okay with that?" she asked.

I inhaled deeply and let it out slowly. "Yeah, I'm okay. Why upstairs though? Does he expect us to hang out in his office all night?"

She climbed off me and I followed her into the office so we could dress.

"They're probably at his place on the rooftop."

"Rooftop?" I muttered. Intriguing.

Talon and Pope greeted us in his office. The two men swarmed her and then shook my hand. Ash glanced my way and blew me a kiss as Pope guided us upstairs.

I tapped the envelope Talon had left for me. "I haven't looked at this yet."

He patted my shoulder. "I understand, Jet. I understand."

My jaw dropped when I entered Tally's living space. "Whoa! Dude. This is impressive."

Ash pressed her body into my side and brought my face down for a kiss. "I need a bath," she said. "See you in a few."

Ash and Pope disappeared down a corridor while Talon showed off his place. I admired every nuance in the interior of his home as he walked me through it. The design was all him. Hardwood floors throughout combined with graphite-gray-colored walls and leather furnishings which were a burnt-orange. The kitchen was modern with black granite counters and chrome fixtures. It was on the small side, which indicated he didn't spend much time in the kitchen.

Unless the bachelor was a foodie, that wasn't unusual. The outside terrace was just . . . wow. He had a barbeque area, a dining table large enough to seat eight, and a lounge area decked out with surround sound and flat-screen televisions. All of which were surrounded by a rooftop garden that wound down a small path and led to a pool. If all of that wasn't enough, the view was fucking spectacular.

"Talon . . ." I gasped. "You've been holding out on me."

He chuckled modestly.

"Seriously, man. This is beyond impressive. Why does Ash need me or Pope when she has you and all this?"

"Ash isn't in it for the money. You know this. She's smart and can support herself. Material things aren't important to her."

"Hell, if she won't marry you, I will."

He laughed. "You have your own money."

"True, but mine is family money. This is all you, Tally. You should be proud." I clapped him on the back.

"Thanks, man," he said.

"I'd toast you, but you haven't offered me a drink. Some host you are." I snickered.

"Get it yourself. Bar's over there." He pointed behind him.

"Over where?" Pope called out. "Our queen wants some wine."

Talon showed us the bar which was beside the kitchen. I perused his wall of whiskey while he opened a bottle of red and poured a glass for Ash. I grabbed a bottle off the shelf, and he arched his brow.

"Only you would choose the most expensive bottle I have," he snarked.

"You said help myself." I grabbed a glass.

"Uh, Jet, no offense but maybe you should jump in the shower. You smell like Aisling and sex. It's making me horny." Pope grabbed the wine and walked away.

Talon tipped his head back and laughed.

"It wasn't that funny," I muttered.

"Go." Talon moved into the kitchen and pulled out steaks from the fridge. "I'll get dinner started."

He fired up the indoor grill and began unwrapping the meat.

"You're not cooking those now are you?" I asked.

"I was. Why? Do you want me to wait, princess?"

"Piss off. That's not how you cook steaks. You need to wait for the meat to come to room temperature before you put them on the grill."

"Do you want to cook?"

"He should shower." Pope returned to the kitchen and took a seat at the counter.

"Yes, I can already tell I'm better at it," I said to Talon then turned to Pope. "And I will. Just let me . . ." I pushed Talon aside and began searching the kitchen and pulling out other ingredients. For a guy who couldn't cook he had a decent selection of things that would turn into a decent meal.

I found a pot and filled it with water. I turned back to find Pope and Talon staring at me with stupid grins on their faces.

"What?" I asked.

"Look at you being all domestic." Talon snorted.

"I think I'm in love," Pope crooned.

"Fuck you guys. You peel the potatoes." I pointed at Talon. "And you dice up these veggies." I pointed at Pope.

"What are you going to do?"

"Supervise," I retorted.

"I think we can handle this. Go shower before Pope jumps you," Talon teased, earning a punch from Pope.

I laughed. "Don't put the steaks on for at least ten minutes." I strolled out of the kitchen and stopped to pick up my gym bag which I'd left in the foyer. I'd gotten a few things from my truck earlier in the day so at least I had clean clothes. Hell, I could move in. I had a suitcase full of stuff.

Don't, Jet. Don't go down that road. Everything is working out just fine.

I scrubbed a hand down my face and found Ash, easing into the bathtub. Her face lit up when she saw me.

"Hi." She smiled.

"Hi, little monster. I thought you'd be soaking by now." I kissed her forehead.

"The water was too hot." She sank into the tub until the bubbles touched her chin and sighed. "Are you joining me?"

I glanced at the separate shower. "Next time. I need to supervise dinner."

"Oh. I can help." She sat up.

"We got this, Ash. Relax. Let us take care of you." I caressed her beautiful face and took a quick shower.

By the time I was done and dressed, Ash was dozing off. I sat at the edge of the tub, admiring the woman I'd come to love.

Admitting it made my heart race. *Easy, Jet. She's nothing like your ex.*

"You clean up nice," Pope said as I neared the kitchen.

"Shut up," I told him.

Talon laughed. They'd done a decent job with the veggies, and I took over making the potatoes au gratin. Once it was in the oven, Talon offered to cook the steaks. I eyed him which earned me a snarl.

"It's just meat. I won't ruin it. Here, you sit and oh I know, look at those files from MPD. I'll even pour you an expensive glass of whiskey." He pointed to a seat at the counter.

"Me too!" Pope chimed in while keeping his eyes glued to his laptop screen.

I opened up the file and began reading the documents while keeping an eye on Talon.

Interesting. I read through one of the reports. "Season first," I said.

Talon, the child, threw a pinch of salt at me. "For good luck."

"Hey! Watch my drink!" I peered into my glass.

"You watch your drink and stop watching me."

"You're doing it wrong," I said.

"Working with you must be so much fun," Talon snarked.

Pope snickered.

"I'm bossy. Ask Aisling."

"We know," Pope and Talon said at the same time.

"Fuck you guys," I chuckled.

I read the rest of the reports twice over just to be sure and set them down.

Aside from the normal kitchen noises, it was silent. All eyes were on me. Pope and Talon watched me with . . . curiosity. No anxiousness.

"This isn't much to go on. It isn't familiar but I have seen a similar gene sequence before. In a textbook. I'd have to look through my library to compare but even that won't provide me with much. It'd be a guesstimate. The sample is too small, or their equipment is outdated."

"And? What does that mean? Exactly?" Pope asked.

"Inconclusive. It is impossible to make an accurate analysis based on this alone. I need more data. Or a larger blood sample."

Pope released a heavy sigh.

"Should we call the chief and tell him that?" Talon asked.

"Sure."

After delivering the not-so-great news to the police chief, I finished preparing dinner, just as Ash padded into the kitchen barefoot, and wearing an oversized t-shirt. Her hair was still damp making it appear darker in the dim lighting of the kitchen. And her cheeks reddened at something Talon said to her. The sunlight streaming through the windows highlighted the golden striations in her eyes. She smiled at me, stealing my breath away.

You made the right choice, Jet.

CHAPTER THIRTY-SIX

POPE

I pulled Aisling into my arms as soon as we were alone. "Don't disappear on me like that ever again," I said, squeezing her to my chest.

"Can't. Breathe," she said.

I loosened my hold and gazed into her eyes. "I was worried. I love you, Ash. And I'm glad you and Jet are getting along, but Christ, reply with an emoji at the very least."

She cupped my jaw. "You're right; I should have replied. I'm sorry."

She tiptoed to kiss my bottom lip. "Forgive me?"

"Of course." I grinned. "So, you and Jet, huh?"

She giggled. "Stop it."

"Stop what? It's not like you two can hide what you've been up to. All day. In your office. Hot, babe. Super. Freaking. Hot. Do I get details?"

Her face turned beet red. I laughed.

"Alright, I'll leave it for now. Here," I showed her the closet. "I know you've been here before, but I was the one who put your stuff away."

"My stuff?"

"Yeah, Talon packed some of your things, while I packed some of my things. I wanted to snoop around and so I used unpacking as an excuse."

"You're the worst." She smacked my belly.

"You wouldn't be scolding me if you learned what I found . . ." I teased.

"What did you find?" She squealed.

"Nothing. Talon is boring," I told her. "Gotcha!"

She smacked me again. "You're so immature."

I showed her which drawers were hers and she paused at the designated space for her undies.

"He packed my lingerie. All of it."

I laughed. "I can't blame him, angel. But, yeah, I think he packed more of that than anything else."

She shook her head.

"Oh, here," I opened a mini fridge which was hidden amongst the bookshelf. "I brought your lady tonics."

"Pope." She threw her arms around me. "You take such good care of me. Do you know how much I love you?"

She sealed her lips over mine before I could answer. Her tongue swirled through mine. She tasted different. Like her but there was a masculine flavor in her mouth. Jet. My cock stiffened, and she hooked her leg on my hip. I gripped her thighs, hoisted her into my arms and laid her on the bed.

I kissed a path from her neck down to her tits. She had hickeys everywhere. I chuckled. "Jet's been busy marking his territory, I see." I kissed and licked each one.

"What?" Ash sat up and peered at her body. "Oh." She ran her hand over her tummy. "He did not!" She spread her legs. "That little shit."

I laughed, then kissed the hickeys on her inner thighs. Then I flicked my tongue over her slit, making her squirm. There was something so hot about licking her after another man came inside her. I brought her pussy lips into my mouth and sucked hard.

"Fuck that feels so good."

I released her pussy and placed a chaste her cheek.

"Hey. I wasn't finished." She pouted.

"Trust me, baby, I don't want to stop." I stood and adjusted my dick. "We'll finish this later. I promise. Let's get you in the tub."

I left Ash in the bathroom and went back to hangout with the guys in the kitchen.

JET WASN'T AS bad as I'd thought he'd be. I was expecting him to be more uptight. He wasn't at all. Sure, he had a bossy side to him, but it was more quirky than irritating.

He fit into our little family seamlessly. There wasn't a moment of awkwardness ever. The banter between us men was refreshing. We gave each other shit and no one got butthurt over anything.

Plus, Jet could cook. Me and Ash were mediocre in the kitchen. And Talon was an order-out kind of guy. His secretary ordered groceries, and Jet whipped up a delicious meal.

Jet also helped us out with the DNA thing the cops wanted him to look at. The chief wasn't really happy with not having a definitive answer but that was all they'd get with what they'd provided. The doc was smart and not one to push around. I was impressed with his knowledge and the way he handled the chief of police. The DNA thing was done and done. He was the expert and unless the victim provided more DNA, they had nothing. Talon and I were relieved to have him on our side.

I never thought I'd ever be in a polyamorous relationship. It always seemed overwhelming and complicated. It wasn't for us, though. Maybe that was due to having the right pieces of the puzzle.

Ash was the best. She managed each of our personalities and needs with grace and surprising equality. With three men vying for her attention, she didn't make anyone feel excluded. It had to be exhausting, but she managed, and we were happy just being in her presence.

We were sitting on one of the loungers out on the terrace, drinking beers, bullshitting, and enjoying the view. Ash had her head in Talon's lap, her legs were draped over Jet's, while I sat on a cushion on the floor in front of her.

"So, Red, are we moving you in this weekend?" Talon asked Ash.

I turned to face them, waiting for her answer.

"Moving in?" she asked. "Isn't that kind of soon?"

I laughed. "Talon and I have been living in your apartment for weeks."

Me more than him, but I wasn't going to rub it in. Talon's wolf might be willing to share but he wouldn't let Ash sleep anywhere without him at her side. My place was across from Ash which meant I was there when she came home. And I was pretty sure Jet wasn't going to be left out.

"Hmmm . . . I guess we have. Well, I don't know, ask Jet and Pope," she replied. "This is a package deal, mate."

Talon laughed.

"I vote yes," Jet said. "Now you won't be late for work."

Ash shoved his shoulder with her foot making him chuckle.

"Me too, this is freaking awesome," I added.

Talon's place was sick. Had I known it was like this, I would have encouraged Ash to move in weeks ago. Or had it been a month? Or more. Not sure. I lost track of time after everything we'd been going through. At some point, I moved into Ash's place. I still kept mine because of my gear. Guess I would continue to keep it.

I rested my chin on the seat cushion, my face level with Ash's tits. She ran her hands through my hair. Her nails gently scratched my scalp and gave me tingles . . . everywhere.

She'd been with Jet all day and probably could have used a break. But . . . damn it. I looked into her eyes, and she smiled. There was that smile. My smile. She traced my cheek with the tip of her finger, and I angled my chin to plant kisses on her palm. And her wrists. She mewled and leaned into me.

I captured her lips with mine. The kiss was gentle. An exploration. A test. We were being watched. And I was curious to see how Jet would react. Sharing Ash with Talon was fun. Adding another to the mix was going to be interesting.

Aisling deepened our kiss. More demanding. Heated.

A hand reached between her legs. I peeked a glance as Talon shoved his hands into her panties. Ash groaned and began humping his palm.

"Fuck baby, you're already dripping."

Jet tugged her panties off her body. "Spread your legs wide, little monster. Show me your pussy."

"What a pretty cunt you have," he breathed.

"The prettiest," Talon rasped while inserting one of his sausage fingers into her wet heat.

I slid in my finger next to Talon's. Jet added his.

We stared at her pussy, mesmerized as she took all three of us at the same time. She was beautiful. So smooth and silky and glistening with her arousal. We worked her into a frenzy. Pushing in together and pulling out together, Ash writhed under our touch.

"I need . . ." She reached for my crotch and palmed my length. The other hand reached for Talon.

"Not yet, baby," Talon groaned.

"Come for us, first," I said as she squeezed my cock.

"You heard him, little slut. Come for us. We want to watch your sweet pussy squirt all over our hands. And then we'll fuck you good and hard."

Ash started to tremble.

On instinct, we sped up our assault on her pussy, jamming our fingers into her core.

"That's it, Ash. Take our fingers like it's all three of our cocks in you right now," Jet said.

This man and his filthy mouth were going to make me come in

my pants. Ash liked it, too. Her pussy contracted, squeezing our fingers together as she came. A flood of her juices leaked out of her cunt and down my hand.

"More," she demanded.

"Be polite, little monster." Jet pinched her clit.

She moaned with pleasure. "More, please."

I dropped my joggers. My cock sprang free. Ash noticed and rushed me. She swallowed my crown and I shoved myself deeper until I hit the back of her throat causing her to gag. Her eyes watered. Normally, I'd feel bad, but I was so fucking needy.

"Fuck, Aisling, you slurp on his cock like it's fucking delicious." Jet licked his lips.

I was on the cusp of coming when a big hand grabbed a fistful of her hair and yanked her off my dick. I glared at Talon. Between the wolf and the warlock fighting for dominance, this was going to get rough. And I liked it.

"I need to fuck you while you eat his dick, baby."

We repositioned ourselves. I backed up, Ash got on all fours and Talon took her from behind.

Jet sat back, stroking his dick, and devoured us with a hungry gaze.

Talon pounded into her from behind. Every thrust pushed me farther down Ash's throat. I placed my hand on the back of her head holding her in place while I fucked her face. We were abusing her body, and she fucking loved it.

I loved it. I was so close to shooting down her throat. I closed my eyes trying to hold off on blowing my load too soon.

"Oh Aisling, my precious little slut. You are so perfect, the way you take two big dicks at the same time," Jet crooned.

God damn that man's mouth. And his dick. Holy fuck. My eyes widened at the sight of his piercings.

Talon saw me staring and glanced at Jet's crotch. "Is that?" he rasped. Our eyes were on Jet, but we didn't stop pumping into Ash.

She was like a rag doll between us being pushed and pulled at our will.

Jet ran a finger down his shaft tracing the Jacobs ladder. "Don't worry guys, you'll get a chance to feel these, too. Ash loves it."

I wasn't sure what he meant but I was dying to find out. I'd never been with a guy before, never been attracted to one, but hell, I'd never shared before either. And I knew with these three, it was a judgment-free zone. I could trust them. And the four of us fucking and sucking was hot as fuck.

I fucking lost it. My hips sputtered as streams of my cum shot down Ash's throat. I pulled out an inch, giving her room to breathe. She looked up at me as she swallowed my seed, drops of it dripping down her chin.

"You're so beautiful." I kissed her deeply, tasting myself on her tongue.

She moaned against my lips as Talon brought her to an orgasm. Her body trembled and her pussy squirted everywhere. Talon fucked her through her aftershocks, not giving her a chance to breathe. His big hands gripped her ass cheeks which would surely leave handprints.

Ash screamed with pleasure. He slammed into her so hard she crashed into me. I held onto her as Talon chased his release. He came with a deep growl that was all wolf.

He folded over her, kissing her sweaty back and shoulders. Not even a minute later she eyed Jet. He crooked his finger.

Ash placed another kiss on my lips and did the same to Talon. And then she crawled to Jet. Her boss. And that fucker was good at playing the role.

Her hair was matted to her face, skin coated with a layer of sweat, cum leaking from her pussy. She was thoroughly fucked, but never looked so delicious as she crawled on all fours. At Jet's feet, she opened wide and took his cock in her mouth. He thrust into her, and she took all of him. Every pierced inch.

My dick began to swell again.

"Up," Jet ordered. Ash stood on shaky legs. He leaned in and swiped his tongue up and down her slit.

I licked my lips, knowing how delicious she tasted, full of Talon's cum.

"Sit on my cock," he told her.

Talon and I braced her arms and helped her take his length.

She sank down on him, her lips parted and began rocking her hips.

"Fuck yes, just like that." Jet's chest heaved with every breath.

Their lips met in a hungry kiss. Talon hooked Ash's chin and forced her mouth to meet his. Jet wasn't going to let the wolf take her for himself; he snaked his tongue in between theirs. Lips and tongues swirled together in a dance of dominance. I was mesmerized and rock hard again.

Aisling broke away and reached for me. Our lips collided while I watched Talon and Jet's heated make-out session. Ash sucked hard on my bottom lip, then teeth pierced my skin. The sharp sting elicited a low groan from my chest.

A warm, thick tongue slipped through my mouth and rough stubble scraped across my jaw. Jet. Or Talon. I didn't look. I didn't care. My cock pulsed, needing to be touched.

I reached down to grip my shaft, but a large hand was already there. Jet smeared my precum all over his finger and then brought it to Ash's mouth.

"Suck, little slut," Jet said.

She sucked on his finger, hollowing out her cheeks.

"That's it, make it nice and wet for me," he crooned, while Talon was kissing and licking her neck and chest.

I spit in my hand and gripped my dick.

Ash rocked her hips over Jet's cock, slow and steady. The warlock gripped her ass.

She let out a sharp hiss. "That feels so fucking good."

Talon and I glanced down her back and saw a finger sliding in and out of her ass. Fucking. Jet.

"Fuck, that's so hot." Talon peppered kisses down her spine. "You like that, babe?"

"Yes," she moaned.

He spread her butt cheeks apart and spit down her crack, giving Jet's digit extra glide to finger her ass.

Ash gasped while Jet fucked her in both holes.

God damn these people were killing me.

Talon got on the sofa with them, and Ash leaned over and took his cock into her mouth while pumping her hips.

"You need help with that big dick, baby," Jet asked. His face close to Ash's mouth and Talon's cock.

She popped off Talon's dick. "Yes."

Jet's eyes flicked up to Talon, asking for permission with his gaze. "Our woman always makes the rules. Suck my cock, Jet."

Jet opened wide and took his length, between his lips. Fuck. I'd never seen anything so erotic.

Ash liked what she was seeing. She bucked wildly and reached for me.

"Cock, please." The way she said please made my cock weep with precum.

I pushed my tip between her lips and pumped her mouth.

She sucked and sucked. And then his lips, his mouth replaced hers. Fucking. Jet. It felt like heaven.

Ash and Jet fucked each other while managing to lick and suck me and Talon. We were connected in a mess of hot, sweaty limbs. Another orgasm raged through my body, ready to burst.

My heart galloped in my chest, and precum oozed out of my dick.

Ash bounced up and down on Jet's cock making the warlock groan.

"Oh fuck, my little slut. Come for us. Come with me," Jet growled. He pumped his hips from below until he came with a guttural moan.

I gripped my saliva-soaked cock and choked it. Stroking myself as if she was riding me.

Ash's body spasmed and she unleashed a strangled cry of pleasure. Talon shot his load all over her face.

I came so fucking hard, emptying myself all over her chest. Streams of cum poured out of me, over and over, until there was nothing left.

Except them.

It was the craziest thing I'd ever done and at that moment, nothing else in the world mattered as long as we were together like this. The four of us.

CHAPTER THIRTY-SEVEN

AISLING

The scent of freshly baked bread wafted through the penthouse, making my stomach growl. I cut my bath time short and went in search of food. I padded toward the kitchen and stopped short. My three men were in the kitchen chatting. Bonding.

I always imagined myself in a traditional marriage like my parents. What I had with my men was something I didn't see for myself in my wildest dreams. I wasn't sorry. I was a little sore but it was so worth it.

The four of us together were effortless. There was an easy camaraderie between my men and the physical chemistry between us was undeniable. Still, sex aside, our relationship wouldn't work if they weren't able to get along without me in the same room.

Oblivious to my presence, I slipped behind the wall, watching and straining to overhear their conversation.

Pope was seated at the end of the kitchen island. His bright eyes focused intently on the screen in front of him as he popped a grape into his mouth. His tongue flicked over his bottom lip, making my breath hitch.

Talon sat opposite him wearing nothing but a pair of distressed jeans. My mouth watered as his biceps flexed while sipping his morning coffee. His hair was tousled and there was a slight stubble covering his chiseled jaw. He looked peaceful. Relaxed.

Jet pulled a baking sheet from the oven and placed it on the counter. He draped the dish towel over his tattoo-covered shoulder and then leaned on the kitchen sink. He, too, was shirtless, revealing a dark patch of hair disappearing into the waistband of his joggers.

Damn, I was a lucky girl.

Pope reached for a biscuit which earned him a smack from Jet.

"Hey! I'm hungry!" Pope complained.

"Give it a minute to cool, geez," Jet said.

"Let him burn himself," Talon added. "That'll teach him."

"Mind your business." Pope threw a grape which hit my wolf square in the nose.

Talon picked up the grape laughing. His arm moved as though he was throwing it back at Pope but in a flash, his hand changed direction and the grape nailed Jet in the eye.

"You asshole!" Jet chuckled and picked up the grape. "Open," he said to Talon.

"No way, that was on the floor." Talon shook his head.

"Seriously? You're a wolf."

"Let me try." Pope plucked a fresh grape.

Talon opened his mouth, Pope threw, and so did Jet.

One grape found its mark.

Pope stood and pointed. "Eeeww, you ate the dirty floor grape."

Jet bowled over laughing.

"Fuckers!" Talon leaned over the counter, snagged the entire bowl of grapes, and began throwing them like rapid fire at Jet and Pope.

The battle of the grapes ensued. My men were laughing their asses off. It was hilarious and heartwarming to witness their bonding moment.

My phone rang. Oops. So much for hiding.

The battle came to an abrupt halt.

I stepped out of my hiding spot, chuckling.

"How long were you back there?" Jet asked.

"Long enough. I didn't want to disturb the battle," I replied.

"Were you keeping score?" Pope prodded.

Talon punched his arm. "Don't listen to him, Red. We all know I won."

"Did not." Pope tagged him back.

"Oh no. Nope." I shook my head. "I am not getting in the middle of your testosterone-fueled competitiveness."

"Don't pay any attention to these two, little love." Jet wrapped his arms around my middle, pressing his bare chest into my back.

I snaked my arm around his neck and tilted my head to kiss his chin. "You are all being . . . boyish this morning."

Talon came around the counter. "Boyish? I don't feel offended at all." He cupped my face and kissed me deeply.

"I love watching you two kiss." Jet rubbed his thickening cock on my back.

"My turn." Pope nudged Talon who relinquished my lips only to plant kisses down to my chest.

Pope claimed my mouth, while Jet's hands slid over my hips and into the waistband of my denim shorts.

Sex with my men was out of this world and constant. We were hungry for each other day and night. I should have been exhausted and, in some ways, I was. In more ways, I couldn't get enough of them.

I moaned into Pope's mouth as Jet's deft fingers inched toward my pussy while Talon pushed my tank top down and flicked my nipple with his tongue.

My phone rang again.

"Who would be calling you on a Saturday?" Talon growled.

Jet pulled my phone out of my back pocket. "Zoey."

"I forgot." I wiggled free of my men, grabbed the phone, and hit the accept button.

"Hi Zozo, we're on our way," I answered.

"Thank fuck. I need backup," she said.

"Is everything okay?" I asked.

"My wife is working, and I have seven kids . . . at a carnival," she replied.

I chuckled. "Be there soon."

"Sorry guys, Zoey needs support." I snatched a biscuit and took a bite. The buttery, flaky goodness melted in my mouth, making me moan. "So fucking good." I licked my fingers.

"You can't make sexy noises and expect us to just stop," Pope complained.

I giggled. "We'll continue this later. Let's go."

Like sullen little boys, they did as I asked.

"Thanks for coming, Ash," Zoey and I hugged.

"Of course!" I greeted the kids while Zoey introduced her husband to my men.

"Alpha." Jacob shook Talon's hand. "Good to finally meet you."

"Talon, just Talon will do." My wolf scrunched his brow. "I'm not Alpha. Or pack."

"Yes, Alpha. I mean Talon." The coyote shifter grinned.

I winked at my mate. He wasn't an Alpha, but he'd be a good one.

"Where to first, angel?" Pope asked. "Rides, games, or food."

He was practically bouncing.

I giggled and looked at Zoey for answers. The county fair was an annual thing. Emily's non-profit organization had a concession stand that raised funds and awareness for their homeless shelter which kept her busy. I'd been attending every year to help Zoey with the kids.

"Rides," Zoey and Jacob said at the same time.

A chorus of cheers erupted from the kids, and we started with the airplane ride.

We'd been at the annual county fair for hours. The lines were long, but the kids weren't fussy. My men were great at keeping them entertained while we waited.

"Look who's here." Zoey pointed behind me.

I glanced over my shoulder and waved at my neighbors, Ty and Nelson.

"I'm glad you made it," I greeted the couple with hugs.

"We wouldn't miss it. Plus," Nelson pulled out a large carafe from his backpack. "We brought reinforcements. Who's ready for a roadie?!"

Jacob went to the nearest food stand to get to-go cups for me and Zoey so that Ty could fill them up. There were a couple of beer stands, but there was nothing like a margarita on a warm sunny day.

Zoey took a big swig of her drink. "I needed this. Thanks, guys."

"What you got there?" Talon asked with one of the boys sitting on top of his shoulders.

I lifted the straw to his lips.

"That's good. Where'd you get those?"

"Oh, you haven't met our—mine and Pope's neighbors." I introduced him and Jet to Tyrone and Nelson. With our neighbors with us, we now had more adults than children. Life at the fair became a lot more manageable. I wasn't sure how Zoey and her spouses did it at home.

After a few more rides, Mama Bear Zoey corralled the crowd and found us a table under the big top.

"Who's hungry?!" she asked.

The kids and my men cheered, making me laugh.

Nelson nudged my arm. "Three men, Ash? I'm proud of you."

"Not just three men . . . three hot as fuck men. Go, girl!" his husband added.

"Details. We want to know everything." Nelson clapped his hands.

"Me too," Zoey chimed in.

"Nope. Not having that conversation right now; besides didn't we stop for food?" I replied. Not that I minded talking about my sex life, but my relationship was new and the kids were around. It wasn't something I wanted to discuss while my men were sitting right next to me.

Talon kissed my reddening cheeks, while Pope squeezed my hand.

"We did. I spied a food truck from one of the restaurants I've been wanting to try." Jet pointed to a truck nearby. "I'm sure they have something kid-friendly, and the line is short."

"MJ Bistro?! Yes! We have to go there," Ty agreed. "Are you a foodie?" he asked Jet.

"I am," my warlock answered.

"I like this one." Ty winked at me. "Is that good, mama?" he asked Zoey.

"Great, let's get in line." She moved to stand but her husband placed a gentle hand on her shoulder.

"I got it, sweetheart. Stay with the kids," Jacob said to Zoey.

Jet patted my butt, and then he, Ty, Nelson, and Jacob went to stand in line, while the rest of us stayed with the kids.

Emily joined us for lunch, which consisted of bacon-wrapped dogs in pretzel buns and loaded fries. For dessert, we stopped at Emily's concession stand to get ice cream, cotton candy, and fried Snickers. With full bellies, our group of sixteen moved on to the games section.

Jet draped an arm over my shoulder and drew me into his side while we watched Pope and Talon play a ring toss game with the kids. "Having fun, little love?"

"I am. You?"

He nodded. "I've never been to one of these before."

I blinked in surprise. What kind of childhood did he have?

"My parents were too busy for these things. And I was either at home with the nanny or in school."

Poor warlock.

"I'm happy you're here now, Jethro. This day wouldn't have been complete without you." I kissed his cheek. "And the children love you."

His smile was so bright it reached his eyes.

"Children were never part of my plan. I didn't think I'd be a good father. Or husband for that matter. Being with you has changed me. Thank you, Ash." He laid a sweet kiss on my lips.

Jacob took Pope's spot at the ring toss game, allowing my hacker to join us. "Carnivals are a lot more fun with kids." Pope grinned.

"So, angel, how many kids do you want?" he asked.

Jet laughed.

My heart stuttered in my chest. *I can't. Or more like I shouldn't. Fuck.* I needed to get back into the lab.

"Definitely not seven," I replied, hoping my voice didn't reveal the unease rolling through me.

"Okay, we'll have eight," he teased.

"Everyone's a winner!" the game attendant announced. Talon fist-bumped the kids and Jacob.

My men were enjoying themselves, and I refused to spoil it by brooding over my problems.

Jet and I walked hand in hand until we came to the railroad train ride, which was a favorite amongst the kids.

"You're up, Jet," Talon said, claiming my other hand.

Jet swooped one of the kids into the air and stood in line with the others.

"No train rides for you, big man?" I chirped.

Talon chuckled. "I can't get one leg in one of those things."

The thought of Talon trying to fit his massive frame into a kiddie ride made me giggle.

While we waited for the others, I found a bench nearby, and Talon went to get me some water. He was a few feet from me when a familiar man in uniform approached him.

"Didn't take the county fair as your type of scene." The chief of police and pack Alpha extended his hand to Talon.

“There’s a lot you don’t know about me, Chief. What’s with the extra patrols?”

I’d noticed the police roaming around the fairgrounds and didn’t think anything of it. Perhaps I’d been wrong.

The chief rubbed a weathered hand down his face. “Being extra cautious. There’s a new drug sweeping the town. It’s unlike anything we’ve dealt with before.”

“Where’s it coming from?” Talon’s gaze narrowed.

“Everything is pointing to Crow Feather trail. I’ve sent patrols, police, and pack, but so far nothing.”

“Good luck with that. Let me introduce you to my mate. Baby,” Talon held out his hand. I grasped it and stood beside him.

“This is Chief Hayes, Chief, this is Aisling.”

“Nice to meet you.” I shook the chief’s hand and studied his face. He looked older than he did on television. Must be the job. “I couldn’t help overhear your concern about this new drug, is there anything we need to watch for? My best friend’s wife works near Crow Feather.”

“There’s no need for alarm. We’re doubling patrols when we can spare the men. Where does she work?” he asked.

“The shelter,” I replied.

A flicker of concern flashed over the chief’s face. “She’ll be fine.”

The chief of police needed to work on his poker face.

As soon as they returned, I warned Zoey and Emily.

CHAPTER THIRTY-EIGHT

AISLING

"Someone's glowing this morning," Zoey sang. "Who's the lucky girl?" She poked my belly.

I grinned. She was right, I was living my best life. For the past few days, I was surrounded by the love and affection of three men. *Three! Go me!!*

"Good morning to you, too." I strolled past her desk smiling from ear to ear.

"Love looks good on you!" she crooned.

I waved her off.

It felt good, too. I was still riding the high from having the best weekend. Being in a relationship with Jet, Talon, and Pope was better than I could have ever fantasized about. Maybe I could have it all. Career, love, family.

Perhaps I should talk to my men about my issues. I buried the thought, not wanting to ruin my good mood. *Yep, queen of avoidance, right here.*

I sat behind my desk, immediately missing Jet's presence. He'd left early in the morning to vacate his rental and pick up his things.

We'd decided to move into Talon's place. It was an easy and

obvious choice. Sure, our relationship was moving fast, but it felt right. And I for one couldn't imagine being away from them. Plus, the penthouse was bigger, more convenient, and flat out amazing.

I fished my phone out of my purse and sent a text to Jet. We hadn't done a stitch of work for days as evident by the countless emails in my inbox and the long list of tasks that were overdue. *Where was my helpful, broody, doctor?*

Despite my long list of things to do, I decided to take advantage of his absence by working on my personal project. I didn't take my tonics once the entire weekend. Life was good. But . . . should I push it? I drummed my fingers on my desk and decided to take one anyway.

The morning flew by and still no word from Jet. Zoey saved me from worrying by dragging me to one of our favorite restaurants. Girl time was always therapeutic and I hadn't fretted over his absence once.

An hour or so after lunch, Talon stopped by.

"Keys for you and Jet. I've given Pope his already." He laid the plastic key cards on the desk.

"Thanks. Have you heard from him?"

"Who? Jet?"

I nodded.

"He's not here?"

I shook my head.

He snapped his fingers. "He did mention he had some business to attend to. Something to do with his rental. I'll track him down." He kissed the top of my head and hightailed it out of the office.

Weird.

I called Jet and got his voicemail. Something wasn't right. I squashed the negative thoughts, focused on my work, and called him an hour later. And again, thirty minutes later. By the time Zoey left for the day, I had begun calling him every fifteen minutes.

My phone rang. I jumped to answer it. "Hi angel," Pope's smiley voice calmed my nerves.

"Hi. Have you heard from Jet?"

"Umm . . . no. I'll ask Talon, I was going to call him next. I'm thinking about ordering sushi from Jade for dinner. Sound good?"

"Perfect. I'll see you soon."

I hung up and called Jet. Then texted him. Worry raked down my spine. An hour and multiple texts later, I went upstairs. No one was home, and I searched the apartment. We all had designated drawers and Jet's was half full as it had been over the weekend. He didn't take anything.

I began pacing and called Talon.

I got his voicemail and received a text immediately after.

He was in a meeting.

I couldn't sit and wait. I got in one of Talon's cars and drove on instinct. I wasn't sure how or why, but I found myself parked in front of a two-story Mediterranean home. It seemed familiar but I couldn't recall ever being there.

Doubts aside, I knocked on the front door. A gorgeous blonde woman answered, and my heart lurched.

"Is Dr. Buchanan here?" I glanced behind her.

"Jet? No, he checked out early this morning."

"Okay, thanks." I turned away.

"Oh, wait. Are you A. Sling?"

"It's pronounced Ash—leen."

"My bad. I was just about to call you. Jet left something." She stepped into the foyer and returned with an envelope.

"Thanks." I took the envelope that had my name and phone number scrawled on it and trudged to my car, the envelope burning a hole in my hand. I knew what it was without even looking at it.

I sat in my car for a moment reminding myself to breathe. The blonde stood in the driveway and waved. "Are you okay?" she asked.

I waved back and started the car. I drove in circles until nightfall, ignoring Pope's and Talon's calls and texts the entire time. Needing a bathroom, I stopped at a fast food joint in a part of town I was unfamiliar with. My appetite was nil, but I hated to use the establishment's restroom and then leave without purchasing something. I ordered two tacos and sat at a table looking at the letter.

My phone rang and I hit the accept button.

"Mate. Where are you? Are you okay?"

"Yes." *No*. "I went to Jet's rental. He left me a note."

"What did he say?" His voice was tight with restrained anger.

"I haven't read it yet. I've been driving."

He exhaled. "Come home, baby. Let's read it together."

"I need some space. I'll be home soon. I love you. Tell Pope I love him, too."

I hung up and then tore open the envelope. I read the note repeatedly until my eyes blurred.

That fucker.

CHAPTER THIRTY-NINE

JETHRO

Sharing wasn't as bad as I thought it'd be. Who was I kidding? It was freaking awesome. I didn't have second thoughts about it at all. At first, the word "sharing" ruffled my ego's feathers. And Ash, well, the moment I laid eyes on her, I wanted to keep her to myself. That would have never happened, though; she wasn't that kind of woman. Working beside her made me realize I wanted a life partner. Being inside her changed everything. The moment I came inside her I knew she was mine for life. My heart, body, and soul kicked my ego to the side and forced me to leap.

Following her to Talon's rooftop residence was the best damned decision I'd ever made. It was odd at first. I wasn't sure how to navigate being around two other men who were also in love with my woman. Turns out, the entire process was smooth and felt natural.

Aisling was our queen in every sense of the word. We adored her, all three of us. When she moved, we moved. If she wanted or needed something, we got it for her. Sometimes even before she said anything. It was our goal to not only meet her needs but to also surpass every conceivable expectation. She was our sun, and we were happy to orbit around her as one cohesive unit.

And Ash, being the kind and generous spirit that she was, returned our attentions in kind. She wasn't a bitchy tyrant. Bratty, yes. But she wasn't a user. She gave as much as she got, which was nothing short of miraculous since the odds weren't exactly in her favor. The three-to-one odds didn't make a difference though. She handled our individual and group demands without leaving anyone to feel neglected. She certainly deserved our undying love and loyalty.

As far as her other men, I couldn't ask for cooler dudes to be in a relationship with. Yeah, relationship. We'd gone beyond crossing swords, thanks to yours truly. I liked playing both sides of the field, and Ash was into it. Her acceptance was a relief. I never thought I'd meet a woman who was okay with my choices. If Ash hadn't been, the relationship wouldn't have lasted long. The added bonus to having Ash's acceptance was having the guys on board. It was the best of both worlds for me.

Sex aside, our camaraderie came easier than expected. I had history with Talon, which helped. We'd been good friends in college. And we were able to pick up where we left off. Pope was one of those men who got along with everyone. You could throw him into any situation and he'd adapt and make the best of it.

I'd never worried about my future or money. Relationships were something I didn't consider after Jess and I had called it quits. Now, with Ash, Talon, and Pope, everything seemed brighter.

So, why was I leaving it all behind to drive to Meridian City? Because of the one phone call that planted a seedling of doubt. Once that had taken root the only thing I could envision was how it would go to shit and it would be my fault.

"You haven't returned yet. I'm disappointed. I thought you were smarter than that. Since you need a little prodding, let me make myself clear. You can't have her, Jethro. I didn't bring Aisling into Buchanan Pharmaceuticals for you. She is mine. I have plans for her. Big plans. You can't compete with me, Junior. Everything you have is because of me. CEO is just a title. I could disinherit you with the stroke of a pen.

Do you want me to come down there and prove it to you? In front of her?"

"Stay away from her. Stay away from Port Midway. I'm coming home."

I scrubbed my hand down my face. I should have told her instead of taking off while she was asleep. But no, I snuck out like a bitch. If that wasn't cowardly enough, I left the note at the rental because I didn't want the guys to find it. Talon and Pope would never forgive me. Would she forgive me? She loved me. I knew she did. Even if she did forgive me, what good would it do? Harlo would disown me because he could, and then I'd have nothing to offer her. And who was I without my family name and my family money? Nothing. And my father knew it. The fucker had sex with my ex-fiancee. He wouldn't hesitate to take everything away and reduce me to nothing. I was born into privilege and wouldn't know where to begin without it.

He controlled me. And her, too. That secret little project of hers belonged to him and I had a feeling he knew what she was working on. I palmed the vial in my pocket.

"Hand me a bottle of water while you're up," Pope said as I got out of bed. Ash and Talon were in the shower and since I was the best cook in the group, I was going to fix something to eat. We'd had ourselves a sexy little orgy, which always made Aisling hungry.

I opened the mini fridge in Talon's bedroom, which was empty aside from little glass bottles filled with liquid. I pulled one out and was ready to open it when Pope said, "I wouldn't do that if I were you."

"What is it?" I asked.

"Ash's lady supplements or something."

I popped the top and brought it to my nose. Herbal with a medicinal undertone. I flicked my tongue over the rim.

"Don't!" Pope warned. "Now you're going to grow ovaries and start laying eggs."

I chuckled. "I'm sure you know this, but I'll say it anyway . . . that's not how it works, Pope."

"Whatever. Don't say I didn't warn you when your boobies get swollen and sensitive and you start shooting eggs out of your ass." He shrugged.

Fucking, Pope. He managed to make everything hilarious. I laughed and snuck a bottle in my pocket.

What were you working on, little monster? I mused as I continued driving to the city.

Whatever it was, I was sure my father wanted it. And I needed to find a way to protect her somehow. She knew whatever was created in that lab of hers belonged to him. She had to. It was in black and white.

I glanced at my phone, which was on the passenger seat beside me. I'd turned it off as soon as I left Talon's. I didn't want to talk to her or any of the guys. I'd wanted to turn around and go back a million times. The minute I heard her voice, I knew I would go back to her. I couldn't. Did she call me? I reached for the phone and then stopped myself. Thirty more minutes, Jet.

Please don't hate me, Aisling. Let me figure this out and figure out how to protect you.

CHAPTER FORTY

POPE

"Thanks, Igor," I said, as he helped me with a few boxes. We were officially moving into Talon's place. I'd gotten a few of Aisling's things while she was working and some of mine, too. Talon's penthouse was larger than mine and Ash's combined. As spacious as it was, the space felt cramped with four of us living in a one-bedroom, so I didn't pack everything. Just the basics. Mostly my gear. I could work with my phone if needed, but it was faster, and I could multi-task with my full set-up. I'd brought enough to get by. I ran my hand through my hair and stared at the five boxes.

"You need me to bring this upstairs, or is the boss setting you up with an office?" Igor asked.

"Uh, let's leave it." I shook his hand, and he exited Talon's office.

I used my keycard and climbed the stairwell to the penthouse, carrying a suitcase of Ash's things. She'd given me a list of things she couldn't live without, which was a bunch of hot girl shit. I smiled thinking about her.

"Jet, you motherfucker. This is the tenth message I've left you in the last fucking hour. Call me back asshole." Talon's gruff voice reverberated through the penthouse.

Uh oh, someone's pissed. What the fuck did Jethro do?

The last few days had been incredible. *Did it already go to shit in less than,* I looked at the time, *eight hours?*

Talon was pacing a trench in his fancy zebra wood flooring. His rage was thick and suffocating. I remained in the doorway to his office and waited a full beat until he realized I was there.

"Do I even want to know?" I asked when he finally met my gaze.

"Please tell me you've heard from Jet?" he asked without answering my question.

"Uhh . . . no. Isn't he downstairs working with Ash?"

"Nope. The fucker has disappeared. He didn't show up at the office. And he hasn't returned my texts or calls. Or Ash's."

"What do you mean disappeared?" I asked. His words weren't making a lick of sense.

He told me about his visit to Ash's office.

"He's not gone. He can't be. Is his stuff still here?"

Talon waved his hand, a see-for-yourself gesture.

Did that fucker leave town? Without telling her? Or any of us?

I went to the bedroom and ensuite. Nothing was amiss. He hadn't brought much, a shaving kit, and a few clothing items, all of which were still where they'd been the past few days. Maybe he was coming right back.

Talon was pacing again, his phone clutched tightly in his hand. I dialed Jet's phone. No answer. Sent a text. No response.

"I don't get it. Did he say anything to you?" I asked Talon.

"Not really. I was up late, working, and heard mumbling. He was in the kitchen, phone in hand. He told me he'd gotten a call earlier in the day from the owner of the house he was renting. They wanted to do a walk-through in the morning before returning his deposit. He said he was leaving a message. It didn't sound like a big deal. He left before any of us woke. That was hours ago."

"Son of a bitch." I tipped my head to face the ceiling, endless possibilities racing through my mind. "Do you think she did something to him?"

"The first thing I did was check the surveillance. He left before six alone. Ash left the building this afternoon for lunch."

"This isn't good. Is Ash okay?"

"No." He huffed out a whoosh of air. "She's acting like she is. But she's not. The pain reflected in Aisling's eyes broke me. She's worried and hurt. I played it off like it was nothing because I didn't want to cause her any more grief. We need to find him."

"Shit. Help me with my gear. I'll see if I can track him."

Talon followed me downstairs to his official office, where my boxes sat off in the corner.

"Is this it?" He scratched his chin.

"Yeah. I only brought a fraction of what I normally work with but it's enough to get the job done," I replied.

"Upstairs or down here. There's a workspace temps use. It's empty."

"Let's check it out."

The space was more than adequate. It was a corner office with a big window and about the size of my loft. All of my gear would fit, and I'd still have room for more.

"This will work," I grinned. "Are you sure this is okay?"

Talon frowned. "Why wouldn't it be? I own the place. But um . . . never mind."

"Tell me, Tal. If this is going to be a problem . . ."

"No," he cut me off. "Not a problem. I thought we needed a bigger place since there are . . . were four of us."

"Are, Talon. There are four of us. We'll find him."

He nodded and helped me set up my system which took a while, with wiring and shit. I also needed to tap into a wifi system outside of the building to ensure I couldn't be tracked. It wasn't difficult but it took time, and the task was important. The last thing I wanted was for my clandestine hobbies to be traced back to Talon and Ash.

Once the system was set, I got to work, searching for Jet via every available system online, which wouldn't be easy since his phone was off. I did what I could while Talon went to his office to make calls. He had everyone at his disposal looking for him.

I sent Ash a text, telling her how much I loved her. She replied right away. I wanted to go downstairs and wrap my arms around her, but fucking Jet.

He was in love with Ash just as much as I was. What would make him leave? Unless he didn't. Had he been kidnapped? Did someone kill him? Was he in an accident? I scanned local 911 dispatch calls and called hospitals. Port Midway wasn't a huge town. The population was not even a half-million. Still, it took a while, and I had only so many screens to work with. Frustrated but determined, I kept at it for hours until Talon came in.

"He was sighted this morning at a gas station near the border," he said.

"What? What the hell does that mean?" I threw up my hands.

"He went home. To Meridian City."

"Without telling Ash or one of us? I swear I'm going to kick that fucker in the balls when I see him."

"Stand in line."

"Why the hell would he just leave? I thought we were good."

"Don't know. And yeah, I thought so. Are you able to access highway patrol feeds? I'm hoping he's fine but if he got into an accident, I'd rather be the one to tell Ash."

Fuck. I switched tactics and broadened the search which covered hundreds of miles. I grabbed a fresh cup of coffee from the breakroom and settled in for the time-consuming search.

I'd been so busy doing my thing that hours had passed, and I realized Ash hadn't responded to my last text.

"Talon!" I covered my phone and shouted.

"What's up?" He appeared at my doorway.

"Have you heard from Ash?"

"Uh no. Shit. Call her."

"I'm on the line with a hospital," I pointed.

"Is he?"

I shrugged. There was an emergency room, about halfway to Meridian City. The nice woman on the phone put me on hold while she checked the list of admittees for the day.

Talon put his phone on speaker and called Ash. She picked up on the second ring.

"Mate. Where are you? Are you okay?" he asked, his voice surprisingly calm.

"Yes. I went to Jet's rental. He left me a note." Her voice was meek and weary.

"What did he say?" Anger oozed out of his pores.

"I haven't read it yet. I've been driving." She sniffled.

My heart fractured.

"Come home, baby. Let's read it together," Talon pleaded.

"Sir?" The operator at the hospital said into the phone at my ear.

"Please hold," I told her and focused on Ash's voice.

"I need some space. I'll be home soon. I love you. Tell Pope I love him, too."

She hung up.

Shit. Talon's shoulders sagged.

"I'm sorry, ma'am," I said to the operator.

"No worries. You're in luck. No one by that name was admitted today. I hope that's good news."

"Yep. Thanks," I replied and disconnected the call.

"What now?" I swiveled my chair to face Talon.

"Track her phone, Pope."

I turned back to my computer station and started typing. My system was in the middle of running facial recognition on Jet and his license plate.

"I don't have my full set-up. I'll need to abandon the search for Jet," I told him.

"Do it. Fuck Jet. If he's hurt, he's hurt. Aisling is our priority." Talon stood behind my chair with his imposing figure.

I switched off the search on Jet and rerouted everything to look for Ash.

"Give me a minute. I'll come get you when I've found something," I told him.

Talon reluctantly left me to do my thing and returned an hour later. "Anything?"

My fingers flew over my keyboard, as I replied, "She turned off her phone. What is with her and Jet turning off their phones?"

Talon groaned.

"Shit." My fingers flew over the keyboard.

"What's wrong?" he asked, standing directly behind me.

"The last known location was here. From almost two hours ago." I pointed to the map. "Why the hell is she all the way down there?" I felt like I ran a thousand miles in the desert.

"God damn it." Talon snarled.

"That's the best I can do. The tracker hasn't moved, it seems." I began typing and found a satellite picture. "She's at a fast-food joint."

"Let's head out," he said.

CHAPTER FORTY-ONE

AISLING

After reading Jet's note, I drove around aimlessly and ended up at the pier in a spot overlooking the water. It was a seedy part of Port Midway where fishing boats docked. It was quieter than being on the Strand, and it suited my mood. I needed a moment. Jet's note left a hole in my heart. It was total bullshit.

> *I love you Aisling. But I have to go home. Forgive me for not telling you face to face. Maybe someday I'll have the courage to explain. For now . . . forget about me, Ash. You're better off without me. Jet*

He had to go home, he said. No explanation as to why. I could have called his father. But Harlo was the last person I wanted to speak with. Hell, I didn't want to speak to anyone. I was lost.

The world felt hazy. And my heart felt like Jet had raked hot coals over it and left the wound open for the crows to pick at it. I wandered around the pier for a while and stopped at a convenience store to buy a bottle of tequila. It was a cheap brand, the type that would get you drunk and leave a wicked headache the next morning. Perfect. I trudged around drinking straight from the bottle concealed in a paper bag. I must've looked like an addict. I didn't care. I wanted to forget it all. I wanted to be numb and oblivious to the world. I wanted to forget Jethro Buchanan.

We were perfect together. Why would he throw it away? Was he married? He didn't act like a married man. Not that I would know. Don't married men wear rings or mention their wives at least once? A slip of the tongue?

I pressed the bottle to my lips and tilted my head until my gaze looked up at the night sky. Nothing came out. I pulled it out of the bag and peered at the bottom. Hmmm . . . no leak. That's weird.

Music blared in the distance. *Oh, look at that. They must have alcohol and I'm fresh out.* I followed the smooth strum of guitars and the melodic voice singing about a "Stairway to Heaven".

The scent of greasy food and stale beer welcomed me into the dive bar. I moved through the crowd and found a seat at the counter.

"What can I get you, miss?" the bartender asked.

"Margarita with salt. And food."

He slid over a laminated paper menu which had three food items. Hot Wings. Cheeseburger. Hot Dog. Healthy options. I ordered some wings, ate a little, and drank a lot more.

The cover band switched to happier tunes and soon I was singing along to "What's Up" and dancing by myself. The sting of Jet's note ebbed its way out of my consciousness and I was having a great time. *Yeah, that's right. Fuck you, Jet.*

He said he loved me. And he left me.

"Who left you, sweetheart?" a male voice asked.

Did I say that out loud? I blinked at the man with a kind voice. He was . . . blurry.

"My boyfriend," I slurred. "One of them."

There was a chuckle behind me, and I swung around to see who it was and the world swayed.

"It's okay, sweetheart, we won't leave you," Chuckles said.

My heart clenched. And I released a deep sob. "I love him."

"Awww. You poor thing."

A warm arm draped around my shoulders. "Would you like another drink?"

"Yes!"

"I'll get it. What are you drinking, gorgeous?" a third man asked.

"How long did it take to grow that?" I reached out a hand to touch his thick beard.

The men laughed.

"You're a lot of fun. Why would anyone leave you?" Beard man said.

"Right?" I agreed.

"Fuck him. Let's drink. Shots!" Chuckles said.

I downed a shot, danced, and made more friends. We sang along as the band did their rendition of "Sweet Child of Mine" and had another shot. Life was nothing but drinks, dancing, and making new friends. And for a moment, I was blissfully floating in oblivion.

The next thing I knew, I was walking down the pier to another party with three men.

"Look! Fishies!" I exclaimed, peering into dark murky waters.

"Careful, we don't need you to fall over," Kind voice said.

He put his arm around me and led the way to their boat.

"Aww are you taking care of me, kind voice man." I patted his face.

"Of course, I would never leave you. Least of all with a note."

I stopped, my hand pressed to my chest. "I love him. I love all of them."

"Hey, now. No more of that. We're going to party and leave all the heartache behind." Beard guy patted my back.

They led the way and I followed. Forget. Forget. Forget. That's all I wanted. That's what *he* wanted of me.

The boat bobbed along with the gentle waves. I sat cross-legged on the wooden deck, drawing ocean air deep into my lungs. As the lights of Port Midway became smaller and smaller, my mind became a little clearer, but my heart was an anchor weighing me down.

"Come with me. The party is downstairs." Chuckles put his arms under my armpits and helped me stand and walk. My legs were useless noodles unable to carry my heavy body.

After a couple of missteps, I managed my way below deck. It was cramped and messy. Food containers and bottles of booze were strewn across every surface. Stacks of unwashed laundry covered the bed. The stench of body odor and cigarettes filled the cabin. And three men surrounded me.

"You're not my men," I slurred. My mind sluggishly tried to catch up with the reality of my situation.

"Your men left you remember. You're with us now. We're going to sail away from all of your problems," Kind voice said.

"No. I don't want to sail away." I shook my head.

"No, you don't. You just want to party, right?" Beard man said.

"Where is everybody?" I asked. *There were other people at the bar, right?*

"This is it. You are the party," Kind voice told me with eyes that were . . . sinister.

I bolted to the door. Strong arms gripped my arms and forced me onto a bed.

Oh fuck, Ash. My foggy thoughts cleared, and I realized this was bad, bad, bad.

I swung my fists and kicked my legs.

"Keep still!"

"No!! Let me go!!" I punched and kicked, desperate to be anywhere but in that boat.

Thwack!! My face stung. Copper-tasting liquid filled my mouth. My vision went spotty. And the rush of adrenaline vanished, leaving me limp and vulnerable.

"Not the face, asshole! No evidence, remember?"

"Hold her down!!"

A strong grip pinned my torso. *No!* I shouted in my head, but the words didn't come out.

A glint of metal flashed in the dimly lit cabin. The sound of fabric ripping echoed in my ears. *No! I don't want this.*

My legs were spread painfully wide. "No. Please, don't do this," I whimpered.

They say people in extremely stressful situations have two physiological reactions—flight or fight. I think they missed an *F*. Because, at that moment, I couldn't do either. I was paralyzed with fear, shame, and regret. Instead of flight or fight . . . I FROZE.

A switch flipped in my brain, and I welcomed the darkness.

CHAPTER FORTY-TWO

AISLING

The gentle sway rocked me with a false sense of safety. I squeezed my eyelids tight as a veil of red filled my vision. The movement made me wince at the tenderness on the right side of my face. My hand clenched around something hard and flat—my lifeline.

Wake up, Aisling!

My inner voice shouted.

You need to get help. Wake up.

I blinked rapidly and grimaced as the room came into focus. Dead eyes stared at me. I bolted upright and scrambled to the edge of the bed, my heart jackhammering in my chest. No, no, no!

Kind voice guy lay next to me, his chest covered in blood.

Fear and revulsion rolled up and down my spine. I brought my hands up to cover my screams and realized I was holding a knife, the sharp edge covered in red. A violent tremor racked my body causing me to drop the knife, my lifeline, my only means of protection in this hell.

Get out, Ash.

I backed away from the dead man, bracing my hand on the wall to steady myself. The galloping of my racing heart thundered in my ears. I stumbled out of the room, trudging through my fugue to find my way. The boat wasn't big, but it felt cavernous in my time of crisis. The corridor seemed to stretch for miles, and it felt like I was looking at the world through someone else's eyes.

A few steps from the bed, I tripped over another prone form. The man with the thick beard lay in a puddle of blood with his belly sliced open and his guts spilling out. The stench of death, blood, and excrement hit me all at once. My stomach lurched and I heaved and heaved, emptying everything I drank and ate earlier in the day.

I scrambled on my hands and knees through the blood and vomit-covered floor, desperate to get far away from the carnage. The sight of the stairway brought tears to my eyes but there was just one problem, another body was there, blocking my only exit.

"No!" The sound of my voice was desperate and helpless and came from the depths of my being.

Chuckles slowly turned his head. "Don't kill me, please," he croaked. Blood dripped from a deep gash on his throat. In his weakened state, he attempted to clamber up the steps. To escape . . . from me.

"Let me help. I'll call the police. Or harbor authority." I searched my crossbody purse, miraculously still draped over my shoulders. Keys, make-up, wallet. No fucking phone. Dammit Aisling.

"Is there a radio? Or a phone?"

"Galley," he gurgled. Blood bubbled out of his wound.

I gagged but nothing came up. I searched the galley and found three phones sitting beside an overflowing ashtray.

I fumbled with the phones and went back to the stairs. "I need a passcode."

The man's head was lolled to the side and his eyes vacant.

"No. No. No. What did I do? Did I do this?" I paced in the small space."Think, Aisling."

I had three phones. Three dead bodies. I hovered the phone in front of the stairwell guy's face. On the last try, it unlocked, and I dialed the only number I remembered by heart.

There was no signal.

Fucking dammit!

I climbed the stairs, inching past the dead body. There was nothing but darkness all around me. The ocean was black—the sky's mirror image. The crescent moon frowned down on me, judging me for my crimes.

I swallowed past the bile in my throat and tried the phone. It rang and rang then went to voicemail.

Please. I pleaded with the universe.

I pressed redial.

"Hello?"

"Pope!" I sobbed.

"Angel?"

"I'm in trouble."

"Tell me where you are, babe, we're coming."

"I don't know. I'm on a boat."

"Shit. Talk to Talon, I need to get on my laptop,"

"Mate, are you hurt?"

"No. But. I . . . I think I did something bad," I cried.

"It's okay, we'll find you, baby. We'll take care of everything. I promise."

"I don't know where I am. I'm on a boat. And I can't see anything." My words came out in a panicked rush.

"I got you, angel. I'm tracking the phone," Pope said in the background.

"Is anyone with you?" Talon asked.

"Not anymore," I stammered.

"It's okay. The main thing is you're alive. And safe. Just stay on the line with me."

"Got it!" Pope shouted.

They muttered between themselves and then Talon said, "I know where that is, baby. You're not far."

"I'm not?"

"Not really. You're a few miles offshore, but close to my mom's. Do you know anything about boats?"

"No."

"Okay, I'm going to walk you through a couple of things. I want to make sure the boat isn't drifting."

I woodenly followed Talon's instructions, not registering what I was doing. It wasn't making much sense. Nothing was. It was like I was in an alternate reality, and I wasn't in my body.

Talon directed and I used the phone light to navigate my way around. I found the helm and turned on the lights. In the distance, buoys were bobbing in the water. He guided me to the anchor. Once I confirmed there was tension on the rope, Talon sounded less stressed.

"Should I . . . call the police?"

"No," Talon and Pope said at the same time.

"Wait until we get there, babe."

There was a lot of shuffling on the line as my men did whatever they were doing to rescue me.

"Keep the line open, angel. I want to make sure I don't lose the signal," Pope told me.

"K." I went to the helm and curled into the ball on the floor.

Tires screeched in the background.

"Ash, we're close. The phone will be on mute but don't hang up. Sit tight."

"Okay." Exhaustion hit, and my eyelids felt very heavy.

The events leading up to the blackout were loud and clear. They were going to hurt me. Rape me. Did they? I didn't want to face reality yet. I wanted to go home and forget.

A thick film of ick covered my skin from head to toe. It wasn't the blood or the vomit. It was *it*. Whatever had happened to me clung to my body like filth-covered saran wrap.

I glanced down at all the blood, which didn't seem to be mine. My body had been numb since I'd woken, so I couldn't tell if I was injured. My tank was barely hanging on my frame, my yoga pants were gone. My panties were in place, which had to be a good sign or so I'd hoped. I hung on to that fantasy with everything I had.

A barrage of conflicting emotions whirled through me on a continuous loop. Shock. *This couldn't be real life.* Fear. *Will my guys find me? Will I die here in the middle of the ocean?* Guilt. *What did I do?* Shame. *How could I be so stupid? I should know better.* Panic. *I'm going to jail for murder. I could claim self-defense, but could I really? I willingly got drunk and boarded this boat with three strange men. Yes, they took advantage of me. Yes, I said no. Yes, I asked them to stop. Would a jury side with me? Or with them?* Pride. *They were going to hurt me. And now they were dead. And I was alive.* Confusion. *How did I do this?*

The reality of it all was too much. I was drowning. Every emotion and every question stole my breath and pulled me under. I couldn't make sense of the situation. So, I just laid there plagued by my thoughts and covered in filth so thick I felt it in my soul.

CHAPTER FORTY-THREE

TALON

It took almost two hours to get to the twenty-four-hour taco joint looking for Ash. She wasn't there but her phone was. The cashier was kind enough to hold the phone Ash had left behind and her food order. I had to snarl at the woman for her to hand over the phone, but she did, and Pope and I resumed our search.

"Where to next?" He packed up his satchel.

"Try her apartment first," I replied.

He drove. It had been hours since we last spoke to Aisling. In a normal situation, I would have respected her wish to be alone. Our Ash was unique and so alone time wasn't something we could grant her.

"She didn't come here. Everything is as I left it when I was here to pack her things." Pope told me and we got back in his car. It was a long shot, but I had to check.

I'd already called Zoey. Pope called Nelson. No one had seen her.

We circled the areas where she'd killed even though Pope had scanned traffic cam footage. We even drove to the brothel on the east side of town. We had just left Jet's old rental and were driving around near the pier when his cell rang. He let it go to voicemail.

"Who was that?" I asked.

"Unknown caller."

It rang again.

"Answer it, it might be her."

"Hello," he answered through his car phone speaker.

"Pope!" Ash sobbed.

My heart skipped a beat.

"Angel?"

"I'm in trouble."

Fuck.

"Tell me where you are, babe, we'll come get you."

"I don't know. I'm on a boat."

Double-fuck.

"Shit. Hold on a sec." Pope stopped in the middle of the street, and we changed seats.

"Mate, are you hurt?" I asked.

"No. But. I . . . I think I did something bad."

I put the car in gear and drove toward the pier, the closest port.

"It's okay, we'll find you, baby. We'll take care of everything. I promise." I clenched the steering wheel anxiously waiting for Pope to pinpoint her location.

"I don't know where I am. It's dark. I can't see anything." The sound of her weak voice killed me.

"I got you, angel. I'm tracking the phone," Pope said.

"Is anyone with you?" Talon asked.

"Not anymore," she stammered.

The meaning of her words was received loud and clear. Pope spared me a glance.

"It's okay. The main thing is you're alive. And safe. Just stay on the line with me."

"Got it!" Pope shouted.

My mother loved the water, and we'd gone sailing a lot when I was a kid. I didn't gravitate toward it like she and my sister did, but I was familiar with the basics.

"I know where that is, baby. You're not far."

"I'm not?"

"Not really. You're a few miles offshore, but close to my mom's. Do you know anything about boats?"

"No."

Shit, the last thing we needed was for the damned boat to drift out to sea. I walked her through a couple of things while speeding to the pier.

"Should I . . . call the police?"

"No," we answered.

"Wait until we get there, babe."

I skidded the Tesla into the parking lot which was empty aside from my car.

"Shit, I'll need to scan this area for security cameras."

"Not now. Ash first."

He fiddled with his phone and then said, "Please tell me you have a boat."

"Nope. We're borrowing one."

"Works for me."

We ran down the pier, and I chose a boat that was old and had been sitting at the dock for a while. My father bought it for my mother years ago. We had to sell it to pay for my college tuition. When I began making money, I wanted to buy it back, but the new owner refused to sell. He had taken good care of the vessel, and it had been his home. He'd died recently and there was a dispute with distant relatives as to who would inherit it.

"Do you know how to drive this thing?" Pope asked.

"It's been a while but . . .." I put the boat in reverse and scraped the dock.

"Move." He handed me his phone and took over. "Put that up here, will ya?"

He pointed at the phone with his chin.

I did as he asked and went below deck searching for things that could be useful to mask a crime scene. There wasn't much, mostly blankets and a few cooking utensils. In one of the storage benches, I found scuba gear and snagged two pairs of diving gloves.

At the helm, Pope navigated the dark ocean. "Almost there." He glanced at the gloves and gave me a curt nod.

Ash wasn't far out. Whomever she was with had taken her to the west of Port Midway which wound its way to Shadow Cove. Local legends say it had been a portal for demons to cross a millennium ago. Now multi-million-dollar homes dotted the shoreline. I purchased an old Victorian-style home years ago at an auction. It had been weather-worn, termite-infested, and mold-ridden. It had been a complete rebuild. My mother loved it, and I'd gifted it to her when the renovations were complete. She and my sister lived in the main house, and I lived in the guest house, which had been the servants' quarters. I didn't need much, and I'd already had my sights on another property that was about to go into foreclosure.

"There it is." Pope pointed in the distance.

Fucking finally. The *Waverider* bobbed peacefully with the rise and fall of the ocean.

Pope brought us starboard and parked as close as he could. "Can you . . ." he began. I was already leaping onto the other boat leaving Pope to deal with rafting the boats together.

I crossed the upper deck to the helm, where I'd instructed Ash to stay until we arrived.

My stomach dropped.

Aisling was in the fetal position shaking like a leaf. She was half naked and her body was covered in blood and muck . . . vomit, I presumed from the smell.

"Hi, baby," I approached warily.

She jolted awake and backed away from me.

"It's me, mate. You're safe now."

"Talon?" She blinked.

"Hi, Red. Let's get you home."

She stumbled into my arms, her body wracked with heavy sobs. I held her close to my chest and carried her to the other boat where Pope was waiting.

He helped me get her settled below deck, and we tucked her in on one of the benches covering her with blankets. She wept the entire time.

"We'll be right back, baby. You're safe here."

"No, no, no, no. You can't. Don't leave me here," she begged.

"I need to take care of something and then we'll go."

"No, Talon. Don't. Don't go down there. Please."

"Pope will stay here with you. I'll be quick." I tore myself away before she convinced me to stay.

Pope was right behind me.

"Stay with her," I told him.

"No, Talon. I don't want you to deal with this alone."

"She needs you here. I got this. You dealt with the others by yourself. I'll do this one." I grabbed a pair of diving gloves and leaped over again.

Not wanting to leave fingerprints, I slipped on the diving gloves and went down the narrow steps of the *Waverider*.

Fuck me dead. There was so much blood. So, so much. I swallowed hard.

The body lying at the bottom of the steps had a deep gash on his throat.

I steadied my breath and kept moving. On the way to what would have been the captain's quarters another body was on the floor. Eviscerated. I bit the inside of my cheek and leaned over to see another body on the bed. Several stab wounds to the chest. A knife lay on the floor covered in blood.

I stepped away from the gruesome scene and scanned my surroundings. It was a small fishing boat the three men had probably lived on. They were scumbags judging by the way they lived. Booze and cigarettes everywhere. Not to mention the soiled laundry. The alcohol and cigarettes gave me an idea and I went to work.

"Talon?" I turned toward Pope's voice. "You've been gone for a while. Ash is asleep and I wanted to . . . holy fuck." He grimaced. "See if you need help."

"Thanks, man. I'm done. Here's what you need to do."

I watched him disembark and sail away, then went back below deck and lit it up. I doused each body with alcohol and covered everywhere in between. I turned up the propane, turned on the engine, and gunned the throttle while the anchor was securely in place. The engine groaned and the anchor started to lift. I hit the retraction button on the anchor, lit the strand of material sticking out of the bottle filled with more booze, threw it below deck, and then dove into the black water.

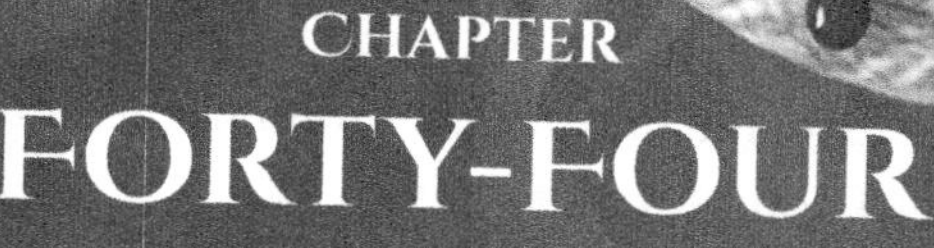

CHAPTER FORTY-FOUR

POPE

"Don't let him go in there. Don't let him see, Pope. Please." Ash sobbed in my arms. I rocked her back and forth and held her as tight as I could.

"He'll be okay, angel. Talon is a tough son-of-a-bitch. He can handle anything, and he'll be back in no time."

"I did bad things." Her voice trembled. "I'm an awful, stupid, bad person."

"Easy, now, you're talking about the love of my life," I said in a stern but quiet voice.

"You shouldn't love me. Wouldn't. If you knew how horrible I am."

"Hey, listen to me, Aisling. I love you no matter what. There is nothing you or anyone else could do to make me not love you anymore. I am always by your side. Trust me, Ash. Trust in my love for you."

She wept until eventually her breathing evened out and her body stopped shaking.

Where the fuck was Talon?

He'd been gone for too long. I knew he could handle himself, but

I was anxious to get home.

I untangled Ash from my arms and laid her on the bench. I hated to leave her, but it was time to go.

The smell hit me before I went below. I took a deep breath which didn't help.

"Talon? You've been gone for a while. Ash is asleep and I wanted to . . . holy fuck." I peered around his broad frame at the grizzly scene. "I wanted to see if you needed help."

He was in the main cabin dousing the dead with a liter of vodka.

"Thanks, man. I'm done." His voice was rough. "Here's what you need to do."

Following his orders, I sped away to what I estimated to be a safe distance, then anchored and waited.

A few minutes went by, and I heard a splash. I shined a light on the water, watching for any sign of him.

Boom!

I dropped to the floor. The *Waverider* went up in flames.

"Pope! Talon!" Ash shouted.

"I'm here, Ash." I crossed the length between us and gathered her in my arms.

"Where's Talon? What happened?" she asked, her eyes taking in the blaze of fire.

"He's fine. Come, you can help." I handed her a flood light and we scoured the surface.

Come on, Talon. Could wolves even swim? Fuck, it should have been me.

"Talon!" Ash rushed to the side of the boat.

I hurried over to help him climb aboard.

Ash tackled him and so did I. We held onto each other as the *Waverider* crumbled into the ocean.

"It's gone," she murmured.

"It's over, angel," I said.

"You did this." Her gaze darted between me and Talon. "For me."

"We'd burn down a fleet of ships for you, Aisling." Talon stroked her cheek.

"Thank you." She stretched her arms around us and sobbed. "I love you. So much."

"Take us home, Pope," Talon said.

I sped back to the pier and parked the boat.

Ash had fallen asleep, and Talon hoisted her in his arms and began walking toward my car.

"Follow me, Pope," he said, heading toward his vehicle parked farther down the lot.

"I should take care of this," I jutted my chin out toward the pier.

"Fuck. How long?"

"Thirty minutes tops."

"Take down my address in Shadow Cove. It's five minutes. We'll be in the guest house. Take the long driveway and veer to the right. You won't miss it."

I typed in his info and then pressed my body against Aisling who was still peacefully sleeping in his arms.

Talon leaned in, resting his forehead on mine. "Hurry, Pope."

He let out a weary breath. I cupped his nape, pressed a kiss to his forehead, and laid one on Ash.

"See you both soon."

Talon double-timed to his car, carrying Ash as if she weighed nothing, and sped away.

I pulled out my laptop and began a search of all cameras in the area. There weren't many aside from the cameras on the main road. There was a bait and tack shop, a sundry store, and a restaurant slash bar. All three establishments had archaic systems that weren't readily online which meant I had to physically go in and dismantle the security feeds. Easy to do. The restaurant had a more modern system. The type of security surveillance that archived video in the cloud. If I had to guess, that was where Ash had met the recently deceased.

A part of me was curious so I scanned the videos starting from the call where she had said Jet left her a note. An hour or so later, Ash walked in and sat at the bar. Even with downcast eyes filled with sadness, she was still gorgeous. And she was drinking. Three men approached her. She kept drinking. She danced and sang along to the band. She was trying to forget about Jet, and she kept drinking. The guys kept buying shots. Fuckers.

I deleted everything. I didn't want to see any more than I already had.

After that, I went to the sundry store, and let myself in through the employee entrance. It was small and they didn't even have an alarm system. The security feed was an old tape-over system. I rewound the video from the day and sure enough, Ash walked in and bought a bottle of tequila. That got tucked into my laptop bag and I replaced the missing tape with another sitting on the shelf.

I did the same at the bait and tackle store, then headed to Shadow Cove.

Not even five minutes later, I was cruising down a long driveway, passing a monstrous mansion, and parking beside Talon's car in front of a smallish home.

My phone rang. I was tempted to answer it but fuck him. I felt like I had been in a twelve-round heavyweight fight. Ash must've felt worse. I hit the decline option and gathered my things.

Unsure of what I was walking into, I crept in and closed the door quietly behind me.

"You happened, you fucking prick." Talon's menacing tone cut through the quiet house. "You have no idea what your actions caused. Stop fucking calling like you care."

The dim lighting was just enough for me to see a phone speeding at my face. I ducked just in time as it crash-landed into the wall behind me.

"Sorry. That wasn't meant for you." Talon gestured to his damaged phone.

I gave him a thumbs up. Jet. I understood.

Ash was in the bathtub, scrubbing furiously at her skin.

Talon pulled me away. "There's another bathroom and shower there." He pointed to the other side of the house. "Help yourself to whatever. We'll be in here when you're ready."

"Thanks." I took one more look at Ash, who was crying into her hands.

Aww, angel. I wish could reverse time for you.

CHAPTER FORTY-FIVE

AISLING

Pope and Talon's presence calmed me, and I slept like the dead. Still, I couldn't keep my eyes open. I woke and Pope asked if I was hungry. It was lunchtime, and I was still exhausted. This was the mother of all hangovers.

Sometime later, Talon crooned in my ear and peppered my face with light kisses. It made me smile, and gave me the strength to get out of bed.

I'd slept for hours and still had bags under my eyes, and the right side of my face was a bit tender, but at least it wasn't bruised or swollen.

I padded through the house following the sound of my men's voices. I'd been told we were in Talon's guest home in Shadow Cove. The exclusive neighborhood where the uber-rich lived. My wolf had stupid money, and although he said it was the designated guest home on the property, it was still huge, which meant the main house where his family lived had to have been at least three times the size.

Pope lifted me off my feet and spun us in a small circle. "Hi, angel."

"Hi."

"Hungry? You must be," he said.

I should have been, but my stomach was still in knots.

"Um . . ."

"Eat mate, at least a little. The chef made some chicken noodle soup and fresh bread."

The heavenly smell hit me waking my senses.

"Chef?"

"My mother has a chef," he began.

"Who he pays for." Pope pointed at Talon with his thumb.

I smiled.

"Anyway, yes, chef. My mom and sister are out of town for another week or so. The staff gets bored."

"Staff?" I asked, unable to hide my smile.

"There it is," Pope said and kissed my cheek.

Talon smiled back at me with his hand extended. I grasped his hand and let him guide me to a glass breakfast table that overlooked a quaint garden.

"This is beautiful, wolfy."

"Are you teasing, mate?"

My cheeks heated.

"There it is." He laid a wet kiss on my lips.

I ate while Talon and Pope ribbed each other about their favorite sports team.

It seemed so normal, except someone was missing. I glanced around the room. There was a kitchen beside the breakfast table and living area to my right and beyond that was where I slept, the bedroom. The penthouse had dark walls with bold accents. This place had a beige base with dark accents. Talon did have good taste.

"Your phone is on the nightstand. Do you want me to bring it to you?" Pope asked.

"I already talked to Zoey, if that's what you're worried about," Talon added.

"Um . . . no, it's okay, I don't need it. As long as Zoey knows I'm okay."

They both nodded. I stuffed a piece of bread in my mouth and asked, "Jet?"

There was no mistaking the emotion that rolled off my men. They were mad. No, livid.

"He's home. I spoke with him briefly last night. He's called us," Talon pointed between him and Pope. "A few times. I texted and told him you'd call him when you're ready."

I kept chewing and chewing, then forced myself to swallow. "Okay."

"Do you want to talk about it?" Talon asked.

"Not yet. I think I'm going to lay down for a little while."

"Whatever you need," he said.

I dozed off for a while and woke feeling restless. A part of me didn't want to face the world but I knew I had to.

The sound of my men speaking gave me comfort and so I dragged my butt to the bathroom. I took a long shower and dressed leisurely. Someone had packed lingerie and a silky robe I never wore but loved. I took my time on purpose. Making every excuse to delay the inevitable. They saw me at my lowest and were still with me. It was time to come clean.

I turned on my phone which had a dozen texts and messages from Jet. My eyes watered. Why was I missing him? I shouldn't.

You have men who truly love you, Ash. Fuck him.

I set the phone down and went into the living room. My men greeted me with warm smiles.

I stood at the edge of the room and let the words tumble out before I lost my nerve. "I uh . . . I have an issue." I pointed at my head. "I'm not sure what it is exactly. I've been trying to self-medicate and so far, it's worked. Well, until recently. Not sure. Anyway, yeah so I blackout, and I don't remember. I think it's a psychological issue. Or a mental disorder. I have these episodes and wake up feeling weird. And the doctors couldn't find anything wrong with me. My mother helped me with this herbal concoction when I was little. And then it stopped working when I became an adult, and then I figured out a combination of human meds and herbs and it was working, and then it stopped. And then um, I'm not sure what happens because sometimes, like this last weekend I didn't take anything and felt fine. And yesterday I realized I hadn't taken a tonic and so I drank one midday. And then I was sad. So sad." My voice trembled and a tear escaped my eyes and traveled down my cheek.

Pope stood. I held out my hand telling him to stay put.

"And so, I just um . . . wanted to forget, so I had a few drinks. And got carried away. And ended up on that boat. And I didn't want to be with them, I swear. I wanted to forget. I wanted to have fun, and it was supposed to be a party or so I thought, but I was alone with them, and then they tried to . . ." I crumpled.

Talon caught me before I hit the floor, and he carried me to the couch. I kept talking, I needed to. "I don't know what happened after that. Honest. I woke up and they were dead. Well, not all. One was dying, and he was trying to get away from me."

I was full-on ugly crying by then. Talon and Pope had me sandwiched between them, their warm bodies pressed against mine offering support and love I didn't deserve.

"I think I did it. I don't know how, but I did. I know I did. I should turn myself in."

My men rocked me in their arms and let me cry.

After the tears had run their course, Pope handed me a glass of water. I sipped feeling shaky and yet relieved. It felt good to speak my truth.

"Do you guys hate me now?" I asked, my voice timid.

"Well," Talon started, and he and Pope exchanged a look.

My gaze switched between them.

"You might hate us," Pope said. "Please don't, Ash."

"What's going on?"

"We know, Aisling. Not all of it, but most of what you said. We already know," Talon added.

I shook my head. Not possible.

"I don't understand."

"This might take a while. And I think I'm going to need some of that expensive alcohol," Pope said.

"You're freaking me out." I sat up.

Talon cupped my face. "Hey, the most important thing for you to know is that we love you. And we're not going anywhere."

CHAPTER FORTY-SIX

TALON

Bringing Aisling home after the boating incident was rough. She was a shell of what she had been less than two days ago. Jet's disappearance was shocking, his note, which I read, pissed me off but had to have been devastating for her. The drinking was no big deal. Dealing with those guys on the boat had to have been frightening. And then to wake to find them dead, and that she caused their deaths had to be confusing and horrifying. And it all landed in her lap at the same damn time.

She slept for most of the day, woke up, and slept again. During that time, Pope and I worked a little. It was difficult to concentrate when she wasn't well. But we stayed close enough for her to hear our voices, assuring her she wasn't alone.

Jet had called and texted a million times. I finally told him she'd call him when she was ready. He fucked up. He knew it. He was sorry. He said something about needing to protect her, and he was working on it. Fuck him. We protected her. He didn't even realize what that meant. What that entailed.

I didn't give a shit about blowing up the boat and all that

evidence. The assholes shouldn't have taken advantage of a drunk woman in the first place.

It would take time for Ash to see it that way though. Even though I knew they hadn't violated her body in that way. I knew every inch of her. I witnessed with my own eyes and my wolf senses what she looked and smelled like before, during, and after sex, with three men. I knew without a doubt those fuckers didn't get that far.

I'd shared that fact with Ash but it didn't seem to register. When she was ready to talk about it I would reassure her over and over until it sunk in. It was important for her to know that she had nothing to be ashamed of. I told Pope and he was relieved. Still angry with those fucks and Jet, but he was relieved she had been spared at least that much.

The biggest hurdle was yet to come. She was aware of her blackout episodes but what she didn't know was how much we knew. Fuck me. That wasn't easy for Pope or myself to talk about. Nor would it be an easy thing for her to forgive. It was possible we could have prevented so much if we had said something in the first place.

Pope was chastising himself hard about it since he'd witnessed the beginning. At least he hadn't had sex with her while her alter ego was in charge. We weren't looking forward to having that conversation but here we were. A bottle of scotch later. All the cards were on the table.

Ash had been pacing during the entire confession, which was good. She hadn't bolted out the door. If she had, I was ready. My wolf was on edge, anticipating her every move.

"Okay, let me get this straight." She stopped pacing and pinched the bridge of her nose. She faced Pope. "You've been stalking me. And you've seen me during this . . . I don't know what to call it . . . blackout state before?"

He gulped his drink and croaked, "Yep."

"And you witnessed me killing people and you covered it up, every single time?"

He nodded.

"Explain Gaius Pope. I don't understand." She threw her arms up and flopped on the sofa.

"I told you I don't know my magic. It just happens. The first time it happened, the guy pulled a knife. It happened so fast. You overpowered him and did your thing. Then you walked away like it was no big deal. I checked on the guy and he was still breathing. He tried to speak. I uh, I did something stupid. I pulled the knife out of his throat. That didn't help. He bled out faster. My prints and yours were on the murder weapon and I freaked out but knew not to leave it there. And so I took it, went to my car, and drove down a block. That's when I began deleting surveillance footage."

"Where's the murder weapon now?" she asked him.

He shrugged. "It's gone. I . . . I disintegrated it."

"What the hell does that even mean, Gaius?!"

"I don't know how else to explain it, Ash. At every incident I witnessed, you left the weapon. And every time, I hold the weapon, wish for it to disappear, and then it turns to dust. I tried to do it again, with other objects, and nothing, it doesn't work. Ask Talon, he saw me do it."

"True story. He concentrates on the object, and it dissolves. It's some kind of magic I'm not familiar with. Like yours but different," I added.

She massaged her forehead. This was a lot to handle.

"Have I done anything else interesting while you've stalked me?" Ash asked him.

"No. Not really." He squirmed in his seat.

"What was I doing if I wasn't murdering random people, Gaius Pope?" she asked.

"There was only the one other time." He tipped his head in my direction.

"I'm sorry, wait. You saw that?" Ash's face dropped.

He nodded.

"Mate, I told you it was at a sex club. Tons of people saw us. But

Pope was the only one who knew the woman behind the mask," I added.

"Jesus, fuck." She moved to sit cross-legged by the coffee table and reached for a glass. "Hit me with some of that."

Pope gave her a trepidatious look, and she frowned. "Gaius, don't even right now."

He poured her a shot and she drank it down in one swallow. *I'm in deep shit if she starts using my full name.*

"And you, Talon Shelby. You didn't think to tell me we'd already had sex?"

"I should have but by the time I figured it out, it didn't matter; I knew you were my mate."

"You mean you didn't recognize me until we had sex?" she squealed. "That makes no sense. Didn't I give you my name at the club?"

"Yep. Mistress," Talon answered.

"Mistress Havoc, more like it," Pope muttered.

Both Ash and I gave the hacker a scathing glare.

"Sorry, bad time for jokes," Pope said.

"Ash, I had a feeling it was you when we met. But I didn't know for sure until we had sex," I admitted.

"How is that possible?" She huffed.

"Mask, babe. Plus you blindfolded me when we went to my private suite."

"Still! Am I that much different in my whatever form? My voice? My hair?"

"It was hard to tell, Ash. There wasn't much talking. And it was hard to hear anyway, the music was loud. The lighting was dim. You snuck out while I was asleep. Your smell was the only way I knew for sure."

"Smell?"

"I'm a wolf. I memorized the smell of your sex." I tapped my nose.

She gaped. "I don't even know how to process that info."

Her cheeks flamed a bright red.

"Ash, angel, the wolf over here committing the smell of your pussy to memory is not a big deal. We've been all up in your guts a million times. The time for demure bashfulness left the building a long time ago," Pope said.

My jaw dropped. *Well, that was one way to put it.*

Her body shook a little as she chuckled. Leave it to Pope to lighten a fucked up situation.

A moment too soon, Ash let out a resigned sigh. "This is too much to process, guys. I'm not sure where to go from here."

"We figure it out together. Whatever you need, we're here for you, Ash," Pope said and refilled our glasses. "I'll get another bottle."

"We love you. I think we've proven how much. We're not going anywhere." I knelt in front of her and caressed her cheek.

"Talon." She leaned into my palm and closed her eyes. "I'm crazy."

I gently swiped her tears. "Look at me, Aisling."

Her watery eyes met mine.

"Your crazy is beautiful to me. You can kill as many people as you want. I will cover it up every single time, and still be madly in love with you."

She threw her arms around me, and we stayed like that until Pope returned with a fresh bottle of scotch.

Pope and I got drunk, because fuck . . . we'd been through a lot.

"Ash." Pope sat between her legs on the floor. "I know it's a lot, but I think I should tell you one more thing."

"You mean there's more?" She groaned.

He nodded.

"Spill it. Tell me everything. Both of you. Just lay it on me."

That was all the incentive Pope needed because his mouth suddenly had diarrhea.

"Here goes; I think there's a correlation between the victims. Maybe."

"What?" I asked. I knew he was working on leads, but I hadn't heard anything because . . . everything.

"Yeah, remember when we talked to a guy who knew the other two guys? The one's from the parking lot brothel."

"I can't believe I went to a sex club. And a brothel," Ash muttered.

"Parking lot. You didn't go in," he corrected.

"And the sex club was hot," I said under my breath.

Ash gave me a flat stare and asked the hacker, "You found info on the victims and talked to who, their family and friends?"

"Associates," I corrected.

"No wonder you two have been getting along so well. You've been bonding over solving murder mysteries. It would be cute if I wasn't the killer," she said.

I couldn't help it, I laughed. Pope laughed with me. Maybe it was the alcohol.

"Guys, seriously, it's not that funny." Ash swatted us half-heartedly.

Once he got the giggles under control, Pope continued. "So, I found out that those two had been wanted by the police. Ask me why. Come on ask."

Ash gave me a look that said, what the fuck?

"Fine, I'll play. Why were the police looking for those men, Gaius?" I asked.

Ash rolled her eyes.

"Because they raped a woman. And beat her. To death," he said dramatically.

"Fuck off," I said.

"Not making it up. I found the police reports. The woman, Sharon, or Shelly, or something, died from her injuries. Somehow, according to reports, she made it to the shelter." His gaze landed on Ash. "The one Emily works at."

"Sheilah. Her name was Sheilah; I was there when she was found. It was a big commotion. The shelter is for the homeless and it was a peaceful day until someone started screaming. We rushed outside and there she was lying in a bloody heap in the parking lot." Ash started to cry.

I punched Pope's arm.

"Owww!" he whined.

"Babe, what Pope is trying to tell you is that you did a good thing. Somehow her story got into your subconscious, and you avenged her."

"Oh." She leaned over and used the hem of my shirt to dab her eyes. "That's not so bad."

I took off my shirt and held it against her nose. "Blow," I said gently.

She frowned at me.

"Seriously, Ash, we've seen it all."

The corners of her mouth curled into a small smile, and she blew her nose.

"Better?"

"Thank you."

"Is there more, Pope?" she asked.

"About the victims? Not yet. But I'm working on it." He rested his chin on her knee. "There is something else though. It's about Jet. I think."

"Quit being so cryptic. Just let it rip." I nudged his shoulder.

"Well, remember the tonics I brought from your place to Talon's?"

She nodded.

"You two were in the shower, and Jet got up so I asked him for some water. He opened the mini fridge and found the tonics."

Ash pushed us away from us and stood. Shiiiittt. Now what?

"And?" she asked.

"He opened it and stuck his tongue in it. I told him he was going to grow ovaries and start shooting eggs out of his ass."

She chuckled, then fell to the floor laughing.

We laughed with her. This had to be good news. Well, nope, not exactly.

"I brought the tonics here, and there's only seven. There used to be eight, right?" Pope continued.

"Son of a motherfucker." She covered her face with her hands.

Ash was a nervous wreck about Jet having his hands on what we learned was her special blend of meds made for her mental condition.

"Explain, Red. I'm not a doctor or scientist."

"Buchanan Pharma could manufacture the blend and claim it as theirs. Not that it isn't since I have a signed contract, but it's not fully proven yet. I was waiting to present it after a few years of successful testing. Buchanan Pharma does good work, but Harlo, Jet's dad, is all about the money. He won't care. He'll mass produce it and as we've witnessed, it's not ready."

"That's why he said he was protecting you," I muttered. Maybe Jet wasn't so terrible after all.

We talked for a while, Pope and I drank a lot more, and Ash fell asleep on the sofa between us. I wasn't sure when I fell asleep, but I woke much too early.

"Get your big ass up!" Something hit me in the face.

"Come on, Talon!" The pillow came down, and I deflected it with my arm.

"What Pope?!" I sat up rubbing my eyes.

"Ash is gone."

CHAPTER FORTY-SEVEN

AISLING

My men were still asleep, snoring away. I woke up an hour ago, showered, made coffee, and they hadn't budged.

After everything they revealed the night before, there was no doubt they were in love with me. So much so that they'd committed crimes to protect me. I couldn't love them more.

I leaned over and kissed Pope's cheek and lips. He rolled over.

Okay.

I did the same to Talon. He muttered an "I love you" then smooshed his face into the pillow.

Their overconsumption of alcohol was due to being nervous about telling me their truths. It was a lot. They kept a lot of secrets and so did I. I called it even. I mean I couldn't blame them for withholding so much information. How do you tell someone you love, "I've been watching you kill people"? I shuddered at the thought and got ready. I packed an overnight back and still no movement from the guys. I wasn't trying to skip out on them, I just needed to get moving. Using my lipstick, I scrawled a hasty note on the mirror and got into my car.

Someone had driven my car to Shadow, filled up the tank, and charged the battery. Sweet. I had a long way to go.

As I drove away from my men, I sent Zoey a text. She called me immediately.

"Hey, bitch. Are you feeling better?"

"Yeah, sorry to bother you so early."

"Girl, I have seven kids. I'm always up at this hour."

I chuckled.

"I have to take a couple more days off," I told her.

"No worries, Ash. You deserve it. You're ahead of the production schedule anyway. Are you sure you're okay? Your men sounded worried, and Jet's been calling."

"Right, about that."

I told her everything as I drove across town and over the border.

"Jesus, Ash. What are you going to do?"

"I'm going to see my parents."

She didn't say anything for a beat. "Did you tell your men?"

"Yes. No. Sort of. I left a note telling them to call me. I won't lie about where I'm going. But I didn't have time to tell them about the situation there."

"Ash, I'm sure they won't care about it one way or another."

"I know. I just hate talking about it and confronting it head-on. I will tell them everything, but I must do this visit alone."

"Got it. Be careful on the road. Text as often as you can. And Aisling, I love you."

"Love you too, babes."

I pressed the pedal to the floor and drove to the Moon Serpent commune.

Minutes after hanging up with Zoey, my phone rang. I stopped myself before answering. Jet. "I love you Jet, but I can't deal with you right now," I said aloud to no one and let his call go to voicemail. A text came through. And another. I set my phone on the seat beside me.

According to Talon, Jet said he was protecting me. From what? From his father? Why? Maybe Harlo had known what I was working on and wanted to produce it. He could have asked, and I would have told him no. Would Harlo go against my recommendations? Yep. No doubt about that. He was a businessman through and through. I knew that about him which was one of the reasons I didn't want Jet to know what I was working on. All in all, I had no reason to distrust Harlo. I respected him. He was like a father figure. Sure there were business dealings I'd learned about over the years that were borderline, but nothing blatantly illegal. Not from what I could tell.

It would suck for them to produce something with my name on it that didn't work. It wasn't ready yet. And it was out of my hands.

I had more pressing matters, like my mental health. *Murders, Ash. Plural.* I shook my head. Hearing Pope and Talon tell me what they'd witnessed was surreal. Pure fiction. It could have been a book. It couldn't go on, though and a part of me had known this for weeks, months now. But I procrastinated and had hoped another visit to the commune wasn't necessary. I waited too long. And others paid the price.

My phone chimed again. Jet. I reached over and turned it off. The more I thought about him leaving and the way he did it hurt my heart, but I couldn't hold a grudge. If he hadn't done what he did, I would have delayed seeking help and continued my late-night shenanigans of killing people. My life was so fucked up. I was a mess.

The closer I got to my turn off, the more nervous I got. It had been months since my last visit. I used to visit twice monthly and that should have continued. But things had gotten worse for my father, and it was too hard for me to be in his presence, for everyone.

"He's slipping, Ash. You should come home," my mother said.

"What do you mean? I was just there three weeks ago?" I replied.

"You'll see when you get here."

That same day.

"He's sleeping, Ash," my sister said.

"I'll just peek in." My father slept peacefully, the rise and fall of his chest, shallow but steady.

I kissed his forehead gently while my mom and sister looked on, and then I crept toward the door, not making a sound.

As though he knew I was making my exit, he woke. His eyes flashed with suspicion.

"Hi, Daddy. I didn't mean to wake you." I slowly approached his bed.

"Who are you? I don't know you!" he spat.

"It's me, Daddy, Aisling. Your daughter."

"No, no, no. You're not my daughter. You're the devil!"

I froze, my jaw hanging open. He'd been losing his memory a little at a time, but he had never shouted at me. And those words. They hurt. He threw a cup at me and a box of tissues.

My mother tugged on my arm and pulled me out of the room.

"He's not himself. Let him rest. You can visit him in the morning."

The morning visit was the worst. He insisted I was a demon coming to steal his soul. He got more and more violent. And those outbursts were reserved for me, the eldest of his two daughters, the redhead.

A month or so later, he was sitting on the deck in his wheelchair staring at the lake. I approached warily as I'd been doing since that first visit where he didn't recognize me.

"Hi," I said softly. "Beautiful day."

"You can't have my soul."

A tear trickled down my cheek.

"It's okay, you can keep it."

I pulled a folding chair beside him and sat down. I didn't say a word, content to be in his presence. He didn't say anything either, but I could feel his eyes burning a hole into the side of my face.

"Look at me," he said.

I inhaled deeply and turned in my chair.

His gaze was hard, suspicious, and full of loathing.

"What you did to her wasn't right. She deserves to know the truth."

The waterworks were on full blast. The words coming out of his mouth made no sense.

"What truth?" I asked.

He blinked.

"Aisling Marie Lovelle." He reached out for my hand.

"It's me, Daddy. I'm here."

"They will kill you. I kept you safe. I won't be able to keep you safe much longer." Sadness clouded his eyes.

"Safe from who, Daddy?"

"Aisling I will always love you, but I can't anymore. I can't pretend."

My heart was breaking into a thousand pieces.

"I don't understand." I swiped my tears and then clasped his hands with both of mine.

"Don't cry. It's just another secret. So many secrets in the house."

"Daddy, don't leave me. You're my only ally in this house."

"I know, I know."

"What's going on?!" My mother stomped toward us. "Aisling, are you upsetting your father?"

He snatched his hand away from mine and cackled. "You brought the devil to us, Gillian, this is your doing. Be gone, devil child!" My father waved his hand dramatically.

My mother whispered an incantation. His eyes rolled back in his head and then he was asleep.

I had a million questions for my mother, but she wheeled him away. I had stayed on the deck awash with sadness and confusion.

A little while later, my mother returned. "Ash, it might be better if you limit your visits. It's upsetting your father."

"Why, mother? It seems like he's trying to tell me something but can't. What aren't you telling me? Am I not part of this family? Am I not of his blood?"

"Don't be ridiculous Aisling. Of course, you are."

"I'm a doctor, mother. I can easily get a blood sample analyzed."

My mother hit me with a blast of her witchy magic. The force of her power knocked the wind out of my lungs and caused me to fall to the ground.

She knelt by my side. "I'm sorry my beautiful daughter. So sorry. Give us time. I'm trying something new. Maybe you can try, too. In your lab. That doctor will give you anything, Aisling. Ask him."

My next visit was worse. Not only did he not recognize me, he was more agitated and more violent, with everyone. My mother kept him sedated with her magic and a special blend of herbs. And I hadn't been back since.

I made a quick pit stop and called the guys.

"Ash, fuck!!! We've been calling for the last hour," Pope growled.

"Sorry, Pope, I turned off my phone because of Jet. I'm sorry."

"Why would you leave without us? Where the fuck are you?"

Oh my. He was pissed.

"Mate," Talon's deep voice rolled through the phone. "Where are you?"

"I'm visiting my family. I have to see if my mother can help me with my tonic. I'm sorry. I wrote a note."

"Why didn't you wake us?"

"I tried. You slept through my kisses and everything."

"You could have waited," he fired back.

"I need to do this alone. My dad," I took a deep breath. "My father has dementia. He doesn't remember me. He gets violent every time he sees me and starts saying weird, mean things. I didn't want you and Pope to witness that. I'm sorry. I waited for two hours this morning, and I just couldn't sit still. I'll be home tonight or at the latest tomorrow morning."

"Christ, Ash." Talon let out an exasperated breath. "Are you okay? No . . . you know."

"No episodes. I promise. And I'll call and text often."

"You better."

"Pope?"

"I'm here," he growled into the phone and then huffed. "Is that why you stopped visiting your parents?" His tone softened.

Of course, my stalker knew my schedule.

"Yes."

"Aisling. Just stop, okay? Stop keeping things from me. It hurts,

Ash. I respect your space and I can't imagine what it must be like to be unrecognizable to the man who raised you. But, Ash, I, we, are your future. Quit fucking shutting us out."

"Okay, I won't. Please don't be mad, Gaius. I'm not perfect. And I'm trying. Honestly, I am."

"I love you, Ash."

"Love you, too."

CHAPTER FORTY-EIGHT

AISLING

I pulled into the commune and rubbed my eyes. Did I take a wrong turn? I checked the sign again and parked my car.

"Ms. Aisling is here." A little girl waved at me from one of the buildings. One of four new buildings.

My mother was the head witch of the Moon Serpent Coven. She was powerful and led a group of over a dozen talented witches. As a child, our living situation had been modest. The community had been comprised of multiple, plain, single-story, structures. Our residences were no more than six hundred square feet, with one bathroom which had all of the modern-day amenities, and no kitchen. The community's largest building was the kitchen, which was shared amongst everyone. It was a simple, carefree life. The women took pride in growing food, making their clothes, and many other things most people, including myself, went out to purchase. The coven made money from selling things that we made at fairs and online. We did well financially. Well, enough for me to afford college and grad school. But this, this had to have cost the coven a fortune.

I approached the closest structure, slowly. "Ash!" My sister Ally waddled over to me. Her belly protruded with baby number two.

"Hi." We embraced. "What is all this?"

"Momma dipped into the coffers and this was built."

"Okay, great. Where is she? How's Dad?"

"She's been notified of your arrival. And Dad is not doing so well. He's umm . . . bedridden." She sighed. "I'm glad you're here."

That's the way it happens. Unless there's a cure, the body succumbs to the disease and soon it fades. The reality of impending death didn't make it easier to bear. I swallowed my tears and followed my sister as she showed me around the new buildings.

As we walked, children swarmed around us. Ally taught basic math and reading to the children, which made her popular amongst the little ones. As we walked, she pointed out new things.

The new structures replaced the older ones aside from the chicken coop, the animal pens, and the smithy, my father's workshop—which hadn't been used since the dementia had gotten worse. We toured each building; one was designated as the community center, also used as the business office where they housed the goods to be sold. Two were communal residences. The units had separate living quarters fully equipped with kitchens and bathrooms. They still did community meals together a few times a week, but for the most part, it gave residents more private time with their families. The fourth building was a home for my family.

"Aisling!" My mother greeted me with a hug. "Let me look at you." She tilted her head and *really* looked at me. "Let's talk inside."

Ally rounded up her students and my mother led me to the new house.

"Business must be good," I said.

"You're not here to talk about business, Aisling. I'll fix us some tea, and we'll go to the gardens."

"Can I see him first?" I asked.

She inhaled a deep breath and slowly released it. "Yes, of course, last door on your left."

On the opposite side of the kitchen was a corridor that led toward the back of the house. There was a room to my right. One glance at the quilted bedspread told me it was my mother's. My father's room was opposite hers and had a beautiful unobstructed view of the lake.

My heart lurched in my chest as I gazed upon the man who raised me, tears springing to my eyes.

His skin was gray, and he was bone-thin and frail. He looked to have aged a hundred years since I'd last seen him. I gently patted his bony hand making sure to use only my fingertips.

"Who are you?" he asked in a reedy voice.

"My name is Ash," I said. Saying I was his daughter felt like it would be too much for him to hear, and I didn't want to add to his already weakened state.

"I knew an Aisling once. She was a good girl. You resemble her. But you're too old. Are you her mother?"

I smiled despite myself. "No. I don't have children yet."

"Come on, Aisling, let's go outside. You can visit again later." My mother ushered me out.

"That isn't Aisling, the demon took her. You know this," my father spat.

I hurried out of the room, needing distance from his ranting. He continued shouting long after I was gone.

My mother found me sitting in the garden that surrounded her new home. She set up the tray of tea and cookies and finally sat down.

"Talk to me, Aisling, I can see your aura requires help. What happened?"

I told her about my episodes. All of it. Including the murders.

Her brows furrowed and she rocked back and forth shaking her head. This was bad news, I expected that, but her reaction was dramatic.

"What's wrong, Momma? You're worked up. What aren't you telling me?" My belly squeezed.

"I can't," she shook her head. "I can't speak of it."

"You must! Tell the truth, Gillian! Tell her now before someone gets hurt."

I whirled around to see my father, standing behind us, leaning on a cane. How the hell?

"Daddy? You can't . . ."

"Donovan! What are you doing out of bed?"

"Tell her, Gillian!" And then he collapsed. I was able to catch him before he hit the ground, but I was no athlete, I wouldn't be able to carry him. My mother ran into the house and got his wheelchair. Together we hoisted him in the chair and got him back in bed.

By then he passed out, and I was exhausted. It had been a rough couple of days.

Later that night, after my sister, her husband, and their son had gone to bed, my mother pulled me into the garden again. We hadn't had a chance to talk, and I was wrung out.

"Ash, I have one final option to help you," she started.

I held up my hand.

"What was Daddy talking about, Momma? What are you not telling me?"

"Aisling, please."

"No! I demand to know. What is wrong with me? I know you know! Daddy knows! Why won't you tell me!!"

She just sat there. I got up in her face.

"Momma I have killed innocents. Do you want me, your oldest daughter to go to jail?! Tell me the fucking truth!"

"He's not your father. Your father is . . . was a," She averted my gaze. "He was a demon. I banished him before you were born."

"A demon. Really?" I scoffed.

"This is not a joke, Aisling!

"Fine. Start from the beginning of this fiction."

"I was seventeen when I met Mischa. He was beautiful. Magical. I thought he was a warlock. He could have had any woman he wanted but he chose me. I gave him my virgin blood. But when that was over, he didn't want me anymore. He wanted you. The child growing in my womb. I was a strong witch by that age and had gotten stronger as soon as you were conceived. I played along with his games and found a way to banish him. After you were born, I did everything to conceal what you are to protect you. The herbs were part of it. I cast a small spell to repress your demon. For most of your life, it worked until you went off to school and the episodes returned. You are so smart. You figured out how to combine our ways and the ways of humans. Still, I intervened. I cast a bigger spell. I had to. It was the only way to protect you. If anyone found out, Aisling, he would return or worse, they would crucify you."

"Who is they? And what kind of spell have you been casting, Mother?"

"Demon hunters, Aisling. There are demons all around us. And hunters are getting more and more aggressive."

Demon hunters made the news now and then, but I'd always thought it was sensationalized media and shrugged it off.

"And the spell? What does it entail?" I prodded.

"I had to . . ." She turned her head.

"Momma?!"

"Your father. I had to use a life force from someone who loves you."

"What the fuck are you saying to me?"

"Language," she said.

"I will say fuck as many times as I want and very fucking loudly. Are you seriously saying that I'm part demon?"

She nodded.

"And you've known all my life."

She nodded again.

"Fuck my ass. You made me think I was crazy!! I thought I had a mental imbalance. I've been taking meds for schizophrenia!"

She sniffled.

"And you've been drawing from Daddy's life force? How? By using his blood as part of the spell? Is that why he's gotten so frail? Why he's been losing his mind?!"

"He told me to. It couldn't be me. I was the caster. He volunteered because he loves you so much. I didn't know it would affect him this way. It got out of hand, and I don't know how to reverse it."

"If you stop this spell-casting, will he return to normal?"

"Not likely but it might delay the inevitable and give him more good years."

"Stop it, Mother. Right the fuck now!"

"I will. But you . . . there's another option."

"If it draws on someone else's life force, hell no."

"It doesn't. It's a binding spell on your demon. It will affect you as well. You'll feel different. How different, I don't know."

I thought about it for a moment. Not sure why, I didn't have any options. My father wasn't getting better, and my episodes were back so that had to stop. As far as my demon side, the bitch was out of control, and I didn't know how else to manage her.

"Do it. Now."

She slumped in her chair. "Give me an hour and then meet me in the basement."

Don't do this, Aisling. My internal voice, no, my demon said.

I ignored her.

Please, Aisling. Please don't.

Too fucking late.

CHAPTER FORTY-NINE

POPE

"Angel." I practically tackled Aisling as she entered the penthouse.

"I missed you, too, Pope." Her arms encircled my waist.

"My turn." Talon bumped me to the side.

The wolf lifted her into his arms and carried her to the living area.

"Tell us everything," he said.

"Wait a minute, first Ash, what can we get you? Hungry? Thirsty? Bath time?" I asked.

She laughed. A tired laugh. I studied her face which was drawn, her eyes were red-rimmed and puffy. What did they do to her? Concern weighed heavily on my shoulders, but for Ash's sake, I kept my expression neutral.

"Bath time. Thirsty. And then food?"

"You got it," I said.

She gave Talon a chaste kiss and climbed off his lap.

Talon and I exchanged a look, and I went to get her something to drink.

After her bath, we moved outdoors to eat sushi on the terrace.

"So," she said. "I am sure you want two are dying to know what happened."

"No," I replied.

"I wasn't thinking about that at all," Talon chimed in.

"My mother revealed that one, my father Donovan, isn't my father. And my real father is a demon," Aisling blurted.

I choked on ahi sashimi. Ash slid a glass of water to me.

"Seriously? Did she not know?" Talon asked.

"She did. She cast a spell that bound my demonic side. The spell has weakened over time, as my father became ill. He was the catalyst," she said.

"What the . . ." I started then stopped. Ash's downcast eyes spoke volumes of disbelief, sadness, and frustration. She didn't need me to say that her mother had wronged her.

"I'm sorry, babe." Talon rubbed her arm. "What can we do?"

"Thanks. And uh . . . nothing. My mother cast a different spell this time, binding my demoness for good," Ash told us.

She proceeded to tell us everything that happened at the Moon Serpent Coven.

After hearing about the ritual and what her father had gone through to help keep Ash safe, I blew out a breath. Her mother sounded scary. And I hope she meant well, and the new spell wouldn't have any negative repercussions.

"So, you're okay now but different?" I asked.

She nodded. "I don't feel different. A little tired. Lethargic is a better word."

She'd been home for all of two hours, and I could already tell, my Aisling was a totally different person. At first, I thought it was the long road trip that had zapped her energy. But after hearing about everything, I wasn't so sure.

It was concerning but fingers crossed it was temporary.

More than a week had passed since Ash's visit to her parents, and she was not the same woman. I mean she was, but she was different. The new spell had changed her. Talon sensed it as well and we were both at a loss on how to help her.

I pulled up some information online about demons and there was some validity to her mother's claims. There were demon hunters out there. According to the internet, people who had been diagnosed with psychological issues were considered demons and vanquished. Or killed. There wasn't solid confirmation out there, just conspiracy theories.

We didn't have any sources on the subject except Jet. He'd been calling and texting. Talon finally texted to let him know she visited her parents and was back. That didn't satisfy his constant pestering. The way I saw it, if he cared so much about her, he shouldn't have left in the first place. He called continuously. I didn't care.

Jet wasn't a sore subject for Ash, nothing was. She was emotionless about him and everything else. It was odd. My fiery, passionate, angel was now subdued and listless.

She didn't even blush. And her smiles seemed forced. Her appetite had changed also. She picked at her food and insisted she ate a late or had a large lunch. I'd have to ask Zoey about that.

And the sex was not the same. I expected that after the trauma on the boat. But she wasn't even affectionate. Not like before. Ash was one of those touchy-feely types. She craved physical contact with one of us at all times. Now she nearly flinched at the slightest graze on her skin. The fire was gone, and she seemed to be going through the motions.

I was beside myself with worry. I liked being proactive, but it was impossible when we had no idea what to do. At least I wasn't alone on this. Talon and I had become close, although there were things we missed about Jet. We weren't going to initiate a truce. That was up to Aisling. Or maybe we'd play that card as a last resort.

All of it was concerning, but we decided to wait it out for a couple more days before bringing it up. Her mother had told her she'd be different for a while, and that things would take time to normalize. Sounded like bullshit, but we had nothing else to go on. And yeah, she was different, but it was better than her killing people.

Her work habits had remained the same. She'd go to work and come home. After that, she was game to do whatever we suggested. The concerning part was if we didn't initiate anything she was happy to read a book and go to bed.

That was the other thing. She slept ten hours nightly. With all the sleep she was getting she still had dark circles under her eyes.

"Everything okay?" I asked, entering Talon's office.

"Not sure," he replied.

"Ash?"

He nodded. "I know we said we'd wait a few more days but I don't like it. She's getting worse, and I'm concerned about her health."

"I agree. I'd rather be overly cautious than wait until it's too late. Should we call Jet? Or her mother?"

"Mr. Shelby," his secretary said over the intercom. "Zoey is on line one."

"Thanks."

He pressed the speaker phone button. "Hey Zoey, everything okay?"

"No. Something is severely wrong with Aisling, Talon. What are you going to do about it?"

"What happened?"

"She's not herself. She's lagging on work, which has never happened. She's listless half the day. And the rest of the day she's staring off into space. When I asked her about it, she said she was fine. Or she hasn't gotten much sleep. I'm concerned."

"Thanks for letting me know, I'm concerned as well. I was about to call her mother," he replied.

"Why? That woman did this to our girl! Don't call her. Call Jet. He's a warlock and has been studying mystics including demons," Zoey said.

"I know that. But, Ash. I'm not sure how she'll feel about having him back." He blew out a breath. "Shit. I don't think we have a choice."

"We don't, Talon. She needs help. Call him and keep me posted."

"Before you go, Zoey. How's um . . . lunch? Have you two been going out to eat daily?"

"No. She's never hungry. I bring lunch from home sometimes for both of us or I'll order out. She never finishes her food. She said she eats a big breakfast and you guys feed her well at night. Is that not the case?"

Talon massaged his temple. "No, it isn't. I'll handle it. Thanks, Zoey."

"That settles it," I said to Talon. "We're talking to Ash about this tonight."

Later that evening, Ash barely picked at her food during dinner.

"Not hungry again, I see," I said pointing at her plate.

"No, big lunch. I need some air." She put her plate in the sink and went out to the terrace.

Knowing she was lying straight to my face hurt like a son-of-a-bitch. Talon and I followed her. She was sitting on a lounger gazing out at the dark blue sky. He knelt at her feet, caging her in with his body.

"Ash, this has gone too far. I think we should talk to your mother about undoing whatever she did. You're not yourself," he started.

I sat beside her and laced our fingers together.

"I can't do that, Talon," Aisling said.

"Why not? You said she could reverse the spell and undo the binding," I asked.

She nodded. "That is true. But I don't want to. I feel better. I like knowing I won't go out killing people."

"We agree with the no-killing part. Maybe we can try something else. You're not you, angel. You sleep a lot, and you are still tired. And you seem . . ." I began then trailed off. It was a delicate subject, and I couldn't find the words.

"Disinterested in life," Talon finished for me. "Before the spell. You had strong opinions about many things. You had a passion for your work. You loved it there. And now, you're falling behind. And then there's the issue with you not eating."

"Did Zoey say something?" Aisling asked.

"Yes, she's concerned."

Ash pursed her lips, her eyes watering.

"You're right. I'm not myself," she finally said. "But . . . the alternative is not going to work. I'll have to watch my back from hunters. I'll have to be tied to the bed every night to make sure I don't go out murdering people at night. The alternative is not an option. I'm sorry to disappoint both of you."

"You're not disappointing us, angel. We're worried and we have every right to be," I said.

"If not your mother, I'm calling Jet," Talon offered.

"Why him? He left me."

"He studied demonology and may have some insights for us," Talon replied.

"He did?" Her eyebrows raised.

That was the first facial expression she'd shown in days.

"He won't help." She tried to wiggle away from us.

"Jet or your mother, Aisling, you decide. Now." Talon's eyes flashed gold. "Or I decide for you."

She bit her lower lip and thought about it for a minute. "Fine. Call Jet. May I?" She tried to stand but Talon caged her in with his broad frame and squeezed her to his chest.

"I love you, Ash. I just want what's best for you," he murmured into her hair.

She hugged him back. "I love you, too." She released him and then leaned against my side. "Both of you."

Aisling trudged into the penthouse, head down and shoulders slumped. Watching her go left a crushing weight on my chest.

"Call him, Talon," I said.

He pulled out his phone and dialed the warlock. Jet picked up on the first ring.

"Talk to me, Talon. What's wrong with Ash?"

"She's unwell, Jet. From what I recall you studied demonology."

Jet didn't miss a beat. "Are you insinuating what I think you are?"

"Yep."

"Shit. Now it makes sense. I'll be there in the morning." He disconnected the line.

"I'll go check on her," I said to Talon and strolled into the penthouse, hoping Jet had some answers.

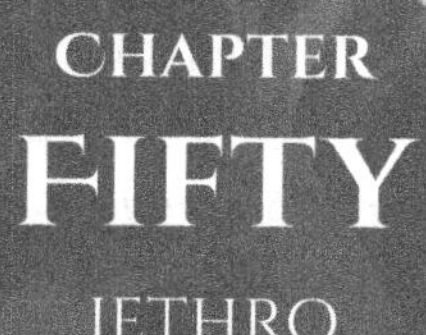

CHAPTER FIFTY

JETHRO

It had been over a week since I'd left Port Midway. I hadn't seen or heard from Aisling and it was killing me. She didn't even return my texts. She hated me. Truly hated me and I deserved it. If that wasn't enough, there was a constant churning in my gut telling me something was wrong.

Talon said she went to visit her parents which raised my hackles. I wasn't sure why since I knew next to nothing about her family. Something was going on there that didn't sit well with me. I almost got in my truck and drove out to the commune, but I busied myself in the lab instead.

I took the tonic she created and studied the ingredients. Despite having the best lab equipment and being a powerful warlock, the process wasn't quick or simple. Using a little science and a lot of magic, I had just enough liquid to decipher ninety-nine percent of the ingredients in the potion. That one percent was a form of sodium and nothing I had been familiar with. I couldn't recall seeing anything out of the ordinary in the lab, but I'd been consumed with Aisling and hadn't thought to look under every jar and bottle in the cabinets.

Even without having info on that last ingredient, I was able to study the others which also took a while. I took each compound and cross-referenced the info with potential uses. The top use for the combination of ingredients was for mental illness. Blackout episodes, hallucinations, and delusions. Was Aisling sick?

She didn't seem sickly to me, nor did she seem to have any behavioral issues, however, we'd just met. And the tonics might have been working. *Was this the reason my father wanted to keep her happy?* It would certainly track. If my findings were correct, Ash's creation would rock the medical industry. And that would make the board of directors very happy.

I called Ash and sent her a text again. No response. I called and texted Talon and Pope and no response from them either.

To keep myself busy, I decided to do some sleuthing in my father's office. He hadn't cleaned it out which irritated the board members, me too, except it worked out to my benefit. All his files were where he'd left them. The arrogant prick thought he'd be back in the chair and didn't need to bother packing up his shit.

I would have rolled my eyes at his hubris but silently thanked him instead. One call to my IT department and his files were blown wide open. The goal was to find anything regarding Aisling.

The HR file we had on her was thin. I wanted to kick myself in the nuts for not noticing that earlier. Even some of the basics were left out like sex, age, and marital status. My father mentioned running a DNA analysis, which was also conveniently omitted.

He had to be keeping her info stored somewhere and after hours of looking through his computer files I found nothing but porn. My father frequented live porn chats often. Yep, total cringe.

I was about to call it a day and decided to look in his desk drawers. More porn. A burner phone. Interesting. It was locked and so I had to come back to deal with that, not that I wanted to. He was probably contacting one of his many mistresses.

Sifting through his desk drawers my hand skimmed over a metal object. A keychain. On closer inspection I discovered the keychain wasn't just any old keychain it was a USB flash drive.

Bingo.

I fired up the drive and read everything twice. What was my father up to?

Talon's name flashed on my phone screen. "Talk to me, Talon. What's wrong with Ash?"

"She's unwell, Jet." He blew out a rough sigh. He sounded tired and if I had to guess, calling me was the last thing he wanted to do.

I ejected the USB drive and exited the office as soon as he hung up.

As grateful as I was for Talon's call, I couldn't shake the dread that had taken root in my gut. Unwell? Demonology? He didn't elaborate and he didn't need to. No matter what had happened, I'd do anything in my power to make things right.

Although I hadn't unpacked my truck since I returned, I went back to my place and packed a few more things. Textbooks on demonology mostly. I'd collected a lot of info over the years which might come in handy.

I got into my truck and said goodbye to Meridian City. If all went well in Port Midway, I'd never see this place again.

It was early morning when I arrived at Talon's penthouse.

The overnight security buzzed me in, and Talon met me at his office, wearing nothing but boxers. He ruffled his hair and yawned. I leaned in for a bro hug and the next thing I knew I was laid out on the floor.

Holy fucking fuck, that hurt.

"What the hell, Tally?" I groaned.

"That's for leaving, asshole. Now get up!"

Fucker lit me up good. It took me a minute to get to my feet.

I hobbled behind him to the penthouse.

"When you said you were on your way, I thought that meant tomorrow," he said.

"It is tomorrow," I muttered.

Talon glared at me over his shoulder. The big man was still pissed.

"How's she doing?" I asked.

"Not good. There's a lot you should know." He pulled a bag of frozen peas out of the freezer and threw it at me.

I sat at the kitchen counter, icing my face when Pope walked in. The hacker wasn't pleased to see me.

I approached him with my hand extended. Pope looked at my offered hand and then his gaze lingered on my aching face. "I'd punch you, but it looks like Talon already took care of that."

He turned away, then said, "Aww, fuck it."

Pope turned quickly and slammed his fist into my gut. I bowled over only to receive a knee in my face.

Motherfucker! I spat blood onto the wood floor.

It took me a minute to formulate intelligible words. I blinked away the stars swirling in my vision and said, "Respect."

Wheezing, I slumped back to the chair and placed the bag of frozen veggies to my face.

"If you think a couple of hits hurt, wait till you hear about what's been going on with Ash." Talon slapped my back so hard it rattled my lungs.

"Why don't you start, Pope." Talon sat on the opposite end of the counter while Pope leaned on the kitchen sink glaring at me.

"Months ago I stalked Ash to a bar called The Last Resort, where I witnessed her first of many murders," Pope said with a serious tone I'd never heard from him before.

He was shitting me. Had to be.

I glanced at Talon, who nodded.

"She's been having these blackouts for a while. Those tonics she was taking, the one you pilfered from my mini fridge, helped her for years. Recently, they stopped working. She's been going on little murder sprees during these episodes. Pope has been covering them up for months before I came along."

I couldn't believe my ears. My aching head whipped back and forth between the hacker and the wolf. "You're not fucking serious."

"I witnessed her do it. We both have," Pope added.

"What the hell."

"A few weeks ago, Ash welcomed her asshole boss into her life, into our lives, and then he pussied out and left. Guess what happened?" Pope glared at me.

This was going to be ugly. Swallowing hard I met his gaze.

"She went to a bar, got fucking wasted, and then these assholes decided to take her to their boat," Pope said.

Yep, the truth hurt a thousand times more than their hits. I gripped the counter, struggling to breathe. "Did they . . ." I couldn't finish my question.

"No." Talon's voice was gruff. "She blacked out and killed them all. When she woke, she was on the boat. With three dead bodies. In the middle of the ocean."

I wanted to puke my guts out. Ash had been murdering people for months and didn't realize it until I, the asshole, had to up and leave, forcing her to confront her issues in the most traumatic way. I choked on a sob. *Fuck Jet. What did you do?* "She must have been frightened. Is she okay?"

"Fuck no. It gets worse," Pope spat.

I swiped my tears, the ache in my face nothing in comparison to the agony squeezing my heart. "Hit me again. I deserve it. I deserve worst."

"You're not getting off that easily. You're going to fix this," Talon scoffed. "Ash went to her mother for help. She revealed to Ash that her biological father is a demon, and she's been casting a spell to bind Ash's demon side since she was a child. The last binding has changed her. Our Ash is not the same woman."

Everything began to click into place. The DNA reports from the police. The tonics. My father.

My mind raced with a myriad of different things I'd learned over the years about demonology. I paced in the kitchen wringing my hands. *Why would her mother bind her demon?* Caging someone's nature was ludicrous. No wonder her demon side was going on murder sprees.

"Can you help her?" Talon asked.

"I will do everything in my power to help her," I vowed. "I have an idea. I'll need her mother's help though."

Pope grimaced. "Is that a must? I mean she did this to Ash in the first place."

"I might be able to unravel the binding but it's risky. Her mother's cooperation would ensure nothing goes amiss."

Talon shrugged. "I guess it wouldn't hurt to ask."

"Can I see her?" I asked.

"No," Hacker and wolf said simultaneously.

"I appreciate you being here for Ash. Still don't expect forgiveness just yet. You need to earn it. I'm going to bed." Pope strolled out of the kitchen.

"Follow me." Talon led me to the guest room on the other side of the penthouse.

"You're sleeping in here." Talon flipped on the light. "Just because you're here and have offered to help her, doesn't mean we've forgiven you. I want to pummel you so badly right now, but we need you. Ash needs you."

I hung my head. I knew it wasn't going to be that easy, but at least I was here.

"Thanks for letting me help. I'll do everything I can."

He crossed his arms over his chest and glared at me. His body language conveyed the distrust flowing through his veins. He was going to make me suffer for leaving her, for leaving them. "Ash doesn't know you're here. You need to mend things with all of us for this to work."

He stomped off.

I WASN'T sure if it was the long drive or the beating, but I slept for hours. Talon left a note stating they were at work and to meet him downstairs.

After a quick shower and a change of clothes, I found Talon and Pope in the big man's office.

I approached them warily. "Is Ash in her office?"

Talon nodded. "We'll go down there with you."

"Won't she feel like we're ganging up on her?"

"We told her that you're here. She peeked in on you while you were sleeping. And she knows we're coming to take her to lunch."

At the lab, Zoey greeted me with a stink eye. *Suck it up, Jet. You deserve worse.*

Tally and Pope entered Ash's office before me and greeted her with hugs and kisses. I stood just outside of the doorway, waiting my turn. Ash's gaze locked with mine, and my heart broke as I took her in. She did not look good at all. Her eyes were puffy, and her face was gaunt.

The need to wrap her in my arms and tell her how much I loved her was so strong that I rushed her, going in for a fierce hug.

My head whipped to the right and a sharp sting bloomed over the side of my face which had been spared from Talon's fist.

For as frail as she looked, I would have never guessed she was capable of delivering a hit with that much force if I hadn't seen her wind up.

I was stunned.

As if he was waiting for the perfect moment, Pope draped a protective arm around Aisling and said, "And you can suck your own dick from now on."

Ash let out a soft chuckle that didn't reach her eyes. Still, the sound was so lyrical and infectious, that Talon and Pope laughed with her. The joke was at my expense, but to see her smile again was worth the agony in my face.

CHAPTER FIFTY-ONE

AISLING

The four of us were together for the first time in almost two weeks. Instead of being filled with lively conversation and laughter, it was awkward. Especially since we were at Jade Gardens. We ordered and sat in silence for a few minutes.

I wasn't myself and I knew it. I didn't know how to be different. I wanted to be me, my old self, but that woman was gone. Vanished in my mother's basement.

My mother had me sit in a salted circle, while she chanted in the old tongue, and thirty minutes later I emerged a different person. Everything was dull. Colorless and tasteless. It was as if someone hit the mute button on all my senses. Food lost its flavor. I used to love my work and now the numbers and alphabets jumbled together and made me tired. More tired. No matter how much sleep I got, I was always exhausted.

On a good note, everything that had happened on the boat with those strange men hadn't bothered me at all. It felt like it had happened to someone else. I wasn't traumatized in the slightest. I didn't feel anything.

My men were supportive and affectionate as always. They were there right beside me and yet I couldn't feel them. It was like my skin was covered with an invisible barrier blocking out all sensation. I hated it, and I couldn't muster the energy to snap out of it.

While the guys talked amongst themselves, I stole glances at Jet. Unlike the other two, Jet had always confused me emotionally. It was a non-stop rollercoaster of relief, resentment, love, distrust, and anger. He'd been in my presence for fifteen whole minutes, and it was already too much to bear. I couldn't decide if I wanted to hug him for coming back or stab him with my chopsticks.

I released a heavy sigh and made a conscious effort not to slouch or rest my head on the table. Talon draped an arm over my shoulder and signaled the waitress while Pope interlaced my fingers with his.

"Come on, baby. Let's go upstairs. Someone will deliver the meal." Talon helped me stand.

Thank god, I almost blurted. I shouldn't have been so relieved, but I was. I wanted to go back to bed.

Pope held my hand and led the way back to the penthouse.

In the foyer, I released Pope's hand.

"This way, Ash, lunch will be here in a minute," Pope said.

"I'm going to change into something more comfy," I replied and went straight to the bedroom where I flopped on the bed.

The bed dipped beside me. "Hi, little monster. You need to eat something."

"You left me," I muttered.

"I had to." He rolled me over and climbed on top of me. "Look at me, Ash. Let me explain."

I squeezed my eyes shut.

"At least you're still being a brat."

My eyes snapped open, and I glared at his swollen, bruised face. *That had to hurt*. "Name calling is not helpful."

"There's that spark, I've been looking for. Granted it was a teeny tiny spark, but at least it was something."

"And I see you're still the same asshole. Get off me." I feebly shoved his shoulder.

"Only if you promise to get out of this bed and have something to eat."

"I'm not hungry." I sighed.

"Why not?"

I turned away from him. He settled his weight on me and hooked my jaw to meet his gaze.

"Answer me, Aisling."

"I'm just not. I'm not . . . myself. You're crushing me."

He propped himself up on his elbows.

"Let me help you, please."

"I don't trust you, Jethro." I squeezed my eyes shut again.

He pressed his forehead against mine. "I'm sorry, Ash. I'm sorry I left the way I did. I'm sorry for not being there for you when you needed me. Let me make this right. Let me gain back your trust."

"No." My traitorous tears seeped out from the corners of my eyes.

He kissed each eye. "You're not yourself, little monster. Let me help."

I kept my eyes closed, hoping he would leave and let me sleep.

"If you prefer, I can just use my magic to assess what your mother's done without your permission," he said.

My eyelids lifted "No, I do not prefer that. Don't you dare invade my body with your magic. Ever. You have a lot of explaining to do, Jet. To all of us."

"Hitting me and making me sleep in the guest room isn't enough?" he asked.

"Not even close," I retorted.

He sighed and pressed his forehead to mine again.

"I made a mistake, Aisling. I was . . . am a coward. I don't know how to love you the way you deserve but I will die trying. Let me help you, it's the least I can do."

"I don't want your help." My voice hitched.

He released a heavy sigh. "Hear me out, Ash, and let me help undo what your mother did. If you still want me gone, I will leave. Please."

"Do you think you can help me? With all of it," I whispered.

"Of course," he answered with confidence.

It wasn't just undoing my mother's spell, it was coming up with something that would keep my demoness in check. If anyone could do it, it was Jethro Buchanan. Did I dare hope? Was it possible for me to live a normal life without my demoness causing havoc wherever she went? The possibility seemed like a fanciful dream.

"When was the last time you had a proper meal?" he asked.

I shrugged.

"I'll explain while you eat. And after that, I'm working my magic." He brought me to a seated position.

"I need to change into something more comfortable," I argued.

"You're stalling. Come on." He pulled me to stand and then swatted my butt.

I gave him a flat stare and trudged to the dining room.

While Jet talked, Pope and Talon ate, and I sipped my miso soup. It was warm and bland, but at least I didn't need to chew.

The words coming out of Jet's mouth should have been concerning. It was a little, but I couldn't bring myself to express what I was thinking. Harlo was a controlling jerk when it came to his son. *Who threatens to disinherit his only child?* I knew Harlo cheated on his wife, which was sad. Harlo treated me differently. He never flirted with me. He treated me like I was treasured. Like I was his favorite child. I'd never say that to Jet. He was hurting. And he was pushing boundaries for me.

He told us of what he found in his father's office, and that made me cringe. Harlo checked my DNA which meant he knew I was a demon before hiring me, years ago.

"What would demon DNA do for someone?" Pope asked.

"As far as mystics go, angelic and demon DNA is on the top end of the spectrum in terms of overall power. I would imagine one vial would have endless potential. That's speculation of course because as you all know, demons were shunned from this realm centuries ago. The texts and manuscripts I've studied have been regarded as pure fiction."

"For argument's sake, what are the possibilities with demon blood or DNA? What would Harlo hope to gain from Ash?" Talon asked.

"Everything. My father is the weakest warlock in Buchanan family history and the company has suffered financially. I found spells on a hard drive that need angel or demon blood."

"Ash has been working for the company, for years. He could have taken what he wanted. Why now?" Talon pulled my chair closer to his and held a fork full of noodles to my mouth.

Like a fussy toddler, I clamped my lips shut and gave him my cheek.

"Eat, Aisling," Talon growled.

My wolf uttered those two words like a command. I opened my mouth, accepted the noodles and chewed. It wasn't horrible, and I had to admit, the more I ate the more energized I felt.

Talon pushed the plate of noodles in front of me and handed me the fork, while Jet answered his question.

"From what I could tell, the spells are specific. Demon DNA is volatile, meaning you can't just throw demon blood into a spell without the risk of cataclysmic effects. I believe he was trying to decipher Ash's demon lineage."

"By doing what exactly," I muttered. My first utterance during the entire discussion.

Jet released a huff of air. "He was trying to get close to your mother."

I choked on my noodles. Talon gently patted my back, and Pope handed me a cup of water.

"Excuse me." I wiped my mouth with a napkin. "Say that again."

Jet cleared his throat. "On that drive, I found bank statements for one of his personal accounts. He was sending her money. A lot in the last six months."

That explained the new building structures. Lunch soured in my belly and exhaustion pulled at me.

"I'm sorry, Ash." Jet regarded me with an apologetic gaze.

"Alright, let's undo this demon-binding thing and figure out how to protect Ash from your father, her mother, and potential demon hunters." Pope stood.

"And myself," I added.

"I think I have a solution for that, but first we need to undo the binding."

CHAPTER FIFTY-TWO

TALON

Ash wanted a shower before Jet did his magic thing, so we decided to have a drink and give her some space.

"You're not doing an exorcism are you?" Pope glanced in the direction of the bathroom.

"No, I'm just going to do a spell to scan Ash's body. That will give me a read on any spells or bindings that have been placed on her," Jet answered.

"Do you think you can help?" I swigged my beer.

"I hope so. You were downplaying when you said she was unwell. She's slowly wilting." His voice trailed off and his gaze darted down the hall.

"I'll go check on her." I went into the bathroom.

Ash was in the tub filled with bubbles, her eyes closed. I admired her for a moment. She was still so beautiful. Demon and all.

"Hey, babe," I sat at the edge of the tub and brushed my lips over hers.

"Hi, is it time for me to get up?" she murmured, her voice faint.

"Yes. Let's do this, baby." I grabbed a towel and held it open while she stepped out of the tub.

She leaned her head on my chest, and I dried her off, then swooped her in my arms and carried her to the bed.

"Would you like help getting dressed?" I asked laying her down on the bed.

"Umm . . . T-shirt?" She tugged on the cotton clinging to my torso.

"This one?"

She nodded.

I took off my shirt and helped her slip it on.

"Do you know how much I love you?" she asked.

"Yes, mate."

She leaned on my shoulder. "I'm scared, Talon."

"Jet won't hurt you, babe. I'll be right here."

"Not Jet. Everything else. What if he can't help me? What if my mother was lying and I'm stuck like this? What if it does work and this Mistress persona goes crazy? Some days I feel like I'm dying, Talon."

My chest tightened, making breathing difficult.

"Don't talk like that, Ash. Never say those kinds of things." I clung to her body and felt her sobbing against my chest. "You're not dying baby. I won't allow it. We will fix this now. Somehow, someway. I'll always fight for you, Aisling. Please, hold on and fight for me. For us, please."

She nodded and I went to get the other two.

Pope was a ball of nervous energy. He couldn't keep still and Jet glared at him more than once.

Finally, the warlock said, "Pope, get Ash something to drink. Actually go downstairs and ask Zoey if there is a fresh batch of tonics somewhere. Please."

Pope hesitantly left the room.

"Do I have to ask you to leave also?" Jet glared at me.

"Piss off and get to work."

Jet sat cross-legged on the bed and began chanting. His face was a mask of serenity.

He finished chanting and then Ash's body glowed for a minute. The warlock tipped his head, and his forehead creased. His lids lifted revealing only the whites of his eyes.

My lip curled into a snarl. My wolf was ready to pounce and protect her from him.

She was resting peacefully, which was the only reason I stayed in place.

A second later Aisling's back bowed, and she gasped. Jet's eyes snapped open and he laid a hand over her forehead, chanted, and then her body relaxed.

"Get her mother on the phone. Now," he snarled without even looking at me.

"Hello," a young voice answered.

"May I speak with Gillian?"

"Mrs. Gillian is . . . not here. Do you want me to look for her?" the kid offered.

"Yes, please."

Minutes later, the kid was still searching for Ash's mother.

"This is ridiculous," Jet growled.

"I don't have another number for her. Do we need to drive up there?" I asked. Whatever was going on seemed dire.

Jet scrubbed his hand down his face and winced. I almost felt bad for punching him in the face.

"No, we can wait," Jet replied.

"I can't find her and my mom's calling me." The kid hung up.

"Fuck!" Jet shouted, waking Ash.

"What's wrong?! Am I dying?" she whispered.

"No, little monster. You're perfect. I need to speak with your mother about the spell. I need her help."

"Elaborate, warlock," I said with an edge in my voice.

I knew it was bad, but we had to know every sordid detail.

"The spell is embedded somehow. I can't access it."

"And?" I prodded.

"We need to undo it. Quickly. It's draining her life force," he added.

I fucking knew it.

"If you find out how she embedded it, can you undo it?" Ash asked.

"I should be able to."

Aisling sat upright and took her shirt off. She gathered her red hair and swirled it into a bun on top of her head. Her bare breasts were on display.

My cock twitched and Jet squirmed uneasily, telling me he was having the same issue. It wasn't the right timing but Jesus she looked amazing, and it had been so long since I'd been able to enjoy her flesh.

Ash turned her back to us, snapping us from our lustful thoughts.

"Back," she said.

I crawled on the bed to get a closer look. "I'm not seeing anything. Jet?"

"Let me try something. Don't touch her while I'm doing this, Tally," he instructed.

I sat on my heels while Jet cast a spell. Ash's body glowed and then the light dimmed revealing a serpentine symbol spanning the length of her back.

"What'd I miss?" Pope walked in. "Holy shit."

"Is it bad?" Ash whimpered.

I glared at Pope, telling him to shut the hell up.

"It's not horrible, Ash. It's going to take me some time. I need to go down to the lab," Jet said.

"Can I help?" she offered. Her voice sounded weak.

"Stay here with Talon and Pope. I got this."

Jet shuffled off the bed and rushed out of the room. Pope took his place and handed her a bottle of water, while I went after Jet.

"Jet," I called out to him as he exited the penthouse.

He didn't stop, making me chase him down the stairs.

"Hey. Wait up." I took the steps two at a time to catch up to him in the corridor. "What's going on?"

He opened the door that led to my private office space. I slammed it shut. "Jet. What the fuck?"

His busted-up face looked stricken. I laid a hand on his shoulder. "Let me help, Jet," I said in a gentler tone.

He inhaled deeply, then he pressed his forehead to my chest. "It's Harlo, Talon. He's such a piece of shit. I'm so fucking embarrassed. I can't face Ash right now."

I cupped his nape. "Jethro, you are not your father. Whatever he did, is not on you. Help me understand. Help me fix this."

He leaned into me, resting his body weight on mine.

"The spell was on his disk drive. He must've given it to her mother. It's not killing her. But it's subduing her. Making her compliant," Jet muttered.

Dread curdled in my belly. My arms tightened around him, needing support.

"Can you fix this? Or should we drive north?" I asked.

He didn't answer me.

"Jet?" I tugged the back of his hair and forced his gaze to meet mine. "Our woman needs us to make decisions she is unable to make herself. I'll take Ash to that damn commune and force her mother to fix this. Unless . . ."

"I can do this. Give me a couple of hours."

"What else can I do?"

"Contact her mother. I need details about the spell. And I have a couple of boxes in my truck." He dug into his pocket and pulled out a key fob. "Bring them to the lab."

After hearing him explain why he'd left, I understood. Sometimes our parents were the most disappointing people. Like me, I knew Jet was determined to be a different man than his father. A better man. And Ash was our glue. She needed us.

Jet gave me a bro hug and then pulled away. "I've got a lot of work to do," he said.

He slapped the key fob in my palm and left me in the corridor.

CHAPTER
FIFTY-THREE
JETHRO

"What's going on?" Zoey stood behind her desk, eyes round when I entered the office.

I may have slammed the door open with more force than I'd intended.

"Sorry, I've got work to do." I waved her off.

"Is Ash okay?" she asked.

"No, but I am going to fix it." I flipped on the lights in the lab.

"Can I help?"

"Um . . . yeah. Turn on the lab equipment for me, and I need a cauldron."

Zoey ran around the lab doing as I asked, and I began working on a counter spell. Creating a spell required a combination of things. One part of it was meant to block a demon's powers by neutralizing it with an object, like an amulet. The other part was meant to make a person compliant. I was worried her mother had used something that would make Ash controllable. Something my father would have access to. It could have been another object or something else like a simple word.

"Done," Zoey said. "Anything else I can do?"

I committed the ingredients to memory, then faced her. She winced as she gazed upon my cheek. "I know I deserved it. It's late Zoey, you can take off for the day."

She hesitated then nodded. "Okay. Save her, Jet. Please."

The great thing about Ash's lab setup was she had all the essentials a witch or warlock could need. I had fresh herbs. Roots and powders in sealed containers. And a batch of remedies. Amongst those vials, I found what I needed. A healing tonic for my aching face and something that would ease the drain she was probably feeling.

I began the process of gathering the items necessary when my three favorite people in the world came into the lab.

"We're going to your truck now. Ash wanted to help," Talon told me.

I gathered her in my arms and whispered in her hair. "I love you. Please forgive me."

She disentangled herself from me without saying a word.

"Thanks," I said to Pope and Talon. They exited and I steered Ash to a stool in the lab.

"Give me one second." I poured her energy tonic into a glass beaker, cast a tiny spell, and watched it spark. Once the smoke evaporated. I turned to Ash. "Did Talon explain?"

"Yes. I know I'm supposed to be angry but it's weird. It's like I'm watching my life through someone else's eyes."

"I'm going to fix this, Ash. Do you trust me?"

She eyed me for a minute. "I shouldn't. I should be mad at you, but everything seems dull."

"What does that tell you, my little love?"

"I'm not myself." She slumped, her eyes watering.

"No, Aisling you're not. But I vow," I knelt before her. "To prove myself worthy of your love. And do everything in my power to help you in any way."

She nodded. The gesture was hesitant, but I took it as a good sign.

"This will fade the fogginess and give you some energy. You don't have to take it, but I might need your help."

She made a gimme motion with her hand. I handed over the potion and she downed it in one swig. She canted her head to the side and said, "Interesting. It tastes like you."

I kissed her cheek.

"What can I do?" she asked.

"Give it a minute or fifteen. In the meantime, relax and maybe try your mother."

The guys returned with the boxes.

"Hi, angel, you look different," Pope told her.

"Jet gave me something. I feel different, sort of. Still weak."

"You need to eat," all of us said at the same time.

"We'll bring down some food," Talon offered. "Anything else?"

I shook my head.

"My phone. I don't know where it is. My mother will answer. I think. Or maybe my sister," Ash told him.

"I know where it is. We'll be back before you can miss us," Pope said.

Aisling gave him a genuine smile. "There it is." He stroked her cheek, then came over and punched my arm.

"Hey! Do you mind?!" I held up my hands, one holding up powdered valerian root, the other a measuring cup. "I'm working!"

"I'm out." Pope scampered out of the lab.

Talon and Ash were in a lip lock. The big man was not about to let her go until Pope returned and dragged him out.

I worked for hours non-stop. Tally, Pope, and Ash helped by reading textbooks, looking for anything that would help with the current potion plus what would come afterward. Her mother never answered, and her sister promised on two occasions she'd have her mother call back. We were still waiting.

Spells were all about intent and precision. I was being extra careful because it was Ash. And she was in this predicament partly because of me leaving the way I did. Which led to the boat incident.

My stomach clenched just thinking about what they all had been through. And then there was my father's involvement. Sure, she had demon blood and her mother had handled the situation poorly all her life, but his actions weighed heavily on my shoulders. He was responsible for her current state.

I took a deep breath and looked at my work.

"Hey." Ash trailed her fingertips along my shoulders sending a tendril of warmth through my body. I closed my eyes savoring her touch for a second. Life would be meaningless without her in it. *I must fix this.*

I gripped her waist and pulled her onto my lap. "I'm sorry, little love."

"I know, Jet. I wish I could tell you all is forgiven but I'm not in my right frame of mind. My thoughts have gotten clearer in the last few hours than they have been in days. And I appreciate everything you're doing right now." She wrapped her arms around my neck. "Thank you, for coming back to save me."

"I won't leave your side again. Ever."

Ash's arms tightened around me for a brief moment and then her body relaxed. She remained seated on my lap and asked. "So, where are we?"

"The potion is done for the most part. It needs a drop of something. Blood. I just need to know whose blood she used. Typically for something like this, it would be the person who will be able to break the spell. It could be someone who loves you, someone in your family. Or someone who would be umm . . ."

"The one to control me. Harlo. I can't believe my mother did this to me." Her voice cracked.

"It wasn't just her, Ash. My father is just as guilty," I said hoping to ease the disappointment she must've felt over her mother's actions.

Ash shrugged and called her mother again. It rang and rang then went to voicemail.

"You know what, let me try." I patted her leg and went to get my phone in the office.

I called the number she gave me and put it on speakerphone.

A child answered. "Hello," he sang into the voice. "Is this Aunt Ash?"

I pressed my finger to my lips telling Ash to keep quiet. She nodded.

"No, this is Dr. Buchanan. I need to speak with Gillian, it's an emergency."

"Okay. Momma? This man wants to speak with Grandma. He said it's a 'mergency."

Who is it? Someone said in the background.

"Dr. Buck."

Buchanan?

"Hello?"

I held up my hand telling Ash to remain quiet.

"Gillian, did you use my blood in the spell you cast on Aisling?"

"Of course not. Listen, Harlo . . . Is this Harlo? You sound different. Anyway, listen no, I did not. I know what using your blood would have meant. I'm not a first-year witch. I would never give you control of my daughter."

Aisling released a loud sob.

"Momma, it's me."

"Aisling, no. Get away from him!" Her voice was frantic.

"It's alright, Momma. I'm with my men. That was Dr. Jethro Buchanan, Harlo's son. He's trying to help me."

The women cried. Aisling's mother apologized and told Ash how much she loved her. Ash cried and promised she was okay.

It was sweet. And I was glad her mother wasn't entirely complicit with my father's scheming. Donovan, Ash's father, had shown early signs of dementia. He received the diagnosis just as Aisling finished her residency. He had been the original catalyst in Gillian's spell to subdue Ash's demon as a child. The impressive spell worked for years which was a testament to Gillian's skill. However, as soon as Donovan's dementia kicked in, the effects of the spell began to wear off.

This had also been about the same time my father had come into the picture. The asshole saw a way to gain Gillian and Donovan's favor by funneling money to the commune in exchange for info on Aisling's demon father. Gillian was a smart witch. They needed the money for Donovan's care and the commune as a whole, so she made a deal. But she hadn't given Harlo the info he sought. She sent my father on a wild goose chase trying to find Ash's father. He'd given her the binding spell, which Harlo had said had to be fueled by the blood of a warlock. Gillian knew better and used Donovan's instead. Ash's father sounded like a good man.

What my father withheld from Gillian was that the spell would not only subdue Ash's demon side, it would subdue her as well. If the binding was left as is, Ash would have been in a vegetative state in less than two months.

I talked to Gillian for thirty minutes going over what I'd done to counter the spell. We didn't need her father's blood anymore. We had three men present, who loved her more than anything. Two who had repeatedly covered up her crimes and then there was me, the man giving up his life and family history, to be with her. My sacrifice was small in comparison to getting rid of dead bodies, but if I had known, I would have done the same thing.

Ash's mother insisted we do the spell in a sacred space so ten minutes later we were in Talon's SUV and heading to Aisling's apartment.

CHAPTER FIFTY-FOUR

AISLING

The tonic Jet had given me helped. I wasn't one hundred percent yet, but at least I could think straight. Ever since I'd left the commune I felt like I was sleepwalking. I still felt tired but at least I could form coherent thoughts.

Per my mother's instructions, we were at my apartment to do the ritual. I was raised as a witch and had carved out a little space for practicing my craft. Under a secret panel in my laundry room, I led my men down to the basement.

"You've been holding out on me, angel." Pope spun in a small circle.

"Demon." I pointed to my chest. "Not angel. And I am half witch. This should have been expected."

"And this?" He plucked a cell phone from one of the shelves.

A burner phone that did not belong to me but probably had my fingerprints all over it. I shook my head. Disgusted. Fucking Mistress. *What else was she doing down here?* I gave Pope a half-hearted shrug which appeased him for the time being and went back to admiring my private space.

My mother, my sister, and at least half of the women in the coven outdid me on the power scale in terms of witch abilities. I had some skill with potions, hence my chosen degree and career path. The lab provided a space for me to do most of my potion work. My basement was where I came to meditate and tinker with simple spells.

A pentagram drawn in white chalk was on the floor surrounded by candles. There were a few floor cushions for comfort while I was meditating. Along the far wall, I had a hearth, with a cauldron poised over a stack of wood. On the opposite side was a row of shelves, which housed books and glass containers filled with dried herbs. I had a workbench for simple potion creations, and mortar and pestles in various sizes.

"This looks important." Jet gestured to a wooden chest with forged iron hardware, which was sitting on top of the workbench where it didn't belong.

I tried to think back to when I may have moved it and came up blank. The Mistress again. A creepy feeling crawled up my spine. She had been everywhere and in everything. I groaned inwardly, hating this being residing in me.

Pausing for a breath, I said a silent prayer. *Please not this.* I cast a simple spell to open the chest that housed my sacred things.

A glass jar filled with red salt was in its proper place and looked untouched. Serpentine salt was from my home and the key ingredient in my tonic. It was powerful and had the potential to create many useful remedies. The red salt came from a brackish plunge pool located in the commune. Moon Serpent Commune was located in the mountains, miles from the ocean. The coven hadn't discovered why there was brackish water in the mountains or what the true purpose of the salt was. It was one of those natural phenomena that remained a mystery for centuries and remained a secret.

The serpent queen, the protector of our coven, guarded the plunge pool and thus the sacred salt. I had to ask for permission to take what I had via a ritual and a little blood sacrifice. The queen was happy to drink up my blood, and it made me wonder if she knew I was a demon.

My other prized possessions were wrapped in distressed leather. I picked up the bundle and swallowed. It felt lighter, which meant . . . I stepped back and pressed up against a hard chest. My men were behind me, looking over my shoulder. Their presence was comforting and encouraged me to speak.

"My father is a blacksmith. Or was. He made weapons. Knives, daggers, and the like. I always admired his work." I began unbuckling the fasteners on the knife roll.

"I used to like watching him work. He was so strong." I wiped my wet cheeks with the back of my hand. "I was a scrawny kid, but he let me work on a few blades over the years. These are a few of them."

My fingertips skimmed along the hilts of five knives, noting that one was missing. *You fucking didn't?!* A restrained sob left my lips.

Strong arms wrapped around my middle. A big hand covered mine and squeezed gently. And someone rested his chin on my shoulder.

"I'm sorry, Ash. I didn't know," Pope whispered.

It took my brain a minute to figure out why he was apologizing and then I remembered. He'd been using his unknown magic to get rid of the murder weapons.

"You did the right thing, Pope. I'd be in jail or an asylum right now if you hadn't protected me," I said.

I inhaled deeply and turned to face them. "Let's get this over with."

After a moment of reassuring hugs and pecks on the cheeks, my men went to work.

Discovering the missing knife zapped the energy boost I had felt moments ago. While the guys prepared for the ritual, I sat wearily on the workbench, thinking about my father. He'd been giving his blood and thus a portion of his life force to save me. I needed to return the favor. The other project I'd been working on was a cure for his dementia. Maybe I could save him, and he and I could replace the knife I'd misused. Yes, misused. My father didn't gift his daughter weapons for her to commit murder. Protect myself, sure. But kill innocents? I tried to shake the thoughts out of my head, which wasn't all that helpful.

"Can I help with anything?" I asked just to be polite.

"Almost done. I want to do a quick review of everything and then we'll get started," Jet winked.

I loved watching Jet work. He was the most powerful magic wielder I knew. Every move was precise and elegant. And no detail was left unturned. Despite the way he'd left, I trusted him to fix me. He was the only person I trusted. It was nice to know my mother hadn't sold me out to Harlo. Still, I'd always be on my guard around her.

Once everything was set to his satisfaction, Jet turned to me and said, "Alright little monster, let's unleash the demon."

I giggled.

"Don't say it like that, geez," Pope grumped.

"You're the worst, warlock," Talon added.

Those two were nervous. They'd never seen a ritual before, and it almost made me want to run around in the circle like a lunatic.

"I can tell by the look on your face you're planning something crazy. Don't. It'd be funny as shit, but you'll give one or both of them apoplexy." Jet smirked and then handed me the potion. "Down the hatch. We'll be done in moments."

I did as instructed, sitting cross-legged on the stained concrete flooring, and closed my eyes. Jet chanted. His voice deep, smooth, and almost sensual. A few seconds went by, then a minute, and another. I lost track of time. My skin felt tingly and then something in me snapped like a twig. The sound echoed in my ears and there was a sharp pain in my back. I crumpled to the ground. The cool concrete pressed against my cheek. A ribbon unfurled in my core and spread through me like a web. I rolled on the ground as the web continued to stretch inside of me. My limbs lengthened as though a puppet master was pulling on the ribbon inside of me. My legs shot straight up, my toes pointed to the ceiling, and then my thighs separated forming a wide V before coming back to the floor. My arms shot to the sides, my fingers splayed, reaching for something and nothing. Then my back arched, my head tipped to the ground. A warming sensation ran up and down my spine.

Thank you, my demon said.

Please don't make me regret this.

And then the world faded to black.

CHAPTER FIFTY-FIVE

AISLING

When I opened my eyes, I was on my bed.

"How long have I been out?" I asked my guys who wore identical expressions of concern.

"Forever," Pope said.

Talon elbowed him in his belly.

"It's only been about ten minutes," Jet answered.

"Felt like forever," Pope muttered.

"What happened? Did it work?"

"You tell us, mate. How do you feel?"

I sat up and rolled my neck and then my shoulders.

"Are you going to do supernatural yoga again?" Pope asked.

A small smile spread over my lips and soon laughter took over which caught on in the room like a yawn.

"I seem good. Yet different. In comparison to the last week, almost two, I feel like my old self. No . . . better. My body feels lighter, and it's like a veil had been lifted," I told them.

"Thank God." Pope pounced, tackling me to the bed. "I missed you, angel."

"I'm a demon, Pope. Not an angel."

"You'll always be my angel." Pope's lips gently grazed against mine.

The contact sent an electrical jolt through my body, igniting every nerve. My senses buzzed to life. Every emotion of my men hit me all at once, and I soaked it all in.

My tongue delved into his mouth, exploring, tasting. He tasted of love and surety that comes when the sun peeks out after a rainy day. Warmth spread through my belly. My legs parted for him. His growing erection rubbed against my core.

He ended our kiss and rolled off me, allowing Talon to take his place.

"And you'll always be my mate." Talon's mouth claimed mine. The weight of his body pressed against me, and I reveled in his unique flavor of protection, my shield protecting me against any storm that would dare touch me.

Talon sat on his heels bringing me up with him.

Jet came up behind me and planted kisses from my shoulder to my neck. "And you'll always be my little monster," he whispered while helping me out of my sports bra.

I hooked my arm around Jet's neck. Lips, tongues, and teeth collided. My warlock tasted of forbidden fruit, sweet and spicy, and oh so addicting.

The oppressive dense fog that had taken over my life since my mother had bound my demoness had been lifted and my thoughts were clear and energy restored. I felt alive.

A heady scent thick with lust filled my nostrils. Arousal pooled in my core and blossomed through my body making me feel light-headed. It felt good to be back. To feel.

"Clothes off," I rasped.

I tugged on T-shirts, buttons, and waistbands.

In seconds, I was naked and so were my men. They laid me back on the mattress, my legs spread wide. The warmth of their skin set my nerves ablaze with want. Their lips were everywhere. Kissing and sucking. Everywhere except where I needed it most.

I reached between my legs. Someone slapped my hand.

"Ours," Jet rasped.

"Is this what you want, angel?" Pope's tongue slid through my wet slit in one slow swipe.

"Yes!" I writhed.

He chuckled. "I don't think you want it badly enough."

I raised my head to glare at him. He gave me an evil smirk and flicked his tongue over my clit.

"You fucking tease," I snarled.

He laughed.

I hooked my leg around his neck and forced his face into my pussy. He devoured me with his mouth. I closed my thighs, keeping him in place, while I pumped my hips.

"That's so fucking hot, little slut. Smother him with your wet cunt," Jet drawled. His gaze fixated on what Pope was doing between my legs. I reached for his length and swiped the precum leaking from his tip, then brought my finger to my mouth.

Talon hissed beside me and fused our lips, forcing me to share Jet's flavor with him.

I bucked my hips, my climax building and building. Pope moaned as though he was eating the most delicious thing he ever put into his mouth.

I reached for Jet and Talon and gripped their cocks. The smooth velvety skin was a contrast to how thick and hard they were.

Talon placed his hand over mine, guiding my movements, showing me exactly how he wanted to be touched, while I ran my fingers over the three piercings on Jet's engorged length, making him groan and twitch in my hand.

Pope continued lashing my pussy with his smooth tongue. Something entered my pussy, taking me by surprise. My orgasm burst out of me, soaking his face.

Jet and Talon made room for Pope as he crawled up my body.

"You're so delicious, angel," Pope said, his voice husky with need. He impaled me with his cock, and I licked his lips, his chin, his neck.

He fucked me hard, the weight of him driving into me. "I love your pussy so fucking much." He groaned. His hips slammed into me, faster and faster.

My ankles locked behind his back, and I clung to his neck as he came, pushing his spend deeper into me.

Before either of us could catch our breath, someone nudged him off me. Pope slid out of me, his cock slick with my arousal and his. Jet eyed his length and licked his lower lip. Giving me an idea.

I exchanged places with Talon, lying him on the mattress, and then squatted over his length. His massive girth stretched me wide as I slowly sheathed him with my pussy.

"God damn, that's a fat fucking cock," Pope murmured, his dick half hard and still glistening.

"Yeah it is, but she takes it like a pro," Jet rasped.

Talon gripped my hips and rocked me over his cock, working me over him in a cadence that had sweat dripping down my spine.

I reached for Pope and cleaned him off with my mouth. Then pulled Jet to me and fastened my lips over his.

"Delicious," Jet groaned. "Both of you."

"You like that?" Pope brought his cock to our lips. Jet and I licked and sucked him together.

Talon fucked me from below. "Fffuck," he hissed.

My body was on fire as another orgasm crested. There were so many sensations and tastes it made me dizzy.

"Not yet, baby," Talon sat up. His lips got into the fray, kissing me, kissing Jet. Kissing Pope's fully hard cock. "I want Jet in your ass. I want to feel his piercings while I fuck you."

My walls clenched around Talon's rigid length. He gasped. "You're killing me with this tight cunt. Get in there, Jet. Before I blow."

"Fuck yeah. You don't have to ask me twice." Jet positioned

himself behind me and ran his tip up and down my crack. "Lay back down, you two. And relax, baby. I'll take it slow."

"Pope, do me a solid and grab that bottle out of my bag." Jet said and then his mouth was on my ass, licking and sucking.

The sensation was different and thrilling. It had always been a no-no spot. Naughty. Off-limits. Taboo. But it felt so freaking good. I began rocking over Talon's cock, encouraging Jet to tongue my back entrance.

"You like this don't you, little slut?" Jet moaned. "Like my tongue in your ass and a big dick in your pussy."

"I'm going to come," I mewled.

"Let me help you with that." Jet slid something in my ass. A finger I presumed. Whatever it was lit the fuse. My pussy contracted as I unleashed and came and came and came.

"God damn, you feel so good when you come, Ash." Talon's lips covered mine, breathing into me while I caught my breath.

Something slick dripped between my cheeks and Jet massaged it in.

He leaned over and feathered kisses over my shoulders and back. "I've been dreaming about this virginal ass ever since we met." His crown nudged into my puckered hole and slipped in.

It stung and I flinched. Maybe this wasn't so good.

"Easy, baby. Let me in," Jet gently pushed. "That's it. Just like that. Swallow my tip with that tight ass."

"Ohmmmygawd," I gasped. The sting disappeared leaving nothing but pure pleasure.

"Feel good, little monster?"

"Mmmhhmmm . . . more." I pushed, taking him deeper.

"Oh fuck." Jet laid a hand on my lower back and slid in another inch, and then another.

"Ash, baby, you look so fucking beautiful, taking his cock. So hot." Pope stroked himself while he stared at what Jet was doing to me.

"Just a little more," Jet said his voice low and breathy. He sank all the way in with a deep groan. "Fuuuck, Aisling." His pelvis was flush against my skin.

I drew in a sharp breath. I felt so full. So connected to my men. And so tight it was on that borderline of pain and pleasure. I rocked my hips, forcing him to move his shaft and lighting up the sensitive nerve endings in my ass.

"Fuck me," I gasped.

"You like that, mate?" Talon asked.

"Yes," I breathed. "Sooo good."

"It feels fucking amazing. I can feel him in you. It's so tight. And those fucking piercings." Talon pumped into me from below.

"Happy to make you both feel good but fuck, little monster. You're squeezing the life out of my cock." Jet thrust into me. "This is going to be shorter than I'd hoped. Feels too fucking good." His hips moved faster and deeper.

"Oh . . . my . . . fuck . . ." I cried out. "Don't you dare stop."

Stars danced behind my eyes. I moaned like a banshee and clawed at Talon's arms.

"Fuck, you guys look so hot," Pope said, stroking his cock.

My gaze landed on his cock as my other two me worked my body from both ends.

"You want this angel? You want me to come in your mouth?"

I parted my lips and stuck out my tongue.

Pope exploded. Ropes of cum shot all over my face and dripped down on Talon's neck.

My orgasm tore out of me. I shattered, coming so fucking hard. My inner walls clamped down on both of my men, wringing their release.

"Fuck yes. I'm coming," Talon roared.

"Damn it. Fuck Ash. You're milking my cock." Jet gripped my hips and drove himself deep into my ass, filling me with his cum.

It was all so much. I was saturated by their love, their desire, their seed. They were consuming me in every sense. Filling my body, my heart, and my soul; I was theirs utterly and completely.

Blissed out, I slumped on Talon's chest. Jet crumpled on top of me. And Pope lounged lazily beside us. We lay there for a while catching our breaths. I slipped in and out of consciousness as my men moved around me. A warm, wet, soft cloth ran between my legs. Someone combed through my tangled locks. And a sheet was placed over my body. I was awash with a sense of peace. For the first time in my life, I was completely *me*. Demoness and witch.

CHAPTER FIFTY-SIX

POPE

Sex between four people was messy. We didn't have multiple bathrooms at our disposal, so Ash, our queen got to shower first. I hopped into the shower with her because . . . just because. The other two were in a post-sex mini coma, also known as old guy syndrome. They weren't that old but being the youngest of the bunch meant I had to give them shit now and then.

After our shower, the guys were still on the bed, eyes closed. Couldn't blame them, I was ready to close my eyes, too, but Ash had other needs.

She was in the kitchen rummaging through her empty cabinets.

"Are you hungry, angel?" I asked.

"Starving."

I chuckled. "Put some clothes on, we'll get some takeout."

"Great idea." She flashed me her beautiful smile.

Minutes later, we were reversing Talon's SUV out of the driveway.

"What do you feel like eating?" I laced our fingers together and placed a kiss on her knuckles.

"Honestly, I would be happy with a cheeseburger."

"Mystic Diner?" we said at the same time.

The drive was short, and the parking lot was full, which on any normal day would have made me choose somewhere else. But Ash was back to her old self, and this was what she wanted.

I hadn't noticed anything odd as of yet, which was normal according to Jet. On the way over to do the ritual, he explained the change might be gradual but he had spells handy for any mishaps or demon shenanigans. They were short-term solutions, he cautioned, but he felt confident about finding something that was long-term. It sounded simple and Ash and her mother were on board with his plans. I was the non-magic user . . . sort of and so I trusted their judgment. The best I could offer was to look after Ash as much as I could.

I offered to drop Ash off at the diner while I parked the car, but she insisted on walking with me, which I preferred. We walked hand in hand just like the old days.

"I missed this," I told her. "Just you and me, hanging out. Don't get me wrong, Talon and Jet are cool guys but sometimes . . ."

I shrugged. All three of us had a role to play in her life. And I was happy to share. She was worth it, and I couldn't imagine a life without them in it.

"I miss this, too." She tucked into my side allowing me to drape an arm around her. "Maybe we should carve out date nights."

"You would do that?" I asked.

"Of course. It can't be easy for all of you to share. And I don't want to neglect any of you." She slipped her hand into my back pocket.

"You really are the perfect woman," I kissed the top of her head.

Mystic Diner was a fast-food joint that had a walk-up window instead of a drive-through. We stood in line, arms wrapped around one another. Talking about nothing important. Ash was hands-down my favorite person in the world. I enjoyed her company more than anyone I'd ever known.

"It'll be about thirty minutes," the cashier said after we placed our order.

Ash and I found a bench and she sat on my lap.

"Did you ever think your life would end up like this? With someone like me?" she asked.

"I wasn't much of a planner. I always knew I'd make money doing something with computers. Marriage and family life wasn't in my periphery until I met you."

"Really?"

"As soon as I met you, I knew you were the one."

She giggled.

"I'm serious. Even though you rejected me. Multiple times."

"I did not."

I gave her a dry look.

"It wasn't rejection, Gaius. I was trying to spare you from dealing with my brand of crazy."

"That would have never worked. Your brand of crazy was like a siren call. I was determined to make you mine. Perseverance worked. Look at us now."

She cupped my face. "Thank you. For never giving up on me. For having my back during my crazy. For loving me."

Her lips fused over mine in a heated kiss. My pulse raced and blood rushed to my cock. I couldn't wait to get her home.

Ash snaked her hand down my trousers. Her soft fingers encircled my shaft and she tugged with a nice firm pressure.

"Pope," the cashier called.

"Dammit," I muttered.

Ash chuckled and fixed her dress as she stood. "I'll get it."

I gave myself a second for my cock to deflate then hurried to the counter to help her with the bags of food.

By the time we arrived at Ash's place, Talon was relaxing on the couch and Jet was bounding down the stairs, fresh out of the shower. We all plopped on the living room floor and ate burgers and fries. Ash ate more than she had in the last two weeks.

"I'm glad you're eating, baby," Talon praised.

"It's so good." She dipped a fry into her chocolate shake and took a bite. "After leaving my mother's, everything tasted so bland. Now flavors are exploding in my mouth."

Jet frowned, then dipped a fry. "That's pretty good," he said, prompting me and Talon to give it a try.

We nodded our agreement causing a big smile to spread over Aisling's face. *God, I missed that smile.*

"So, we were talking, Talon and I, about where we are going to live," Jet began.

"We're moving? From the penthouse?" I asked.

"Yeah, it's too small for all of us," Talon added.

Ash gave me a knowing smile. We were fine with living in our modest apartments. Well, in comparison to Talon's penthouse, our places combined were hovels. I imagined Jet lived in similar if not more lavish housing.

"What did you have in mind? Your place at Shadow?" Aisling asked.

"No. I won the bid for a property near it though. It's a renovation, and my crew is ready to go. It will be a couple of months, but I'd like for all of you to see it and voice your needs and wants," Talon said.

She turned toward Jet. "And you're okay with this? Living here in Port Midway?"

"Yes. But my father is going to be pissed with my resignation which means I will be out of a job. I have some money tucked away, which will help him," he pointed in Talon's direction, "with the house. I'll need to figure out what to do for cash flow at some point. Maybe I'll teach at the university."

"Or like I said to Ash, I can fund another lab."

"How much money do you have?" I asked with my mouth full.

"Billions."

I choked.

"Let him fund a new lab, angel," I added as soon I'd gotten over my shock. Billions. Wow. Look at me shacking up with a sugar daddy.

"I can't go anywhere. I'm under contract. I doubt Harlo will let me go," Aisling said.

"Already took care of that," Jet said under his breath.

All eyes focused on the warlock.

"I submitted an amended contract when I was at the office, giving you the option to leave whenever you wanted. And I took out the clause about your projects." He chugged his water and then added. "And yeah, I may have signed your name."

My gaze switched back and forth between Ash and Jet. And then Talon and Jet. I wasn't the most experienced business person in the bunch, but even I knew forgery was illegal.

Aisling set her burger down and eyed Jet. "I can leave anytime I want and take all of my projects with me?"

He nodded.

"And you forged my signature?" She narrowed her gaze.

"I had to. I had to backdate it so there's no question about the document's validity. Everything was *signed,*" he made air quotes with his fingers, "when I had the authority to make the decision." Nervous energy rolled off the warlock.

Aisling hopped into his lap and kissed him all over his face. "Thank you, Jet. For protecting me. For coming back. For saving me. Thank you for everything."

I released a relieved sigh. We were together, the four of us, as we should be. Everything was going to be okay.

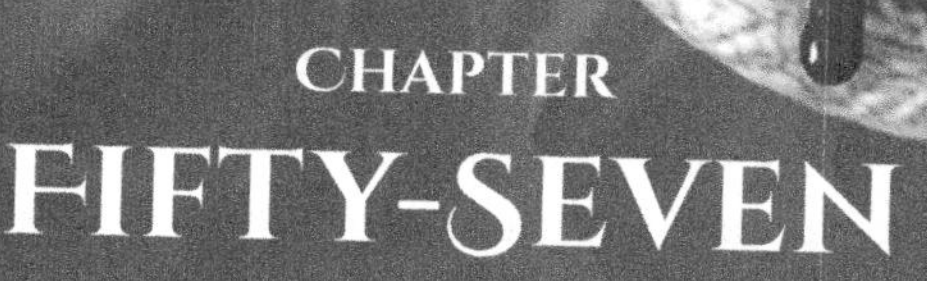

CHAPTER FIFTY-SEVEN

AISLING

The air felt oppressive as though the bar was living up to its name. The Last Resort. The people though, the people were my kind of crowd. Drunk and living like there was no tomorrow. Most of the patrons were cross-country truckers stopping at the border of Port Midway before getting back on the road in the morning.

Making new friends was easy, and they were all so generous. I hadn't paid for a drink or food all night and one guy even offered to give me five hundred dollars for a blow job. I didn't need the money though and as far as sex, I was weighing my options.

I leaned over the pool table and called my shot. "Eight ball corner pocket."

The bar went silent. I sunk it in. Of course.

The room erupted in ooohs *and* aahs. *Everyone was impressed except there was one resounding* Bitch!

"Pay up." I rounded on my opponent. Ball Cap Wearer had a nice truck and I wanted it. And I won fair and square. Okay maybe not exactly fair, but I did win and that's all that mattered. I held out my hand, palm up.

"You cheated!"

"I did not. The entire bar witnessed me whipping your ass. Twice. Keys. Don't make me ask again."

"Or what?"

Or else, I'll kill you, *I thought but didn't say.*

"Fuck off, little girl. You're not getting shit." Ball Cap Wearer brought his beer bottle to his lips and turned his back to me.

"You're a sore loser." I walked out of the bar and waited.

An hour later, the sore loser stumbled out of the bar. He ambled into the parking lot and swerved his way to the motel beside the bar.

Instead of going to his room which was a few feet away, he disappeared behind the building. I rounded the corner just as he whipped out his dick and began peeing on the brick wall.

I waited until he zipped up his pants and then cleared my throat.

"You want some of this." He gripped himself. "Well, come here little girl. Come to Daddy."

Gross.

"At first I just wanted my keys, to my truck. But now you've pissed me off. You want to know why?"

He frowned.

"You have the fucking nerve to ask me to call you Daddy. My daddy is a good man. And you're not even close."

I slashed at him with my pocket knife. He dodged and the blade grazed his arm.

"If you're going to attack someone with a knife, use a real one." He pulled a hunting knife from his boot and rushed me.

I blocked his arm and gripped his wrist then twisted his arm behind his back. He dropped the knife. With speed he didn't expect, I picked up the knife and ran the blade across his inner thigh.

The man reached out, gripped my neck, and squeezed. I sliced him across his neck. He staggered back. I stabbed him again and again and again. Blood sprayed, dousing me with crimson liquid.

"I'M HERE about the Smith family. I have the money they owe you." I placed an envelope on the table.

He looked at it and shook his head. "Too late. I already leased the apartment to someone else."

"You kicked out a single mother and her two young children. For a thousand dollars?"

He shrugged.

"I'll pay you double." I tapped on the envelope.

"Quadruple. No, fifty thousand." He drank his beer.

Greedy fuck.

"You do not want to piss me off," I warned.

He shrugged one shoulder. I took the envelope, walked away, and waited.

Soon I was awash in red liquid which had a metallic tang.

This was getting easier and easier.

"SOMEONE CALL 911!"

Her face was a mass of angry red and purple. Her eyes were swollen shut and her cheeks were puffed like a chipmunk.

"Oh my god, Ash, is she?" Emily asked.

"She's breathing. Her pulse is faint but she's still here." I smoothed her blood-soaked hair from her face. "Who would do this?"

"She's been in here before. It wouldn't be a surprise if Raul did this."

She lay in the hospital, unable to breathe on her own. Her ribs had been broken and her windpipe had nearly been crushed.

"Don't worry, I'll find who did this and make him pay," I whispered in her ear.

I CARESSED the sharp planes of his jaw. He was beautiful, every inch of him. My gaze roamed his naked form, committing every inch of him to memory.

Come find me, mate. I need you.

Slipping into his button-down shirt, I gathered my belongings and crept out of the club. My heels clicked with each step as I skipped to my car, his scent lingered on my skin and I could still feel his touch. The wolf. My wolf.

"Whore," a male voice snarled.

"Excuse me?" I turned to see a man leering at me.

"You heard me. You should be ashamed of yourself. Walking around town with fluids dripping down your leg."

A strangled cry pierced the air. I cut it off short with another blow to his head with my crowbar. I hit him again. His body flopped. I struck him once more. Something in him cracked. I struck him repeatedly, the sound of bones crushing filled my ears.

I jolted awake, my heart slamming in my chest. My gaze swept the room. Talon's room. My men were sound asleep beside me. I inhaled deeply and held it for a few seconds, then released it slowly.

Dream. Just a dream. I laid back down and stared at the ceiling.

You know it wasn't, my demon said.

Not you again.

Yes, me. It is time for you to face the truth.

Darkness ebbed into my vision. Panic gripped me by the throat. I couldn't move, couldn't breathe. The smell of bitter sweat invaded my nostrils. Cold air prickled over my skin as my leggings were violently ripped off my body. No! No! No!

I snapped my head forward, head-butting the man with the deceptively kind voice. Blood spurted from his nose. The bearded man lunged at me, knife in hand. Using my smaller frame, I rolled out of his grasp, gripped his elbow, and yanked at his wrist so hard bones cracked. He let out an agonizing cry. That's right asshole, I'm smaller but stronger. I took the knife from his hand and slammed it into his gut. He stumbled back.

"You broke my nose," the deceptively kind voice man said.

"It's an improvement." I crashed into him, pinning him to the mattress, and stabbed him repeatedly in the chest.

The bearded man was crawling on the floor, gasping for breath.

I kicked him in the face so hard his body turned on its side.

"Please," he begged. "Have mercy."

"You were about to rape a broken-hearted woman who had too much to drink and now you want mercy. Fuck you." I sliced his stomach open and pulled out his entrails.

"What the fuck!" Chuckles appeared in the cabin, his body trembled with fear.

I smiled at him.

"You're a psycho." He ran out of the cabin, which made me laugh.

I tackled him to the floor.

He scrambled, trying to get away from me.

I grabbed a fistful of his hair and yanked.

"Not so funny now, right Chuckles? What did you guys think you were going to do? Kidnap a drunk girl, take her out to sea, use her body, and then what? Discard her into the ocean?"

"No! It wasn't me. It was them. They like to have someone aboard for entertainment."

"Just them? Do you really expect me to believe that?"

"Yes! I . . . only did it the one time. And tonight."

"You guys have done this before? At different ports?"

"Only once."

His lies smelled just as putrid as his breath. I sliced his throat just enough for him to bleed out slowly.

"Ssshh, mate," Talon's raspy voice woke me. "It's just a dream."

His arms encircled my torso as I lay on top of his body while Jet and Pope lay beside us sound asleep.

"Talon." I buried my face into his neck trying to muffle my sobs. His skin was warm, yet I shivered as a dark cold had settled into my bones.

He rolled out of bed bringing me with him.

"I got you, baby. It's going to be okay." Talon cooed as he carried me out of the room.

I clung to my wolf, soaking up his strength even though I knew life as a demon would never be that simple.

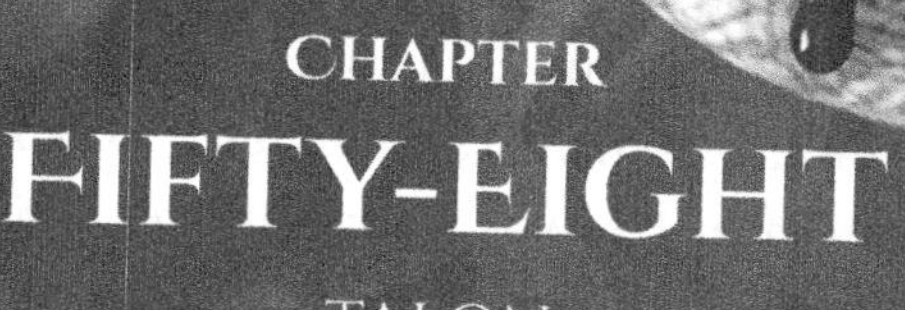

CHAPTER FIFTY-EIGHT

TALON

We came back to the penthouse after dinner. Ash's place was cute but not comfy for four. While everyone got settled, I went to my office. Over the last few days, I'd been preoccupied with Ash and had neglected my businesses. My staff stayed on top of things so I wasn't worried, but I liked keeping a close eye on things.

"Knock, knock." Ash leaned on the doorframe to my office.

"Hey, babe, I thought you'd be sleeping by now." I glanced at the time and realized I'd been in the office for a couple of hours.

"I was about to." She strolled over to me, her eyes tired. "I wanted to wait for you."

Her hair was piled high in a messy bun, and she wore a tank and white cotton panties, her go-to sleepwear.

She perched on my lap, and I dipped my head into the crook of her neck, inhaling her strawberry-scented skin.

"Do you have a lot more to do tonight?" she asked.

"No. It can wait until morning." I swiveled the chair and closed out my files. I'd gotten a lot done. It was time to call it a day. It'd been long and exhaustion was creeping up on me, too.

We climbed into bed. Jet and Pope fussed about who got to sleep on her other side. It was my bed, so I claimed her right. In the end, the other two decided to switch nightly.

Ash wiggled between me and Pope, making herself comfortable, and was soon asleep. I lay there for a while staring at the ceiling, thoughts of our future running through my mind. We needed a bigger house. Ash and Jet needed a new lab. And Pope . . . was low maintenance. He was happy in my office for now. Ash snuggled closer to me, the steady thump of her heart lulling me to sleep.

Ash's whimpers woke me. Her eyes were closed telling me she was having a nightmare. I rubbed her belly, and she settled down.

Sometime later, I woke again. This time Ash was thrashing around the bed. I pulled her into my arms, surprised neither Pope nor Jet had woken. I held her tightly and murmured sweet words into her ear.

"Talon," she said. She was shivering and my neck felt wet.

Without making a sound, I rolled out of bed and carried her into the living area. My mate needed soothing, and I wanted her to speak freely without disturbing the two sleeping beauties in our bed.

Instead of settling on the couch as I originally planned, I went out onto the terrace. I gently placed Ash on one of the loungers and she clung to me.

"Don't go," she sobbed.

"I'm not going anywhere, mate." I reached under the table for a basket and pulled out a blanket. It was early morning and windy. I settled on the lounger, bringing Ash on top of me, and laid the blanket over us.

"Do you want to talk about it?"

She didn't say a thing, but her tears spoke volumes and there was nothing I could do but hold her.

I rocked her in my arms, stroking her hair.

After a while, her sobs abated enough for her to speak. "I remember Talon. I remember all of it. Every kill. It was awful. It was brutal. And . . ." Her voice hitched and tears streamed down her cheeks.

She was facing her demon. Something that probably shouldn't have been taken away from her in the first place.

"Talon, I . . . I can't be allowed to live like this. My demon, this part of me is evil."

"Don't talk like that, baby. We just broke the binding. We need time to find a permanent solution. You can't just give up. I won't let you."

"You don't understand. It's evil. And powerful. There was so much blood. And a part of me . . . liked it. Liked killing." She sobbed again. "I can't deal with it. I can't deal with what I did. And risk what I might do."

"Babe, listen to me." I cupped her face. "You are only part demon. The part of you that is not a demon is good and strong. You can control these urges. I know you can."

She started to shake her head, and I tightened my hold, keeping her still.

"As a shifter, I was born with this sixth sense. A knowing that grew with me. The best way for me to describe is, it's like having another person living inside my body. Like a split personality. My wolf is all animal and I had to learn to control those primal urges. It took time to establish trust and communication. And dominance as well. I have to be in control of my beast to survive in this world. It wasn't easy, especially during puberty, hormones are all over the place for wolf and boy. But eventually, my wolf and I came to an understanding. We had years to establish a bond and now we agree on most things. There are things I cannot do that he can. There are things he can't do that I can. And there is a level of trust that I have with him, a bond so undeniable that I rely on him and vice versa. It is essential when you are dual-natured.

"My beast is such an integral part of me, Ash, I cannot imagine what it would be like if he had been hidden from me as a child. And then to finally meet him in my thirties. It would be a constant battle between man and wolf fighting for dominance. The thing is one cannot survive without the other. I'm sure she meant well, but your mother did you a grave disservice by binding your demon and keeping the truth from you. But here we are. And we make do with what we have.

"It's not all bad, Aisling. I imagine it will take time for you and your demoness to bond. It won't be easy. It won't be quick. But you're smart and strong. Give yourself some time to get to know this other side of you. It won't happen overnight. And that's okay, you have three men who will help you along the way. Grant yourself some grace for the things that you had done when you weren't in control. As you said, some of it was brutal, which must be jarring to relive. But I have to remind you that sometimes brutality is necessary when it comes to saving your life. I'm not the least bit sorry about you wasting those three assholes on that boat. Those fuckers deserved it, right?"

She nodded.

"Of course they did. We all, humans included, battle with the good and evil in each of us. The key is knowing the difference and making the right choice. The guys on the boat chose badly, and in the end, they got what they deserved.

"You see things as good and bad. And if I had to guess, your demoness likes to wade in the seductive morally gray waters and makes snap decisions to protect you as a whole when needed. Both sides are important, and both have skills necessary to survive."

"Talon, I'm scared," she whimpered.

"As you should be. I'd be worried if you weren't. Taking a life, whether it was justified or not, is never easy. It takes a rare breed of individual to hurt another living being and waltz away unaffected. The woman I know and love is good to her core. My mate doesn't go out on murder sprees. My mate delivers justice when it's necessary. You and your demoness may not always agree, and you'll probably duke it out but the main thing to remember is that you, Aisling Lovelle, are loved and supported no matter what. Don't take each burden on your own. Even when it comes to reliving what has already happened. If it helps and I think it will, talk to me. Or Pope. Or Jet. Talk to us about what's going on with you. Let us help. You're not alone."

She repositioned herself to look into my eyes.

"You're an amazing man, Talon Shelby." She cupped my face and pressed her lips against mine. "I remember you from that night at Nirvana. She or . . . I recognized you as my mate. It's like we were fated to find each other."

"We were destined to be together, Aisling. You were always meant to be mine." I kissed her deeply, conveying everything she meant to me that words couldn't begin to describe.

CHAPTER FIFTY-NINE

JETHRO

I woke before dawn. Ash, Talon, and Pope were sound asleep beside me. I spared them a glance, my heart swelling with new sensations I'd never experienced before. Belonging. Love. Family. It was surreal.

Reaching over Pope, I gently brushed a strand of Ash's hair away from her face. She angled her cheek into my hand and pressed her lips to my skin. As much as I wanted to stay in bed with them, I decided to go downstairs for a run.

City running wasn't as mind-clearing as running by the ocean. I shouldn't be so picky, I was surrounded by people who loved me for me, and I was finally free from Harlo Buchanan. Sort of. I hadn't bothered to read his texts or listen to his messages since I left Meridian City.

Thinking about my father had me sprinting back to Shelby Centre, where I stopped at the lab. The guys had mentioned Ash was behind on work. And she was. It wasn't bad, between her and I, we would easily be able to get caught up in a day maybe two. Did we want to, though?

Probably better to do so and then Ash could give her notice and leave on good terms. It was still early so I got started on a few things. Lab work was soothing for me. It took focus, and everything else going on in my life faded into the background.

"Jet? Where's Ash? Is she okay?"

"She's fine, Zoey." I glanced at the time. Two hours had flown by. "She should be awake by now."

"Oh okay. Why do you look homeless? Did you sleep here?"

I chuckled. I'd thrown a lab coat over my shorts and T-shirt. I probably stunk, too.

"No, I went for a run and decided to get a headstart. I'll uh, get cleaned up."

"You do that." Zoey adjusted her glasses and went into the breakroom.

On my way to the penthouse, my mind churned with the long list of things to do. There were plenty of details to sort. That was where Talon came in. He was a clever businessman and an even better attorney.

The attorney, our demoness, and the hacker were awake and they looked panicked.

"What's wrong?" I asked as I entered Talon's penthouse.

Aisling rushed me and wrapped her arms around my waist.

"I thought you'd left us again. We tried calling you for the last hour and you didn't answer." Her voice trembled, and I felt like shit.

Holding her tight to my chest, I smoothed her hair and planted kisses on the side of her face.

"I'm sorry, little love. I should have left a note. I wasn't thinking. I went for a run and stopped at the lab," I said. "And I had my phone off."

"Don't do that again, Jethro Buchanan," she muttered.

"I won't," I promised her. I'd always been a selfish man who only cared about himself but my life was different now. I had to make an effort to be more considerate.

Someone cuffed the back of my head. "For being an asshole and making all of us worry, you're cooking breakfast," Talon snarled and pulled Ash into his arms.

"Fine by me. I was planning to anyway." I leaned over and kissed Ash on the lips. "Let me take a quick shower."

After my shower, I found everyone in the kitchen unpacking a box of bagels.

"We didn't want to wait," Pope said.

Ash hip-checked him and said to me "Not true. We love your cooking. We just don't have anything to cook."

I opened the fridge and sure enough, it was bare. That would have to be changed. "I'll order some stuff," I muttered while making a list of necessities in my head.

"So, Jet, we need to start planning." Ash cut her lox and bagel and slid half to Pope. They shared food a lot, which was a reflection of how much history they had. They were always in sync. "I just got off the phone with Zoey, and she said you already finished a bunch of projects."

"Are you guys still working there? I mean, I thought the plan was to get away from your father," Pope asked.

"Yeah, eventually. I was thinking we, you and me, Ash, could get the lab caught up. It won't take long and then you could give your notice. I don't want you to leave on bad terms because of my relationship with Harlo," I said smearing cream cheese on an everything bagel. "What are your thoughts, Tally? You're the attorney. How should we do this to keep Ash protected?"

"Why do I need protection?" Ash asked with her mouth full. "Excuse me."

I leaned in and kissed her stuffed cheeks.

"He's right, mate. You don't want to tarnish your professional relationship by leaving on a bad note. Plus, I'm sure there's money you're entitled to."

"There is?" she asked.

I chuckled. "Yeah, there is. You get a percentage of profits from everything produced in your lab."

"Interesting." Ash scrunched her brows.

"I know that look," I said to her. "What's on your mind?"

She huffed out a breath and slumped. "I realize separating from Buchanan Pharmaceuticals is a good thing, but I need to ask." She paused then flicked her gaze to meet mine. "I've been working on a couple of projects. The tonic for me, which could still be useful for some. And the other was for my father. For dementia. I'm getting close but there are things I need that I know the corporate office has. Equipment and some other resources. I don't want to abandon that project."

"I knew you were working on side projects. Come here, you brilliant scientist." I pulled her to my side and squeezed. "If you trust me, I will take a look at it and see what can be done. Depending on what's needed, we may need to come up with a different strategy."

"As I mentioned, I am happy to build another lab for you two." Talon chimed in.

"You will. To replicate what we—I mean they—have in Meridian City, it might take years. If Ash's project is close, we may need to come up with a different plan. Keep in mind, Ash's contract has been modified. She's protected."

"Good point. We just need to keep Harlo in the dark about your relationship with us." Talon pointed at me and then pointed at Ash. "And Ash needs to maintain her work relationship with Buchanan Pharma."

"I should get to work then." Ash stepped away only to turn back, her face scrunched with concern. "Wait a minute. What about Zoey? If I leave, there won't be a lab for her to work in. She needs the money. I can't leave her with nothing."

"She'll be fine. Her contract is with you, which means she can leave anytime. And I made sure that if for whatever reason the lab should close temporarily or permanently, she would receive a generous severance package." I assured her.

She hopped in my arms and kissed me all over my face. "Thank you, amazing, super-smart, warlock. Thank you for thinking about my best friend."

I chuckled, then set her on her feet.

Once she was out of earshot, Talon asked, "What about your father, Jet?"

"I'm not sure. I haven't returned his calls. And well, I wanted your thoughts on the situation. I mean yeah, I can tell him to fuck off. That's easy enough. As far as Ash goes, not sure."

"To make things simple, I think you leave on your own accord. Don't mention Ash at all. Don't even tell him you're here. That might buy us some time. Will your separation from the company be that easy though?"

"I can't imagine anyone in the company making a fuss about it except him. As far as the board of directors goes . . . they may not like it. But fuck. Not my problem."

"You're really going to give up your family legacy?" Pope asked.

"It's not a decision that I'm making lightly, but I'd rather leave it all than be associated with him. Profits have tanked because of his lack of leadership. But if staying with the company makes it easier for Ash to finish this project for her father, I'll suck it up."

"I don't understand how this corporate thing works. You're the CEO but he's still in charge?"

"He's the majority shareholder of the company. He holds sway in the company's bottom line. As the CEO, I can make decisions regarding day-to-day operations, like with Ash's contract."

"Interesting," Pope said. "Complicated but interesting. Makes me glad to be working for myself. So, I had another question, since we're talking about lab shit."

I glared at the hacker. "Lab shit?"

"No offense." Pope bit into his bagel.

I leaned against the counter waiting for Pope to ask his question.

"So." He finished chewing then wiped his mouth with a napkin. "Do you have stuff here that can test my magical DNA?"

My eyebrows shot to my hairline.

Pope was open about being adopted and his magical abilities. What threw me was the way he casually brought it up like he was asking for a bag of chips. The test wasn't a big deal, what it had the potential of revealing was. Case in point, Aisling. Having demon heritage was no small thing. Talon and I gave each other a look, just as our demoness returned to the kitchen dressed in a pencil skirt and button-down blouse.

"You look nice." I kissed her neck. "What's the occasion?"

"I haven't done laundry." She gave me a sheepish grin.

"I'll handle it, baby," Talon offered.

"Thanks." She blew him a kiss, then asked, "What's going on? There's odd energy going on in here."

"I just asked your warlock scientist if he could test my magical DNA," Pope said, non-plussed.

"Great idea. I'd do it for you if I had the equipment." She smiled at him, then asked me. "Are you coming?"

"I'll be down soon." I winked. "And Pope, I'll see what I can do."

"Cool." He draped an arm around Ash and the two left for the lab.

"I think you should talk to your father," Talon said as we cleaned the kitchen. "It might appease him for the time being."

He wasn't wrong. If Harlo didn't get the attention he felt he deserved, he'd throw a tantrum. And I had two reasons to remain on his good side. "Sure, I'll send a text."

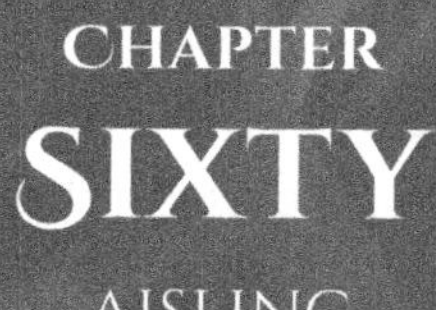

CHAPTER SIXTY

AISLING

Before going to the lab, Pope insisted we stop at his office, the space Talon had given him to work in.

"Look at you. It's almost like you're a legit business person. We should get you a name placard for your desk and maybe one for the door," I teased.

"Excellent idea. Makes it official." Pope grinned.

"I'm glad you're getting along with the guys," I told him as we took the elevator to the fourth floor.

"Me too, as far as boyfriends go, they're not so bad," he said.

Zoey rushed me as soon as I entered the office.

"I was so worried, Ash." She hugged me.

Pope wrapped his arms around both of us for a group hug. "I'll leave you two to catch up." He pecked my cheek and took off.

"Thank you for everything, Zozo. For talking to the guys and for holding down the fort. How are you? What can I do for you?"

"I'm good Ash, Jet came in and got a headstart. I'm sure you two will get us caught up in no time."

"Right. I'm on it. We need to talk though. Give me an hour or two and then we can do a girls' lunch?"

"Two hours, babes. I have things to do also." She returned to her desk, and I went to mine.

Jet had accomplished a lot this morning and there was still plenty to do. I rolled my neck and got to work. My warlock came in an hour later and we worked side by side until Zoey came and got me for lunch.

As soon as we walked out of the building, I told her about the heavy stuff. My demon and unleashing the beast.

"A demon? Seriously?! That's badass," Zoey exclaimed. She wasn't concerned at all.

"No. It could be a bad thing," I told her.

She shrugged. "Sounds like you went after bad people more than good ones. If the scumbag deserves it, I say show no mercy."

"You are ruthless. And that's why I love you. But seriously, I probably should stay away from the shelter."

She shook her head. "I say you need to spend more time there. There are a lot of psychos creeping around. Police patrol the neighborhood more than they used to. And they hired another security guard, but that's not enough. This new drug that's going around has been making people crazy."

The conversation with the chief of police at the carnival weeks ago flashed into my mind.

"That doesn't sound good. Is Em okay? Is there anything we can do? Maybe Talon has some insights."

"Em is fine. Stressed but she loves her work. I'll ask her if she needs anything. In the meantime, maybe you can go over there and be like Catwoman or Harley Quinn or something."

"You watch too many superhero movies."

She shrugged. "They're entertaining and everyone could use a superhero in their life."

I chuckled.

"Well, on top of the demon thing, there might be changes in the work department. We're thinking about opening a lab of our own. And you're coming with us," I said.

Zoey's eyes widened, and I proceeded to tell her everything about Harlo and leaving Buchanan Pharma.

"This is exciting Ash! And thanks for including me in your plans," she said.

"Of course. But you should be thanking Jet. He made sure your contract and mine were secure before he left Meridian City."

"I suppose he gets a pass for being a bitch and leaving you with a note."

"Yeah, I guess he does. I love them. All three of them, which is weird for me to say. But they're meant to be mine. Each of them has a different quality I value and need in my life," I admitted.

"Hey, you don't need to explain yourself to me. I have a wife and a husband. It keeps things interesting." She wiggled her eyebrows.

"You are too much, Zozo."

"So, three of them huh? Nice job, Ash. I am impressed. Too many dongs for my taste but hey if you're happy, then I'm happy."

I laughed.

"How does it work with three of them? One in every hole? Or do they, you know . . ." She brought her fist to her mouth, made a jerking movement, while bobbing her head and pushing her tongue on the inside of her cheek.

"O. M. God. Zoey! Will you stop?! This is a family restaurant!" I smacked her hand. It wasn't but the cafe was crowded, and people were giving us *looks*.

She laughed. "Well, answer me. How does it work?! I told you the deets when I married a man and a woman."

My cheeks heated and I shook my head. "Not the time or place. We need wine for that conversation."

"I can't wait!" She rubbed her palms together.

"You're a fiend for sex gossip." I laughed.

"So are you. That's why we're great together."

We cut our girl time short. One hour. Ugh. And went back to work. Zoey clocked out a little earlier to do momma duties and Jet and I slaved away for hours.

Working beside Jet was the best. It'd been years since I had a lab partner and had gotten accustomed to doing things my way. For the most part, Jet and I had the same style, which made everything flow. We were the perfect pairing.

He was still an edger though. The sex talk, the glances, and the subtle and not-so-subtle brushes against my skin made the time pass quickly. I was a sopping mess for him all afternoon, and of course, he wouldn't grant me my release.

I wasn't going to lie, though, I loved the way my arousal built and built and built.

Hours after Zoey left, he finally granted me my release. I was spread eagle on our desk, writhing and panting when my phone rang.

He fumbled through the items that had gotten tossed on the floor. By the time he found it, my phone stopped ringing.

"Who is it?" I rolled into a seated position.

"Don't know." He kissed my forehead before handing me my phone.

I glanced at the number and shrugged. "Don't know either. Probably a sales call."

I tossed the phone into my purse and then went to the bathroom.

"Little monster, your phone is ringing again," Jet called to me.

"Can you answer it? I'm a little busy." I flushed the toilet and used the baby wipes we stocked to clean up.

Jet opened the bathroom door and said. "It cut off before I could answer it." His gaze roamed over my nakedness. "I can't get enough of you."

He crossed the small space and placed kisses all over my neck and chest and down my belly. My phone rang again.

I groaned. Same number. I didn't want to answer it. Especially since Jet's lips were so close to my pussy . . . again.

"Answer it, Ash. It might be important." He stood.

I hit the accept button.

"ASH!!" Zoey screamed into the phone. "I need you!"

"Zoey? What's wrong?" The phone went staticky.

I pushed away from Jet and went into the office looking for my clothes.

"Ash something's happened. I don't have time to explain. You need to bring the amphetamines. All of it."

"What? Why? Where are you?"

"We've been kidnapped. Millie and I. I had to get something from Emily's office. When we got back in the car, someone was waiting in the backseat. I told him about all the drugs we could get him from the lab. For free."

"That's enough!" a sharp voice said in the background followed by a loud thump.

Zoey screamed in pain and there was more whimpering in the background. Millie, Zoey's seven-year-old.

"Hey, asshole! Do not touch them! I'll bring you your fucking drugs."

"You need to go to Crow Feather Trail. Three miles west, there's a dirt road, follow that until you see the trailer. Thirty minutes."

"Crow Feather is more than two hours away. I need more time to get there."

"Ninety minutes. Don't be late. No cops. And only you. We'll be watching the trail. If I see anything other than one woman driving down that trail, Mommy gets a bullet and her daughter, well, let's just say she'll fetch a pretty price."

"Fuck you! Do not touch them. I'm on my way, Zoey."

I was already dressed and walking out the door.

Talon, Pope, and Jet were waiting for me in the lobby.

"I called them; we heard everything, Ash. We're coming with you," Jet said.

"If you heard them, you know the trail is being watched. That means I do this by myself."

Pope handed me a bundle of clothes and a pair of running shoes.

I dropped my skirt right there and redressed in leggings, and a sports bra and wrapped the hoodie around my waist then stepped out of my heels and into my shoes.

"Not an option, mate. We're coming with you."

"We don't have amphetamines. But I packed the sugar pills." Jet held up a small bag.

I shrugged. "Real or not, that fucker is not getting shit from me."

CHAPTER SIXTY-ONE

AISLING

We drove in silence. Pope was behind the wheel, Jet was in the front passenger seat, and Talon and I were in the back of his SUV. Crow Feather Trail was at the edge of the Woodlands. It was a dense forest which ran along the southwest border of Port Midway. It was vast and many mystics, along with a few humans, made it their home. Mystics liked it, especially shifters because it allowed their animal nature to roam free. Humans liked it because there were no rules. That being said, they had a rustic and simple way of life.

Growing up at Moon Serpent commune was ultra-modern in comparison. Witches interacted with outsiders frequently. We regularly conducted business at Farmers Markets and online, and we abided by local and federal laws. The forest dwellers, made their own rules. The occupants of Woodlands governed themselves and had chosen to live off the grid. They typically stayed away from the city and weren't welcoming to strangers. For a group to venture into Midway and abduct humans was odd and disconcerting. Port Midway was a relatively peaceful town, welcoming to all—mystics and humans alike. Local authorities left Woodlands residents alone as long as they didn't bother Port Midway. What changed? It had something to do with drugs, I presumed and certainly not something I cared to involve myself in. I had my own problems.

I'd been to Crow Feather Trail once while in college. Zoey and I and a few college friends had gone to a bonfire for winter solstice. It was one of the few occasions they welcomed outsiders. The party itself had been a good time. There were lots of booze, drugs, sex, and entertaining fights from sundown to sunup. Most of it was a blur . . . except the location. The forest skirted the edge of the cove near what was rumored to be the demon portal. I recalled the prickly sensation on my skin back then which I cleverly masked with a lot of alcohol and random sex. It worked.

Looking back made me wonder if my demoness had been reacting to the proximity of where my ancestors had come from. The thought made my stomach curdle. There were so many unknowns when it came to my demon side I didn't know where to begin. A large part of me was so deep in denial that I didn't want to know. Hell, I hadn't fully admitted it yet. Saying it was one thing. Living it was something I wasn't ready for. Would my refusal to accept me as I am bite me in the ass?

Of course, it will.

My demoness spoke to me in my head. I ignored her. I didn't need her input, now or ever.

At thirty-two years old, my life was good. Great, in fact. Did I need to accept this demon part of me?

You seriously know nothing, do you?

Fuck off. No one asked you.

Talon had offered sage advice. He of all my men would understand this duality. I honestly had no clue how to merge my two halves and was reluctant to do so.

I glanced at my men. Pope was tapping on the steering wheel. Jet was asleep. Talon was absently making circles on my knee with his thumb. I had everything.

Of course, you do. Thanks to me.

You fucking wish. My men love me. They would love me regardless of your being here or not.

Finally, a real response.

Listen, you. Quiet. I don't need you distracting me. Zoey is important.

Do you think I don't know that?

I contemplated her question. My question. Fuck, it was so confusing in my head. The truth of the matter was, I honestly didn't know jack shit about this other side of me.

Finally, an intelligent thought. You don't know, so don't presume.

Talon squeezed my knee.

"Wanna talk about it?" he asked.

I blinked at him.

"You were frowning, babe," he added.

"How do you speak with your wolf?" I asked.

He tapped his head. "He's always right here. He doesn't use words much unless it's important. It's mostly pictures and emotions. Why is she speaking to you? The, uh, Mistress."

I nodded. "When I was little, I thought I was just crazy. My mother agreed and had me on special herbs which blocked her voice. Now I know she blocked this part of me completely. It's weird. I don't trust this voice in my head. And hearing it, speaking to it, makes me feel insane. I don't know how to shut her up. I don't know if I should."

"It's only been a day. I imagine she's going to be more assertive now that she's free. You're stronger Ash, set boundaries, and don't let her push you around. And give it some time to establish the bond," he told me.

Taking his words to heart, I leaned into his side and stared out the window. He spoke the truth; I just didn't know how to implement them. Taking drugs was easier. Not the smart or long-term solution, though. I sighed.

Lost in thought, I hadn't realized we stopped.

Pope parked a mile from the Crow Feather Trail turn off and we exited the car.

"Ash, you're behind the wheel," Talon said. "Jet is going to cast a concealment spell on him and Pope. They'll be in the back. I'm going to shift and run alongside the vehicle. Emily and Jacob are already on their way. They'll stay out of sight until one of us contacts them."

"You called them? I hadn't even thought to let them know," I said. I'd been lost in my head, dealing with my own bullshit, and didn't think about it.

"We have your back, babe." Talon winked and began undressing. I stared, admiring all the muscles. In the next second, he disappeared, and in his space was a large black wolf with a patch of white fur on his chest and golden eyes. He was huge. Almost the size of a pony.

"Talon." I gasped. "You are beautiful." I stroked his glossy fur, which was surprisingly soft.

He licked my face, making me giggle.

"Here, Ash." Jet's voice had me turning to face him. He held out a familiar chain with a familiar ring dangling from it. "Mine and Pope's. I cast a spell on them so that you can see us. We'll test it first."

He grasped Pope's hand and chanted. In less than a minute, they disappeared.

I blinked. "This is incredible." I stepped to where they were standing moments ago and bumped into hard muscle.

"This is fun," Pope said as I groped his abs.

Jet laughed. "Playtime later. This spell won't last forever. Turn, Ash, let me place this on you."

I did as he asked, and tingles ran up and down my spine as his fingers grazed my nape. As soon as the necklace was on, my men appeared. Fucking magic.

"You're pretty amazing, warlock," I praised.

"Let's go save your friend." His lips slid over mine.

We hopped back into the SUV, and I began driving down the trail, with nothing but the moon illuminating the path. I kept glancing out the window, hoping for some sign of my wolf. It would really suck to run over my mate. I noticed a flash of golden eyes in the woods and sighed with relief as my wolf ran alongside of the car.

The dirt trail wound through the forest in a seemingly endless path. The terrain was rocky, and the road soon narrowed to a single lane just wide enough for the SUV. I hadn't remembered driving this far for winter solstice, but that had been years ago.

I slowed down to a snail's pace and kept going. Pope had gotten us to the trail much earlier than anticipated, and I thought we had plenty of time before the ninety-minute deadline when we stopped. There was no trailer in sight and there was no indication or landmark that helped guide my way. I breathed uneasily.

"We're good, angel," Pope said, somehow sensing my unease.

After another thirty minutes, a row of dirt bikes came into view with a trailer off to the side. "This must be it."

"Roll down the window, little love. We'll need to climb out." Jet tapped my shoulder.

As Jet asked, I rolled down the window, then turned off the truck, and exited.

My men were the best. They'd thought of everything. I was thinking I'd just show up and . . . I don't know. Throw the bag of fake drugs at them and walk away with my bestie and her daughter? What would I have done without my men?

I shrugged off my fleeting thoughts, grabbed the bag, and walked toward the trailer. The door opened and a man stepped out.

He was of average height, gangly with dark brown shoulder-length hair. He wore dirt-stained jeans that hung halfway down his ass and a faded blue T-shirt with holes in it.

"That's far enough." He pointed a shotgun at me. "Leave the bag right there."

Yeah right.

A strange quietness came over me. The calm before the storm. A switch flipped in my brain and my vision tunneled to a single-minded focus.

With strength and speed I didn't know I was capable of, I

sprinted to the man, took the shotgun out of his hands, and snapped his neck.

In the next second, I was in the trailer. Four men rose to their feet. I shot one, dodged to my right and grabbed one man by the hair and pivoted, putting his body in front of mine just as another shot rang in the air, hitting his friend in the torso.

Releasing his soon-to-be-dead friend, I sprang in the gun holder's direction pulled the weapon from his hand and twisted his arm behind his back. The other guy bolted out the front door.

"Wait! Wait! Don't kill me, I know where your friends are." The man in my grasp squealed as I pressed the gun to his head.

"They're not here?!" I snarled through clenched teeth.

"They are. We have an underground workshop."

"Lead the way," I told him.

A dozen feet from the back entrance of the trailer was an access door to a storm shelter.

The fluorescent light swung from the ceiling as we descended into the musty workshop. "Zoey?" I called to her.

Muffled grunts reached my ears. Shadows and darkness concealed two hunched forms. I knocked the man on his head with the butt of his gun and stepped over him as he crumpled to the floor, rushing to Zoey's side.

"Aunty Ash?" Millie whimpered.

"I'm here, Millie," I assured her while tugging the blindfold down and untying her restraints.

"Help my mom, Aunty. She hasn't said a word since they shoved us down here," my god-daughter said.

"Zoey." I patted her face gently after releasing her from her restraints. I pressed two fingers to her neck and felt a weak pulse.

Shuffling down the steps caught my attention.

"Ash?" Jet called out. Pope followed behind him.

"I need help with Zoey. She's unconscious," I replied.

Millie blinked at me like I was crazy. "Jet, lose the concealment spell. For Millie's sake."

He chanted under his breath. Millie clung to me, startled.

"It's alright, Millie. Just a little magic," I told her.

She didn't budge.

Pope carried Zoey and took her to the surface. Jet picked up a twig from the dirt floor and turned it into a daisy. "For you, young lady."

She shot him a grateful smile, took the flower, and allowed him to guide her up the steps.

The man who led me to the workshop was still unconscious. I paused, taking in his appearance. He was of nothing to note. Late twenties or early thirties. He was human for sure. All of the men were so far. If they had magic, they would have used it against me. I studied the workshop, which wasn't interesting either. Dusty with a few wooden benches and shelves. It wasn't a workshop; it was more of a dungeon. At that thought, I aimed his gun at his face and pulled the trigger.

As I rounded the trailer, the guys were already helping Zoey and Millie into the SUV. Something in my periphery caught my attention, I stopped short. Talon? I scanned the woods.

Bullets pinged the side of the SUV. Millie screamed.

"Get them out of here!" I shouted and sprinted into the woods behind the dungeon.

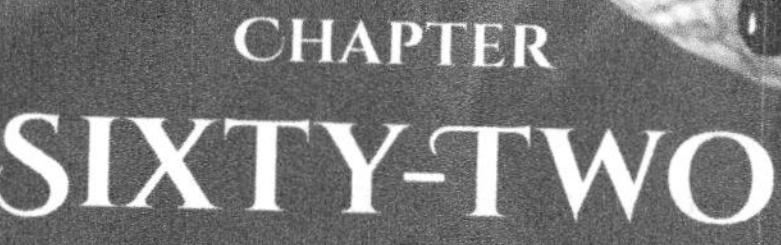

CHAPTER SIXTY-TWO

JETHRO

As soon as the human stepped out of the trailer and pointed the gun at Ash, she was no longer in control of her body, her demoness was. The dead gave away was the change in her eye color. Ash's light-brown eyes glowed an emerald green. Seeing her take out the man holding the shotgun was equally arousing and terrifying. She was powerful.

After that, everything moved fast. Talon in his beast form ripped out the throat of a guy who had been trying to escape. Ash took someone else hostage and went into a storm shelter.

Pope and I did a quick perusal of the trailer and found dead bodies. Ash's handiwork. Watching her work was impressive. The aftermath was a bit perturbing.

We went into the storm shelter and helped Zoey and Millie to the car. Between the gunfire and Millie's screams, I barely heard Aisling's voice. She had taken off just as I jumped behind the wheel. Pope was already in the back seat tending to Zoey while Millie sat up front with me.

Bullets peppered the vehicle, but they barely made a dent. Bullet-proof. Fancy motherfucker.

I hit the start button but the engine didn't turn over.

"What's going on, Jet?!" Pope asked in an urgent tone.

"Fucking thing won't start." I tried again. Bullets kept coming. A tire popped, but the windows and the doors held. "Millie, on the floor and keep your head down. We need to sit tight for a little bit okay?"

She did as I asked then gave me a pitiful look. "Is my mom dead?"

"No! She's fine. We're taking care of her."

"Jet?"

I turned to face Pope and followed his gaze. "She's burning up," he said to me in a grave voice.

"Stay there, Millie." I crawled over to the backseat.

Zoey was feverish. I lifted her lids to see her pupils were dilated. Needing space to work, I said to Pope, "You should move to the front, I need to use my magic."

He didn't hesitate, and I used my magic to scan Zoey's body. Something was circulating in her blood and my magic couldn't heal her.

"Millie, did they give her something?" I asked.

"I don't know. I couldn't see. But . . . they said something about a brick. Maybe they hit her over the head." The little girl answered.

I checked Zoey's head and didn't find any injuries. The kidnappers demanded amphetamines which meant they were cooking drugs. They had to have given Zoey something. I checked her pulse again. Faint, but still breathing.

"We need to get her to a hospital," I muttered.

"Truck's not starting, but they stopped shooting at us. I can run out and check under the hood." Pope gazed out the windows with one hand on the door.

"Don't!" I warned him. "I can't watch Zoey and cast a concealment spell on you, too. Give me a minute and let me think."

A phone rang.

"Tally's," Pope said. "It's in the back."

I leaned over and found Talon's phone sitting on top of his folded clothes and shoes.

The phone stopped ringing and started going off again. "Should I answer it?" I asked. Talon was a busy man, the last thing I wanted was to answer an important business call while we were getting shot at.

"Here, I'll do it. Keep an eye on Zoey," Pope offered.

I placed the phone in his hands, and he accepted the call.

"Talon! Where are you guys?!" A shrill voice came from the other end.

"Mommy!" Millie shouted.

"Baby, are you okay?" Emily shouted into the phone.

"Emily, it's Pope. We've got Millie and Zoey with us. We'll be heading down the hill soon." Pope covered the phone and asked me. "Should they come up this way?"

I shook my head about to tell him no when Zoey stopped breathing.

"Oh shit," I cursed and started CPR.

"Em, how soon can you get up here?" Pope stated into the phone.

"We're on the main highway," Emily replied.

They were a good thirty to forty minutes away. Not good. Not good at all.

"Head this way and keep your phone on." Pope hung up the phone.

Sweat beaded my brow as I continued compressions on the small woman's chest.

"I'll take over when you need a break," Pope said. I paid him no mind and continued pumping Zoey's chest and breathing into her mouth.

Aside from Millie's muffled sobs, all was quiet. The gunfire stopped but I couldn't spare a glance out the window. I would not let Zoey die.

Pump. Pump. Pump. Breathe. Pump. Pump. Pump. Breathe.

"I'm checking the truck. Millie stay down," Pope stated.

He opened the door. A flood of light illuminated the SUV's interior. I continued compressions while Pope slipped out.

I breathed into Zoey's mouth. She was pale and unresponsive.

"Come on, Zoey."

More compressions. And then finally she gasped.

"Battery's gone," Pope said returning into the car.

"She's breathing," I replied fatigue rearing its ugly head.

"Thank fuck." Pope huffed out a breath. "No sign of Talon or Ash. No sign of anyone."

No car. Zoey's life was hanging in the balance. And Millie . . . poor kid would be traumatized for life. At least the car was bulletproof.

"This is the safest place for us until Emily and Jacob arrive," I stated, wiping the sweat from my brow. "How are you holding up, Millie?"

She raised her little thumb in the air. "Is my mommy okay?"

"She's still alive, kid. She'll be fine," I said, keeping two fingers over the pulse points on Zoey's wrist.

I could keep her alive until help arrived.

Something heavy landed on the roof of the SUV, making my heart hammer in my chest.

CHAPTER SIXTY-THREE

TALON

The hunt filled me with an exhilaration I hadn't experienced in too long. I missed it. Missed the wind whipping by my body, the sound of leaves crunching under my paws. My senses were heightened. I saw every nuance around me. Every fallen branch, every divot in the ground. And the smells. It was earthy and felt like coming home. There were mystics in these woods. A dozen of them hid and waited with anticipation. Their erratic heartbeats filled my ears, and they smelled of caution and fear.

I waited eagerly as my mate got out of the car. She had the backpack filled with the drugs and approached the trailer cautiously. The door swung open, and a man pointed a shotgun at her.

He sneered and threatened Ash. Not giving his words a second thought, she attacked. She moved so quickly, her movements blurred and then he toppled to the ground with his neck snapped to the side. I rounded the trailer as she went in.

Through the window I watched Ash take on three men without batting an eye. One ran and I pounced on him before he got two feet from the door and tore out his throat. Blood coated my muzzle and dripped from my fangs.

Ash and her hostage went to an underground bunker. As soon as the door opened, I smelled them, Zoey and her daughter. Millie was understandably frightened while Zoey was intoxicated. There was a putrid scent embedded with her own that made me sneeze.

I stood guard as the other men went down to help, their scent giving them away despite the concealment spell. The breeze carried the scent of others. There were so many of them. Human and mystic. I crept into the woods and found over two dozen men with guns moving toward the SUV.

I pounced on the man closest to me doing what I could to muffle his cries of pain. The others fired their weapons just as Pope and Jet got Zoey and Millie into the car.

Ash didn't follow. She was too far away. Instead, she darted behind the trailer. I took out two men in, covering her. She paused, her eyes an eerie neon green, met my golden gaze for a second and then she winked at me. She ran deeper into the woods, using her demon strength and speed to go after the enemies.

I caught up to her, fighting by her side. She didn't need my help. She was fast and strong. She easily disarmed them and used their weapons to take their lives. Blood sprayed. It was violent and brutal, yet sexy.

The SUV didn't move. Why weren't they moving? I couldn't go to them. They were safe, the bulletproofing would hold, and my mate was pursuing men who were retreating into the woods.

Ash didn't hesitate; she kept going, picking them off one by one. Bodies littered the forest floor. One man begged for his life. Ash cackled. She raised one hand, sharp claws extended from her fingertips, and she eviscerated him with a smile.

She was unhinged. When she woke from this, she would be consumed with guilt. I needed to intervene.

Survivors ran for their lives. Mystics. Witches and warlocks, I presumed. They had speed but it wasn't enough to outrun a demon or a wolf. They weren't my concern, Aisling was.

She tipped her head to the sky and sniffed. She had supernatural senses, too. Great. I stayed on her tail, tracking her every move. She blurred through the woods unbelievably fast. I had to run at full speed to keep up.

A woman scrambled up a tree using its branches to get to safety. The woman had climbed nearly ten feet high. That wasn't enough. Ash leaped into the air, snatched the woman by her ankle, and yanked her out of the tree.

The woman plummeted to the ground and landed with a thud. Her legs were bent at odd angles.

Ash pounced on the woman and raised her claws again. I bowled into her, knocking her off the nearly dead woman.

Ash rolled with me then came up in a crouch. Demon eyes and wolf eyes engaged in a silent war of wills. I wasn't sure I was going to win this, and a part of me didn't want to. I wanted to give Ash whatever she wanted. But the Mistress had taken over my love, and she would be appalled with her actions.

"That was my kill," she snarled at me.

I shook my muzzle and said in my head, "No, Ash. This is over. You've killed enough tonight."

Ash tilted her head to the side and blinked.

"You can hear me?"

"Yes. Mate bond. Why would you do this? Why would you go against me?"

"Aisling, my mate, I am never against you. Ever. I would die for you and with you, without hesitation. I will help you deliver justice to those deserving of it. But these kills are not justified. You've won. Zoey and Millie are safe. This is over."

Her gaze narrowed and her posture told me she was ready to lunge. I dug my paws into the earth, preparing myself for her attack.

Her shoulders relaxed and I released a huff of breath. The sound of a motor reached us, and Ash dashed in its direction.

Shit.

I ran after her. Ash went toward the oncoming vehicle. A truck sped up the trail toward the trailer. A panicked face gazed out the window. Emily.

Ash ran straight toward them moving through the woods with agility and untiring speed. My chest heaved, and saliva coated my muzzle.

The trailer was a few feet ahead. I leaped and landed on the roof of the SUV before Ash reached the area. She stopped short, glaring at me.

I jumped off the SUV, breathing hard, and shifted, then opened the back.

"Fuck, Tally. You asshole. You scared the shit out of us," Jet cursed.

Ash approached us warily, not a drop of sweat on her.

"Are you guys okay in there?" I threw on a pair of sweats while tracking Ash's movements. Her green eyes regarded me with suspicion.

"Zoey needs help. The battery's gone. Emily and Jacob are on their way."

"They're almost here." I stepped toward Ash.

The SUV doors swung open, and I sensed Pope getting out of the car.

"Aunty Ash!" Millie shouted and ran past me.

Ash's gaze snapped toward the little girl. Recognition flashed over her face, she blinked rapidly, and her brown iris returned.

Headlights announced Emily and Jacob's arrival and shone a garish spotlight on Ash's blood-covered body.

Millie came to an abrupt halt. She covered her mouth which failed to hide the gasp she released as she took in Ash's appearance. Fear rolled from her tiny body in thick choking waves.

Ash looked down at her torso. Her eyes widened with shock as reality sunk in.

In a cautious tone, I ventured. "Millie, your mom and dad are here."

On cue, Emily and Jacob called their daughter.

Millie ran to them.

"Where's your mother?" Jacob's worried voice reached my ears.

"She's here," Jet called out. "She's stable, but she needs medical attention."

I glanced over my shoulder as Jet and Pope moved Zoey to the other car. She was pale and listless. From where I stood, I sensed her pulse, faint but steady, and that smell of toxic poison oozed out of her pores.

"Take her to the nearest ER. She's been drugged. I did all I could," Jet said.

"We would have taken her ourselves, but some asshole stole our car battery," Pope added.

"Hop in," Jacob offers. "We'll make room for you."

The guys looked at me for an answer, and I turned to look at Ash.

"Ash?" I called out and scanned the darkness. A futile attempt because Ash was already gone.

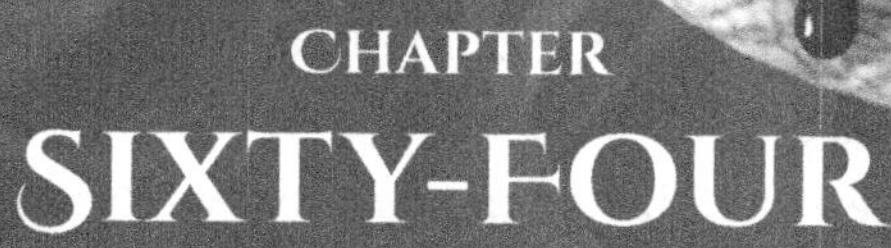

CHAPTER SIXTY-FOUR

AISLING

Free. For the first time in thirty-two years, I was free. Sure, my warlock released the bindings over twenty-four hours ago, but my witch half had held the demoness back. The witch was strong, disciplined, and controlled. As a demon, I was stronger. And now I was in control.

All my senses were heightened. I felt invincible, even though I wasn't. I knew I was mortal and thanks to my witch half, somewhat vulnerable. Still, humans and mystics were no match for me. I made quick work of my prey using sheer prowess. I hadn't used demon magic, hell I wasn't even sure what type of demon power I had.

My wolf had been killing alongside me and then he thwarted my last kill and wanted me to stop. It was that damned consciousness so many on this planet seemed to have. That unfettered need to do good. And that was . . . disappointing. It made me want to kill more just to spite him.

I ran through the woods toward the oncoming car intending to hurt the newcomers. My speed and strength propelled me forward. I was fast. So fast, I was leaving the wolf behind. My wolf.

He surged forward and leaped into the air. It was impossible. Yet he did it and landed gracefully on the roof of his vehicle.

I slowed my approach. My mates were there, waiting for me . . . or were they waiting for the witch? They loved Aisling, the smart, lovable doctor. What was wrong with me? We were the same. Weren't we? Sure, I had savage tendencies. I'd been suppressed since I was a child, I was bound to be unhinged.

Still, my mates were important to my witch half and me too if I was being completely honest. They'd have to accept me as I am. The Mistress. There would be no holding me back. No more playing by the rules. I had control now. And I had zero fucks to give.

My wolf tracked me with his gaze. There was so much emotion in those pale green eyes. Love. Caution. Hope. His body language was tense. He was ready to pounce if needed. At me. Why? I wouldn't hurt my mates. Anyone else was fair game. And I wasn't done killing yet.

Zoey's daughter called me. Relief was apparent on her face as she ran in my direction. Toward *me*. My god-daughter was safe. Something softened in my chest and doused the fire that fueled my need for blood.

Bright light flooded the area. Millie froze in place. She covered her mouth with trembling hands. Shock and fear poured out of her in a heady explosion and smashed me in the face.

My sweet Millisandre was afraid of *me*. I glanced at my body and swallowed the hot bile rising in my throat.

Viscous scarlet liquid coated my skin and saturated my clothes. The coppery metallic scent invaded my senses. It was in my nostrils and on my tongue.

I was revolting. Shame and disgust wrapped around me like a second skin.

As soon as Talon took his eyes off me, I dashed into the woods, bypassing dead bodies on my way. So much blood. And guts and dismembered bodies. My kills. *I did this.*

I turned up the speed. The need to get away from the carnage I'd caused propelled me forward. I ran and ran until my lungs felt like they would burst.

I'm a monster. I slowed to a walk, my thundering heart threatening to leap out of my chest.

Don't be so dramatic.

I'm a crazy, fucked up lunatic who talks to herself. I inhaled a lung full of salty air.

You're part demon.

I'm a killer. A cold-hearted killer.

Killing is part of your nature.

"No! No, it's not. I cannot live like this!" I shouted to the forest.

You don't have to use your voice to speak to me. I live in your head. Talking out loud just makes you look crazy.

I crumpled to the ground. *"Shut up. Shut up. Shut up!"*

You can't make me. Aisling . . . I am a part of you. Stop shutting me out.

"I can't be a part of this."

You already are.

"No. I am not. I would have never killed all those people."

They were all bad people.

"You don't know that!"

And neither do you.

"That doesn't give you the license to kill at random."

Why not? Together we are stronger than any mystic or human.

"There are other uses for strength."

It's not as fun.

"There are other fun things to do."

Perhaps. Enough with the theatrics, already. Your poor me attitude is ruining my high. Demons are killers. That's what demons do.

"I don't want this."

You don't have a choice.

"I always have a choice. This is my body. My choice. And I refuse to live this way. I refuse to give in to this bloodlust."

You can't outrun me, Aisling. You can't pretend I don't exist.

I sobbed into my blood-covered hands. "*This is disgusting. I am disgusting. This cannot be my life. I refuse to live like this.*"

The sounds of the waves crashing on the reef below called to me. I stood and walked woodenly to the cliff.

No Aisling.

"*Shut up.*"

Don't do this. Please.

"*Fuck off. I've heard enough from you.*"

With the last amount of mental strength I had, I ignored my inner demon. That voice was still there. But it was muffled like she was speaking behind a closed door. I imagined her pounding on walls demanding to be heard. Fuck her. Fuck me.

It was too much. The constant voice. The blood. So much blood. I just couldn't anymore. I couldn't face the past. Couldn't face the present. And I didn't want to look at the future which held nothing but *red*.

A soft breeze swept strands of my hair across my blood-smeared face as I peered over the cliff. The half-moon above provided just enough light to see the shadowy darkness below. The ground was so far away and yet so close. Jagged rock seemed to smile up at me, beckoning. And then there was the ocean. A vast stretch of darkness. All that water to wash away the blood I'd spilled, to cleanse my sins and purify my soul. I was bone weary. Tired of fighting. Tired of trying. Tired of all of it. I could end it all with one step. My life, for countless others. It would be so easy. I closed my eyes and stretched my arms to the side.

CHAPTER SIXTY-FIVE

THE MEN

TALON

As soon as I realized Ash was missing, my wolf whined and began pacing in my chest. A desperate warning churned in my gut.

I wanted to shift but I needed help. The dirt bikes sitting off to the side of the trailer caught my eye.

"Bikes! Now!" I commanded.

Jet and Pope didn't hesitate. They didn't offer pleasantries to Emily and Jacob who were sorting themselves out. I couldn't either. Ash was in trouble. Big trouble.

"I need to shift to track Aisling," I told them, shrugging off my sweats and throwing them at Jet. "Keep up. She needs us."

My wolf burst forward, sniffing her trail. I spared a glance at Jet and Pope who were gunning the bikes. I nodded and took off at a sprint.

The rushing wind and the sounds of the motorbikes accompanied me as I tracked my mate. Her trail went deep into the woods in a senseless path, which meant she ran aimlessly with one intent. To run from something. Herself.

Remembering the murders she had committed were like nightmares. What she had done tonight was the experience in real time. She lived it all: the sounds, smells, the inner rage combined with that weird satisfaction from killing. The dead bodies and all the blood were right there for her to face. There was no pretending it didn't happen.

There was a high mystics got when using our power. It was addicting and at times difficult to manage. Ash's demoness had been taken from her since she was a small child and now as an adult, it had to be overwhelming.

I knew it would come to this. I hoped we'd have more time to ease her into this side of her. Zoey's situation didn't grant us that luxury, and Ash was thrust into dealing with the demon she didn't understand. Millie's reaction, although warranted, reflected everything Ash was afraid of. The monstrous side she didn't want to confront, let alone allow others to see it too.

Something in my chest keened. Sorrow. Despair. Her emotions hit me like a sharp blade to the gut causing me to lose my footing. I stumbled, rolled, and shook it off. I turned on the speed, pushing my body harder and faster than I'd ever run before.

Hold on, mate. I'm coming.

JETHRO

The moment I learned about Ash's demoness being suppressed by a spell I knew without a doubt it had to be undone. You can't stifle someone's true nature by force. If Ash had been aware and accepted it willingly that was another story. But she learned about her true nature days ago after her demon had been acting out to put it lightly. Something that was bound to happen.

I knew undoing the spell would have side effects. From the stories I'd been told by the guys, the Mistress was a menace with an

"I don't give a fuck" kind of attitude. I considered this when I undid the binding and had plans to deal with it. As we passed the dead bodies littered on the forest floor it made me second-guess myself. Sure, no one could have predicted a dire emergency involving her best friend. Still, it felt like it was all my fault. I should have prepped a spell or potion in the lab today. I wanted to kick myself and would if I weren't on a bike speeding through the woods.

As soon as Talon and Ash returned to the SUV, I'd known something was amiss. Talon kept his gaze trained on her, even while talking to us. And she approached the SUV like a predator.

Despite the blood covering every inch of her skin, seeing her whole settled the unease in my gut. I wanted to run to her and wrap her in my arms, but Zoey's pulse was erratic and she needed a hospital. I had the mental capacity to handle one crisis at a time it seemed and was glad to be on Team Wolf.

We'd been following Talon for miles, solid proof of Ash's strength and stamina. Talon set an unbelievably fast pace for which I was grateful. He led. I followed. It was hard enough to navigate the rough terrain let alone track her scent. My magic was practically useless to me or Ash at the moment.

I was admiring Talon's agility and speed when something soul-deep cracked. I slumped over the bike barely able to hold on. Talon stumbled then rolled. I glanced at Pope who eased off the throttle, one hand clutching his chest. Aisling.

Was she? Nope. No, Jet. Don't even think about the D word.

POPE

The minute Ash disappeared I knew something was wrong. I was overwhelmed with a sense of not knowing. I had no idea where she'd gone. Or why. Or how to get her back. Thankfully Talon was there. His wolf-slash-mate connection with her set us on a path. I followed his commands willingly, trusting his leadership and his love for our Aisling.

The headlamp barely illuminated the path before me. Branches scraped my skin as I sped by maneuvering around rocks, fallen trees, and dead bodies all while pushing the bike harder to keep up with Talon. We'd been going for miles. How was that beast still running at top speed, let alone breathing? It was a cool night, and I was on a bike and yet my heart was thudding away like I was running a marathon.

A heavy weight crushed my chest. I slowed the bike and held a hand over my heart, drawing deep breaths into my lungs. Tears stung my eyes, and I blinked them away.

Talon rolled then got back up and ran full tilt. Gasping for air, I said a silent prayer, *please be okay Ash* and opened the throttle, chasing Talon. Jet kept up with me.

We continued our pursuit, the terrain sloped taking on a slight incline. The bike groaned as I forced the climb.

Ahead, Talon disappeared over the top of the hill and howled. I felt his despair in my bones.

Jet and I arrived at the top at the same time. Talon was running toward something with all his might.

It was too dark to see clearly. I trusted my gut and Talon as I opened the throttle again. Less than a quarter mile away the clouds parted, and the half-moon shone on the lone figure standing at the edge of the cliff, arms spread wide.

My heart stuttered in my chest.

No, Aisling! I screamed.

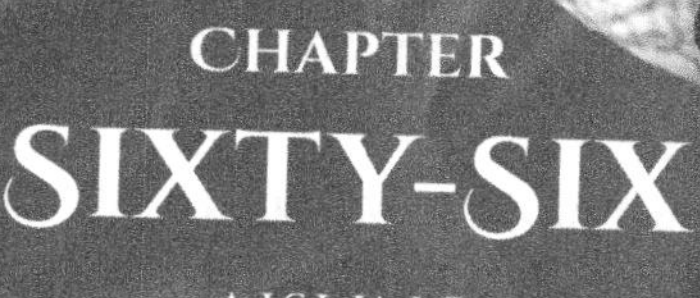

CHAPTER SIXTY-SIX

AISLING

Something hard and heavy crashed into me from the side, knocking the wind from my lungs.

"Ash!" Someone shouted my name.

A heavy, hot, ball of fur, weighed heavily on my chest.

I wheezed, panting for air.

"Ash. Are you okay?" Jet asked. His voice was frantic. "Talon, move. You're crushing her."

Talon's wolf form moved slightly, allowing me a bit of reprieve from his weight. He pushed my cheek with his muzzle, whimpering while licking my face.

Jet was behind me. He raised my head enough to prop me on his lap. "You scared the shit out of us, Ash. What were you thinking?" He smoothed my matted hair from my face.

"I don't know," I said, my voice hoarse.

"Well, don't fucking do that again. Ever," Jet said. "Talon, move. We need to get farther from the edge."

Talon rolled off me, panting, wolf drool coating his muzzle. Jet picked me up, walked toward a tree, and settled me between his legs. He rocked me back and forth, sobbing.

"Aisling." Talon settled beside me. "Explain."

Jet loosened his hold, allowing me to sit upright. Everything hurt. My body. My soul.

Shame and guilt swam in my veins as I took in Talon's tormented face.

I was ready to end it. End my life. It made him sad. Both of them. Where was Pope?

My gaze darted around the woods. He stood a few feet away. He turned his back to me as soon as our eyes met. He looked broken.

My fault. I did that. Knowing I'd hurt him sent a shot of pain through me so raw it gnawed at my bones.

"Aisling," Talon gave me a stern glare. "Talk to us."

"I don't know how to do this. I don't know how to be a good person and be a demon. My demon likes to kill, which means I like it, too. And that scares me. It's confusing. And overwhelming. I just can't." I sobbed into my hands.

Two pairs of strong arms wrapped around me. My men surrounded me with their love and support, whispering words of encouragement. Except Pope.

"And death is your answer? To punish yourself for being who you are, you're going to jump off a cliff?" Pope's words sliced through the night and stabbed me in the chest.

His face was a mask of sorrow.

"You would rather leave me behind, all of us, instead of giving this part of you a chance?" Pope's voice was hard and full of undisguised pain.

"It's not like that, Pope. It's not about you, any of you."

"Right. I get it." He stared at the ground. "No, that's not right. I don't. I . . ." He threw a rock over the cliff. Then he looked at Talon. And then at Jet and then he nodded.

"Okay, Aisling. If that's what you want." He extended his hand to me, helping me stand. Talon and Jet stood beside us.

"I can't either, angel. I'm ready when you are." Pope kissed the back of my hand and stepped forward.

"I have plenty of blood on my hands. If you deserve to die for what you've done, so do I." Talon grasped my other hand. We continued toward the cliff.

I glanced over my shoulder at Jet.

"I finally found a life worth living and that's because you're in it. If you go, I go." Jet stepped up behind me and placed a hand around my waist as we walked forward.

"You jump. We jump with you. All of us. We won't live this life without you Aisling. If death is the answer, then death it is." Talon squeezed my hand. "For all of us."

I stopped. "No!" My voice quivered.

My guys urged me forward.

"No. Stop. That's not what I want. That's not what I'm saying. You can't. No, no, no. You have people who love and care about you."

"Not true. My father doesn't give a shit about me." The sad truth of Jet's words knocked the air from my lungs.

"I don't even know my real parents. They must've hated me before I was born to give me up as an infant." Pope's words pierced my heart.

"I think my mother and sister love me. They'll be well provided for when I'm gone. That's all that matters."

"Stop it. All of you." I stood my ground and faced my warlock. "Jet, fuck your father. He doesn't deserve you. Your brilliance and magical talent will do amazing things for this world. You're a good, honest man, Jethro. You're nothing like him."

I cupped Pope's face. "I'm sorry about your birth parents. Who's to say why they did what they did? And who cares. It's their loss. You light up every room, every situation. You've become a loyal loving man who protects the people you love, without their presence in your life. If they could see you now, they would be so proud."

"Talon, the man you are in here," I patted his chest. "Is more valuable than all the money in the world. The world needs more men like you."

"None of you can leave this earth. Not yet. Not for many, many years," I told them.

"Neither can you, Ash. You surpass me in intelligence and together *we* could do great things for this world." Jet caressed my face.

"You're right about my birth parents, Ash. I don't need their acceptance or approval in my life. I've been fine without them. But your father has been giving you a part of his life essence to protect you all these years. How do you think he would feel if you suddenly ended it?" Pope said.

I staggered on my feet as though he punched me in the face. Pope's words struck a chord that resonated deep within me. *Dammit, Aisling. How can you be so selfish?*

"You have plenty of people who love and care about you. You have three men who love you and would risk anything for you. Your parents. Your family. Zoey and her children. If that doesn't matter, why should any of it matter to me?" Talon added. "Life isn't easy, babe. Whether you're a shifter, human, warlock, or part demon. It's tough for all of us, we make mistakes, and we do our best not to repeat them. The good news is we have each other."

"We won't let you go through this alone." Pope squeezed my hand.

"We're in this life together, little love. Good or bad, we're a team. You make the call." Jet snaked his arm around my middle and rested his chin on my head.

I didn't need to think about it. Individually my men were unique, special, and valuable to me. And they were willing to die not just for me but *with* me. Their love for me was so deep, it transcended all levels of reasoning and I'd be a fool to give up because life was suddenly harder than it had ever been. I had to fight. My men were worth fighting for. My life was worth fighting for. It always had been. And it would always be.

"I'm sorry. I'm so sorry. I don't want to die. Truly, I don't. And I don't want any of you to die, either. Let's go home. Please."

My three men wrapped their arms around me and the broken pieces within me mended together, making me whole.

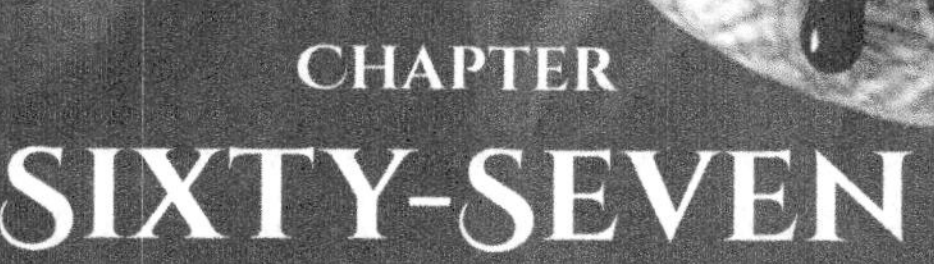

CHAPTER SIXTY-SEVEN

AISLING

A WEEK LATER

I'd like to say life was super great after my suicide attempt but that would be a lie. I did however have a greater appreciation for my life, but it wasn't all rainbows and unicorns. A week had passed and residual emotions were lingering in the back of my mind and my men's as well. We were treading water carefully, which kind of sucked. But it was real, and it would take time.

"Are all these cars here for Zoey?" Pope asked as he drove past Zoey's house. "I thought this was a small gathering,"

"Small gathering when it comes to Zoey's family is a relative term," I replied. "She has seven children. Her wife has two brothers and they both have children. And Jacob's family is huge. He's one of nine kids, and if I'm not mistaken each of his siblings has children as well." I drummed my fingers on Talon's knee who kept his eye out for a parking space. "Plus their parents."

"Sheesh, that's a huge family. We have some catching up to do," Jethro turned in his seat to face me and shot me a wink.

I blew him a kiss.

“I see a space three houses down on the left,” Talon said to Pope, who seemed to always be our driver.

My guys and I strolled into Zoey’s place and were immediately greeted by everyone. There were a lot of people, which I expected, and perhaps I should have prepared my men. Especially since the kids were running amuck like they were at the peak of a sugar high.

Zoey had recovered from her near overdose. They pumped her stomach and kept her overnight for observation. I visited her while she was still in the hospital. Her spouses insisted on having a recovery party for her which was sweet. My bestie wasn’t so keen on the idea, but she was outvoted.

“Aunty Ash!” Millie ran toward me.

I knelt and enveloped my goddaughter in a hug. I visited Zoey the morning she was being released from the hospital but hadn’t seen Millie since that night. Out of everyone in attendance at this shindig, I was most nervous about seeing her. Her enthusiastic greeting set my nerves at ease.

“Thank you for saving me and my mom.” She clung to my neck and sniffled. “I’m so glad you’re okay.”

I drew away from her and swiped the tears streaming down her cheeks. “Hey, I will tear down the world to keep you and your family safe Millisandre. Always. And I’m glad you’re okay, too.”

“I thought you were hurt.” She wiped her nose with the back of her hand. “There was so much blood.”

“Oh. You were worried about me.” Water filled my eyes. “Thank you. That um . . . wasn’t mine. I thought I scared you being all monster-like.”

She giggled. “You’re a good monster, Aunty Ash. The beat-up bullies kind of monster.”

My heart swelled. I pulled her in for another hug. “Thank you, Millie. I’m happy to beat up bullies for you anytime.”

The brief moment had to have been one of the most precious few minutes of my life.

"Go be a rambunctious kid." I released her with a peck to her forehead.

"You good, angel." Pope eyed me warily.

I gave him a big smile and nodded. "Great. I needed that."

He put an arm around me and said, "Good, let's go find us some alcohol."

Hours later, the kids were winding down and the adults were on clean-up duty. Zoey pulled me aside and led me to the front porch.

"Tell me everything about that night," Zoey said as we sat down on the swing bed.

"Didn't we have that conversation? In the hospital?" I replied. I hadn't told her everything. The last time I saw her she was in the hospital, her spouses were bedraggled, and she looked like she just had her stomach pumped.

"Stop it. You know what I mean." She gave me her *mom* glare.

"You know about the trailer stuff and the bad guys. And the part about my demon taking over."

"Yep. Skip that part."

"I . . ." My tongue felt thick. "I wanted to jump off the cliff. Almost did. My guys saved me."

She clutched a hand to her chest and her eyes watered, making her glasses foggy.

"Aisling." She took off her glasses and then grabbed my hand. "Talk to me."

I told her everything. I told her about all the crazy thoughts going through my head. I told her that my men offered to jump with me. I told her how I decided not to jump, that I realized with their help that my life was worth living.

"Please tell me you'll never do that again." Zoey rested her head on my shoulder and I leaned my head on hers.

"I don't want to, Zoey. I am trying to figure all of this out. I really am." I inhaled deeply. "I appreciate you and my guys, but I think I should see a therapist."

Zoey sat up and said, "That's a great idea, Ash. I mean fuck, you've been thrown a whole lot of shit all at once. I can't imagine dealing with it. Emily knows a good therapist who works with mystics, I could ask for a referral."

"That would be helpful, thanks."

"Have you heard anything more? From your demon half," she asked.

"Not a single word. I think the near-death experience settled her."

"Interesting. Guess that incident wasn't so bad after all."

I shrugged. It almost felt like my demoness was waiting for the right time to pounce.

"So, I should probably tell you. I kind of knew." She wrung her hands together, eyes glistening. "My seer magic, you know. When you returned from your mother's and were not yourself, I kept getting these messages about reading tea leaves and well, you know how much I hate that. Anyway, I ignored it and then the night before we got abducted, I dreamt of you standing at the cliff. You weren't sad, you were peaceful. I didn't know what that meant until you came to the hospital. I knew something had happened. I'm sorry."

She dropped her chin to her chest.

"There's nothing to be sorry about, Zozo. You couldn't have known."

"Yeah but maybe if I didn't shun my gifts I could have been more helpful."

"Maybe if I didn't shun my gifts, I wouldn't have felt so suicidal." I chuckled.

Zoey gave me a dry look, then the corner of her mouth curved into a smile. "Some pair we make."

We laughed.

"Let's make a vow, Ash." She held out her pinkie. "Let's vow to have the courage to accept the parts of ourselves that might be uncomfortable to face."

"And to grant ourselves grace for the mistakes we're bound to make," I added.

We interlaced our pinkies and sealed our vow with a hug.

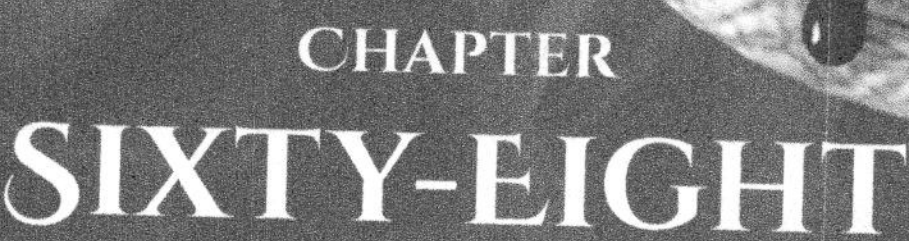

CHAPTER SIXTY-EIGHT

POPE

The wind whistled in my ears in a frantic rush. I was flying through the air, moving faster than humanly possible. My breath came in ragged pants and every muscle ached as I pushed faster and faster.

Ash! I shouted at the top of my lungs. Ash! Get back!!

She didn't hear me. She didn't respond at all. She was too far.

Faster. I must move faster. Sheer desperation fueled my limbs. Almost there.

Aisling! She turned toward me. Her beautiful face was stricken with sorrow so deep I felt it as though it was my own.

I stretched my arms, extending them as far as they would go. The smile on her face was like sunshine breaking through the clouds. Except, there was no sunshine. Only darkness. And Ash was gone.

No, Ash. Come back. Please. Come back to me.

An invisible weight crushed my chest. She was gone. She left me.

"Ssshh . . . I'm here, Gaius." Warm arms cradled my body, and her sweet scent filled my nostrils.

"Ash?"

"I'm here, Pope. I'm right here." Soft lips pressed on my skin.

Aisling. My Aisling. She was here. She hadn't left. I tightened my hold on her and drifted off to sleep.

I ROLLED over and clutched my pillow to my chest.

"Good morning," Ash purred. She stroked my scalp with her nails making me hum.

"Morning, angel." A deep sense of peace settled in my core.

Ash was lying on her side, assessing me with her golden-brown eyes, which appeared amber in the morning light.

"Come here." I tossed the pillow aside and pulled her into my chest.

Aisling scooted closer, allowing me to snuggle into her breasts.

"How'd you sleep?" she asked.

The recurring dream popped into my head. It wasn't just a dream. I'd seen it. Witnessed it. I shoved the images of her on that cliff to the back of my mind and crushed her to me.

The thump, thump, thump of her heartbeat soothed my soul. *It was only a dream, Pope.*

"Aren't you supposed to be at work like the others?" I asked, ignoring her question.

"They've already gone. And I took the day off. Do you want to talk about it?" She asked.

Since that night, I'd been sleeping fitfully, thrashing around, waking her and the guys. Every morning she and the guys asked if I wanted to talk about it. And my response was always the same.

I shook my head.

"What are you going to do today?" she asked softly.

"The guys have some projects for me but . . . I don't know, I'd rather spend it with you." I smiled against her chest.

"Hey." She tugged on my hair, making me face her. "Maybe you can take me to my therapy session and then we can go to lunch."

I smiled at her which she returned.

"I'd love that." I kissed her neck and ground my morning wood into her pelvis.

"Pope, that feels good, but we have to leave soon."

"Right now?"

"Not right this second, but . . ."

"I can be fast." I snaked a hand under her panties and stroked her warm, wet pussy.

She groaned and pushed her panties off her hips. "Pope, baby, we need to hurry."

I didn't waste another second. I rolled on top of her and sank into her wet heat.

"Ash," I breathed her in.

She locked her legs and arms around me, fusing our bodies. I thrust into her, my full weight crushing her into the mattress. I didn't care. A desperate need had risen within me since the night on the cliff, and I ached to make her mine in a way I couldn't explain. It was primal and visceral. I wanted to be soaked with her juices. I wanted to wear her skin. I wanted to brand my soul with hers. I needed to consume her body and soul. It wasn't just my need to love her. It was more.

"Never leave me." It wasn't a request. It was a demand.

"Never, Pope. I'm yours forever," she breathed. Her walls closed in around my cock. She was close and so was I.

I sped up my thrusts as my climax rose.

"Promise me, Aisling."

"Promise" she panted into my mouth.

She was here with me and all around me. Her breath, her taste, her scent. I needed it all and more.

Her perfect body molded against mine, as I drove into her pushing and pulling. Her cunt gripped me, squeezing and pulsing around my length as she came.

"Ash." I groaned, biting her lip, blood filled my mouth and I sucked, drinking her life source while flooding her with my seed.

I peppered her face with kisses.

"When I said I wanted to spend the day with you, I didn't mean in bed." She gave me a lazy smile.

"Do you know how much I love you?" she asked.

"Yes. I love you, too."

She smiled. "Come on, Pope. We have to go."

After a quick shower, we rushed to her appointment.

AISLING

I laced my fingers with Pope's as we drove to see Dr. Ross, the therapist Emily had referred me to.

Therapy had been helpful for me to deal with some of the residual emotions I had difficulty reconciling. My men were great. Loving. Supportive. They were there when I needed them. They gave me space when I needed it. Still, the cliff incident left some emotional scars that needed time to heal for me. And them. Particularly Pope.

After a couple of therapy sessions, I mentioned to the guys that it was an option for them as well. My men refused saying it wasn't necessary. My wolf and warlock seemed sure about their decision, but Pope was hesitant. I had a feeling he was putting on a brave face in front of the other two.

Pope had been having nightmares, and he wouldn't speak to any of us about it. I was hoping to ease him into a therapy session.

Dr. Ross said therapy might help him, and he might be more willing to come in for a couple's therapy session. I wasn't sure if he would and so I came up with a brilliant idea to trick him into it. Dr. Ross didn't think it was a good idea but he penciled us in for a morning session on one of his normal days off.

"Everything okay?" Pope asked.

"Uh-huh."

"You seem nervous. I thought you enjoyed therapy."

"I did. I umm . . ." I exhaled hard. *This isn't right, Ash, and you know it.*

I pulled my phone out of my purse and sent a cancellation text to the doctor.

"Pope, can we go somewhere? I just . . . I just want to be with you today."

His posture stiffened and he white-knuckled the steering wheel.

After a moment, he turned off the freeway heading toward the Strand.

He parked in a free lot, and we walked in silence. The tension between us was too much to bear.

"Pope." I tugged on his hand to face me. "I'm sorry . . ."

"Don't. Do not tell me this isn't working and you're done. Don't." He stomped away from me.

I stood in place. Stunned. He thought I wanted to leave him . . . again. My heart fractured in a thousand different places.

"That's not what I was going to say." I caught up to him. "Pope, stop."

His long strides created more distance between us.

"Do not walk away from me, Gaius!"

"Why not! You did. And you still want to," he responded without turning to face me.

"I do not! That's not what this is about." I jogged to catch up to him.

"What is it then, Ash? I feel like you're this close," he held his thumb and pointer finger a centimeter apart. "To giving up again."

I hopped into his arms. "Pope. Please. I'm not giving up, I promise you."

He huffed and then released me, refusing to meet my gaze.

I led him to a nearby bench. "I was going to trick you into going to therapy. You aren't sleeping well. And you don't speak about it with me or the guys. I think it would help you."

He propped his elbows on his thighs and stared at the ground.

"It's helping me, Pope. Therapy helps me talk about what's going on inside my head without holding back. I'm not saying talking to you and the guys or even Zoey makes me feel like I can't speak freely, it just helps to have a non-biased third party to vent to. I won't lie, Pope. It's hard. But I swear the last thing on my mind is leaving this world. I'm learning to deal with my demon side and am making progress. And I plan on winning this with you beside me. Please, don't give up on me. I'm right here."

I moved to sit on his lap while he sobbed.

"I believe you, Ash. I do. I know you're trying but that night haunts me. I keep seeing you on the edge of that cliff, and I can't get to you fast enough. It kills me."

"Pope. I'm so sorry I did that. That's on me. Not you. You aren't responsible for my mistakes. It was a mistake. A stupid, selfish one. I can't erase what I did. If I could I would. The best I can do is be better. I hope that is enough to give you some comfort." I held him tightly until the tear well dried up.

"A part of me fears it's my fault. Like I should have done more to help you from the beginning." Pope's soft voice was filled with remorse.

"None of it is your fault, and you did everything you could with the information you had. I am eternally grateful for all of it. Your love and protection are everything."

"Is it enough?" His words were heavy with doubt. It nearly broke me.

"It is, Pope. It is. What can I do to convince you that it is?"

"Marry me." His voice was low, almost timid.

"Yes. A thousand times yes."

He flashed me his brilliant smile. "You would do that?"

"Of course. Right now."

He chuckled. "I think the others have to be on board with this too."

"If you want them to be."

"They're good guys. I don't mind sharing with them, Ash."

"They're great guys. And I love all of you very much. And I know they would understand if we decided to have ourselves a mini wedding. Just you and me. Right now. There's a chapel nearby."

"It would be a fake wedding. It wouldn't be an official marriage. It wouldn't be legal. It wouldn't be binding in any way," he mused and then released a heavy sigh. "But it would mean everything to me."

Pope and I stopped at the drugstore and bought two cherry-flavored ring pops and fake flowers on our way to the chapel. There we found a pastor willing to walk us through our vows after telling us it wasn't a legal marriage three times. We rented a cheap motel room to consummate our marriage and then had the guys meet us for a happy hour reception at a random dive bar.

It wasn't fancy nor was it real, but it was a spur-of-the-moment decision. And it was us. Just two crazy kids doing something to cement our love in a way only we understood.

Jet gave me a questioning gaze. "You know this isn't a real thing."

"We both know it," I replied. "But it makes Pope happy. And I need him to be happy and to sleep well."

Pope returned to the table with a bucket of beers.

"Well, I hope you two know we're doing this again . . . a real wedding with all of us," Talon added.

I laughed. "Considering no official proposals have been made . . . I just might keep my options open."

The guys groaned. Talon reached for me as I stepped away from the table.

"Dance with me, fake husband."

Pope joined me on the dance floor even though he hated dancing. Later that night, he slept like a baby.

CHAPTER SIXTY-NINE

JETHRO

After that night at Crow Feather Trail, we'd taken time off to laze around and regroup. Ash, however, didn't do much recuperating. Soon after she began studying demonology, and I was happy to teach her what I could. She added therapy sessions as well, which she seemed to like. Her determination to conquer her demon side's outbursts was inspiring and we did all we could to support her in any way.

In addition to all of that, she and I were still working for Buchanan Pharma until we could figure out our next move. Talon was taking on that task since me and Ash were in catch-up mode at the lab working long hours even on the weekend.

I wasn't bothered by it though. We were all busy, and I was the lucky duck who got to work beside Ash every day. We both enjoyed working in the lab, which was equal parts science and magic.

Magic was pretty amazing most of the time. Sometimes it was a moody bitch. I'd been working on the same formula, Ash's tonic, for weeks and it wasn't doing shit for me. She didn't need the tonic any longer, but I had some ideas we thought would amplify its effectiveness. Plus it was the base for her father's remedy.

At first, we tried adding my magic to what she had already created. It made the entire tonic impotent. We then decided that perhaps I needed to create the tonic from scratch. I'd followed her instructions precisely, countless times, and each time the results were the same. Nothing. My magic would negate every benefit of each compound, making it inert. Utterly fucking useless. It wasn't my magic though. It was that mother fucking red salt. Ash's mother told us it may have something to do with it being an ingredient gifted by their coven's guardian of which I was not a member. I respected magic and its laws of nature but that was bullshit. I loved Aisling. Hell, I shot my load in her daily and drank her cum. How much closer did this stupid guardian want us to be? With one wide swoop of my arm, I shoved my work tools off the lab desk, making a loud ruckus and a bigger mess. Glass shattered and papers flew everywhere.

"Aisling!" I tugged on my hair wanting to pull out the strands by the root. I needed her to show me the process again as though I was a child learning magic for the first time.

My woman ignored me. "Ash! Get your ass out here, I'm not in the mood."

"Don't shout at me, Dr. Buchanan, if you want or need something ask politely." She leaned on the doorframe with her arms crossed over her chest.

My brain short-circuited as I took in what she was wearing. Long legs peeked out of her lab coat; if I wasn't mistaken, there was nothing but bare skin under there.

During our time off, Talon had a crew come in to fix the AC unit. The temperature in the lab wasn't freezing cold anymore, meaning Ash wore less clothing to work.

I stumbled out of my chair, trying to get to her, but the little monster walked into the office and shut the door.

As if that was going to keep me out.

I turned the doorknob which was locked. *Oh okay, I liked this game.*

Typically, I could use a little telekinesis to unlock the damn thing but my ego was still riding the bucking bronco called frustration. I punched through the door with my magic instead, sending wood shards flying all over the place.

Ash gave me a dry look.

"Is this going to be a regular thing? Because if it is, I'll need you to mark the calendar under Jethro's Tantrum Day, so that I know to schedule myself a spa day instead of coming here to deal with your mood swings."

"What are you wearing?" I said through clenched teeth.

"You mean this?" Ash stood. "This here is a standard issue lab coat commonly used by doctors."

Said lab coat opened just enough in the chest area to give me a teasing view of her big tits.

My cock inflated into a stiff rod.

"Hmmm . . . that outfit could be considered sexual harassment."

Ash put a hand on her hip revealing black lacey panties. "Would you rather I wear my turtlenecks again, Jethro?"

"Nope. I'd rather you work naked." I crossed the small space and reached for her just as she disappeared.

Fucking demon magic. Ash was coming into her powers, and we discovered she could *bamf* herself short distances. Sneaky minx.

I stalked out of the office and found Ash sitting at the lab desk, spinning around in the chair.

"You've made a mess," she said without looking at me.

I lunged for her and met with a brick wall. She was also able to create a force field around her body. It was temporary, and I wasn't a first-year magic student. I'd broken through it with ease before.

As I worked a spell to defeat her magic, Ash scooted the chair close enough for her to run a heeled foot along my length.

"You've been a bad boy, warlock," she replied in a sing-song voice. Then a pulse of magic hit me knocking me back a couple of feet.

Ash spread her legs wide and pushed her panties to the side. My gaze was glued to her wet, pink pussy.

"Okay, game over. You win." I licked my lips.

"Of course, I win. You need to pay up. Get naked, warlock."

Yes. I stripped in record time.

"On your knees and crawl to me," she directed while gently fingering herself.

I wasn't too proud to beg.

The floor was covered with glass and paperwork. I didn't care. I crawled over the mess I'd created not paying any attention to the sharp nicks and cuts on my skin.

At her feet, I leaned in, salivating for a taste of her cunt.

Aisling, put her foot on my chest holding me back. "Good boy," she praised. "Now clean up your fucking mess."

Hell no.

I gripped her knee and spread her legs apart with one hand. With my other hand and a little magic, I reached out and tore her panties off.

She blocked my attempt to access her pussy once again. The little monster was fucking edging me.

She moaned, her half-hooded gaze full of arousal. "That was so hot. You almost made me come right then. And as much as I want you to continue. No reward until you clean this shit up."

"Ash. You're killing me."

"Me too. Jethro. Me too." She ran a finger down her slit and slipped into her hole.

"Fuck. Come on, Ash."

She placed her wet finger into my mouth. "Be a good boy and fix this before I make myself come."

Before she could utter another word, I snapped my finger triggering a simple and often-used cleaning spell.

"Cheater," she sneered.

I shot her a grin, dismantled her shield spell, and devoured her whole. She tasted of the sweetest nectar and drank it down. Licking and sucking and licking and sucking until she exploded in my mouth.

I crashed our lips together. There was something so hot about sharing her flavor with her after she came. My cock ached to be inside her.

I picked her up and bent her over the lab desk.

"I love the lab coat, little slut. I think this should be your uniform every day." I pushed the hem of the coat past her hips and lined up with her eager hole. "And the heels complete the outfit."

She glared at me over her shoulder. "No heels."

I grinned then slammed into her tight cunt. "You will wear the heels if I say so," I pumped into her stroking her walls with my piercings.

"You're not the boss of me."

"Is that right?" I slowly pulled out and teased her pussy with my fingers.

"Alright, alright. I'll wear the damn heels. Now, fuck me, good and proper," she hissed.

I gave my woman what she wanted. What we both wanted.

Somewhere between the thrusting and the kissing and the dirty talk, the lab coat came off. And much too soon after, Ash's pussy was choking my cock milking me dry as we came together.

We fell into a pile of limbs on the floor, holding each other close while we caught our breaths.

"Jet?" Ash tilted her head to look at me.

"Yes, little monster."

"I have an idea about the salt issue."

I nodded, asking her to continue.

She tucked her face into my neck and said in a soft voice. "I uh . . . was thinking, that maybe you needed to meet the guardian. All of you."

I gave her a nudge and hooked her jaw with my finger forcing her to look me in the eyes. "Aisling Lovelle, are you asking me to meet your parents?"

She nodded.

"I'd love to."

She gave me a sweet smile that lit up her whole face.

CHAPTER SEVENTY

TALON

I landed on my back with a solid thud. *Time to turn up the heat, Tally.* I rolled to my right dodging a foot that landed where my head was moments ago. Bloody hell, she almost stomped my face.

I sprang to my feet and lunged at Ash. She ducked and delivered a bone-crushing hit to my left flank I felt it in my kidneys. Before she could get in another shot, I side-swiped her legs making her wobble. I caught her before she hit the sand and hurled her into the surf.

She came up sputtering and laughing. She was drenched, her hair was matted to her face, and sand clung to her body. She looked like the most beautiful, drowned rat I'd ever seen.

"Game over, Tal. I'm done." She crumpled to the sand, chuckling.

Thank fuck. I was done, too.

My mate was determined to mesh with the Mistress, combining her witch and demon abilities. I recommended we do some physical training and she jumped at the chance.

Ash and I had been practicing with her demon powers for the past several weeks. There was no question about her strength and speed, I'd witnessed both at Crow Feather Trail. The goal was to get her to access these abilities at will and control it without her demoness going off the rails.

We worked on fighting techniques and weapons training. She took to all of it with ease and oftentimes, she kicked my ass.

I lay next to her on the sand, unable to stifle the groan from the shooting pain on my left.

"Come here, wolf." Ash gently rolled me to the side and made small circles over my kidney area. Her healing magic seeped into my body, like cool water running down my throat on a hot day. We discovered undoing the binding on her demon side had amplified her witchy powers. Ash had been able to work her spells with greater ease and had noticed new magical abilities.

She kissed the area and then ran her fingers all over my body, inspecting for additional injuries and healing me if needed. It was unnecessary since I was a shifter and could heal myself just fine, but I'd never refuse her touch and attention.

While she worked, I drank her in with my gaze, admiring the woman who had captured my heart and soul. Months had passed since Crow Feather and my mate had made tremendous progress with healing her emotional state.

She continued with therapy and roped Pope into joining her. He hadn't had a single nightmare since their fake wedding, but shortly after, Ash encouraged him to give therapy a try. He'd done a few sessions on his own, and they would often go together. He was her emotional support more than me or Jet. I wasn't sure why that was. It may have something to do with their history. Whatever the reason was, Ash needed it, and I was glad she had Pope.

Jet and I were just as scarred as Pope was from that night. We, or at least I, knew without a doubt that had been a one-time incident. In many ways, it had to come to that pivotal point for Ash to deal with her dual nature. Sure, we all had hoped for a smoother and gentler transition, but fate had other ideas in mind. There was no playbook for this situation, and being thrown into the deep end meant we didn't have time to fuck around. Ash knew this more than any of us and she'd taken her recovery seriously.

She'd been soaking up everything Jet had on demonology and had even ordered textbooks from all over the world. Jet was our expert on the subject. He helped her with the magical aspect of things when it came to using her demoness powers and combining them with her witchy powers. It was cute to watch the two science nerds pour over countless books for hours.

We all had our place in her life. Pope was her emotional support. Jet her intellectual equal. And then there was me, the physical challenger. It was worth every scrape and bruise. And I had to admit it was a fun thing she and I could do together. Just us.

"There," she said with a self-satisfied smile. "All brand new and ready for me to kick your ass again."

Chuckling, I rolled her on top of me and brought her lips down to meet mine. "Is that what you think happened? Next time I won't take it easy on you."

I swiped my tongue through her mouth, savoring her sweetness mixed with a touch of salt from her sweat and the ocean. Ash ground herself into my already stiff cock. I pushed her sports bra off her small frame, freeing her tits from the stretchy fabric. She pushed her leggings off her body and straddled my waist. My hands cupped the heavy globes. The grainy sand was abrasive on her smooth skin. Sex on the beach was not fun without a blanket under your ass to shield your private parts.

I got to my feet in one fluid motion keeping her in my arms. She wound her legs around my middle while I stepped into the cool water.

We floated for a while, making out, allowing the ocean to wash away the sand.

Ash pushed my shorts down just enough to pull out my cock and threaded me into her core, impaling herself with my length. She was insatiable, my little demoness. I cupped her ass, guiding her hips to rock back and forth over my dick. The tightness of her sweet pussy had me teetering at the edge. I slipped my fingers down her crack and massaged her back entrance. Using the slickness of the water, I slid a finger into her ass, filling her the way she liked.

She moaned my name, begging for more. I slid another finger into her ass, stretching her. Filling her to absolute fullness. She bounced on my cock and my finger, fucking herself. Fucking me.

Her nails scored my scalp. Her teeth grazed my jaw.

I sucked on the mate mark I placed on her neck. My fangs elongated. I wanted to mark her again. Was that even possible?

Ash tugged on my hair and gazed into my eyes. She leaned in, her tongue flicked over and under my canine teeth. Her eyes flashed green, and she said, "Bite."

She angled my head to her shoulder while her hips moved frantically over my cock. Her walls tightened and I was cresting. I bit. My fangs sank into her flesh. She tossed back her head moaning. Blood filled my mouth. Metallic, but sweet and spicy. We exploded together. Coming and coming and coming. A warm ticklish . . . shimmy rocked my core. My wolf.

My vision went hazy, and I tightened my hold on Ash and dug my toes in the sand.

The next thing I knew I was lying on the shore. The waves tickled my feet.

"Ash?" My eyes snapped open.

"Here." Her fingers linked with mine. "I'm here."

"How'd we get here?" I rolled to my side and then pulled her closer.

She shrugged. Her skin was cold and covered with sand.

"Let's get inside, mate. We need a shower."

She muttered an adorable complaint, and so I carried her back to the house.

Our new house in Shadow Cove was nearly done with renovations. It had access to a private beach where Ash and I trained, and I had the outdoor shower finished for us to use. As soon as the warm water kicked in, I stood under the spray with Ash still in my arms. She clung to me like a koala.

Aisling groaned as the water trickled down her back. "That feels nice." She wiggled free, placing her feet on the ground. "Did we pass out in the ocean?"

"I think we did," I replied.

She laughed. "So much for water safety."

We showered, and dressed, and then I gave Ash an updated tour. I'd been working with a new construction crew on the renovations. We were making progress and ahead of schedule. We'd be able to move in within a couple of months.

"What's this?" She jiggled a door handle.

"No." I steered away from the purposely locked door.

"No? What do you mean *no*?" A little line appeared between her brows.

"I mean no. It's a surprise."

Ash froze in place, with her arms crossed. Her toe tapping impatiently on the newly installed wood floors. My mate didn't like secrets. Or surprises. Even the good ones.

I mimicked her pose. "No. Means. No. You can't see it until it's ready. And don't bother asking. I'm not saying a word."

She narrowed her gaze. "Fine. Keep your secrets."

CHAPTER SEVENTY-ONE

AISLING

Tears pricked the back of my eyes as we traveled the long winding road away from the Moon Serpent Commune. *It's not goodbye forever, Ash. Just goodbye, for now.* I reminded myself.

I blinked back the tears and glanced at the men in the car with me. Jet was behind the wheel, focused on the road ahead. Pope sat next to him, headphones on and his focus trained on the tablet on his lap. Talon sat beside me, one hand on his phone, the other hand resting on my thigh, his thumb tracing a lazy path in an almost hypnotic pattern.

Releasing a contented sigh, I leaned back and reflected on the past few months. We'd been through so much since the night at Crow Feather Trail. My main priority had been to overcome my demons.

The work I was doing to understand my duality had paid off. Through therapy, I learned to integrate both sides of myself. My demoness had been relatively compliant as she needed me to survive. Communicating with my internal voice was odd at first but with time and patience, I began to trust this part of me that needed to be heard and seen. Giving her . . . the Mistress, a voice made life so much easier. I'd been able to do more with my witch magic and had gained a few magical abilities as well. And she hadn't fought for control like she used to.

Studying demonology was also eye-opening. I was eager to learn everything I possibly could. Most of the texts were folklore or fiction but there were some truths I gathered based on what I was experiencing. There was still so much to learn.

My quest to understand my demon side kept me occupied. Fortunately, I had three men to lean on. They handled the normal day-to-day things at home, like cooking meals, cleaning the house, and doing laundry. They even handled business matters and our upcoming move all of which helped me focus on making myself well. It was a major transition period for all of us, and I was grateful to have their support.

We'd been on the road for the past week, a necessary trip for business and to visit my family. Our first stop was the commune. I introduced the guys to my family and the rest of the coven. My mother was the perfect hostess and my men the perfect gentlemen.

We hiked to Serpentine Falls where I harvested the red salt and camped for a night. There was no sign of the guardian. I expected as much since it wasn't a full moon. Jethro was disappointed but got over it when he realized there would be many full moons in our future.

My father seemed to be physically stronger although his dementia hadn't changed. Merging with the Mistress had taken precedence over everything in my life. I hadn't had a chance to focus on his meds. He finally recognized me on the last day, which was better than nothing. My men used the opportunity to ask for my hand in marriage which made him cry happy tears. A part of me wanted to get married then and there while he was coherent, but we weren't ready for a wedding and my father had wanted to spend the time working in his smithy. He directed my men, who did the heavy lifting and they managed to forge their very first weapons. I was so proud of my father and of my men. I took videos and photos documenting the precious moment which was too short. After dinner that same day, the dementia reclaimed my father's mind.

As much as I appreciated those small moments, it was bittersweet. He was there and then gone. Leaving the commune had weighed heavily on my heart, and yet it encouraged me to find a cure for him and make that task a top priority. I'd be happy to at least formulate something that would give him some clarity and more moments like those.

I squirmed in my seat, inching away from Talon's warm body, and glanced at the clock on the dashboard.

"Pull over at the next gas station, Jet." Talon tapped on the driver's seat headrest. My wolf was always attuned to my body's needs without me having to say anything. I gave his thigh a reassuring squeeze.

Jet caught my gaze through the rearview mirror and winked. He drove past a gas station and pulled into a diner less than a block away.

"Cleaner bathrooms and they have decent coffee," he said, pulling into a parking space.

"Thanks!" I hopped out of the SUV and beelined for the ladies' rooms.

By the time I was done, the guys were waiting for me with coffee in hand.

"Coffee and donuts are in the back." Pope held my door open.

"Thanks. How much longer?" I asked, sliding into the backseat, next to Talon.

"Another hour or two," Jet replied.

I sighed. We were heading to Meridian City to deal with Jet's father and Buchanan Pharmaceuticals.

We drove the rest of the way in a comfortable silence. Both Talon and Pope were working away on their tablets and I cozied up next to my wolf with a book. After one chapter, I was fast asleep.

Some time later, the car slowed and jostled me awake.

"We're here," Jet said, pulling up to a building easily twice the size of Shelby Centre.

"Is this your office?" Pope asked from the front passenger seat.

"Nope. This is all residential. My condo is here," Jet replied as he stopped at the valet.

We exited the SUV and took the elevator to the forty-fifth floor. The elevator doors opened depositing us into a narrow corridor with double doors.

"This isn't the rooftop terrace Talon has in Midway, but it should be comfortable for us for the next few days." Jet unlocked the door and let us in.

The open-planned space had white marble flooring with gold and silver veins running through it. The white walls were devoid of art and aside from the L-shaped black leather sofa, glass coffee table, and the big screen television, the living space was bare.

"There are two bedrooms down that way." Jet pointed to a hallway. "I'm assuming we're sharing the same bed, which is to the left. Help yourself to whatever, wherever. But don't get too comfortable. Harlo will be here in ninety minutes."

"This is perfect. Thanks, Jet." Talon clapped him on the shoulder.

He and Pope moved down the hallway with our luggage and I strolled to my warlock.

"Are you okay?" I snaked my arms around his waist.

He rested his chin on my head. "I'm good. Just anxious to get this ordeal with my father over with."

During the past few weeks, my men had devised a brilliant plan to deal with Harlo Buchanan.

While they strategized, I continued working for the company despite knowing what Harlo had planned. It took longer than they had thought, but it wasn't a hardship for me, since Jet had already revised my original contract which included Zoey.

Jethro had appeased his father with lies. He told his father he'd been working remotely, which he was, he just wasn't honest about his location.

Pope did his hacking thing making it seem like Jet was overseas. Receipts from restaurants, rideshares, and even a hotel in London. Pope also set up an overseas phone number that Harlo liked calling randomly to check in. His father seemed happy thinking his son was nowhere near me.

The hacker's work didn't end there. He dug deep into Harlo's finances and found proof of his illegal use of company funds. He wasn't just funneling money to my mother, he was also secretly funding various personal projects. And now, we were going to confront Harlo directly.

I was uneasy, not so much for myself, but for Jet. His father had been controlling him his entire life and he was about to change their dynamics forever.

Dr. Buchanan arrived precisely ninety minutes later. As we had planned, I remained out of sight while my men greeted Jet's father.

"So, Jethro," Harlo said with a condescending tone. "You asked me here. What is this about? Or is this a coming-out party?"

His last question made my skin crawl. I peered around the corner to see the disapproving scowl on Harlo's face. He was such an asshole. *How did I not pick up on that?*

"No. This is about you. I have evidence of you embezzling funds from the corporation." Jet gave him a flat stare.

"Bullshit," Harlo scoffed.

Pope laid out the documents he'd collected on the coffee table.

"Bank transfers, emails, and we have videos and recordings as well," Pope said.

"This is ridiculous! I am your father, Jethro. I can disinherit you and I will!" Harlo stood, a glimmer of magic crackled around his palms.

Jet tossed his head back and laughed. "No, Harlo. Your control over me ends now."

Harlo clenched his fists and began muttering under his breath, working on a spell judging by the glow surrounding his body.

I inched around the corner and began working my magic to

counter his, but Jet beat me to it. With a small flick of his wrist, Jet blasted his father with power, squelching his magic and forcing him to sit.

"Don't even think about it. I'm stronger than you. Talon is my attorney, he's drafted paperwork for you to sign." He gestured to Talon who was casually sitting back with a bored expression on his face.

Harlo glanced at the paperwork and shook his head. "I need time to review this."

"No. You do this now, or I go to the authorities and you can sit in prison for the rest of your life." Jet replied.

Reluctantly, Harlo scribbled as directed. When the last set of documents were presented, he shook his head again. "No. No. No. Not Aisling. She is mine."

"No, she isn't. Everything Aisling has done, past, present, and future, is hers alone. You have no power over her, now, or ever." Jethro told him.

Harlo stood. "I've given you Buchanan Pharmaceuticals, control over the Buchanan fortune. Aisling has nothing to do with any of that. She is mine!"

Harlo sent a wave of magic into the room, that made the walls quake. The television cracked and fell to the floor. The glass coffee table shattered, sending paperwork flying.

Jet's magic shielded him, Talon, and Pope. He smothered his father's magic and slammed him into the wall. Harlo wailed in agony.

"Don't ever use your magic against me and mine, ever again." Jet snarled.

"Please, son," Harlo begged. "Aisling's family owe me. Their payment is her. She's mine."

Oh no, he didn't. I stepped into the room. "I do not belong to you, Harlo. Never did. Never will. And my family owes you nothing."

"What is this? Aisling? I . . ." He sputtered. "I've given you everything!"

"You've manipulated me and my mother. No more, Harlo." I stood beside Jet, lacing our fingers together.

Harlo frowned and then he began laughing. "Oh, I see what's happening now. You fell for his charms. Well, news flash. He's gay. You have no future with him."

I cuddled into Jet's side and said, "I love him, exactly as he is. Jet *is* my future. They all are." I reached out to Pope and Talon who came to stand beside us.

Harlo's jaw dropped. "Three of them," he muttered. His gaze darted between me and my guys.

"Sign the documents, Harlo," I told him.

Jet released his hold on his father and Talon showed him which documents to sign.

Before leaving, Harlo glanced back at me with pure disgust on his face. "Whore," he spat.

A split second later, Talon shifted and had his fangs on Harlo's throat.

"No!" I shouted.

I stepped toward my wolf. "No, mate. He's not worth it."

Talon released Harlo's neck, blood dripping down his muzzle. He came to my side, while Pope and Jet hauled Harlo off the floor and showed him the door.

"I would have let him kill you." Jet spat and slammed the door in his father's face.

Early the next morning, we went to Buchanan Pharmaceuticals.

Talon had offered to fund Jet and me a lab of our own, but after looking into Buchanan's financials, the savvy attorney decided it was a better option for him and Jet to take over.

With Pope's help, they gathered compromising information on the board members which swayed them to sell their shares to Talon for peanuts.

With our arsenal of information, we marched into a board meeting and took over. Jet owned forty-five percent, and Talon forty percent of the company. The remaining fifteen percent was divided between Pope and I who got a generous salary as well. Pope was assigned the task of overhauling the corporation's online presence and internal computer systems. He was ecstatic to have a legitimate job and grateful the men had included us in this corporate takeover. We didn't invest a penny and came out of that meeting with millions. Being a board member came with a new set of rules and tasks which was something we both had to acclimate to. Thankfully we had two men who were pros at it.

Once all the necessary paperwork for the take-over was complete, Jet deemed it safe to test Pope's DNA. Something about not wanting to risk the information getting into the wrong hands. My warlock was right. Buchanan Pharma had a very expensive and very rare device called a Mystic Scanner. It had the capability of testing all forms of mystical DNA. It was linked to a worldwide database which could be disabled by the CEO. Thankfully, Harlo had hidden my results when he ran mine. It was illegal since I hadn't authorized the test; however, if the news had gone out, I would have been fucked. Mystics and humans would have been gunning for my demon head.

Pope was in a similar situation. His results were just as mysterious and coveted as mine. Even Jethro, our scholar was at a loss. The best we could do was begin researching . . . Nephilim. My hacker was part angel. I should have guessed that because he had been more of a guardian angel to me than a stalker. Pope, being a go-with-the-flow kind of guy shrugged it off like it was nothing.

"I don't feel different," he said then turned to face me. "Does this change your love for me?"

"Of course not, Pope." I caressed his cheek.

"Okay then. Let's go home."

As much as I wanted to leave Meridian City right then, there was more work to do.

CHAPTER SEVENTY-TWO

AISLING

It had taken us nearly three weeks to get the newly formulated Buchanan and Shelby Pharmaceuticals LTD organized according to the attorney's and the warlock's satisfaction. My men vetted new leaders they could rely on to get the job done without us having to be there watching over their shoulders. Pope made it possible to monitor everything in the office, but we would have to return monthly, maybe more often. There would be a lot of back and forth between Port Midway and Meridian City which wasn't all bad because that meant I could visit my family as well. Still, I was anxious to get home.

"Did you go to the bathroom?" Jet asked me for the millionth time.

"I already told you I did, Jethro." I yawned. It was early morning and we had a long drive home.

He laid a wet kiss on my cheek and patted my butt while I climbed into the backseat.

"Come here, baby. You can stretch out and go back to sleep." Talon folded his hoodie on his lap making a little pillow.

I smiled gratefully at my wolf and settled in for the nearly ten-hour ride. If I wasn't in the car the guys could probably cut the time shorter, but what could I say, I needed pee breaks.

Talon reached around my waist buckling me in, while Pope laid a blanket over me. I had the best men. I shimmied, making myself comfortable, and closed my eyes.

Despite the early hours, sleep evaded me. I rolled to my side, then the other. I was still restless and tried sleeping on my back. I was about to give up on sleep when Talon snaked his hand under my sweater and pressed his warm palm gently against my belly. A soft moan escaped me and I breathed in deeply willing my body to relax. That didn't work.

Talon's touch had arousal swimming through my blood. I spread my legs and guided his hand to my core. He didn't need any more encouragement than that. He began stroking my pussy through my leggings. I nuzzled my face into Talon's lap, smiling to myself as he began to harden.

"Fuck, baby, you're soaking through your pants," Talon groaned. He applied more pressure on my pussy, making me moan.

I pushed down his sweatpants and swirled my tongue over his fat tip. He hissed. I spat on his crown and took him into my mouth while pumping him with my hand. My head bobbed up and down, sucking, and stroking until precum oozed from his slit.

Talon wormed his hand into my leggings. His fingers found my clit. I ground my throbbing cunt over his palm while salivating over his delicious cock.

"That feels so fucking good." Talon pumped his hips, forcing his cock deeper into my mouth.

My climax soared bringing me closer to the edge. So close.

Talon removed his hand from my leggings and slapped my pussy.

"Get naked and sit on my cock, babe."

I wiggled out of my leggings, then sat up to remove my sweater. Talon watched me undress. His arms flexed, muscles bulging while he stroked himself.

I straddled his lap, realizing then the car had stopped and we had an audience. I glanced over my shoulder and met Pope and Jet's half-hooded gaze.

"Ride that big dick, angel," Pope rasped.

Talon hooked my chin to face him and captured my lips with his. I threaded his cock into my entrance and slowly slid down to the base taking all of him.

My lashes fluttered and I groaned giving him access to my neck. He gripped my waist, rocking me back and forth over his length.

Beads of sweat dripped down my spine as I fucked him hard. Bouncing up and down on his thick shaft.

Smack!

My pussy contracted as a sharp sting bloomed over my left butt cheek.

"Fuck him good, my little slut. I want you filled with cum when I eat your pussy." Jet delivered another slap to my ass.

"Oh, fuck," I groaned.

"That's it, baby, soak my cock with your cum., Talon grunted.

I arched my back, leaning over the center console. Talon fucked me from below and his lips latched onto my nipple. His teeth grazed the sensitive flesh. Pope and Jet's mouths were on me. Licking and kissing all over my face and neck.

My nails dug into Talon's forearms as I came undone, panting for air.

Before I could catch my breath a cool autumn breeze filled the SUV. "Come here, angel." Pope stood outside of the car, his cock threaded through the opening of his joggers.

Talon lifted me off his shaft, placed me on the seat beside him, and exited through the opposite door.

My Nephilim didn't waste time, he grabbed my ankles and dragged me toward him. I was laid out in the backseat with my hips hanging off the edge.

The blunt head of Pope's dick pushed at my entrance and then he shoved himself deep inside me. Each thrust was more punishing than the last and I loved every second. My inner walls closed around his cock.

"Angel," he breathed. "Watching you fuck drives me insane. I can't hold off." He slid his arms under my arms and gripped my shoulders.

The weight of him pressed into me as he drove his body deep into mine.

"Pope," I cried, tugging on his hair. My body shattered as my second orgasm burst out of me.

"Ffffuck," Pope groaned as he found his release. His hips sputtered. With a ragged breath, he kissed my cheek and moved aside, allowing Jet to take his place.

My warlock's lips sealed over mine. He breathed into me, giving me air, and then nipped my lower lip. "I should probably let you rest after being double fucked, but I'm sure you can handle it."

He slid two fingers into my channel and massaged my clit with his thumb.

I mewled.

He withdrew his fingers and stuck them in his mouth. "Fucking delicious."

He kissed a trail from my sweaty neck, down to my pelvis, and fastened his lips over my pussy. His tongue lashed my clit, making my body tremble.

"Let it go, my little slut. Push out all that cum in your pussy, and let it drip into my mouth."

Fucking. Jet. My warlock did the dirtiest things and I was fucking addicted.

He pinched my clit. "What did I say?"

My walls contracted and a flood of fluid dripped out of me.

"Good girl." He praised. "So fucking beautiful." He kissed my pussy. "So fucking tasty."

He licked and sucked and slurped while moaning with deep satisfaction.

"Jet," I placed my hands on the back of his head and pumped my hips. His dark gaze met mine. "Oh my god, Jet."

I came all over his face, drowning him with my arousal.

He lapped it up. Every. Single. Drop.

"More," I begged.

He crawled up my body, his face glistening with my juices.

"Is this what you want?" He slapped my pussy with his pierced cock.

"Yes!" I cried.

He chuckled. "Ask nicely." He slapped me again.

"Please, fuck me."

He released a dark chuckle. "Taste yourself, little slut. Lick my face clean, while I fuck you."

He pressed his lips to mine. His pierced cock easily slid into my slick, cum drenched cunt.

I sucked on his lips. His tongue. His jaw.

"God damn, you feel so fucking amazing." His voice hoarse. "I love the way your pussy chokes my cock."

Jet folded over me, fusing our bodies. He stroked himself inside me. His piercings lit up every nerve ending in my cunt. "Aisling, baby. I . . ."

His thrusts became wild. Unrestrained. I gripped his shoulders, hanging on for dear life until he spent himself inside me. I followed him over the edge. My body trembled as I floated in and out of consciousness.

Jet slumped over me, his heart thumping away in his chest.

"Are you okay?" he asked.

I nodded. "Sleepy."

"Rest, little love. We'll be home soon." Jet kissed me and slowly got out of the car.

The door behind me opened and Talon appeared.

"Hi baby," Talon pressed his lips to my sweat beaded forehead.

"Where are we?"

"Some rest stop off the highway."

"Oh my god. I hope we're alone."

He chuckled. "We're good babe. There's a bathroom that's clean-ish if you need it."

I nodded and my wolf covered me with the blanket and carried my naked ass to the bathroom.

HOURS LATER, Pope, nudged me awake.

"Angel, we're home."

I stretched my limbs and rubbed the sleep from my eyes. The briny scent of the ocean wafted into the SUV.

"Why are we at the cove?" I asked Talon who stood outside, holding the door open.

"Welcome home, baby." He helped me get out of the car.

"The house is ready?" I perked up.

"It is." He grinned.

Jet unlocked the front door and made a sweeping motion with his hand. "After you, our queen."

The new house was nothing short of amazing. I expected it to be from the tours Talon would give me as it was being built. Plus, my man had good taste in everything that had to deal with construction and home decor. Still, my imagination hadn't come close to the final result.

Jethro got his dream kitchen fit for a chef. Pope got his game room and a mini-work space. Mini was putting it generously because it was bigger than the one he had when we lived on Cedar Mill Lane. And I got a library. Located in the west wing of the house was a vast room with shelves lining three walls. The other wall was all glass, overlooking what would blossom into a charming garden.

"Jet ordered more books to add to your collection. And we decided to give you space to add more later." Talon hit a hidden lever which made a row of shelves retract into the wall while another row of shelves replaced it. "They all do that." He gestured to the other shelves.

"Talon." Tears welled in my eyes. "This is . . . I'm speechless. You thought of everything."

"It wasn't just me, Red," Talon said. "We worked together to design this for you."

"I love . . ." I stopped mid-sentence noticing something over the hearth. *Is that?* I strode towards the fireplace my gaze fixed on a photograph mounted on the wall.

"When?" My voice trembled. "How?"

"Awww, little love," Jet wrapped his arms around my middle pressing his chest to my back. "We didn't mean to make you cry."

Talon took one of my hands in his, while Pope used his shirt to dab my tears.

"It's so, perfect."

Out of everything in the house, the one photograph was my favorite thing. I could look at it for hours, had actually, since it was on my phone. It was a candid photo of the four most important men in my life.

Talon Shelby my protective, wolf. Gaius Pope my loyal, guardian angel. Jethro Buchanan my brilliant, warlock. And Donovan Lovelle, the man who'd been offering his blood to protect me my entire life. He wasn't my biological father, but he would always be the father of my heart and soul and the only man deserving of that title. He looked strong, healthy, and happy. They all did. They wore big smiles on their faces and there was a bond between them that was so beautiful.

They were good men, and I was so blessed to have them in my life. They recognized something in me that was worth saving. Something clicked in me and for the first time since I'd learned about my demoness, I felt it in my bones that I was worth saving too. They'd sacrificed so much for me, and I wasn't about to let their efforts be in vain. I vowed to prove to them for the rest of my long life that their efforts were appreciated, seen, heard, and felt.

"Thank you, all of you for showing me that my life has meaning. Thank you for giving me so much to live for. And thank you for loving all my dark, rough edges." I sniffled.

They crowded around me for a group hug as their love for me soaked into my soul.

"Aisling, my beautiful mate, our lives have meaning because you're in it," Talon said.

"And because of you we have a future to look forward to," Pope added.

"You're equal parts of light and dark, smooth and rough," Jet said. "Just like us."

"We love you," they said simultaneously.

I felt their hearts beating a reassuring rhythm that matched mine.

Mine. My men. My loves. Together we tamed my demoness. Together we could overcome anything.

A Note from the Author

Thank you for reading Aisling's story. I'm glad you made it to the end and hope it was a satisfying and entertaining read.

When I began my author journey, I knew Dr. Jekyll and Mr. Hyde was going to be my first retelling. As you have probably guessed, my version isn't a retelling, but more of an inspiration based on the classic.

My original title was *Everything in Reverse* because it is a complete reversal of the original. For starters, I wanted the protagonist to be female, and instead of making a potion to give her powers or strength, I wanted the potion to be a remedy to cure unwanted behavior.

The classic is also quite dark and I wanted to write something different. Initially, Ash's story was supposed to be fun and flirty. But exposure to unsavory situations changed my creative trajectory and the dark themes began to unfold. I'm not the type of writer who drowns in the dark waters of storytelling, but those things do exist and are sometimes necessary. To soften the dreariness, I added the paranormal element to give it a deeper fictitious feel. In my crazy head, the darkness feels less real if there are magical elements in the story.

I'm a lover of romance novels, particularly, why choose. In the original, the other characters (the attorney, the doctor, and the butler) are witnesses to Dr. Jekyll's transformation. In contrast, I wanted these characters to not only witness the FMC's transformations but also have an emotional attachment to the FMC, making her journey a part of theirs as well. The perfect groundwork for why choose romance.

Unlike most popular retellings that are based on romance or fairytales, I chose this classic which is more of a horror/thriller novel. Both of which are not in my wheelhouse. And thus, I gave it a romance flair, allowing for sexy times, and a happily-ever-after ending where love overcomes dark and all sits well in the world.

Thank you for indulging me on this journey. I hope you join me again on my next writing excursion back to Port Midway for another retelling.

If you liked Aisling's story (or not), I would love to hear your thoughts. Please leave a review as I'd greatly appreciate your feedback. As a new author I am whole heartedly interested in what my readers have to say. Your feedback helps me hone my craft and publish books you'll enjoy reading. Connect with me on my website at: genaviecastle.com

Your book friend forever, Genavie

RESOURCES

Sexual Assault

If you've been the victim of sexual abuse, help is available.
Call The National Sexual Assault Hotline at:
800-656-4673
Or visit them online at:
https://www.rainn.org

RESOURCES

Suicide and Crisis Lifeline

The 988 Lifeline is a national network of local crisis centers that provides free and confidential emotional support to people in suicidal crisis or emotional distress 24 hours a day, 7 days a week in the United States.

Contact them by phone by dialing:

988

Or visit them online at:

https://988lifeline.org/